STINKY CECIL

IN OPERATION POND RESCUE

STINKY CECIL

IN OPERATION POND RESCUE

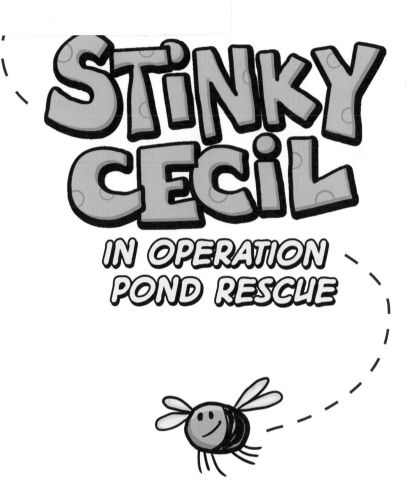

PAIGE BRADDOCK

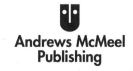

Andrews McMeel
Publishing
Kansas City • Sydney • London

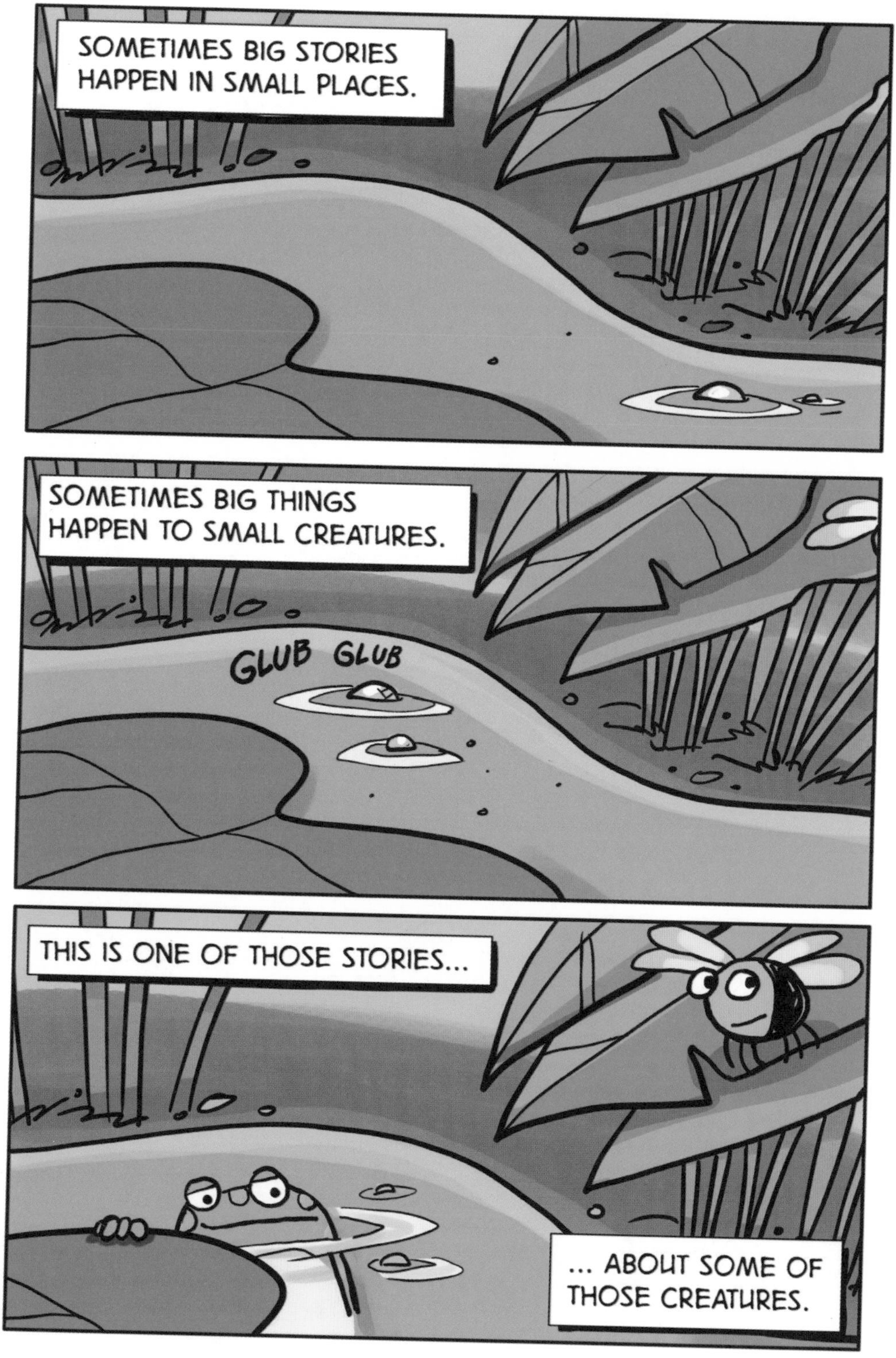
SOMETIMES BIG STORIES HAPPEN IN SMALL PLACES.
SOMETIMES BIG THINGS HAPPEN TO SMALL CREATURES.
GLUB GLUB
THIS IS ONE OF THOSE STORIES...
... ABOUT SOME OF THOSE CREATURES.

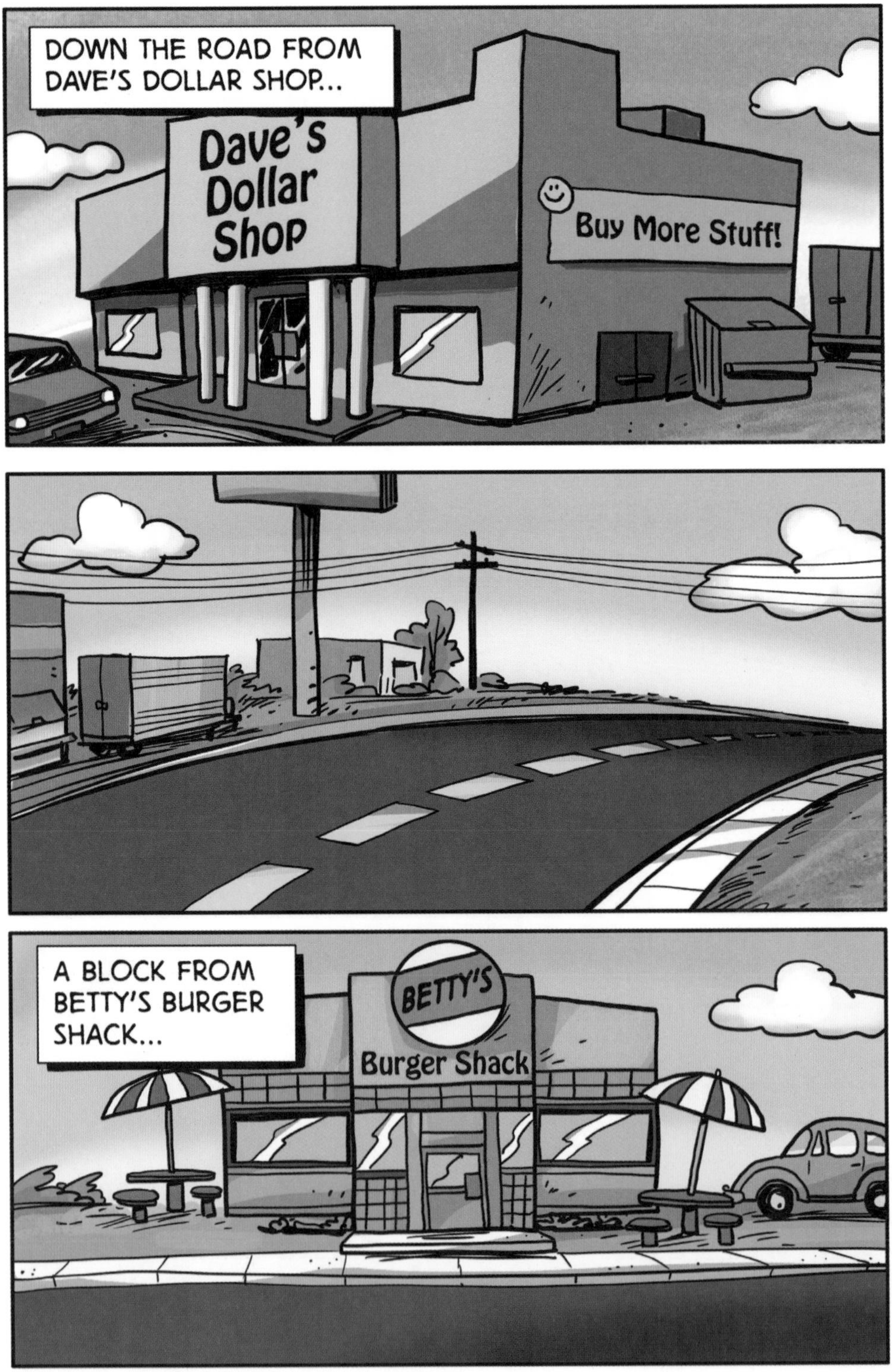
DOWN THE ROAD FROM DAVE'S DOLLAR SHOP...
Dave's Dollar Shop
Buy More Stuff!
A BLOCK FROM BETTY'S BURGER SHACK...
BETTY'S
Burger Shack

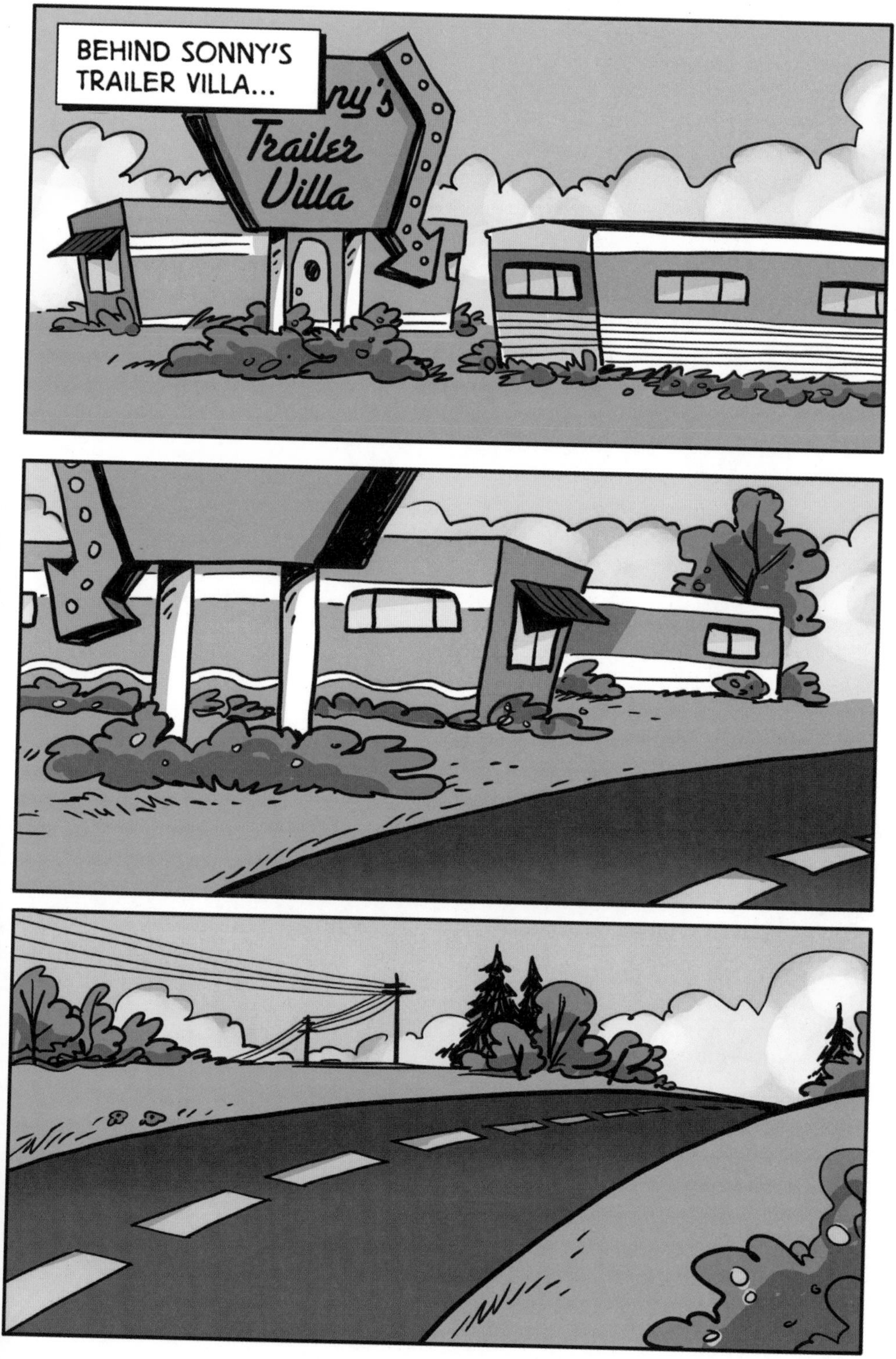
BEHIND SONNY'S TRAILER VILLA...
Trailer Villa

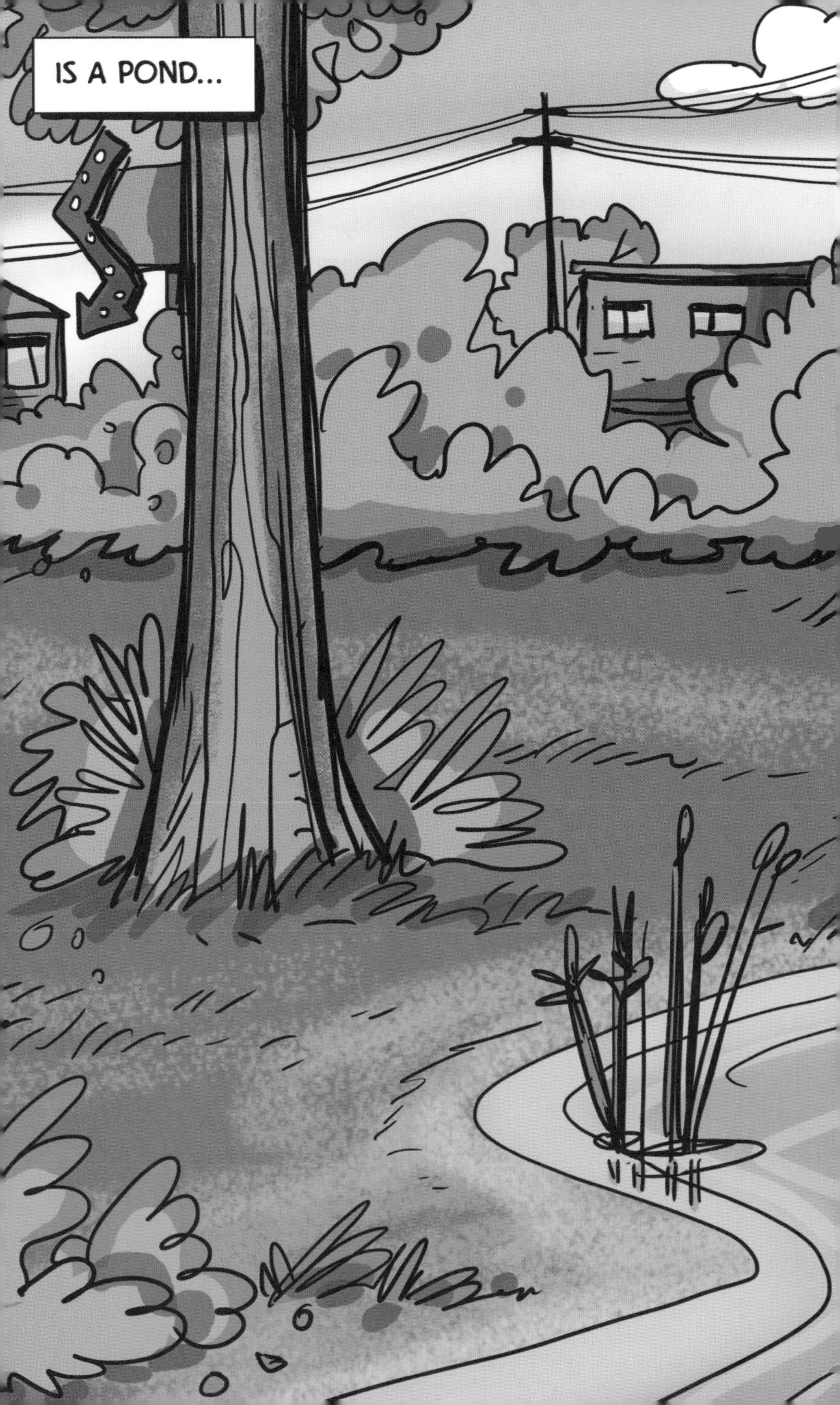
IS A POND...

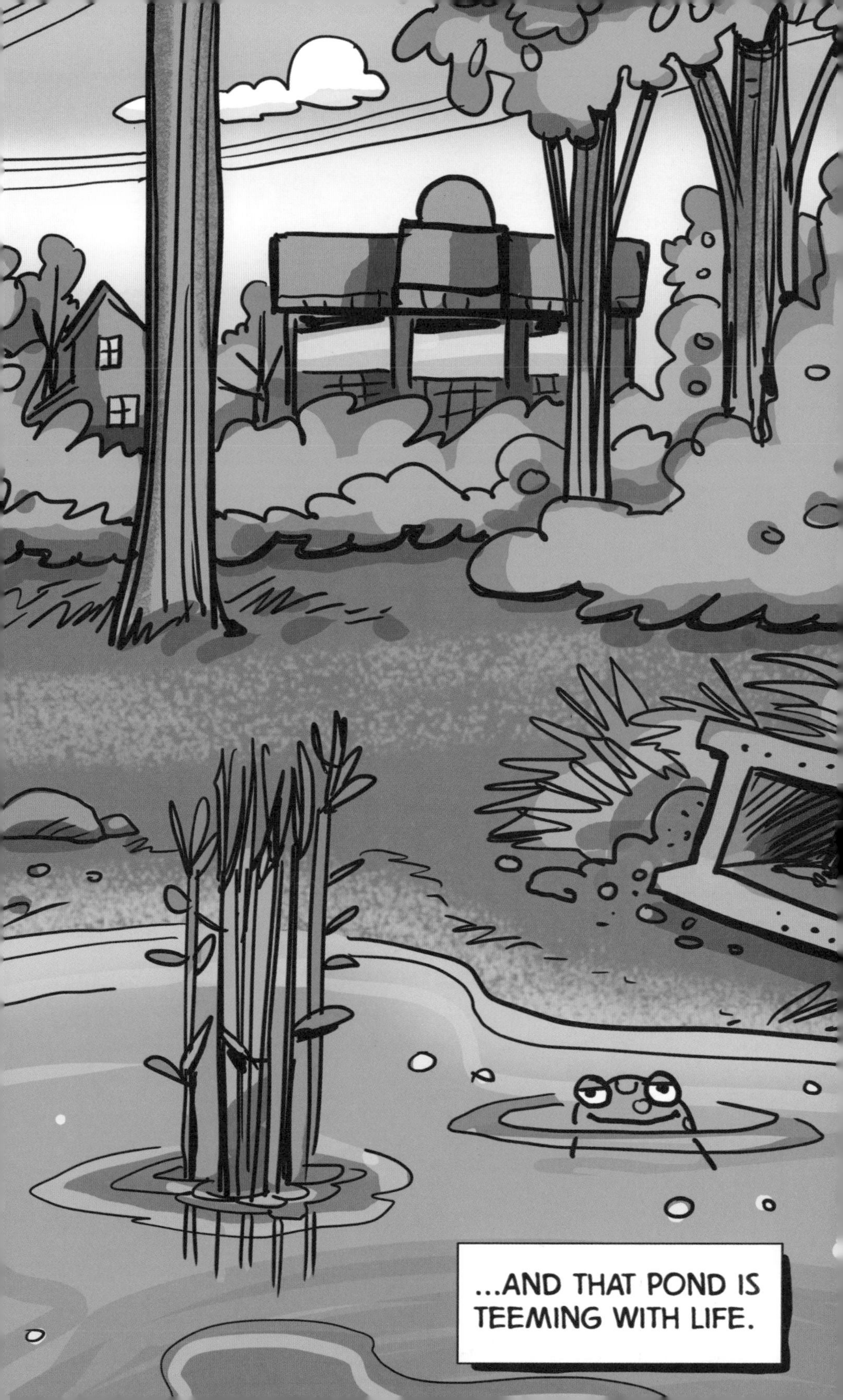
...AND THAT POND IS TEEMING WITH LIFE.

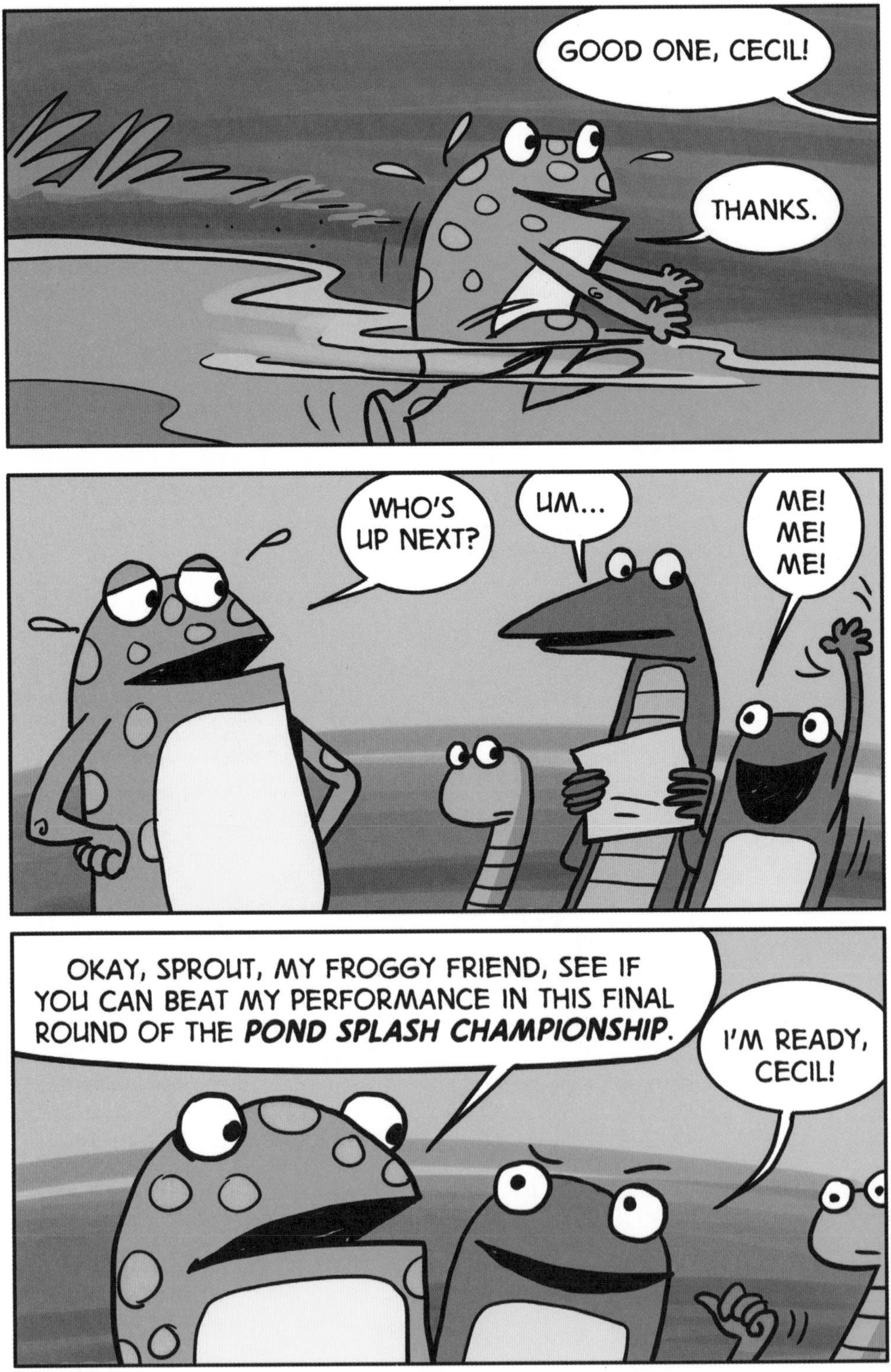
GOOD ONE, CECIL!
THANKS.
WHO'S UP NEXT?
UM...
ME! ME! ME!
OKAY, SPROUT, MY FROGGY FRIEND, SEE IF YOU CAN BEAT MY PERFORMANCE IN THIS FINAL ROUND OF THE ***POND SPLASH CHAMPIONSHIP***.
I'M READY, CECIL!

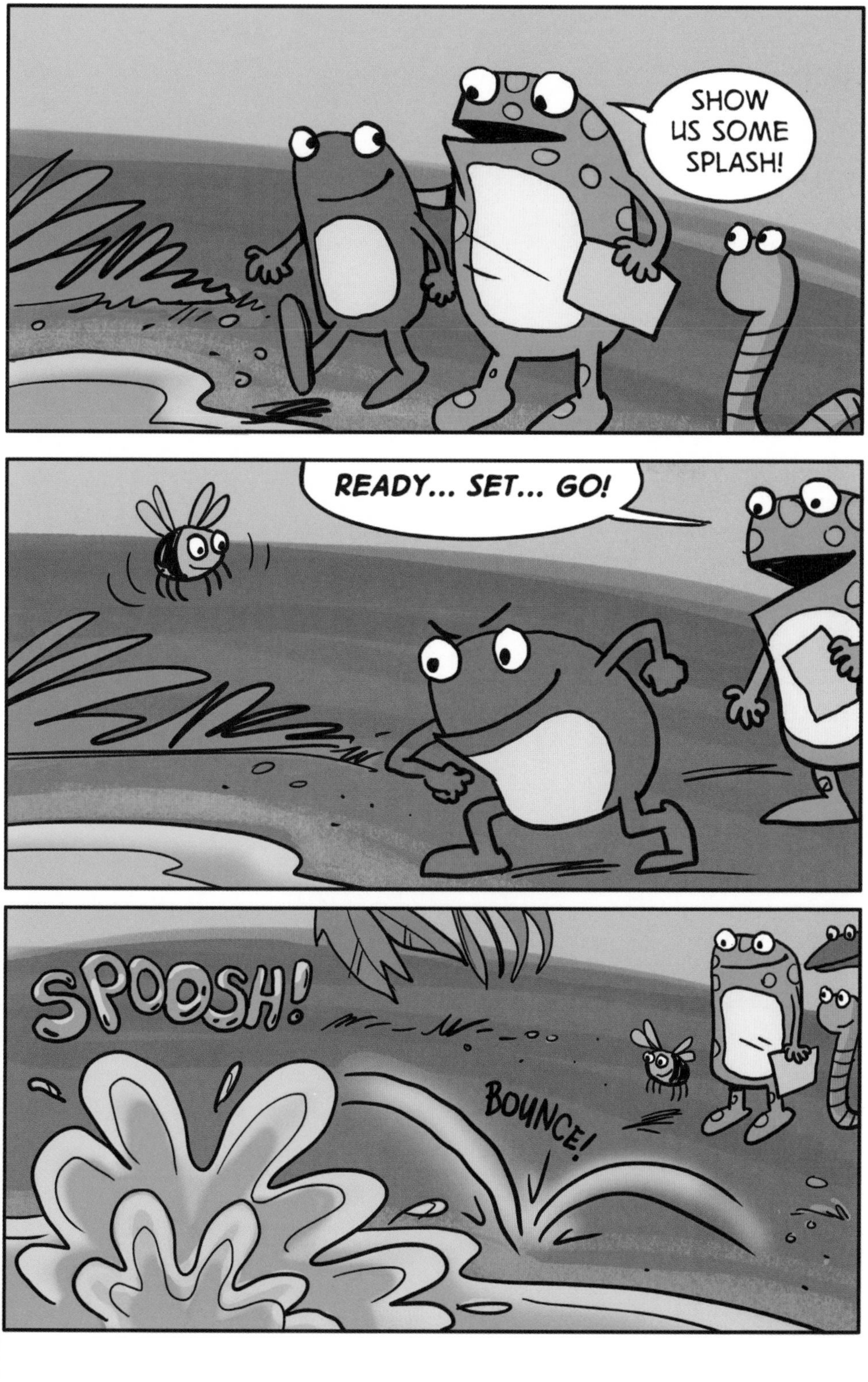
SHOW US SOME SPLASH!
READY... SET... GO!
SPOOSH!
BOUNCE!

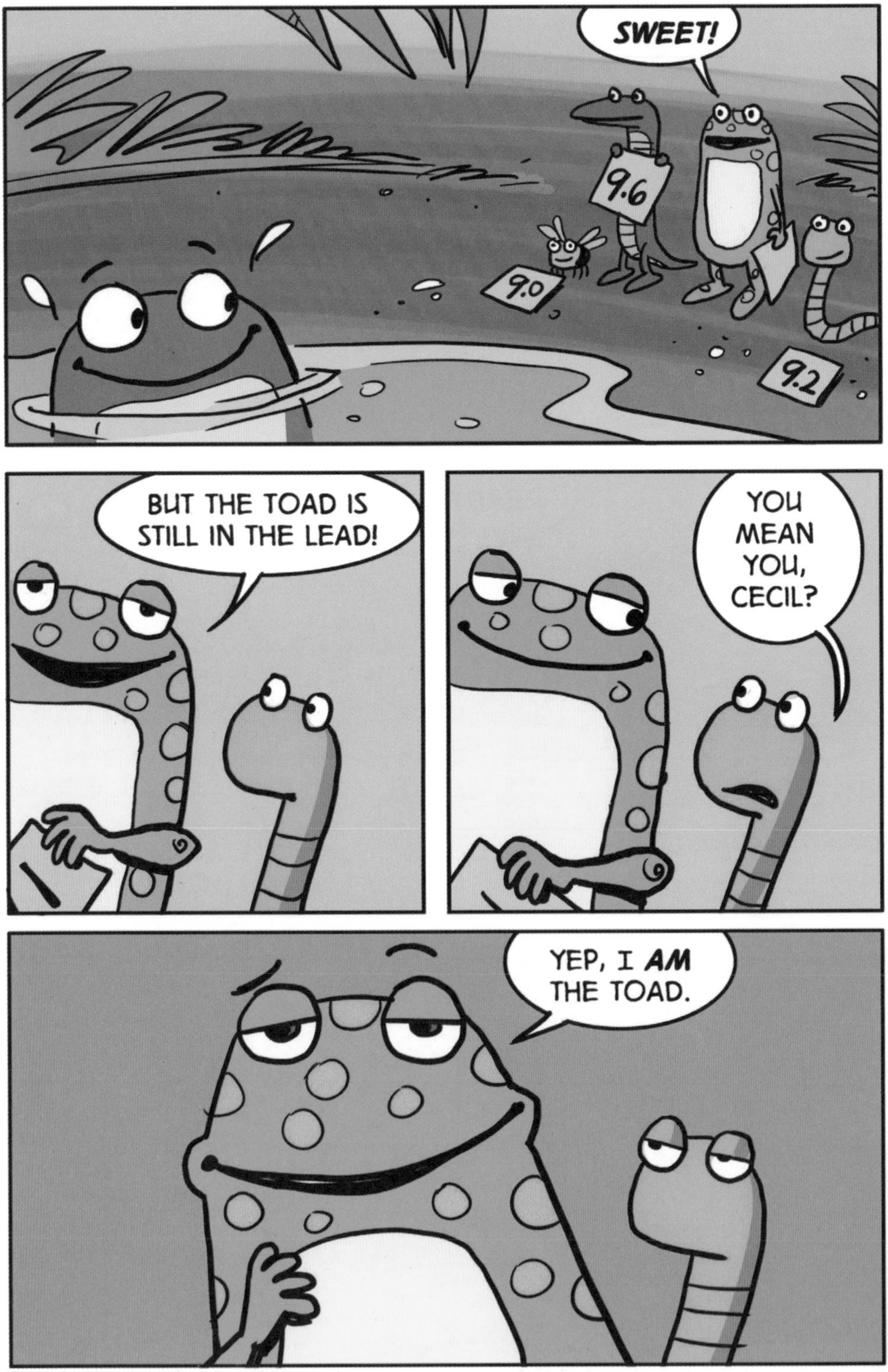
SWEET!
9.6
9.0
9.2
BUT THE TOAD IS STILL IN THE LEAD!
YOU MEAN YOU, CECIL?
YEP, I **AM** THE TOAD.

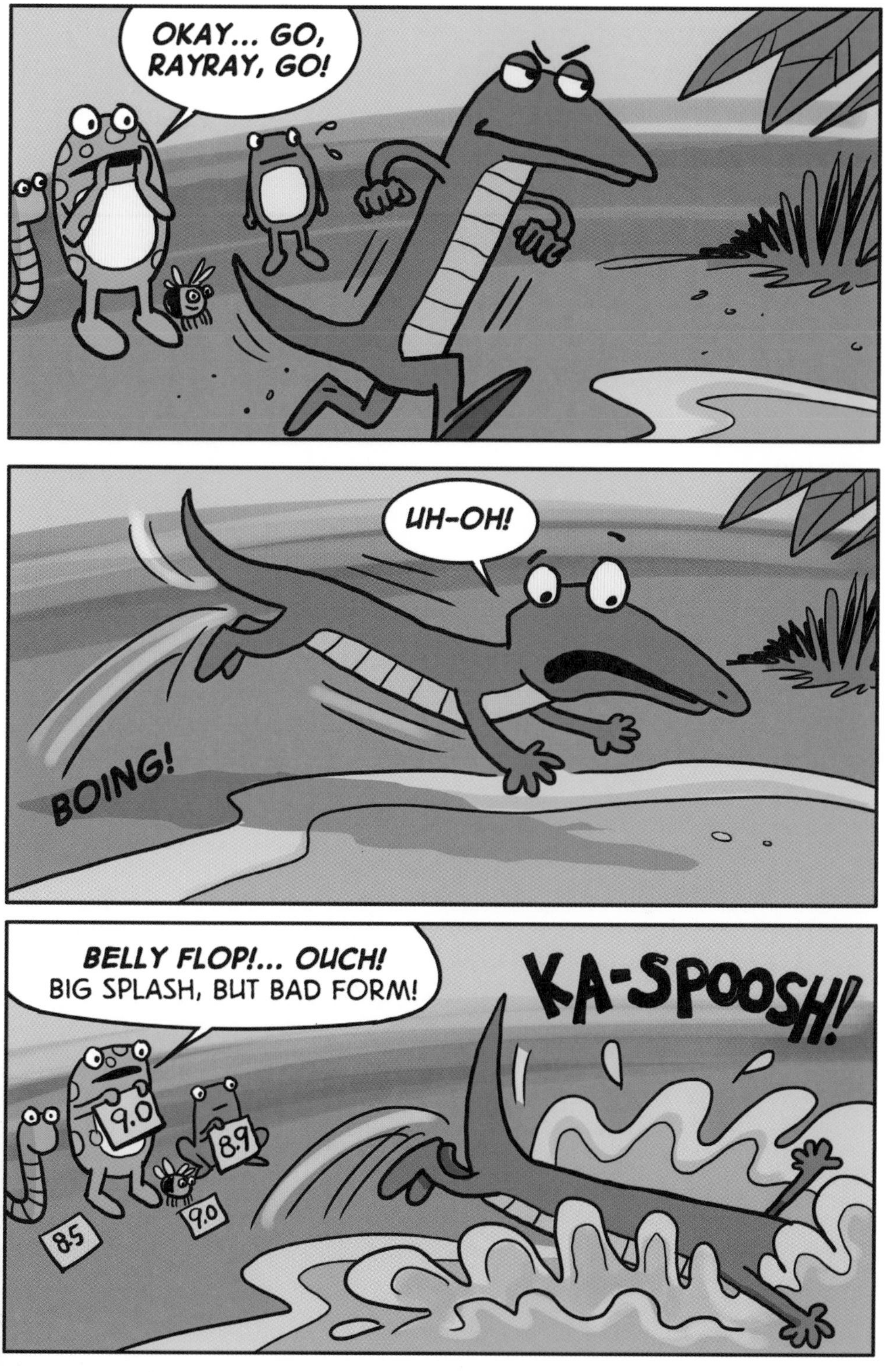
OKAY... GO, RAYRAY, GO!
UH-OH!
BOING!
BELLY FLOP!... OUCH! BIG SPLASH, BUT BAD FORM!
KA-SPOOSH!
9.0
8.9
9.0
8.5

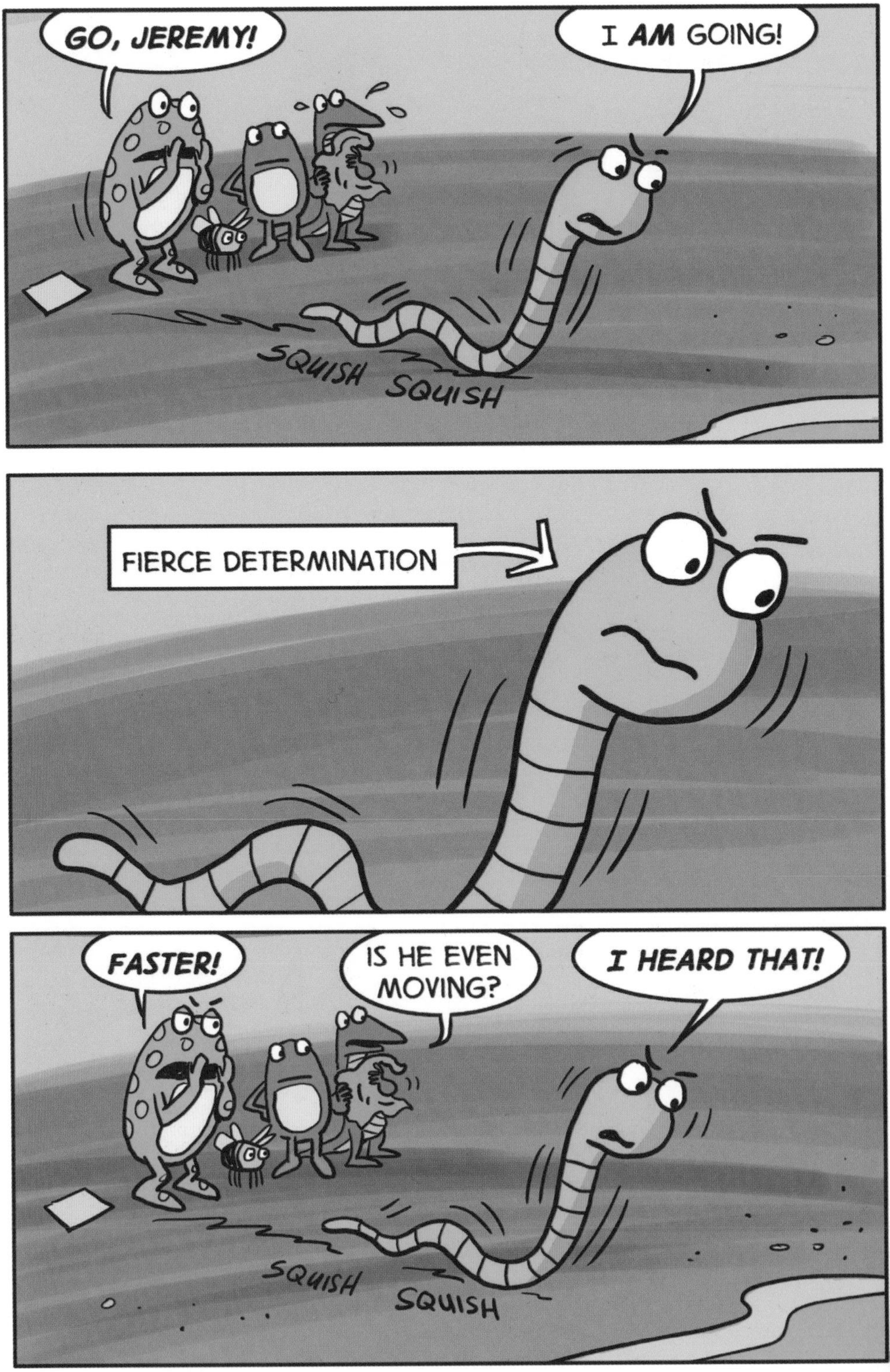
GO, JEREMY!
I AM GOING!
SQUISH SQUISH
FIERCE DETERMINATION
FASTER!
IS HE EVEN MOVING?
I HEARD THAT!
SQUISH SQUISH

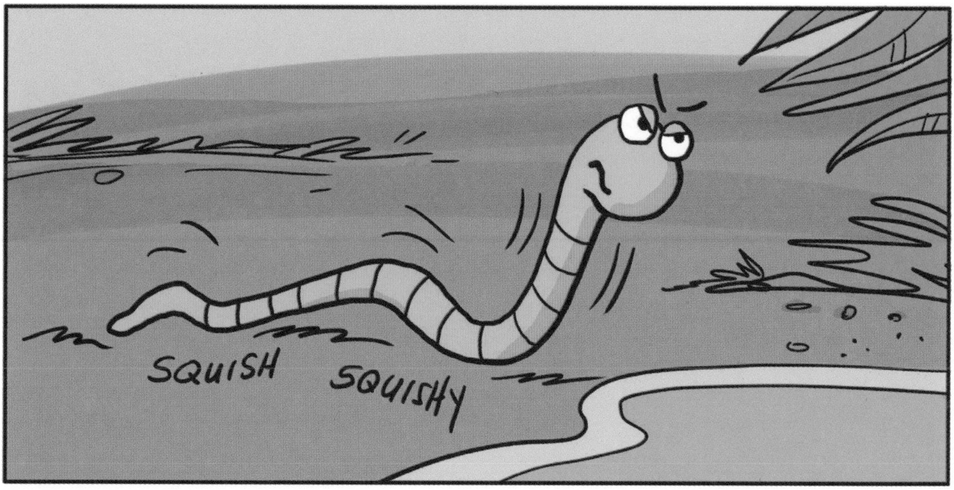
SQUISH
SQUISHY
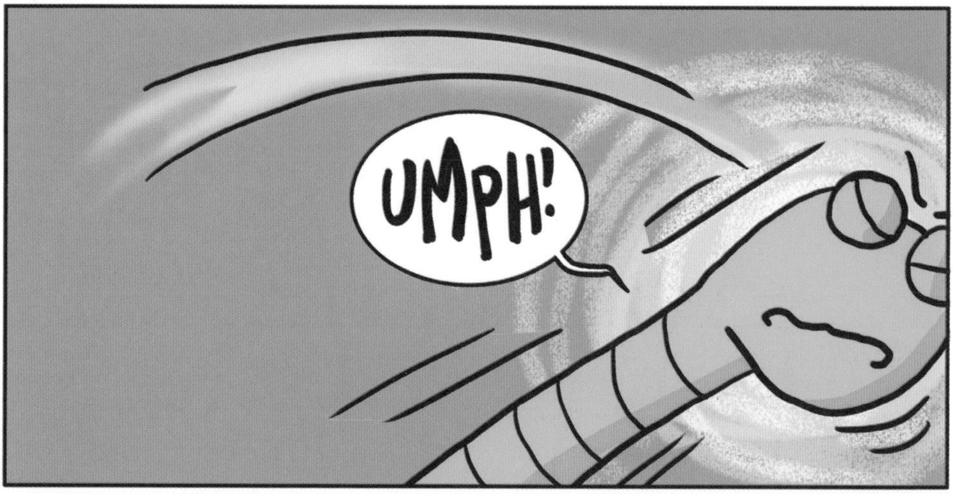
UMPH!
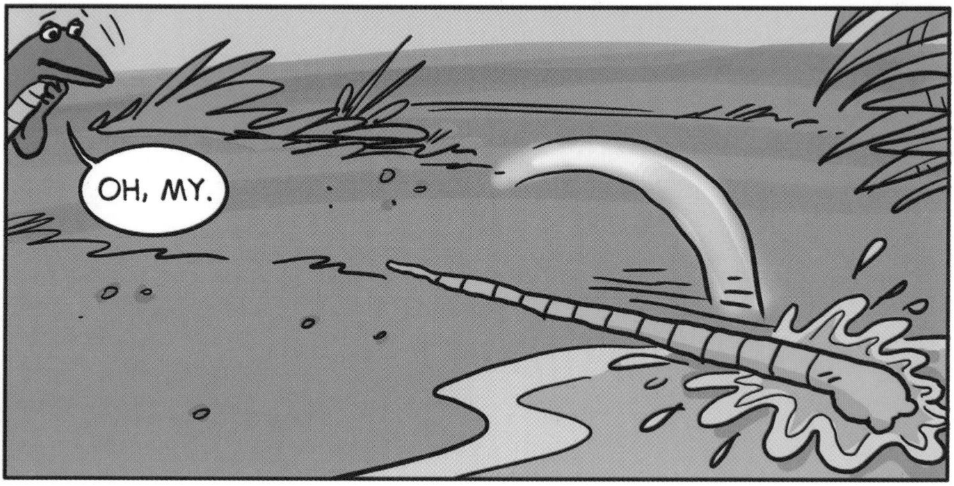
OH, MY.

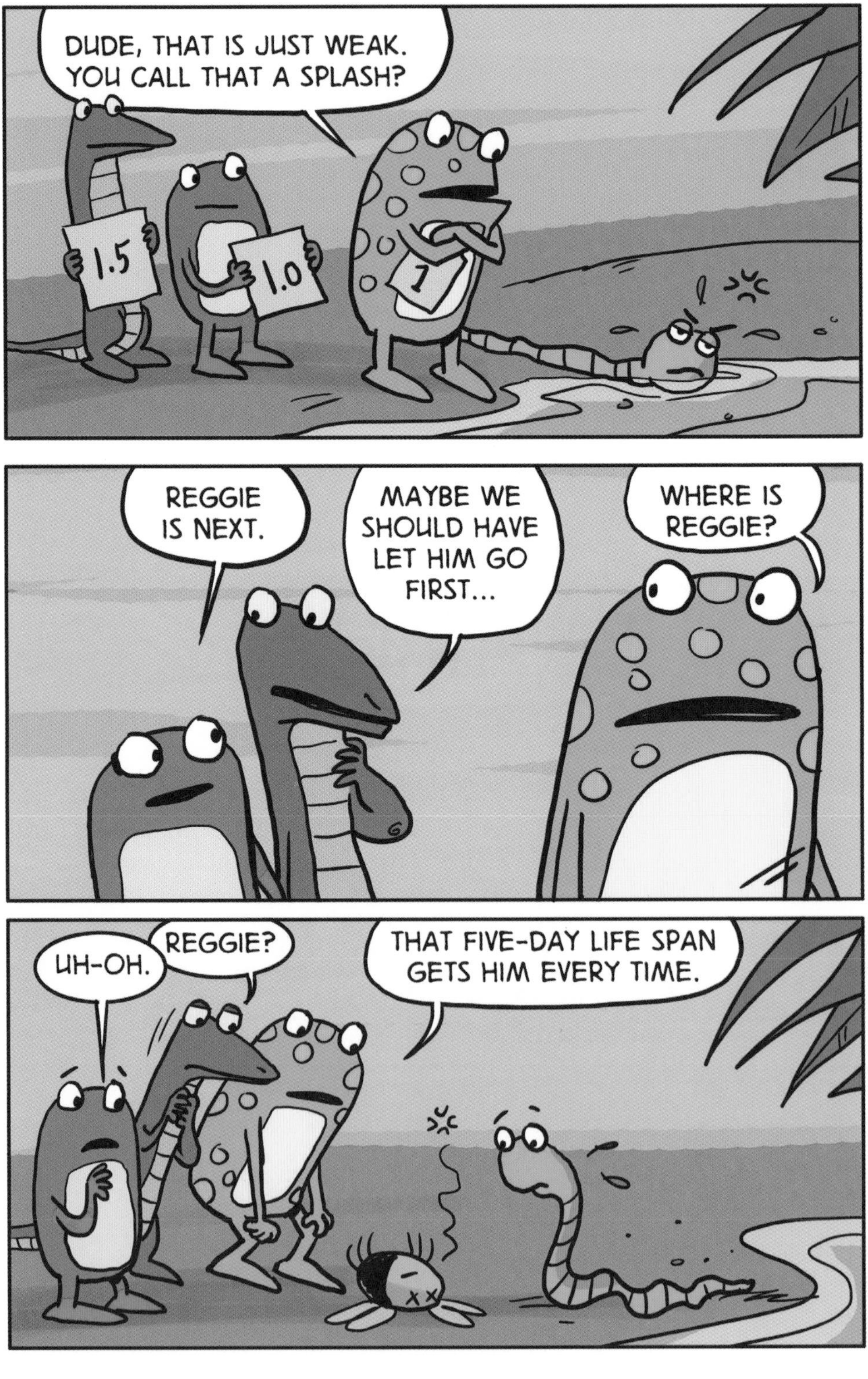
DUDE, THAT IS JUST WEAK. YOU CALL THAT A SPLASH?
1.5
1.0
1
REGGIE IS NEXT.
MAYBE WE SHOULD HAVE LET HIM GO FIRST...
WHERE IS REGGIE?
UH-OH.
REGGIE?
THAT FIVE-DAY LIFE SPAN GETS HIM EVERY TIME.

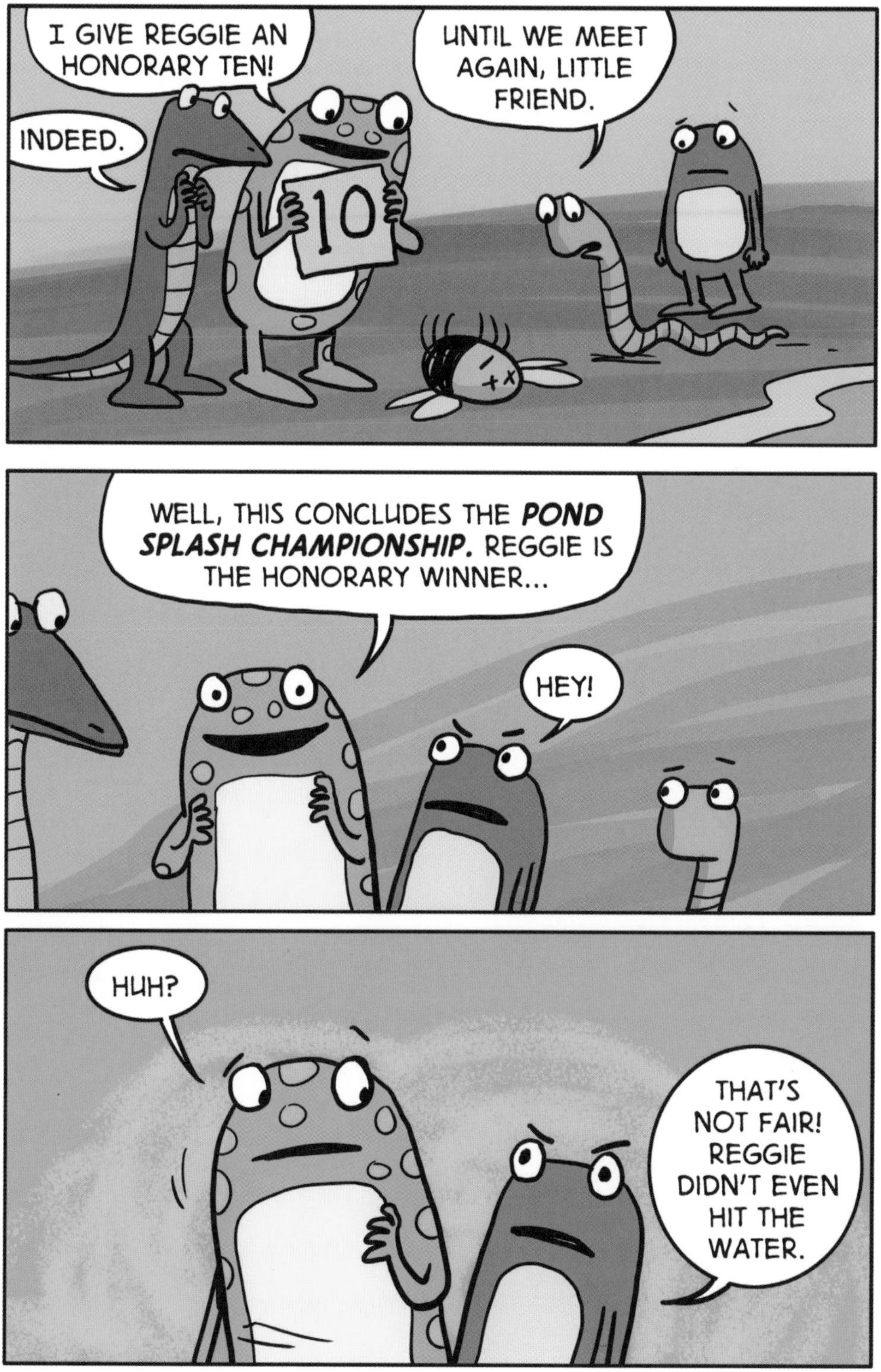
I GIVE REGGIE AN HONORARY TEN!
INDEED.
10
UNTIL WE MEET AGAIN, LITTLE FRIEND.
WELL, THIS CONCLUDES THE ***POND SPLASH CHAMPIONSHIP.*** REGGIE IS THE HONORARY WINNER...
HEY!
HUH?
THAT'S NOT FAIR! REGGIE DIDN'T EVEN HIT THE WATER.

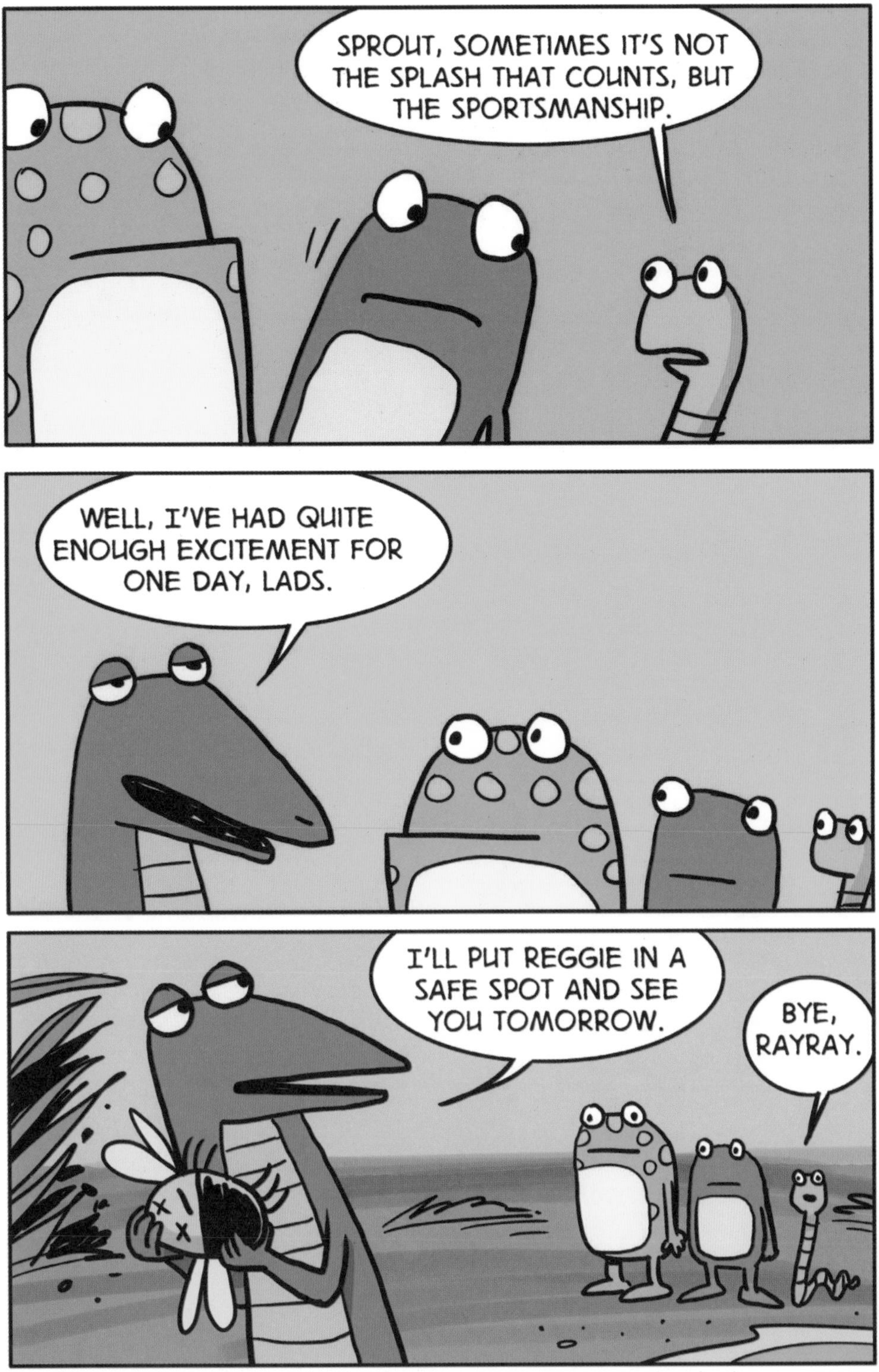
SPROUT, SOMETIMES IT'S NOT THE SPLASH THAT COUNTS, BUT THE SPORTSMANSHIP.
WELL, I'VE HAD QUITE ENOUGH EXCITEMENT FOR ONE DAY, LADS.
I'LL PUT REGGIE IN A SAFE SPOT AND SEE YOU TOMORROW.
BYE, RAYRAY.

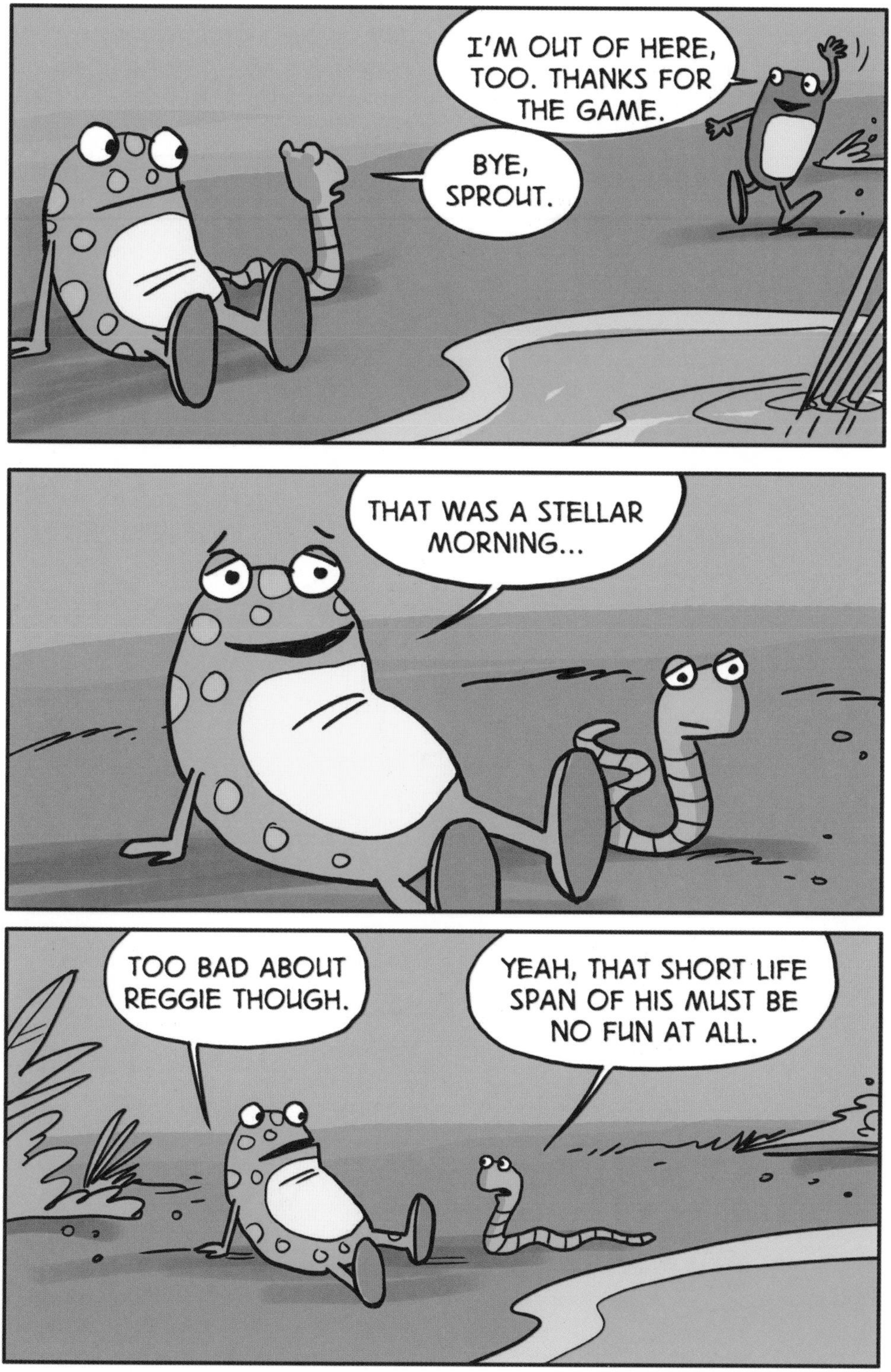
I'M OUT OF HERE, TOO. THANKS FOR THE GAME.
BYE, SPROUT.
THAT WAS A STELLAR MORNING...
TOO BAD ABOUT REGGIE THOUGH.
YEAH, THAT SHORT LIFE SPAN OF HIS MUST BE NO FUN AT ALL.

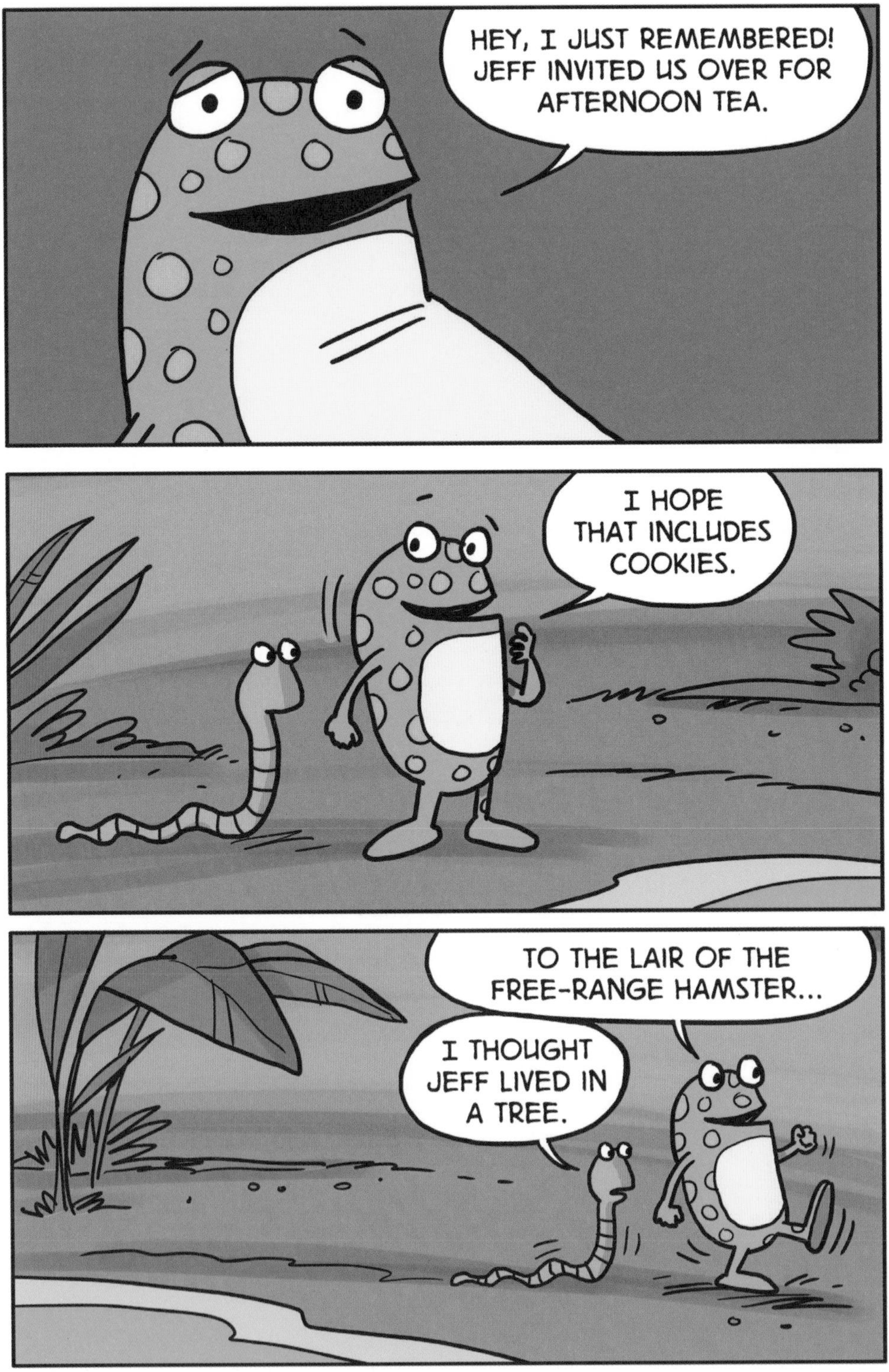
HEY, I JUST REMEMBERED! JEFF INVITED US OVER FOR AFTERNOON TEA.
I HOPE THAT INCLUDES COOKIES.
TO THE LAIR OF THE FREE-RANGE HAMSTER...
I THOUGHT JEFF LIVED IN A TREE.

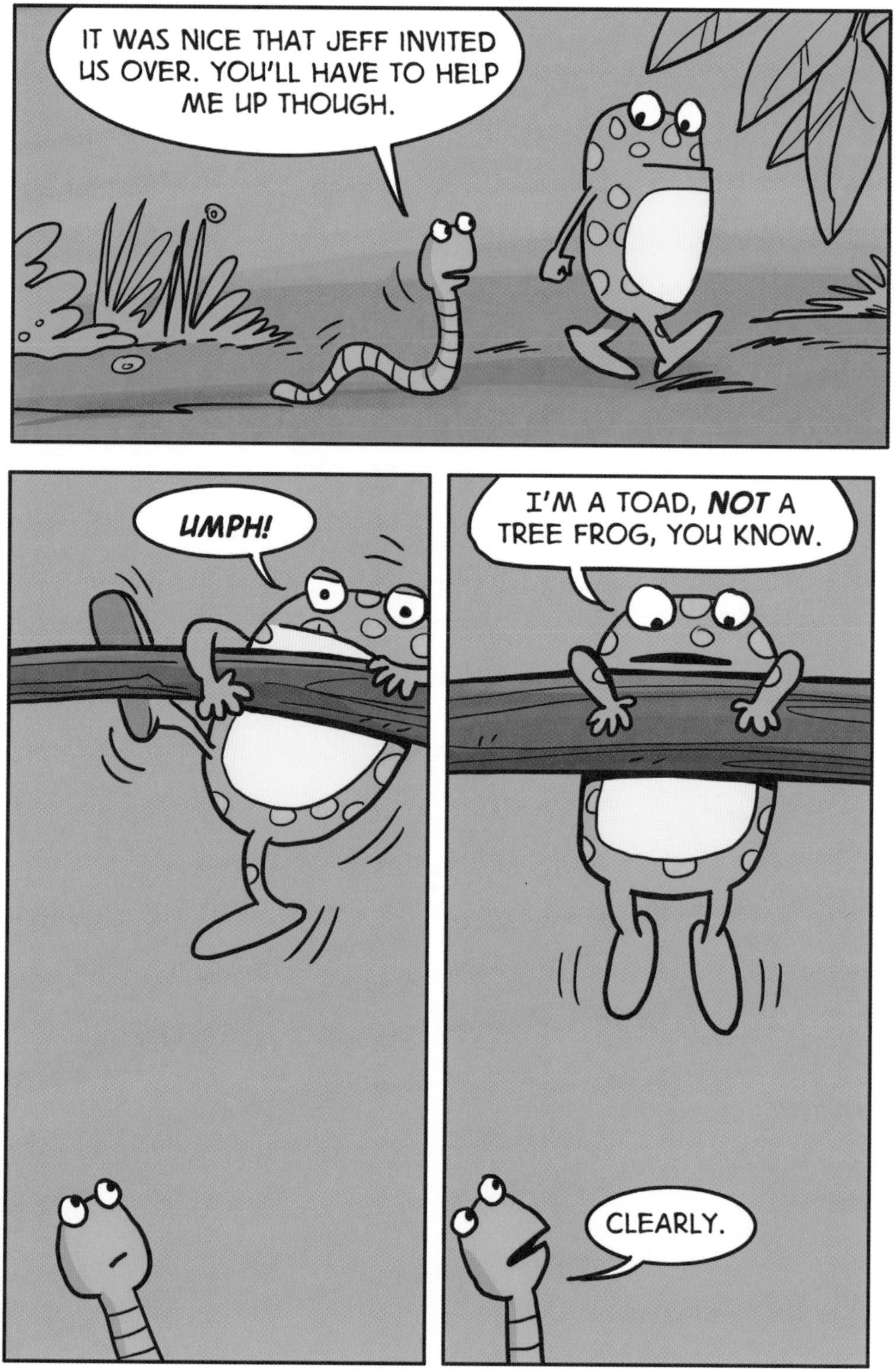
IT WAS NICE THAT JEFF INVITED US OVER. YOU'LL HAVE TO HELP ME UP THOUGH.
UMPH!
I'M A TOAD, **NOT** A TREE FROG, YOU KNOW.
CLEARLY.

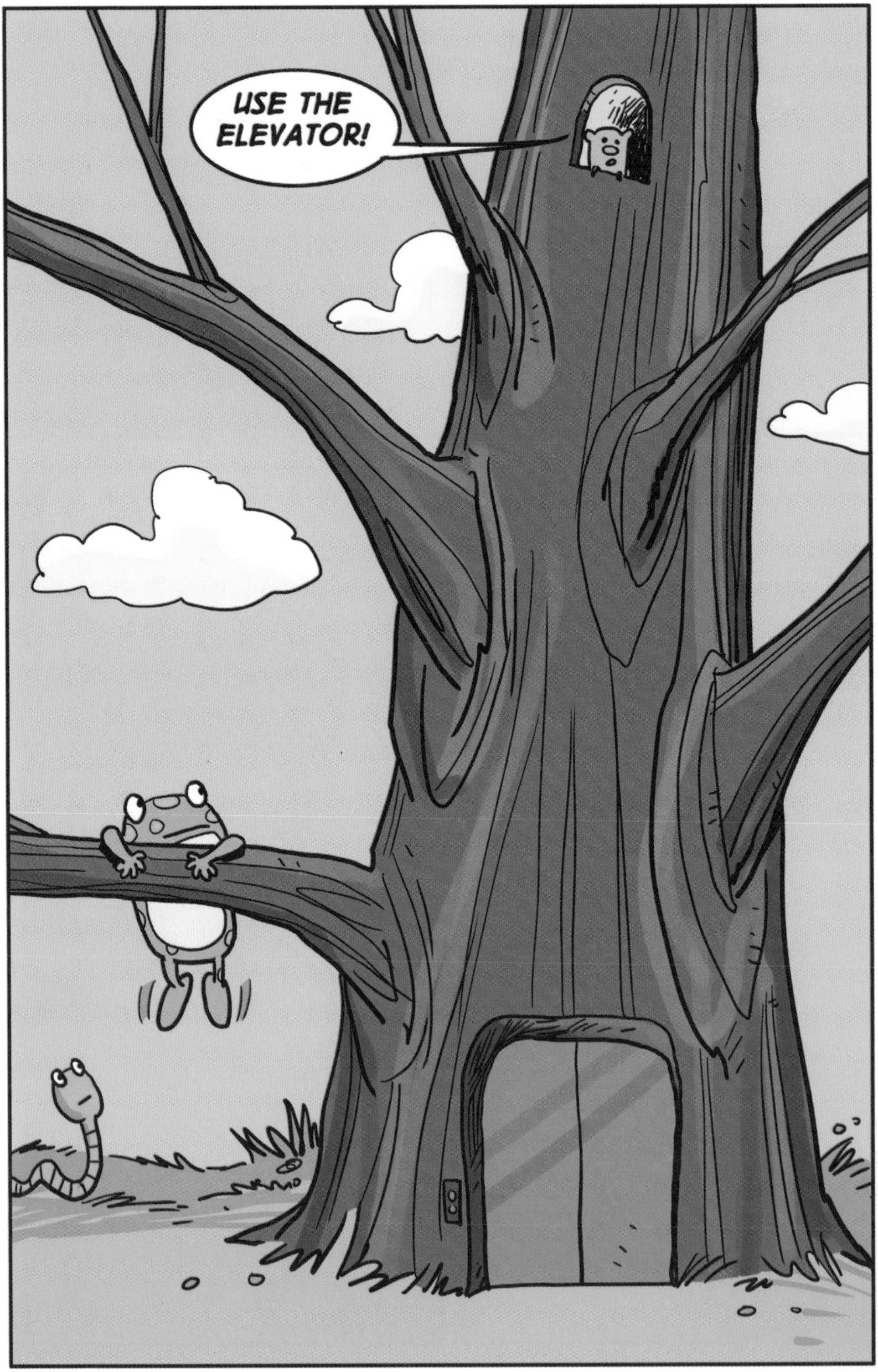
USE THE ELEVATOR!

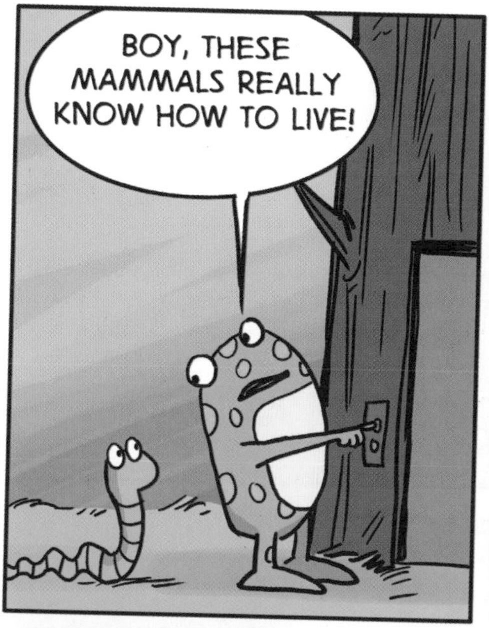
BOY, THESE MAMMALS REALLY KNOW HOW TO LIVE!

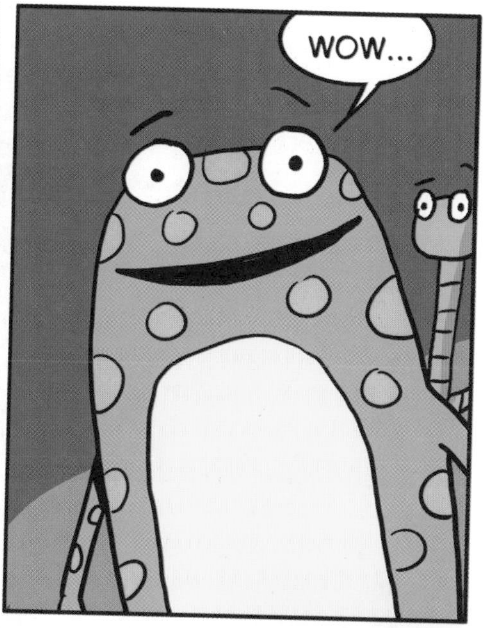
WOW...

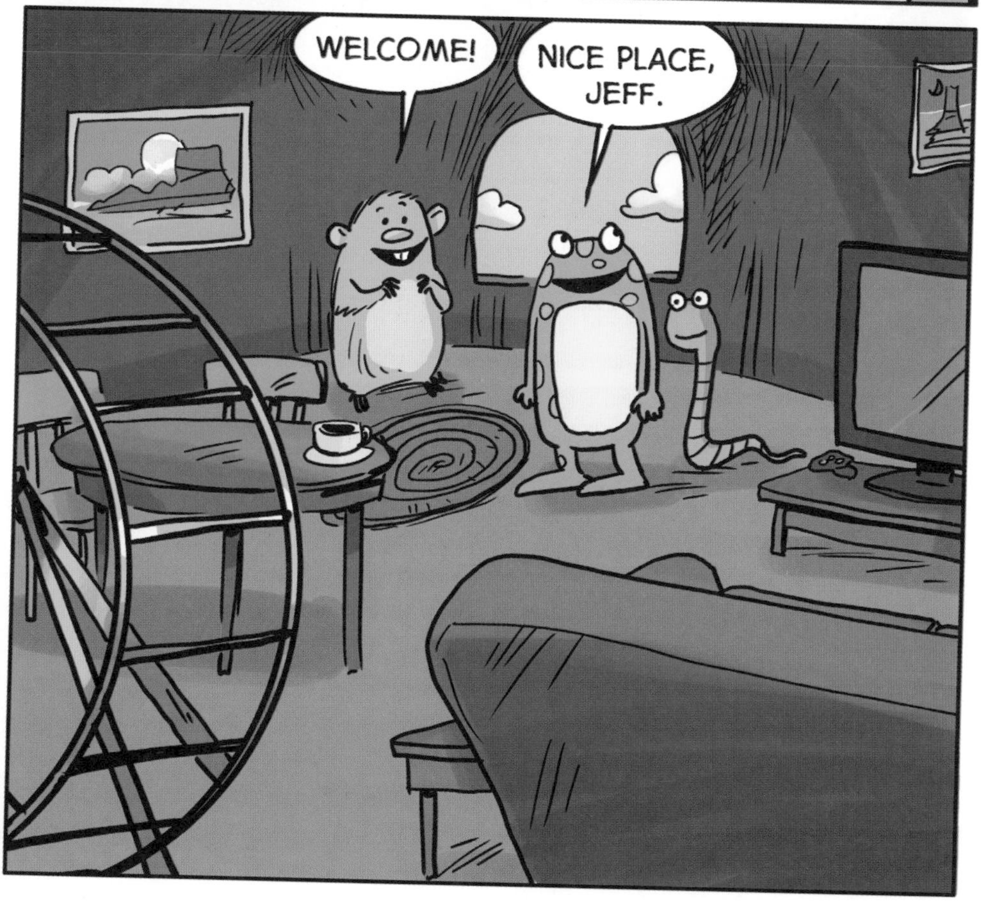
WELCOME!
NICE PLACE, JEFF.

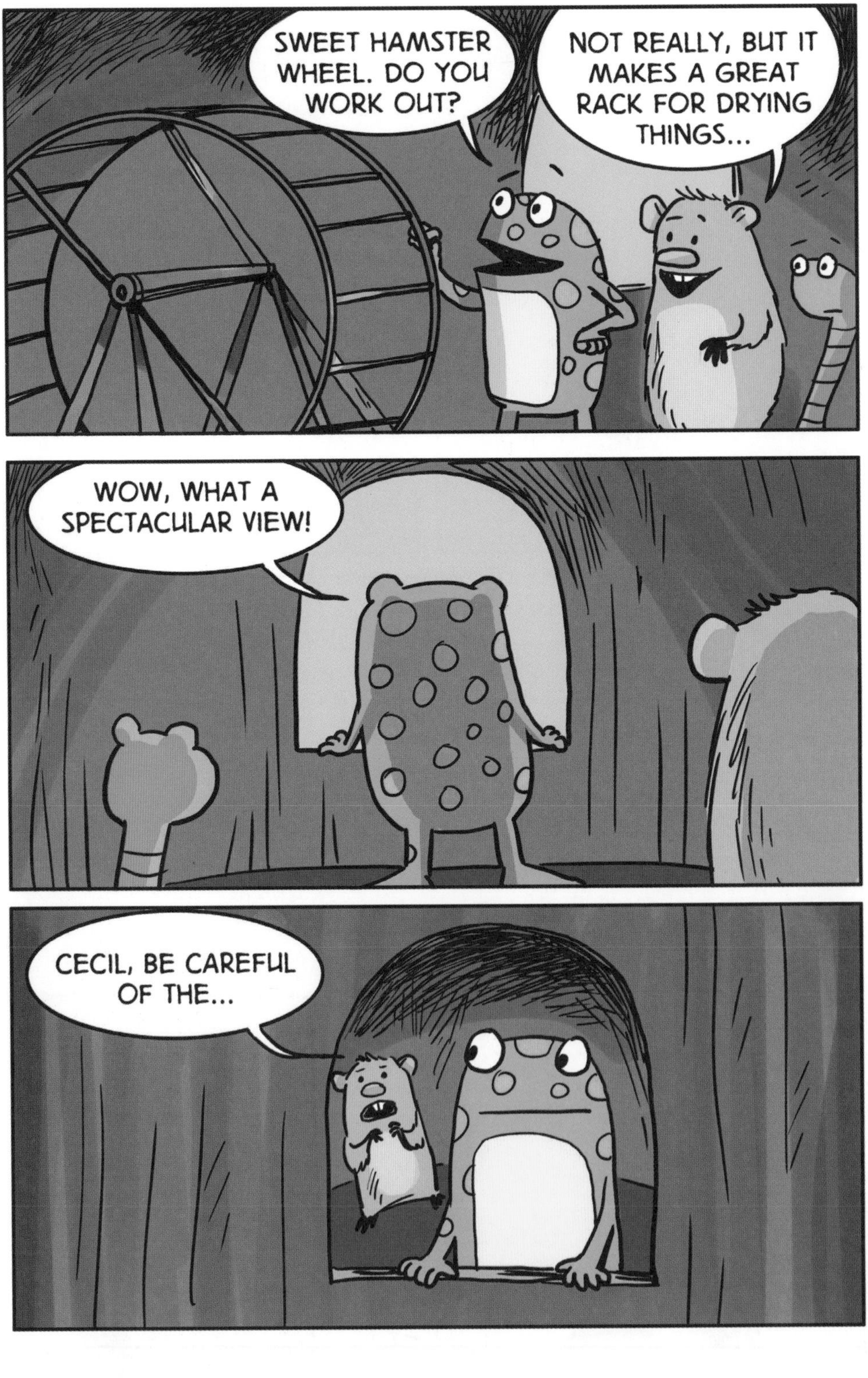
SWEET HAMSTER WHEEL. DO YOU WORK OUT?
NOT REALLY, BUT IT MAKES A GREAT RACK FOR DRYING THINGS...
WOW, WHAT A SPECTACULAR VIEW!
CECIL, BE CAREFUL OF THE...

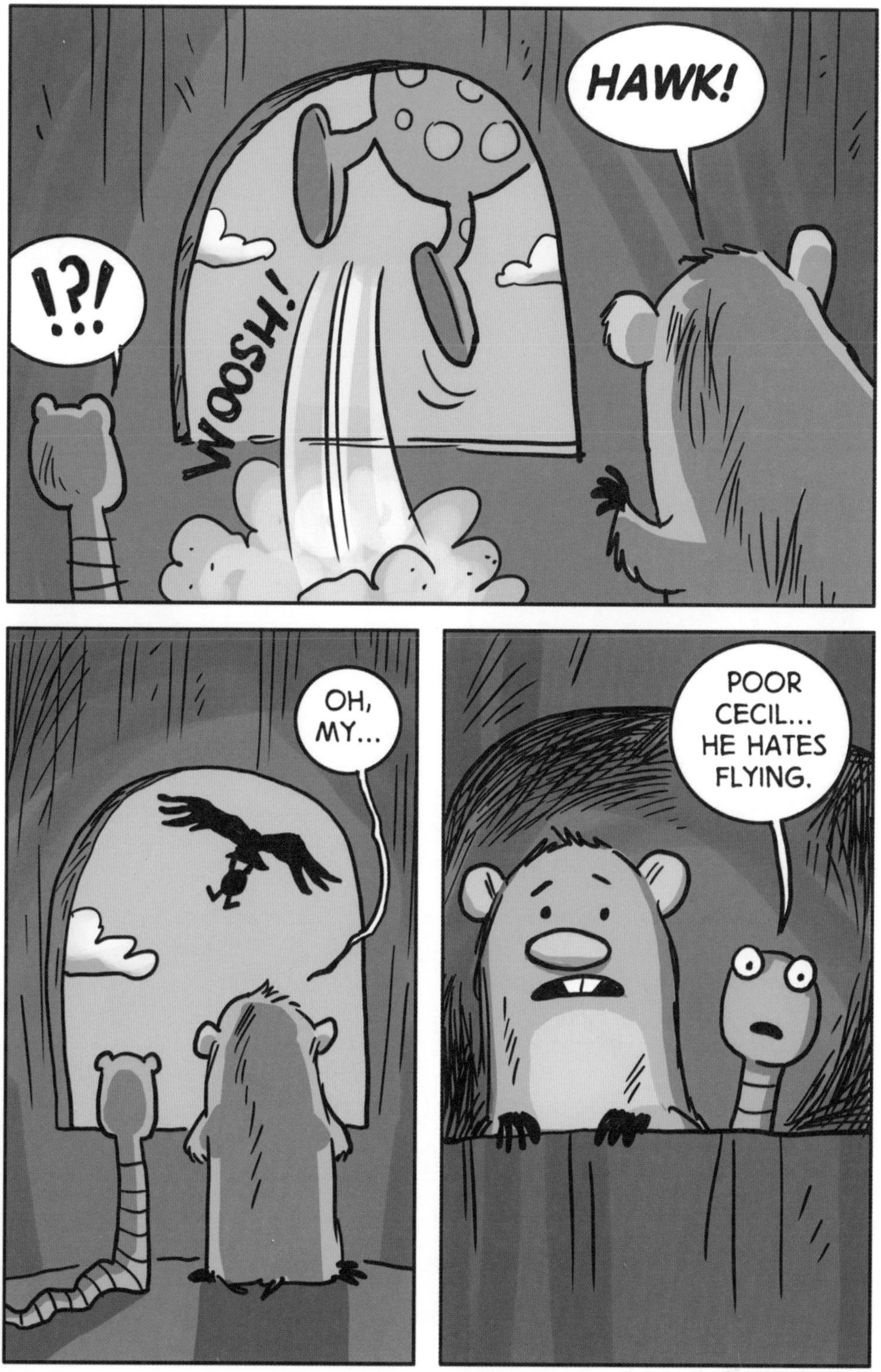
HAWK!
!?!
WOOSH!
OH, MY...
POOR CECIL... HE HATES FLYING.

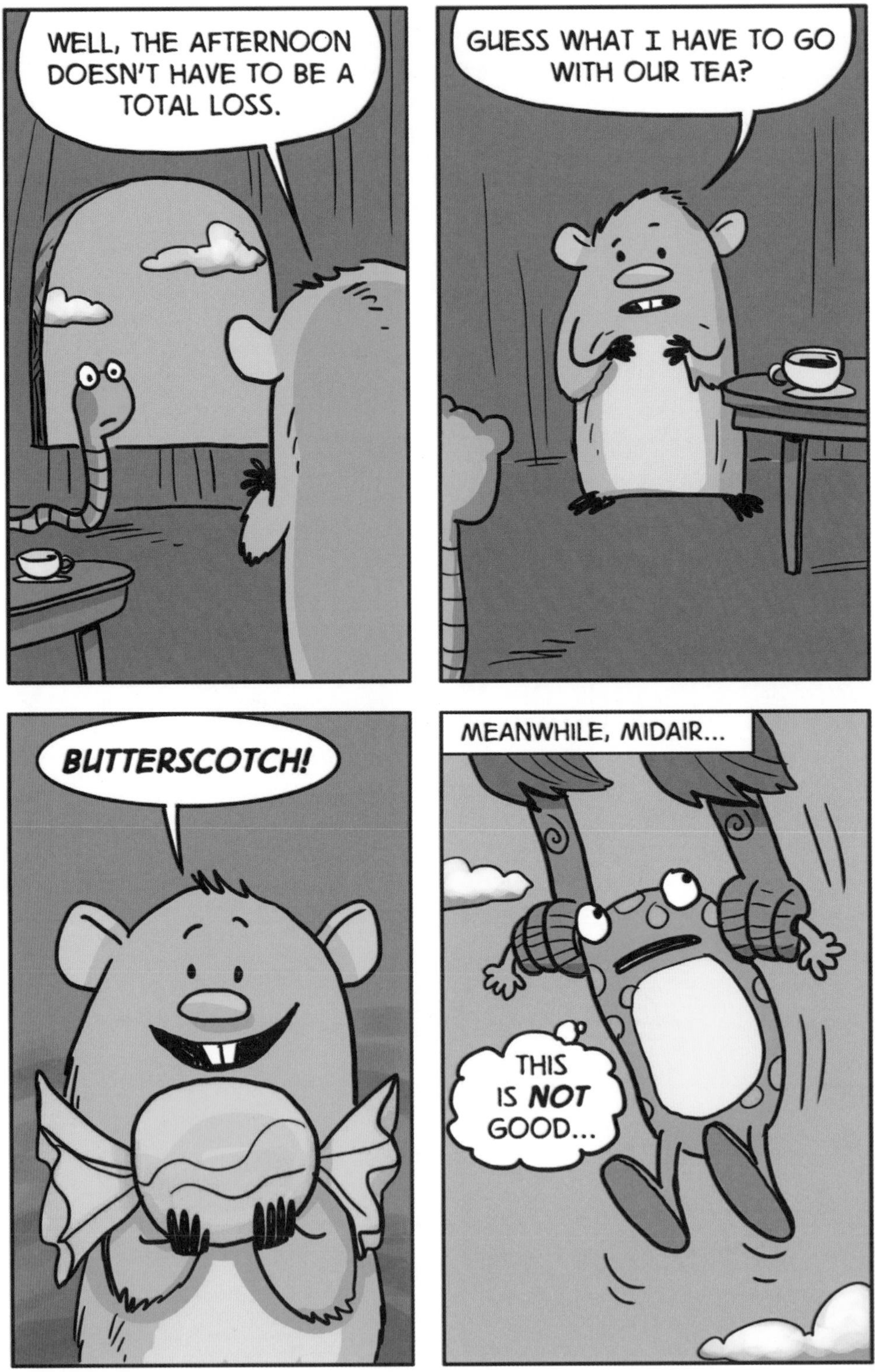
WELL, THE AFTERNOON DOESN'T HAVE TO BE A TOTAL LOSS.
GUESS WHAT I HAVE TO GO WITH OUR TEA?
BUTTERSCOTCH!
MEANWHILE, MIDAIR...
THIS IS NOT GOOD...

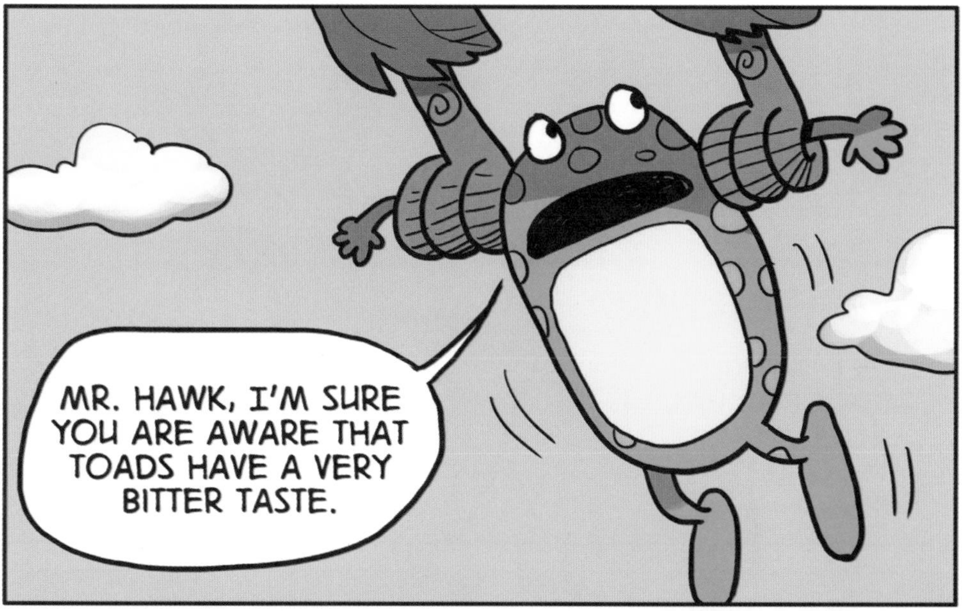
MR. HAWK, I'M SURE YOU ARE AWARE THAT TOADS HAVE A VERY BITTER TASTE.

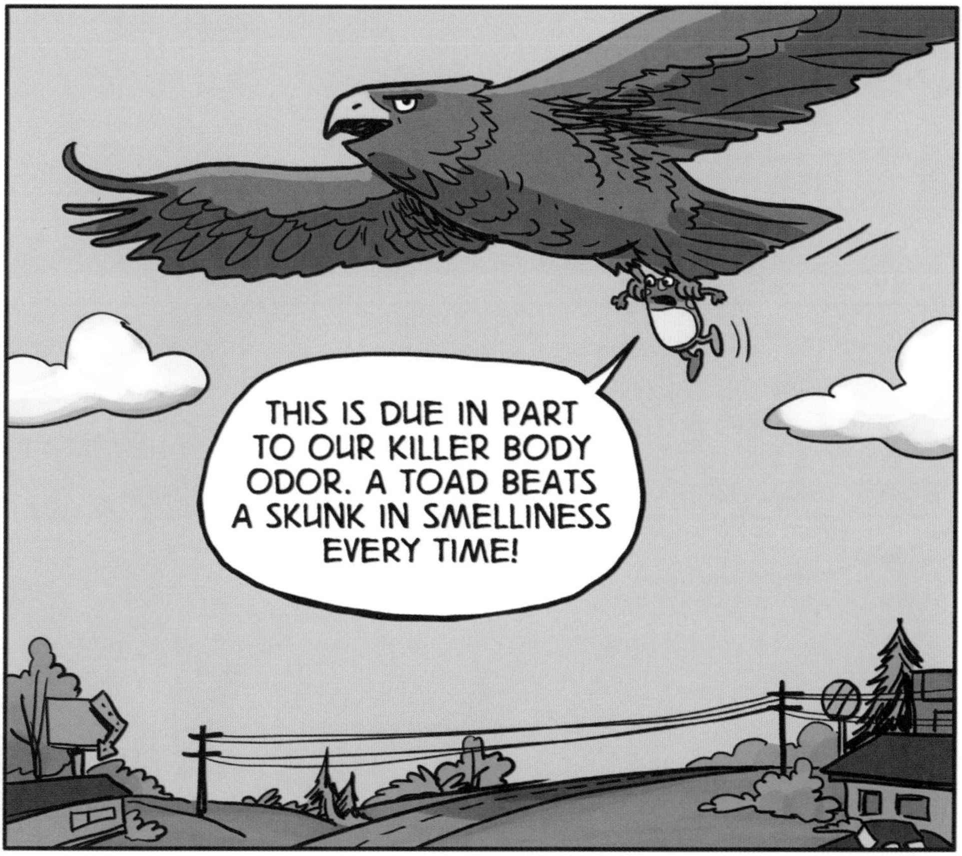
THIS IS DUE IN PART TO OUR KILLER BODY ODOR. A TOAD BEATS A SKUNK IN SMELLINESS EVERY TIME!

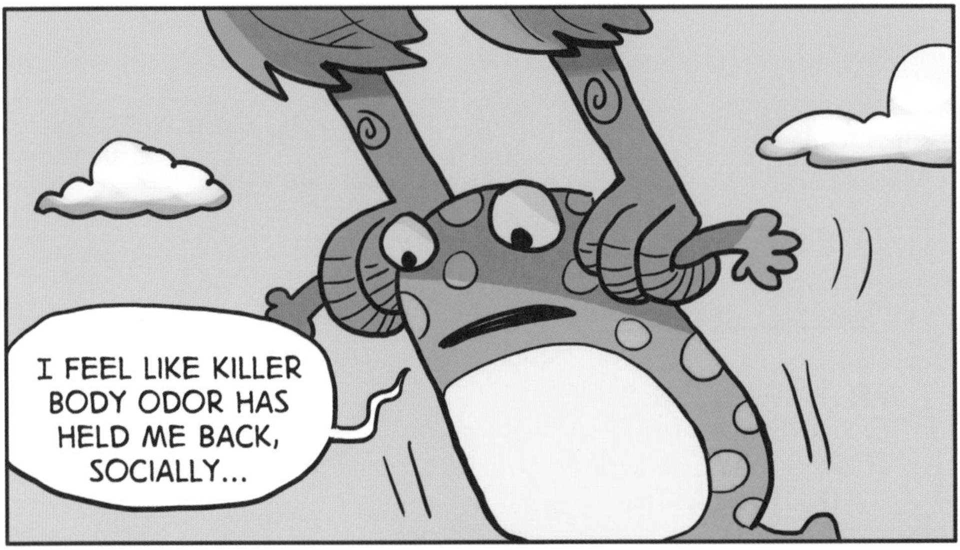
I FEEL LIKE KILLER BODY ODOR HAS HELD ME BACK, SOCIALLY...

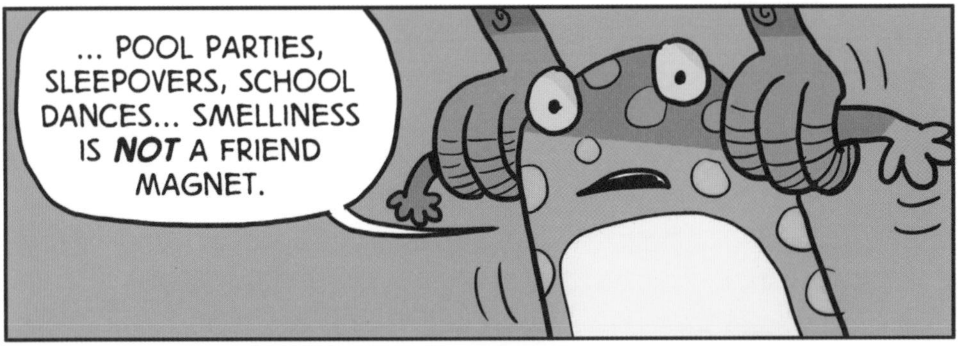
... POOL PARTIES, SLEEPOVERS, SCHOOL DANCES... SMELLINESS IS ***NOT*** A FRIEND MAGNET.

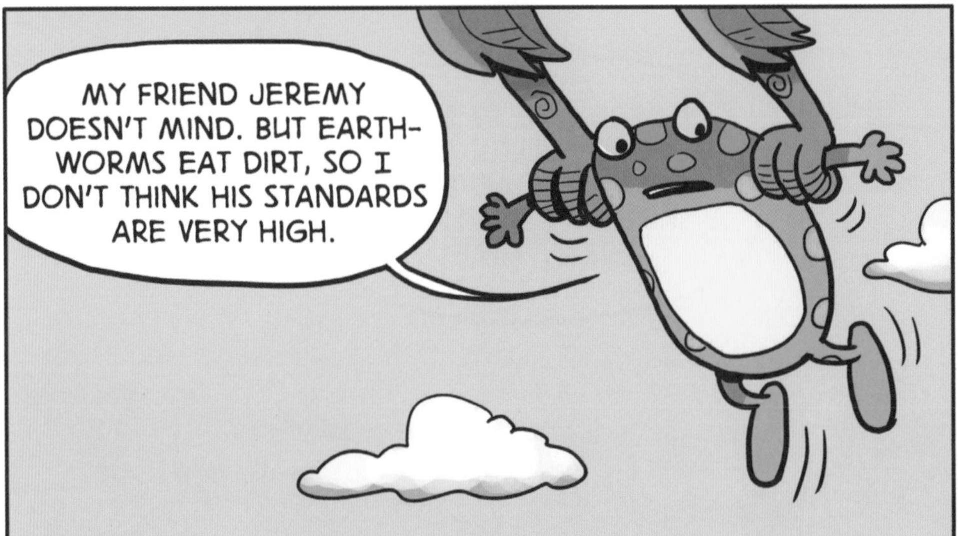
MY FRIEND JEREMY DOESN'T MIND. BUT EARTH-WORMS EAT DIRT, SO I DON'T THINK HIS STANDARDS ARE VERY HIGH.

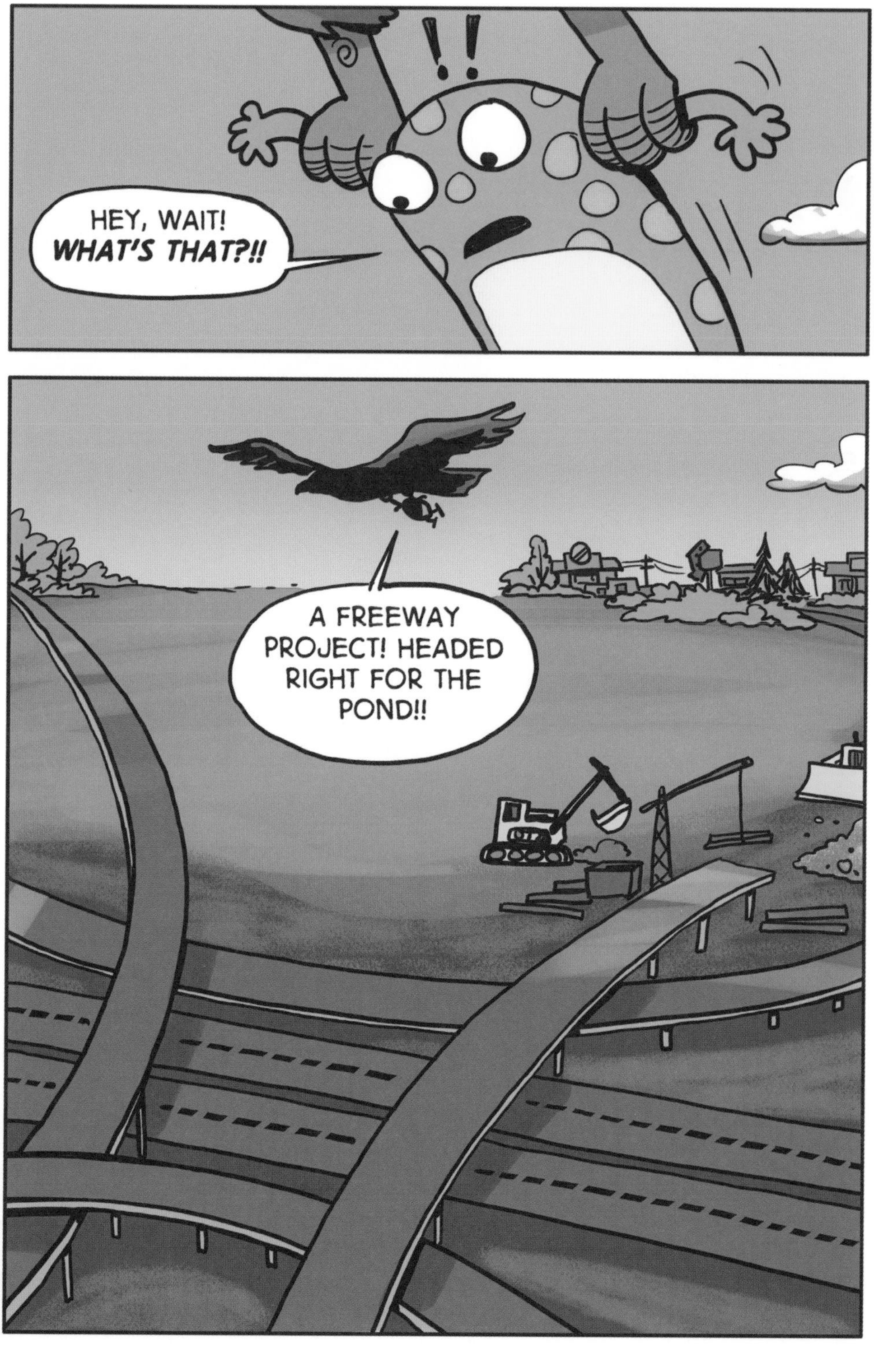
!!
HEY, WAIT! ***WHAT'S THAT?!!***
A FREEWAY PROJECT! HEADED RIGHT FOR THE POND!!

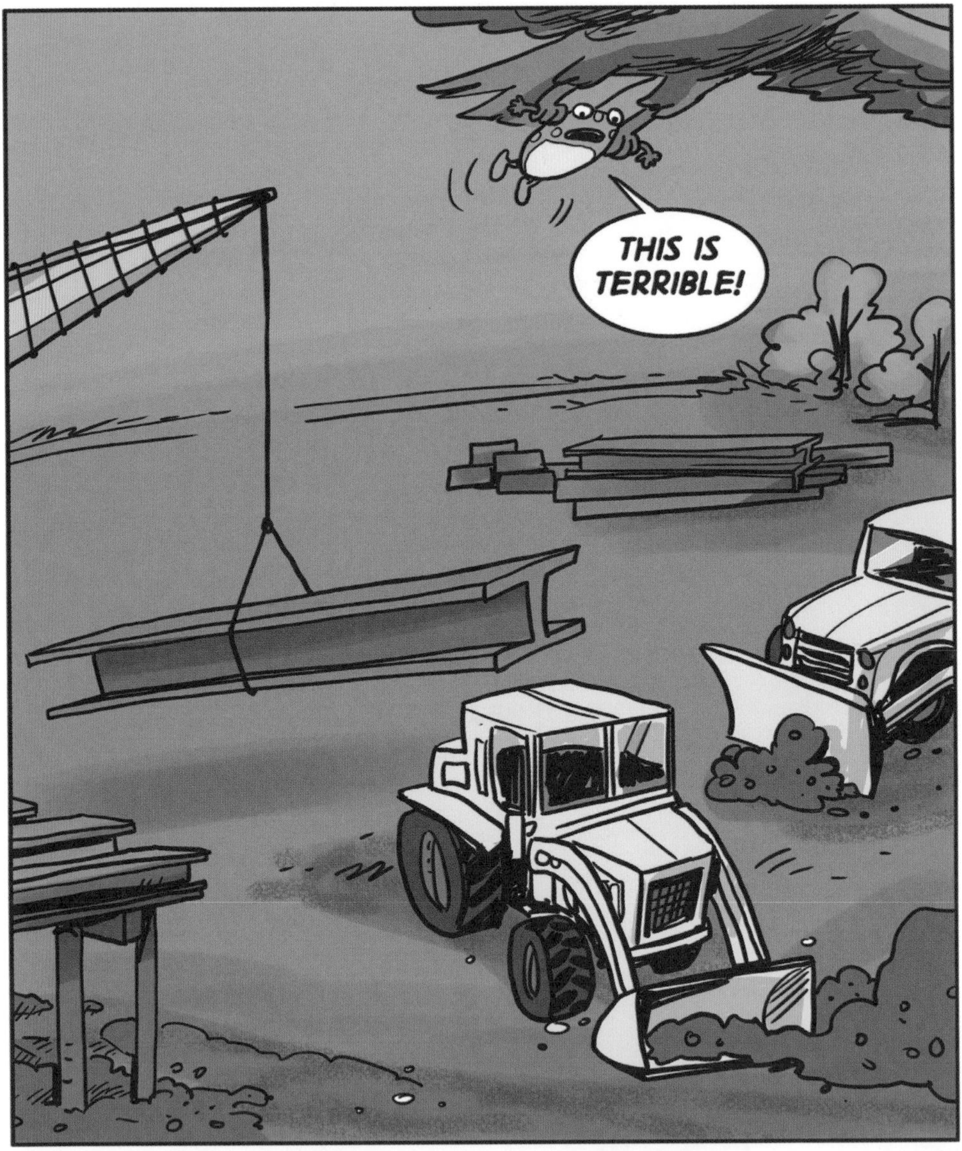
THIS IS TERRIBLE!

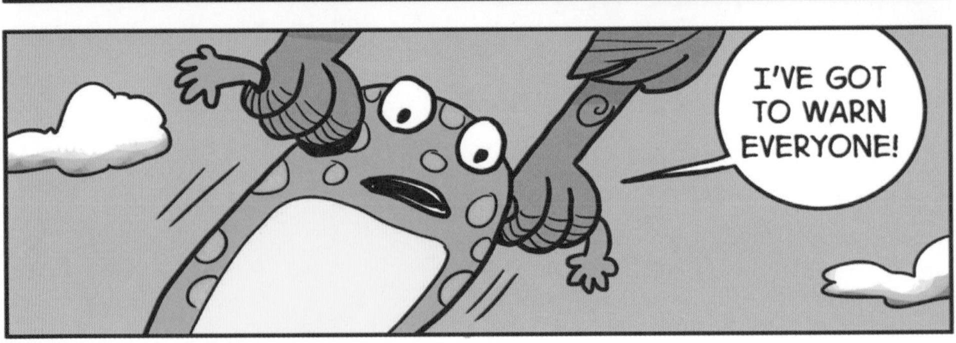
I'VE GOT TO WARN EVERYONE!

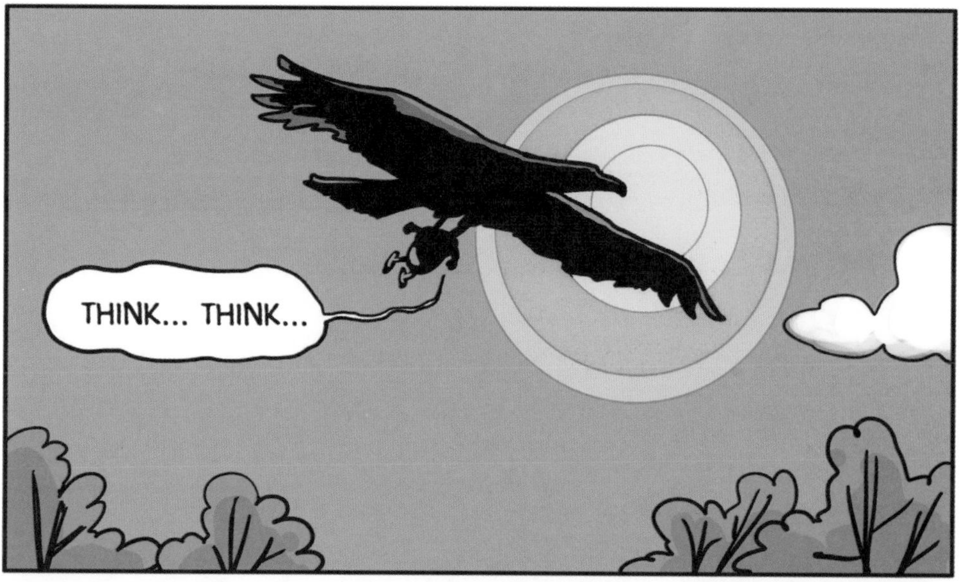
THINK... THINK...

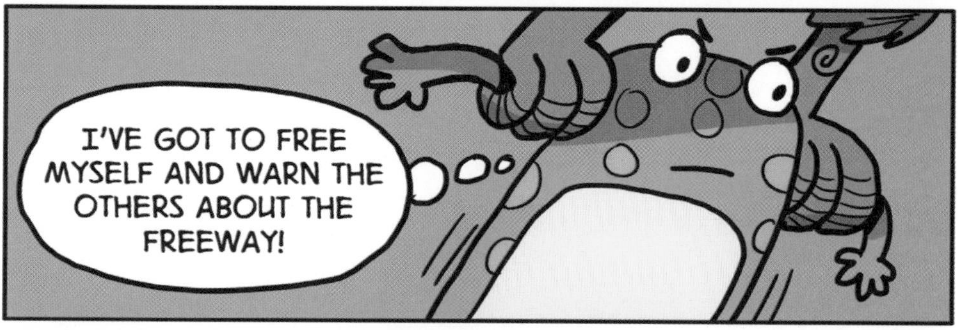
I'VE GOT TO FREE MYSELF AND WARN THE OTHERS ABOUT THE FREEWAY!

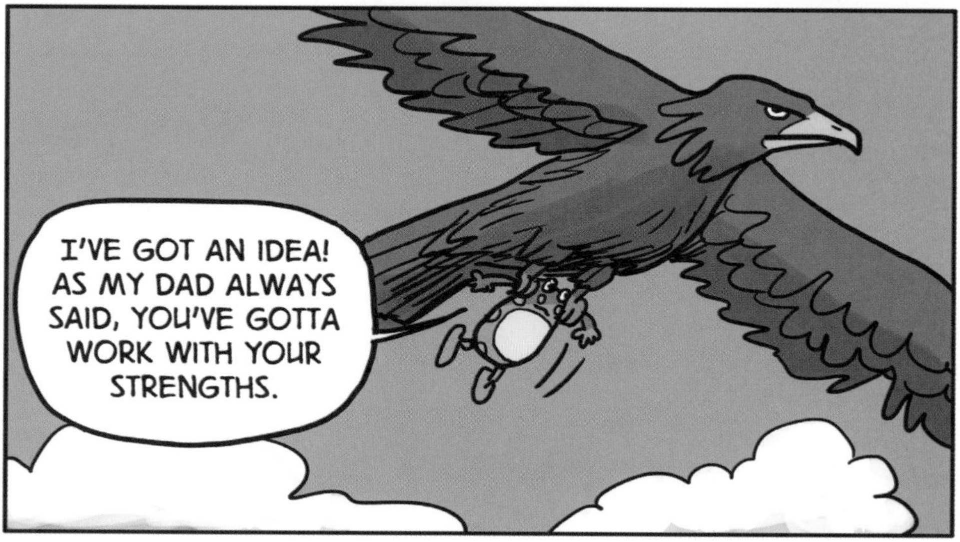
I'VE GOT AN IDEA! AS MY DAD ALWAYS SAID, YOU'VE GOTTA WORK WITH YOUR STRENGTHS.

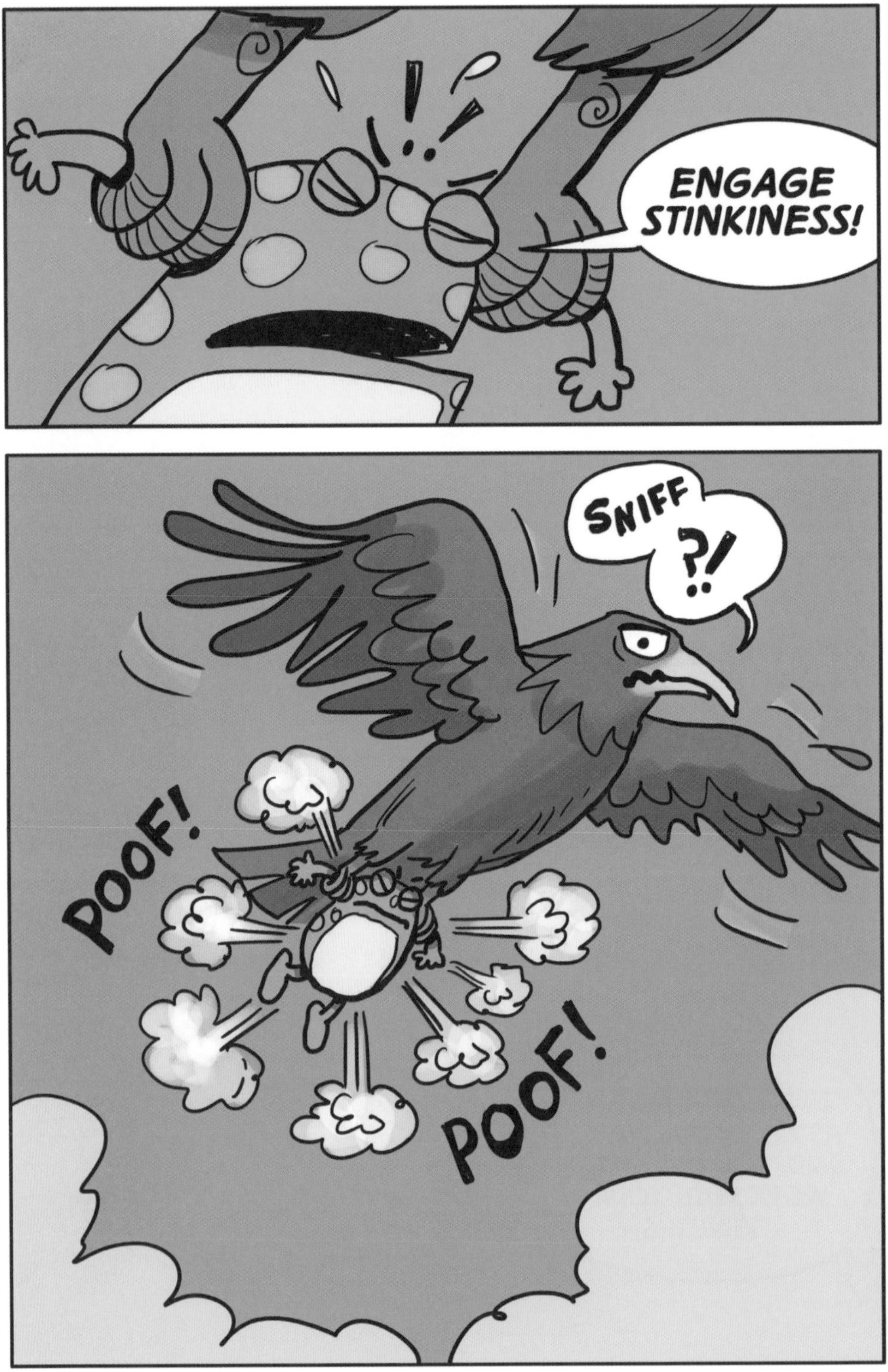
ENGAGE STINKINESS!
SNIFF
?!
POOF!
POOF!

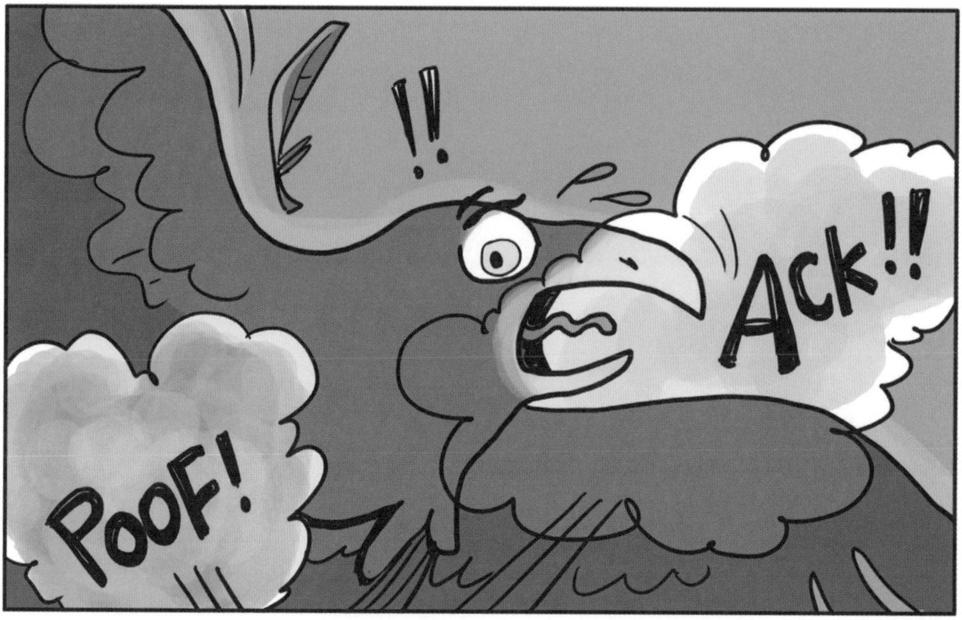
!!
ACK!!
POOF!

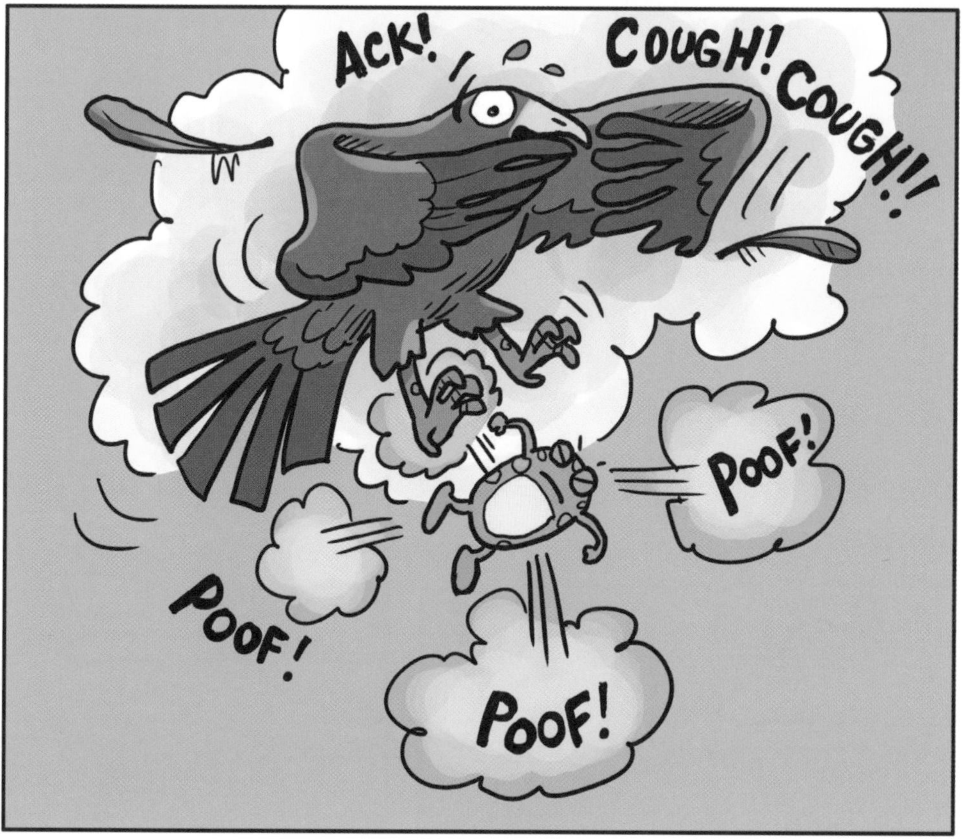
ACK!
COUGH! COUGH!!
POOF!
POOF!
POOF!

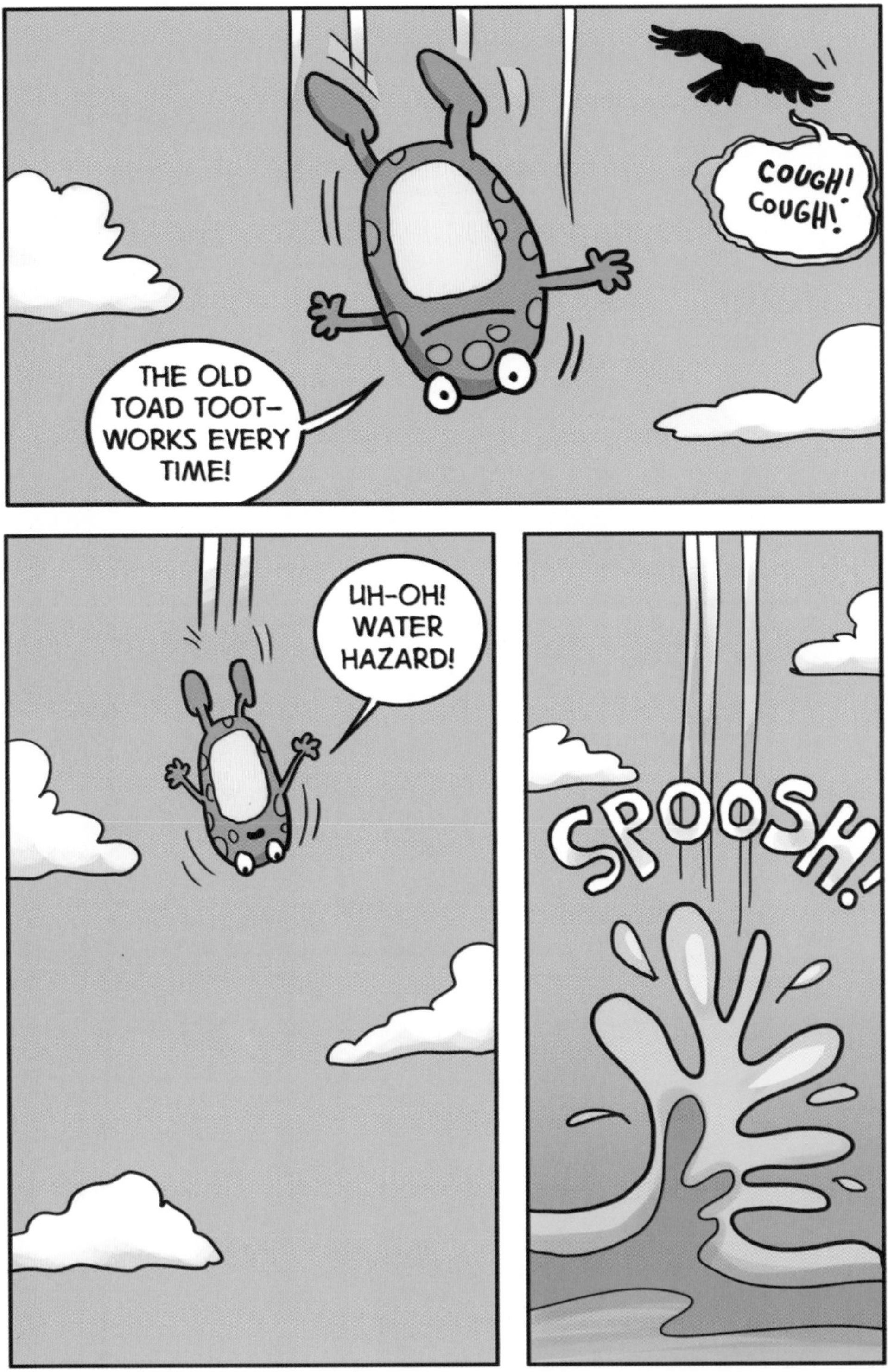
COUGH! COUGH!
THE OLD TOAD TOOT- WORKS EVERY TIME!
UH-OH! WATER HAZARD!
SPOOSH!

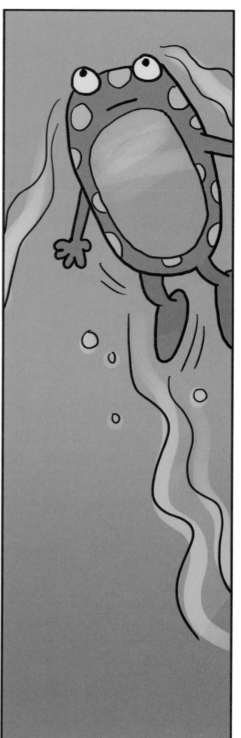

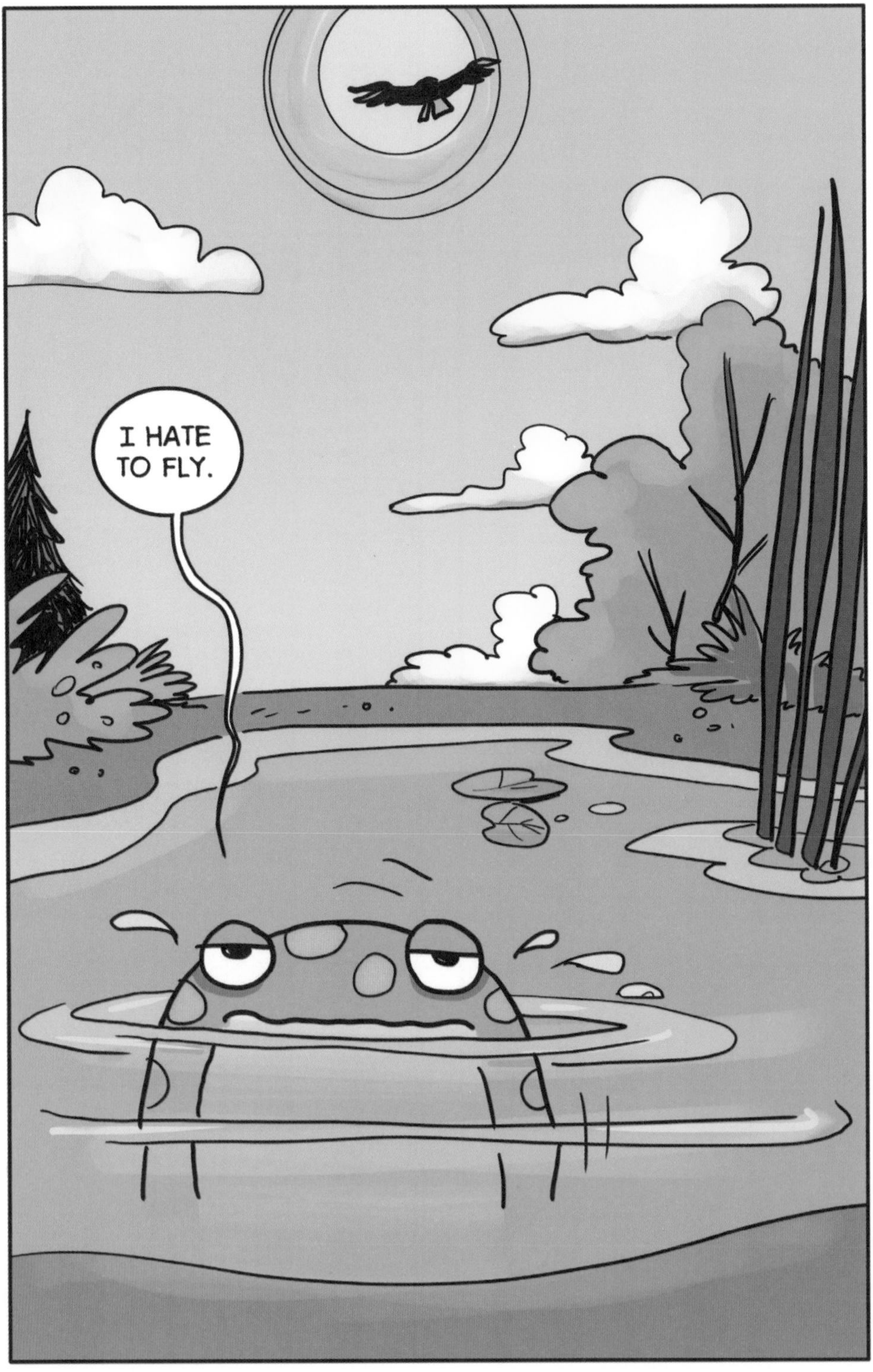
I HATE TO FLY.

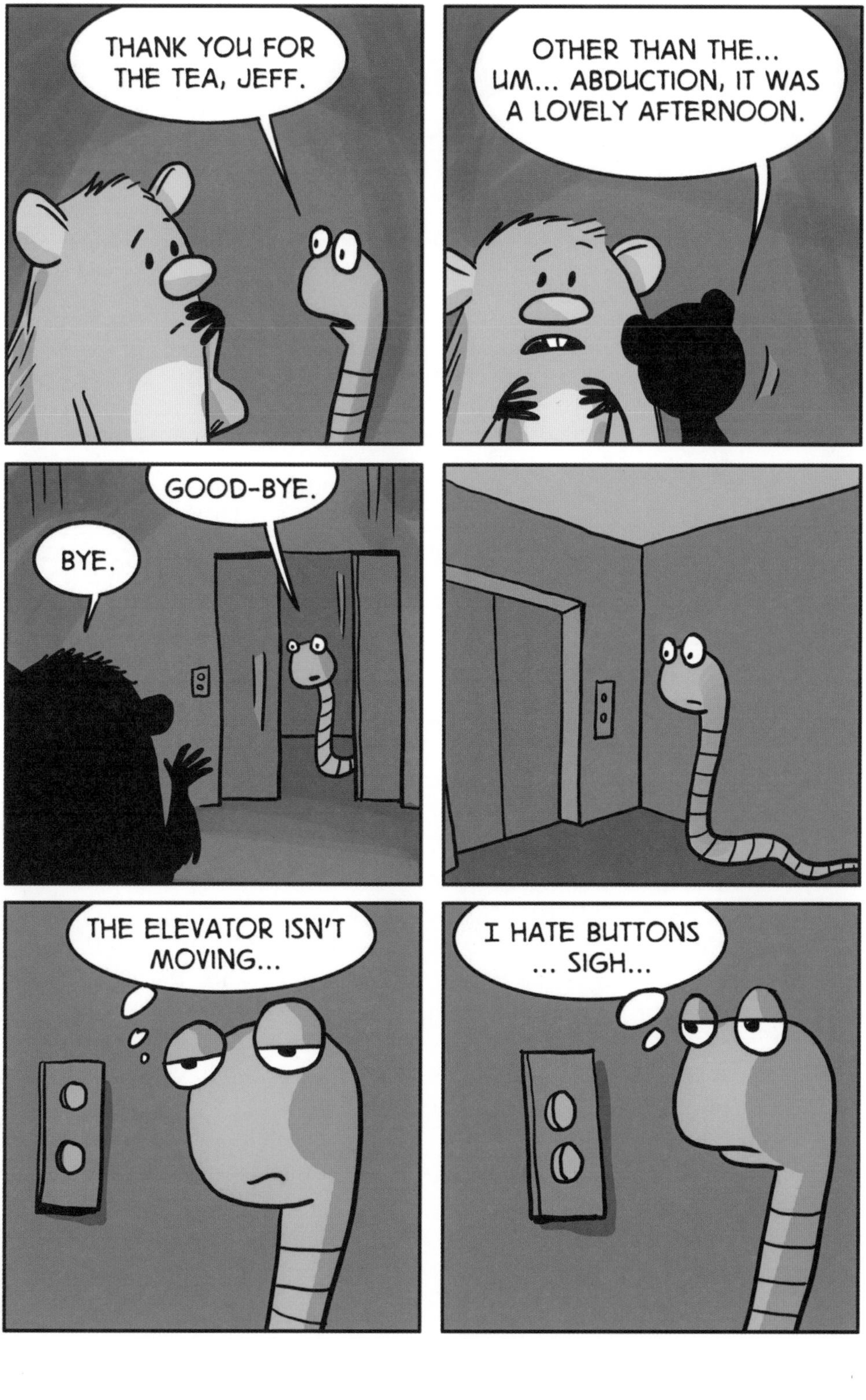
THANK YOU FOR THE TEA, JEFF.
OTHER THAN THE... UM... ABDUCTION, IT WAS A LOVELY AFTERNOON.
GOOD-BYE.
BYE.
THE ELEVATOR ISN'T MOVING...
I HATE BUTTONS ... SIGH...

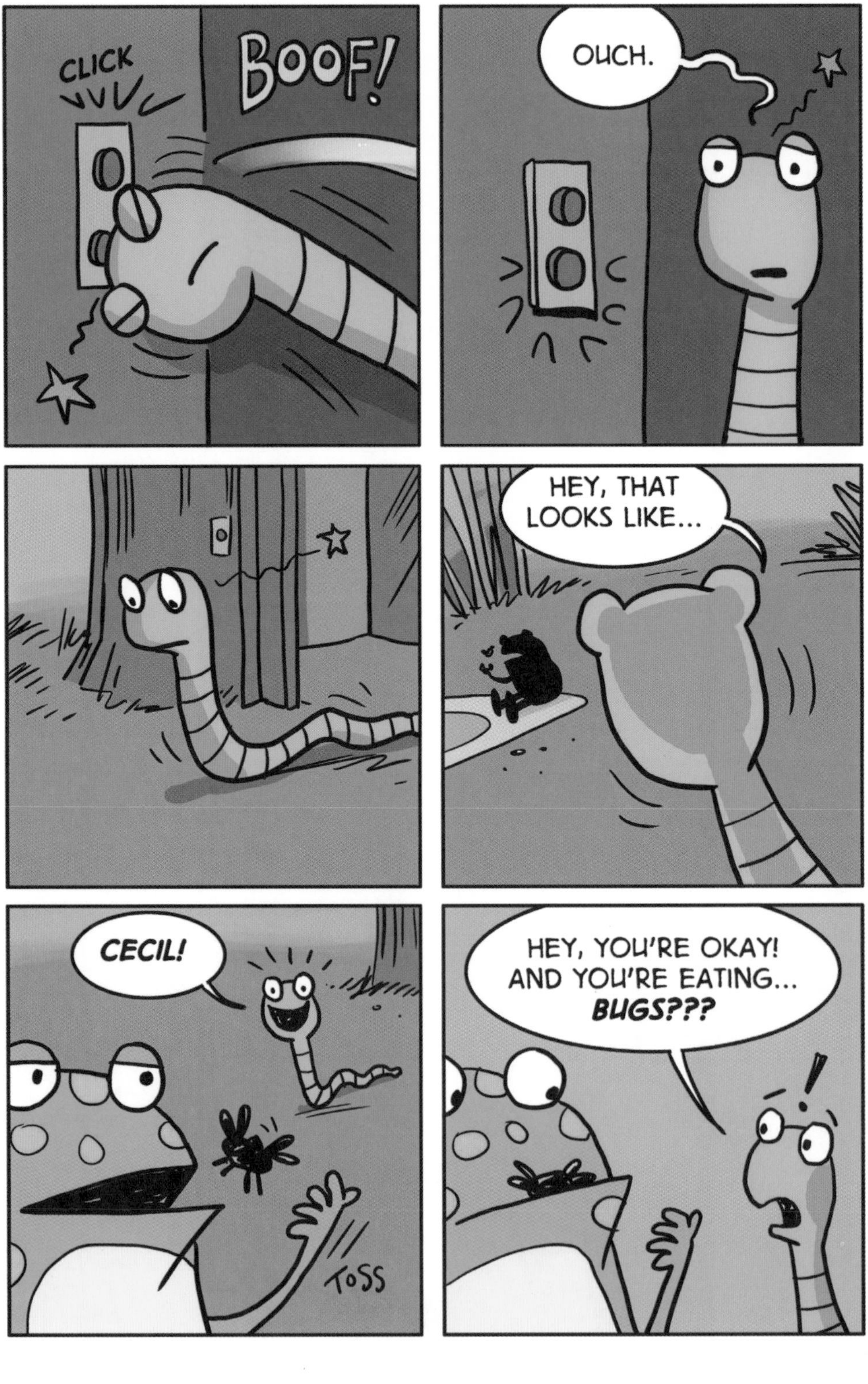
CLICK
BOOF!
OUCH.
HEY, THAT LOOKS LIKE...
CECIL!
TOSS
HEY, YOU'RE OKAY! AND YOU'RE EATING... BUGS???

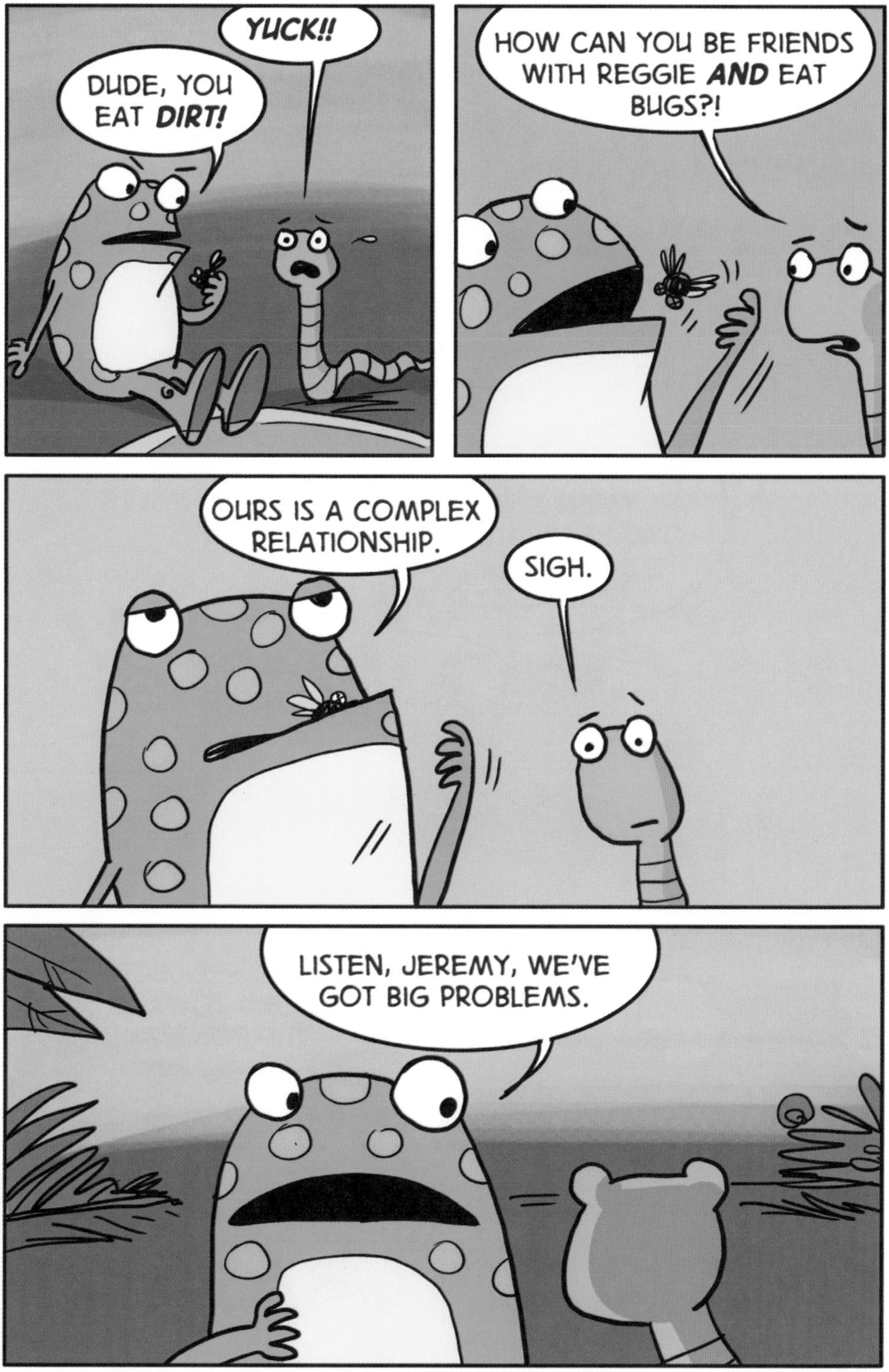
DUDE, YOU EAT *DIRT!*
YUCK!!
HOW CAN YOU BE FRIENDS WITH REGGIE *AND* EAT BUGS?!
OURS IS A COMPLEX RELATIONSHIP.
SIGH.
LISTEN, JEREMY, WE'VE GOT BIG PROBLEMS.

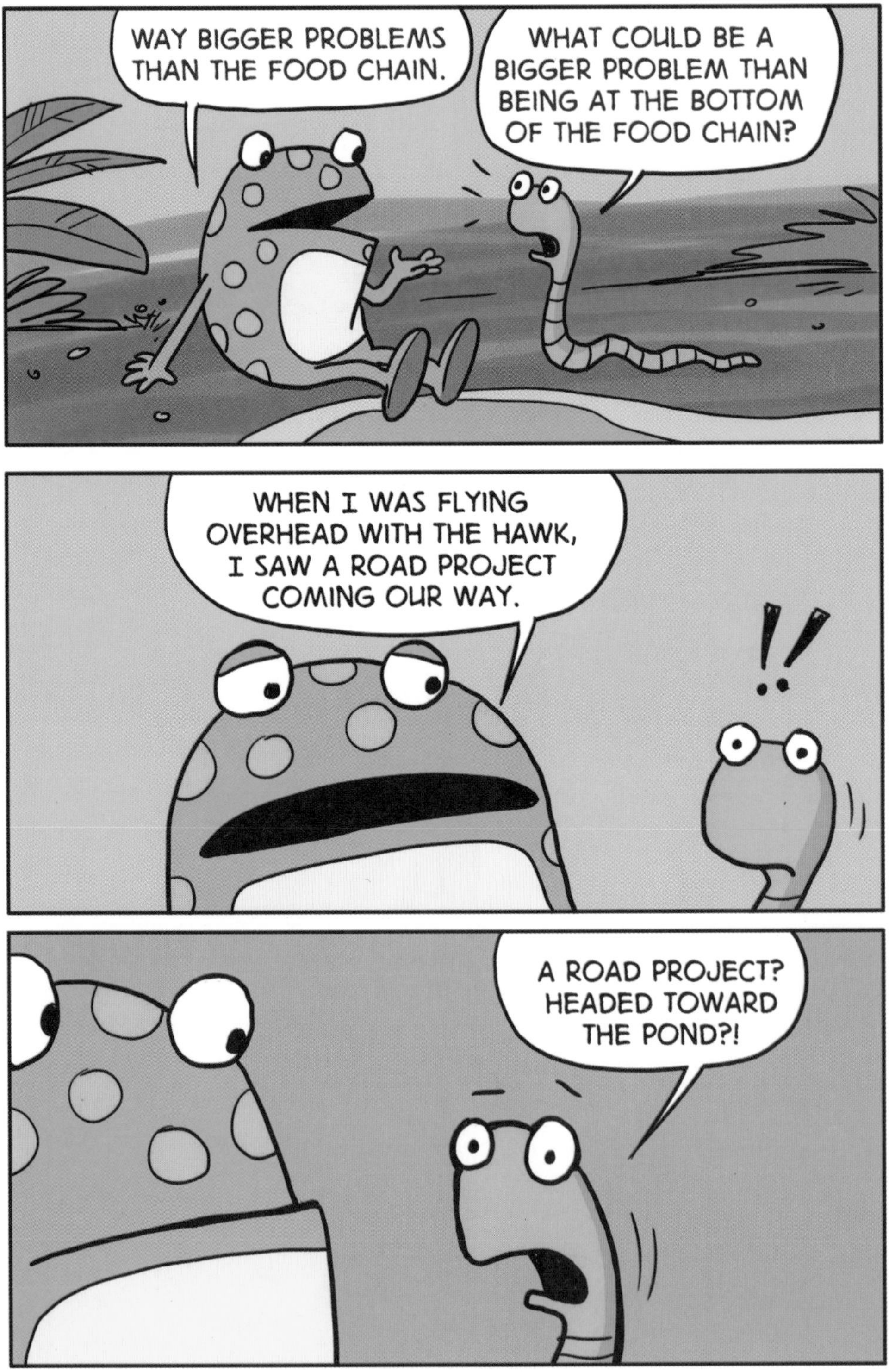
WAY BIGGER PROBLEMS THAN THE FOOD CHAIN.
WHAT COULD BE A BIGGER PROBLEM THAN BEING AT THE BOTTOM OF THE FOOD CHAIN?
WHEN I WAS FLYING OVERHEAD WITH THE HAWK, I SAW A ROAD PROJECT COMING OUR WAY.
!!
A ROAD PROJECT? HEADED TOWARD THE POND?!

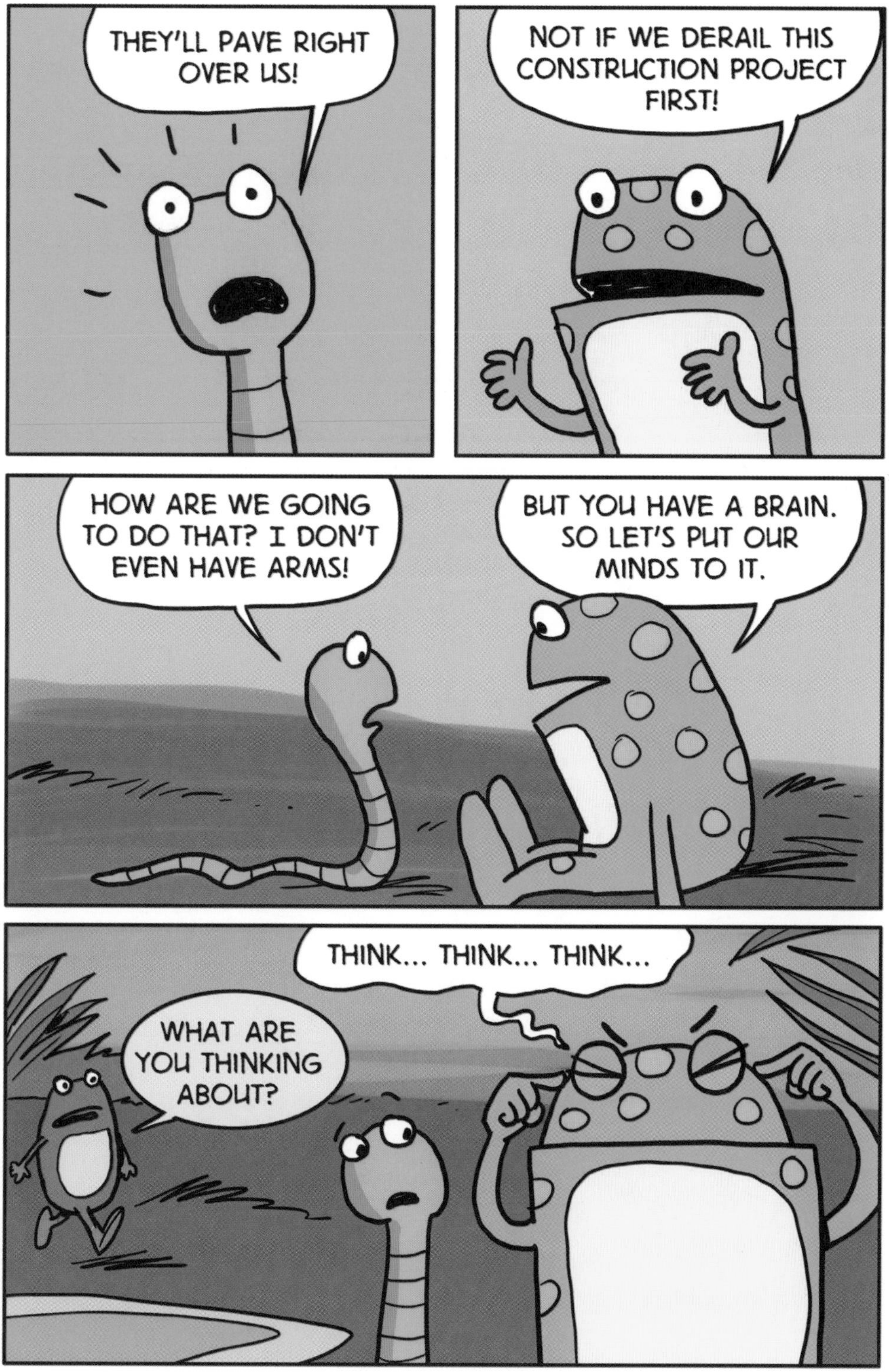
THEY'LL PAVE RIGHT OVER US!
NOT IF WE DERAIL THIS CONSTRUCTION PROJECT FIRST!
HOW ARE WE GOING TO DO THAT? I DON'T EVEN HAVE ARMS!
BUT YOU HAVE A BRAIN. SO LET'S PUT OUR MINDS TO IT.
THINK... THINK... THINK...
WHAT ARE YOU THINKING ABOUT?

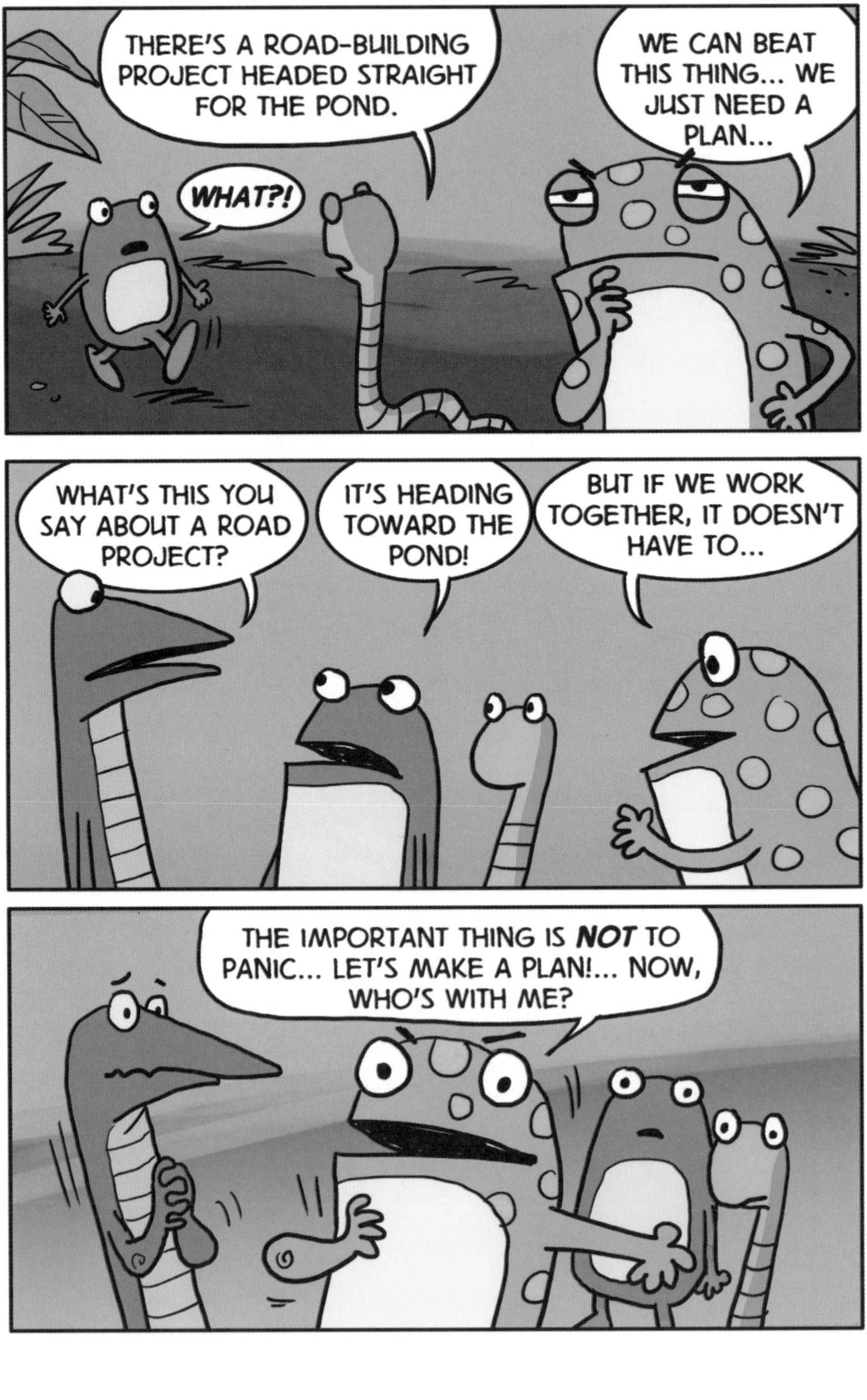
THERE'S A ROAD-BUILDING PROJECT HEADED STRAIGHT FOR THE POND.
WHAT?!
WE CAN BEAT THIS THING... WE JUST NEED A PLAN...
WHAT'S THIS YOU SAY ABOUT A ROAD PROJECT?
IT'S HEADING TOWARD THE POND!
BUT IF WE WORK TOGETHER, IT DOESN'T HAVE TO...
THE IMPORTANT THING IS ***NOT*** TO PANIC... LET'S MAKE A PLAN!... NOW, WHO'S WITH ME?

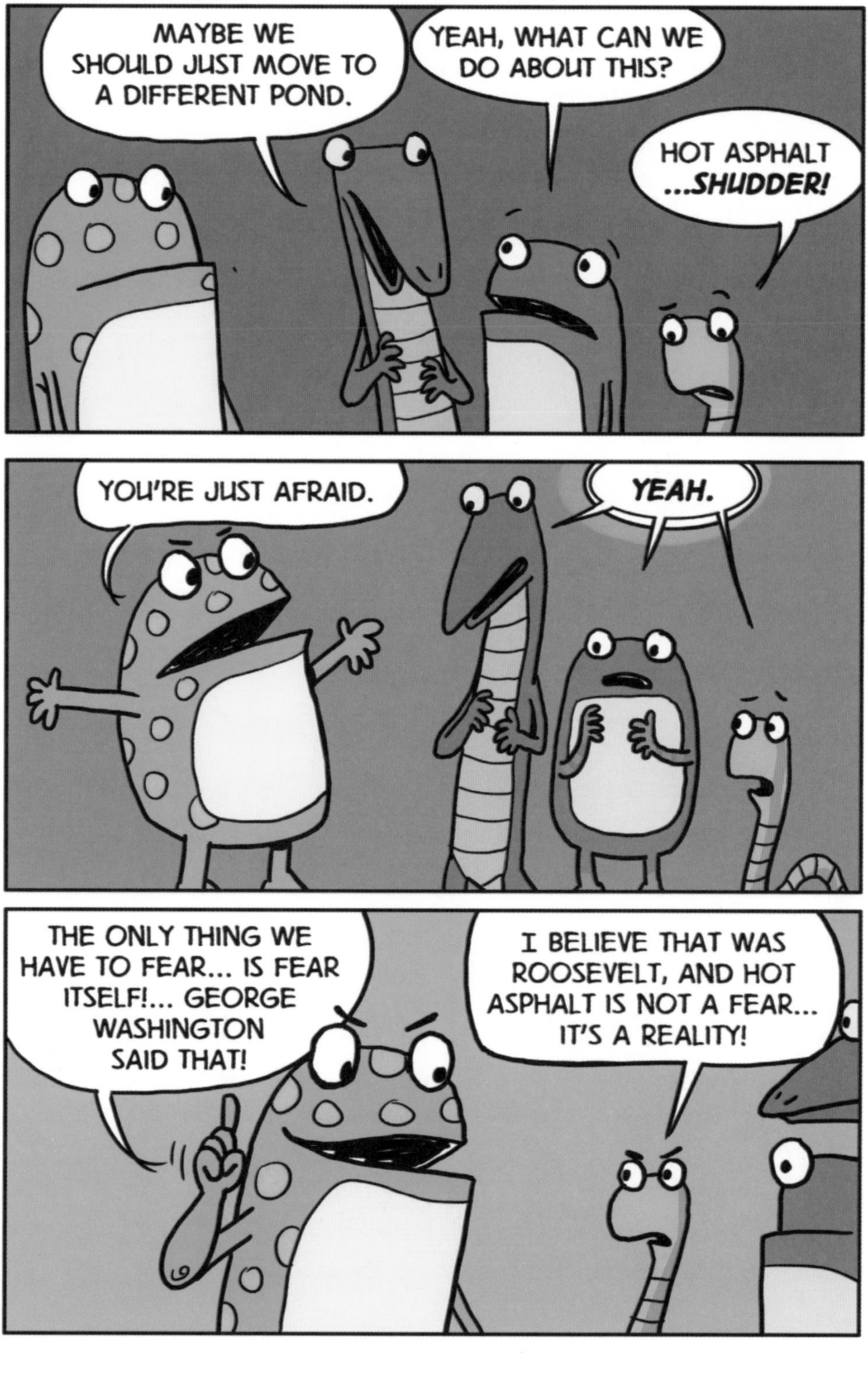
MAYBE WE SHOULD JUST MOVE TO A DIFFERENT POND.
YEAH, WHAT CAN WE DO ABOUT THIS?
HOT ASPHALT ...SHUDDER!
YOU'RE JUST AFRAID.
YEAH.
THE ONLY THING WE HAVE TO FEAR... IS FEAR ITSELF!... GEORGE WASHINGTON SAID THAT!
I BELIEVE THAT WAS ROOSEVELT, AND HOT ASPHALT IS NOT A FEAR... IT'S A REALITY!

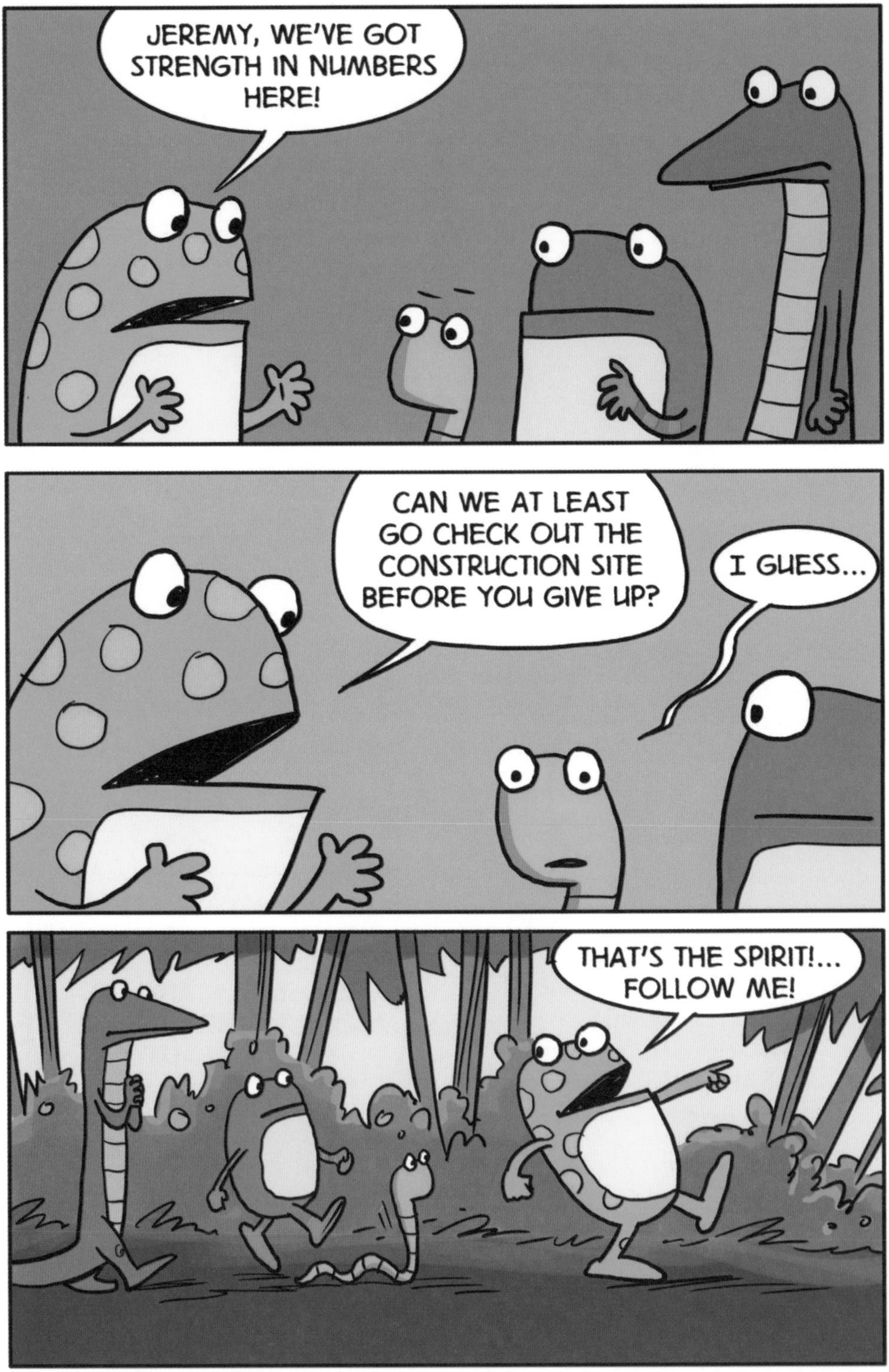
JEREMY, WE'VE GOT STRENGTH IN NUMBERS HERE!
CAN WE AT LEAST GO CHECK OUT THE CONSTRUCTION SITE BEFORE YOU GIVE UP?
I GUESS...
THAT'S THE SPIRIT!... FOLLOW ME!

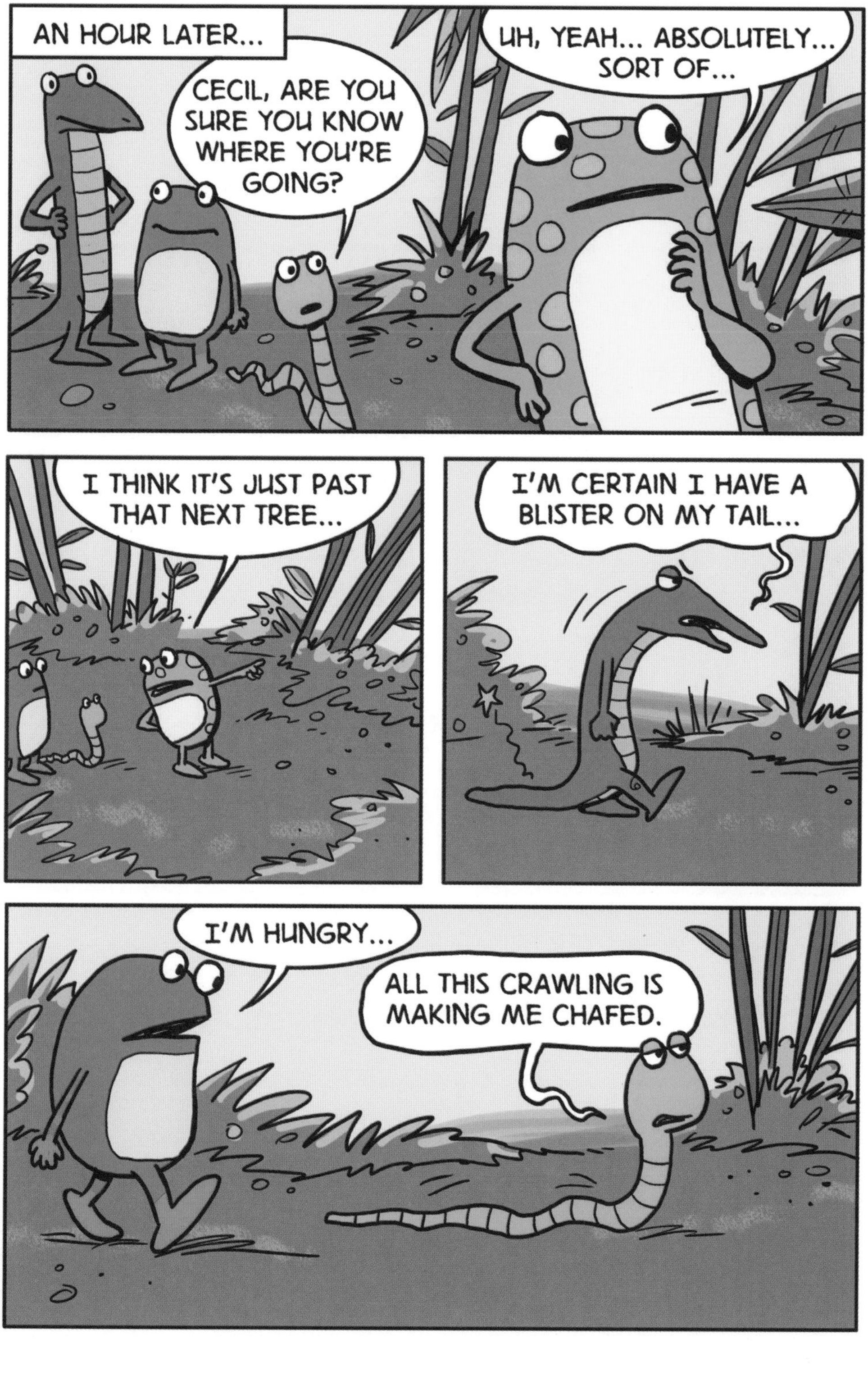
AN HOUR LATER...
CECIL, ARE YOU SURE YOU KNOW WHERE YOU'RE GOING?
UH, YEAH... ABSOLUTELY... SORT OF...
I THINK IT'S JUST PAST THAT NEXT TREE...
I'M CERTAIN I HAVE A BLISTER ON MY TAIL...
I'M HUNGRY...
ALL THIS CRAWLING IS MAKING ME CHAFED.

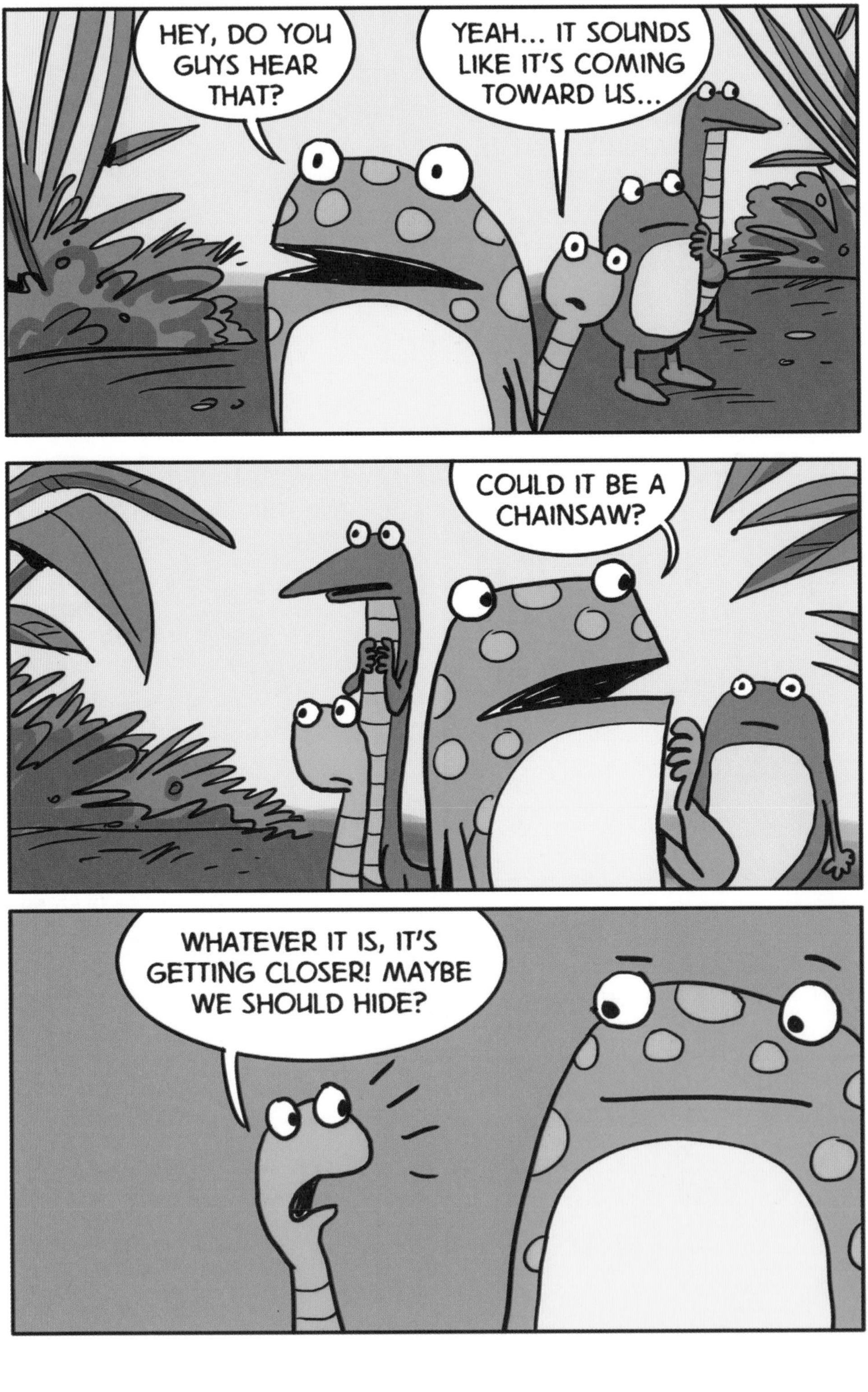
HEY, DO YOU GUYS HEAR THAT?
YEAH... IT SOUNDS LIKE IT'S COMING TOWARD US...
COULD IT BE A CHAINSAW?
WHATEVER IT IS, IT'S GETTING CLOSER! MAYBE WE SHOULD HIDE?

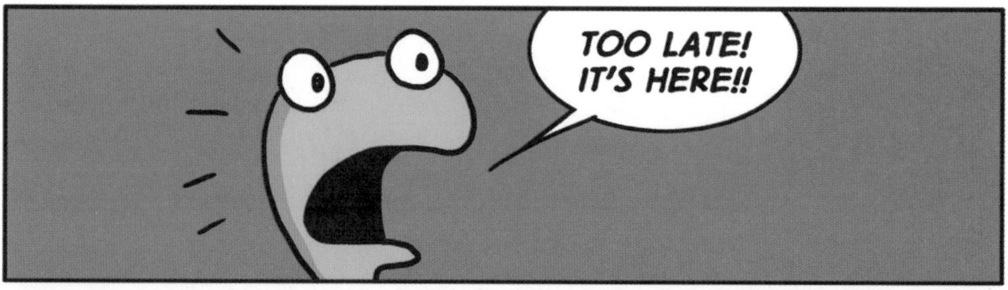
TOO LATE! IT'S HERE!!

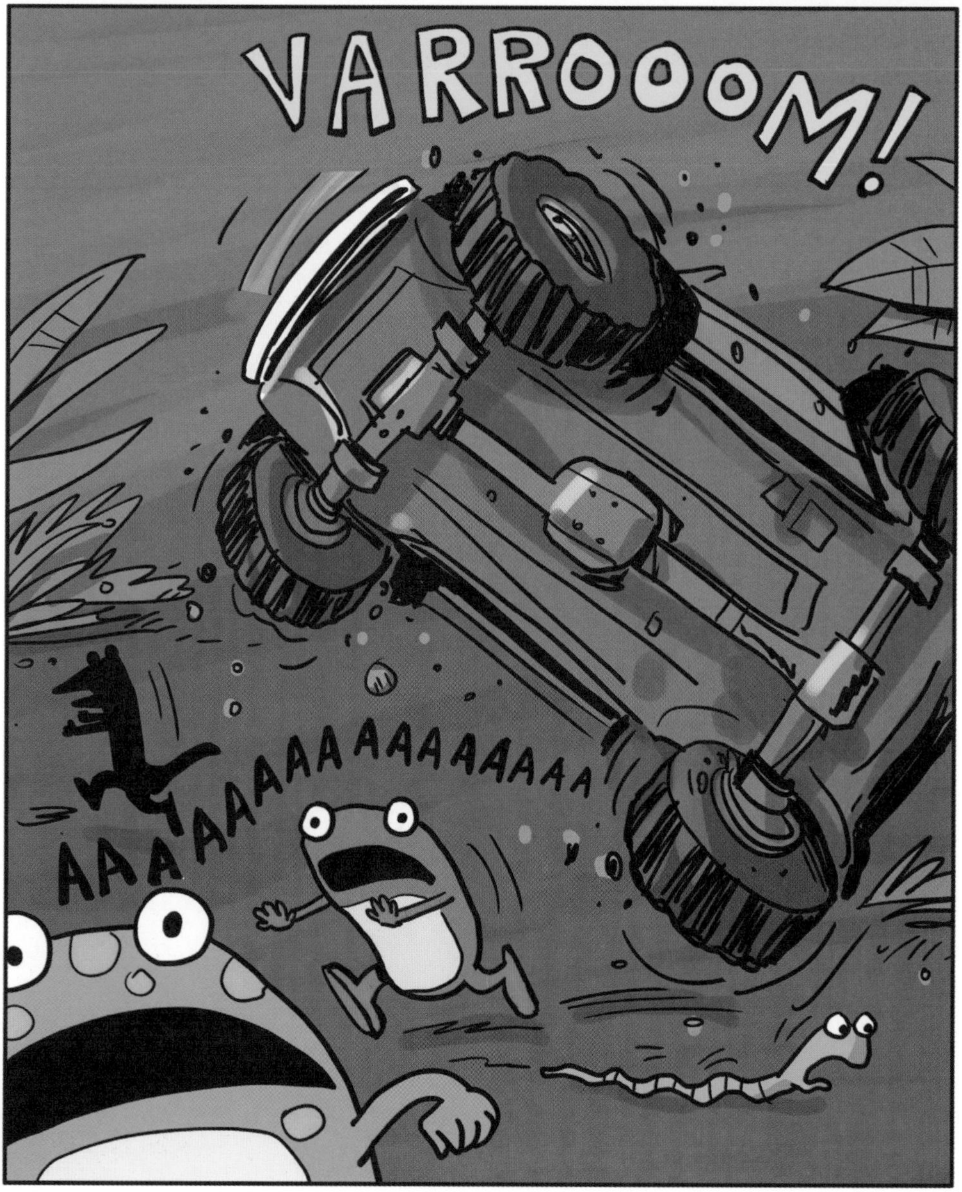
VARROOOM!
AAAAAAAAAAAAAAAAAAAA

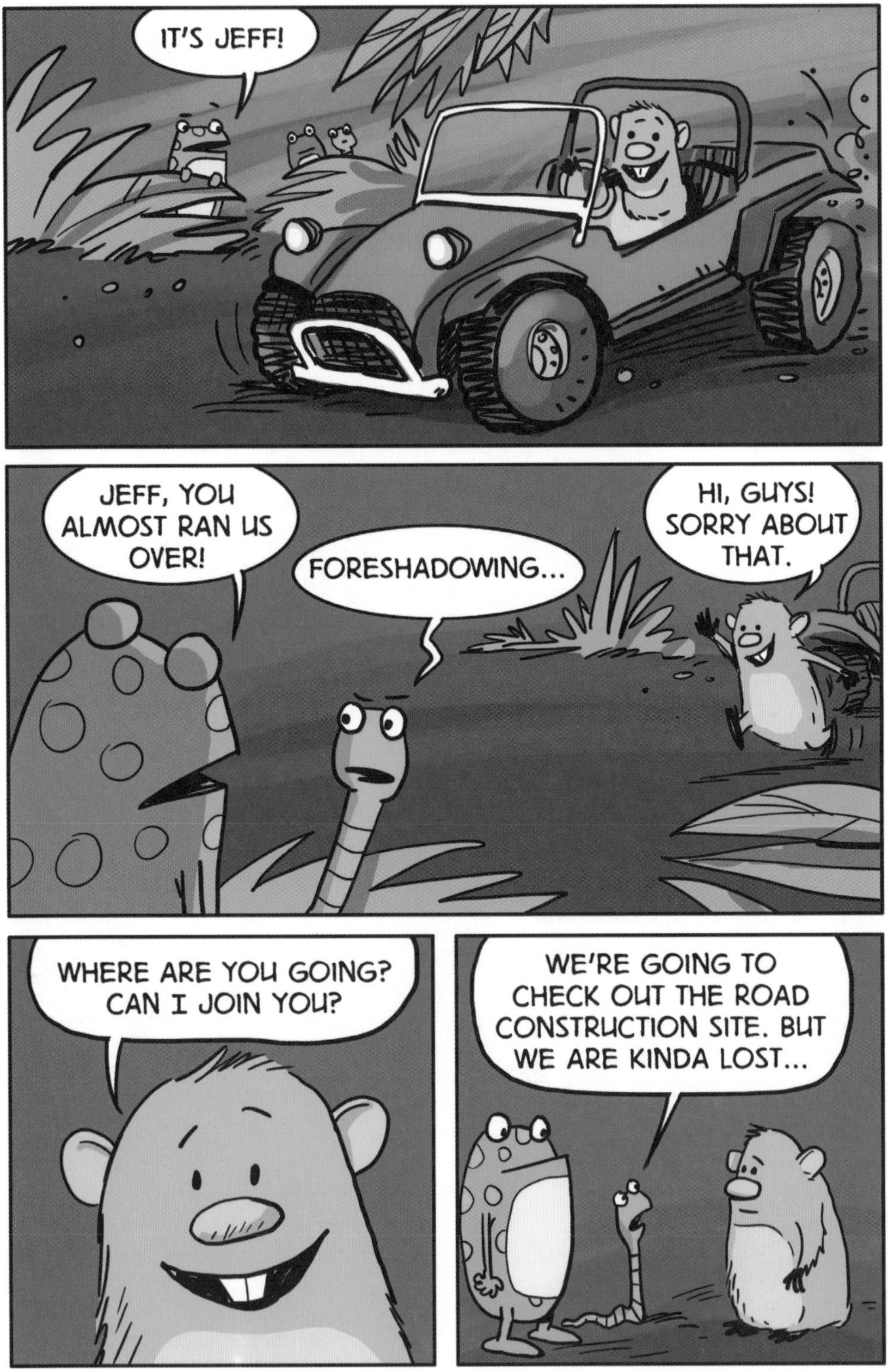
IT'S JEFF!
JEFF, YOU ALMOST RAN US OVER!
FORESHADOWING...
HI, GUYS! SORRY ABOUT THAT.
WHERE ARE YOU GOING? CAN I JOIN YOU?
WE'RE GOING TO CHECK OUT THE ROAD CONSTRUCTION SITE. BUT WE ARE KINDA LOST...

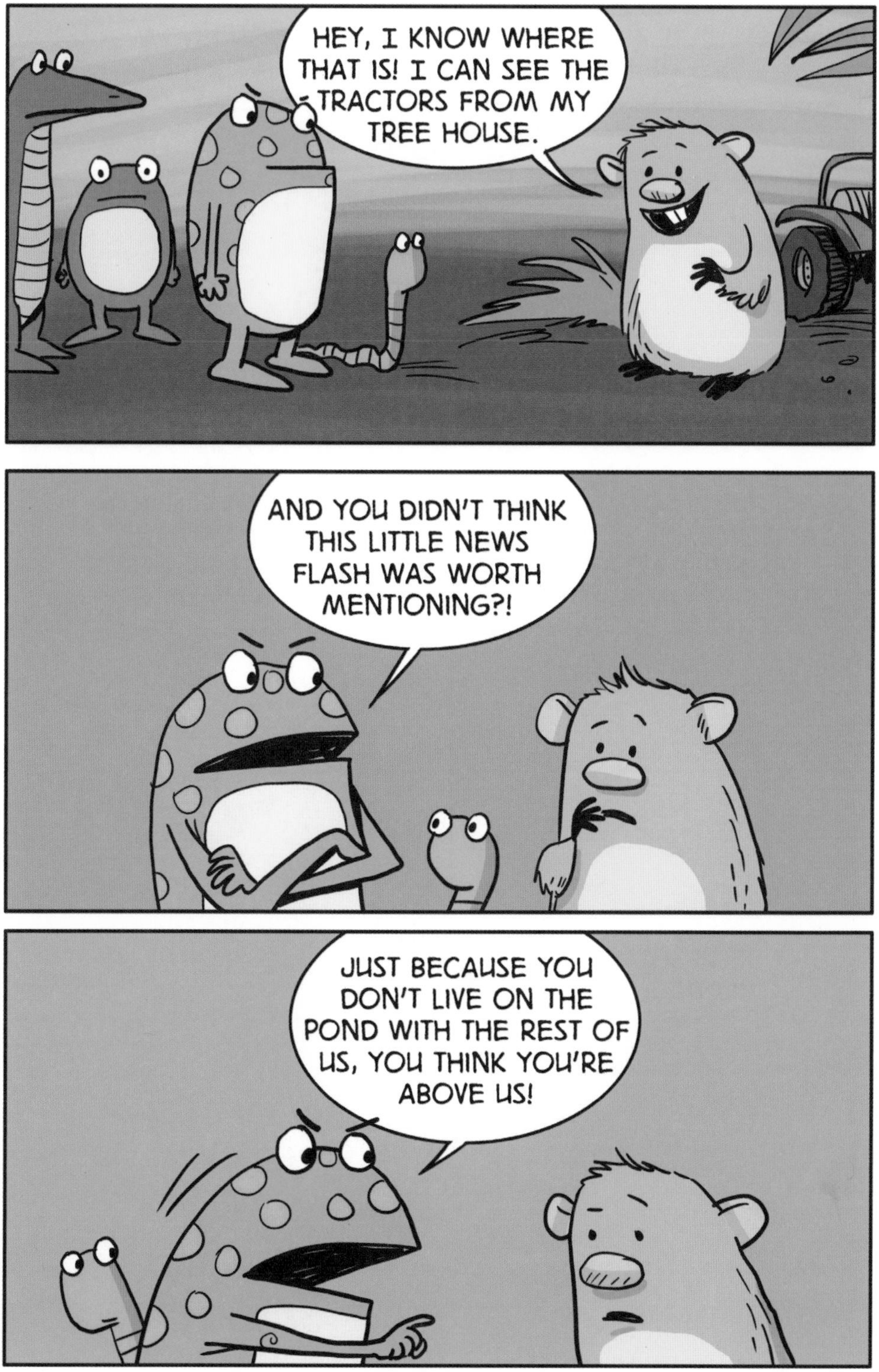
HEY, I KNOW WHERE THAT IS! I CAN SEE THE TRACTORS FROM MY TREE HOUSE.
AND YOU DIDN'T THINK THIS LITTLE NEWS FLASH WAS WORTH MENTIONING?!
JUST BECAUSE YOU DON'T LIVE ON THE POND WITH THE REST OF US, YOU THINK YOU'RE ABOVE US!

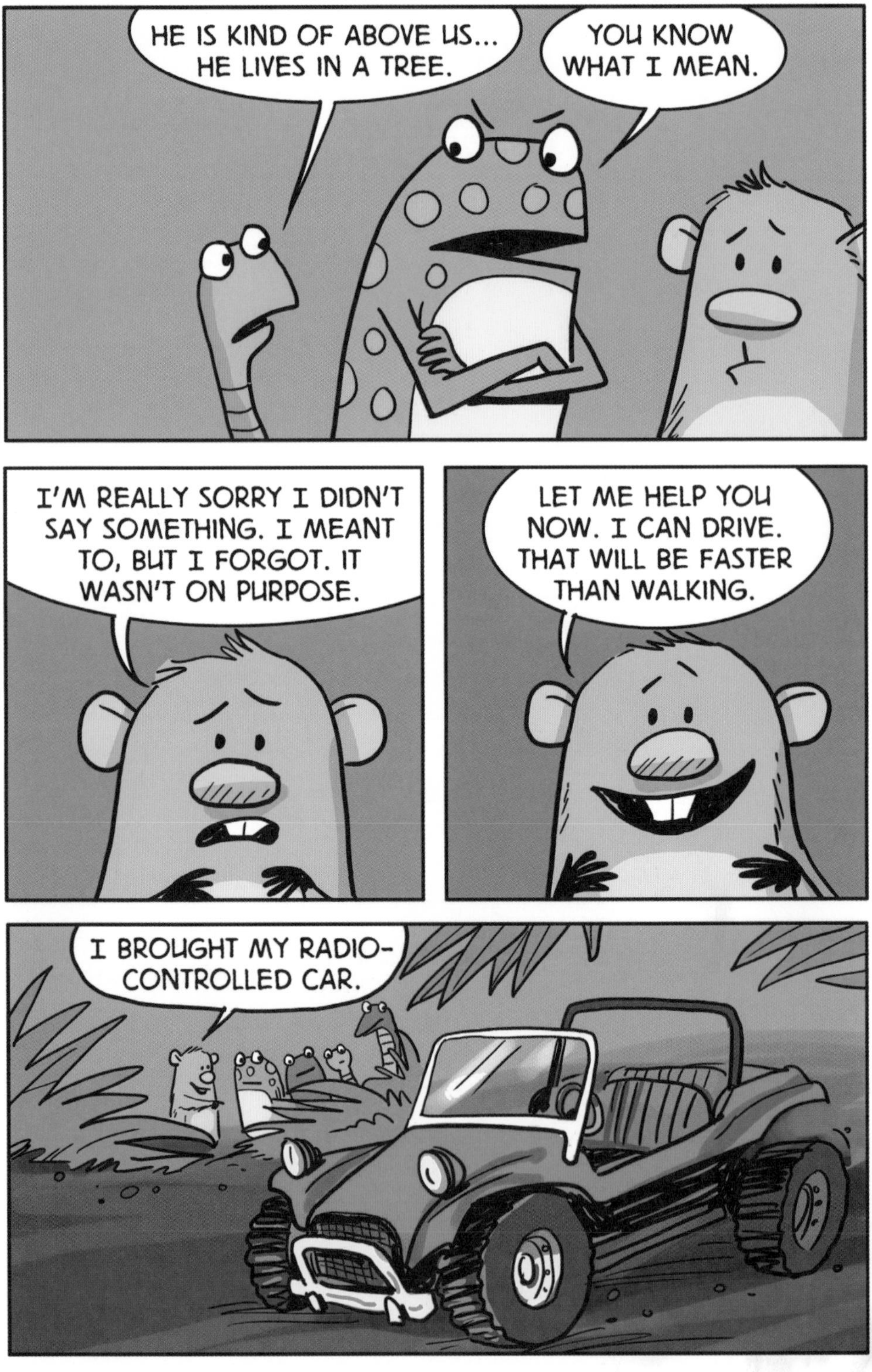
HE IS KIND OF ABOVE US... HE LIVES IN A TREE.
YOU KNOW WHAT I MEAN.
I'M REALLY SORRY I DIDN'T SAY SOMETHING. I MEANT TO, BUT I FORGOT. IT WASN'T ON PURPOSE.
LET ME HELP YOU NOW. I CAN DRIVE. THAT WILL BE FASTER THAN WALKING.
I BROUGHT MY RADIO-CONTROLLED CAR.

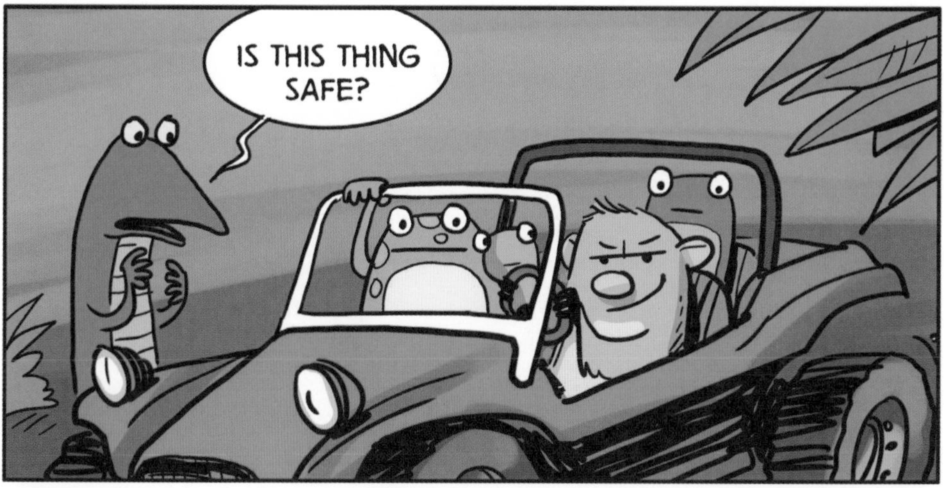
IS THIS THING SAFE?

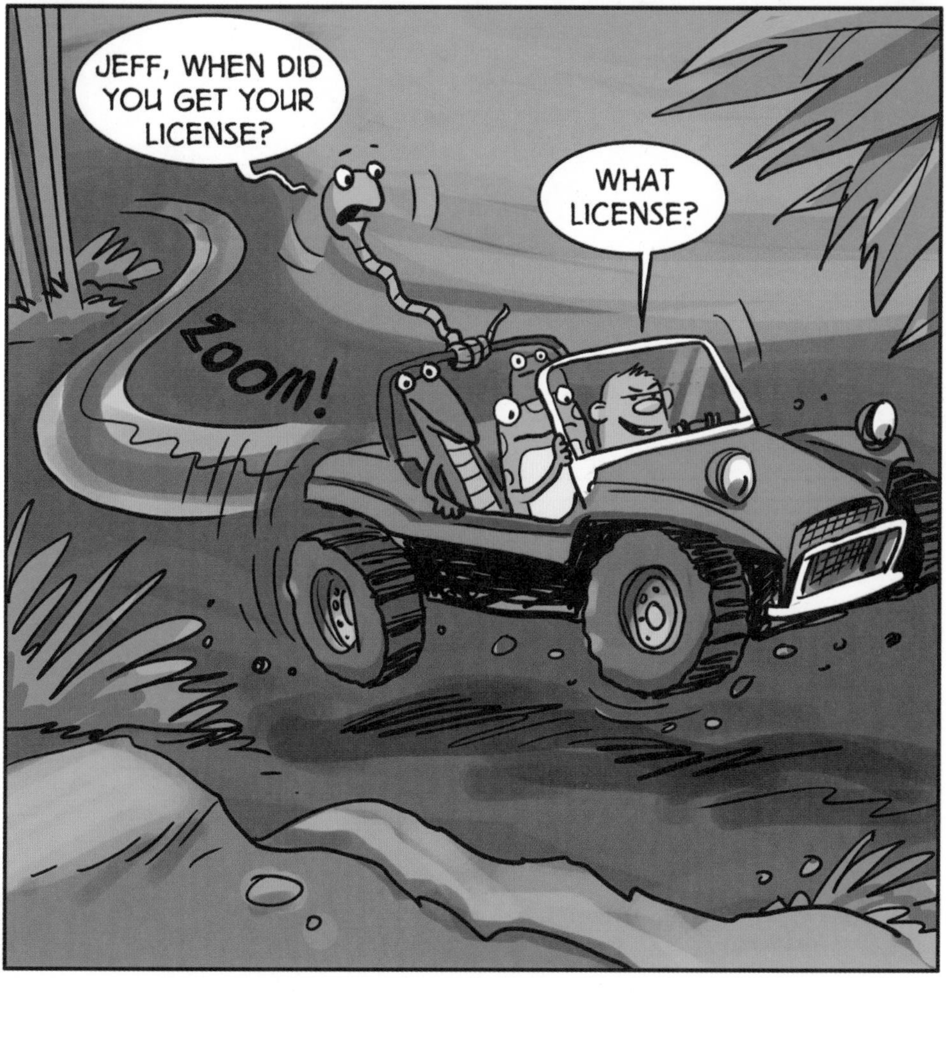
JEFF, WHEN DID YOU GET YOUR LICENSE?
WHAT LICENSE?
ZOOM!

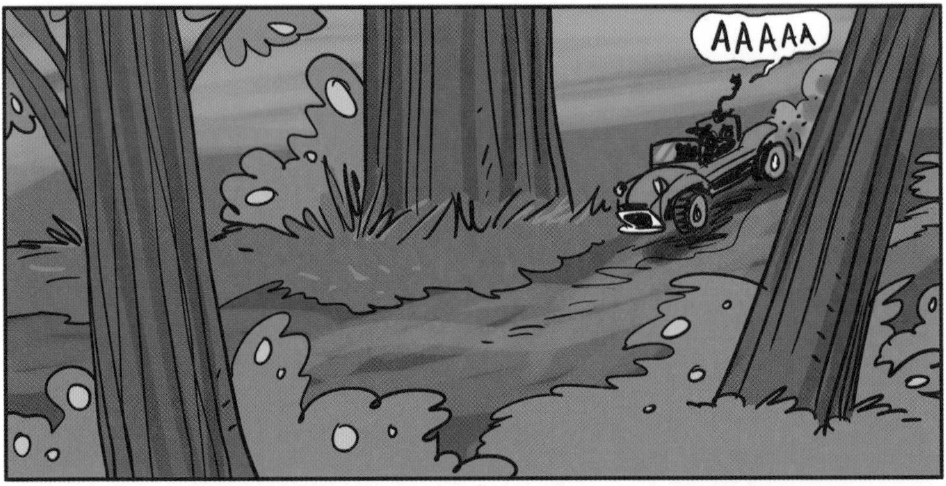
AAAAA

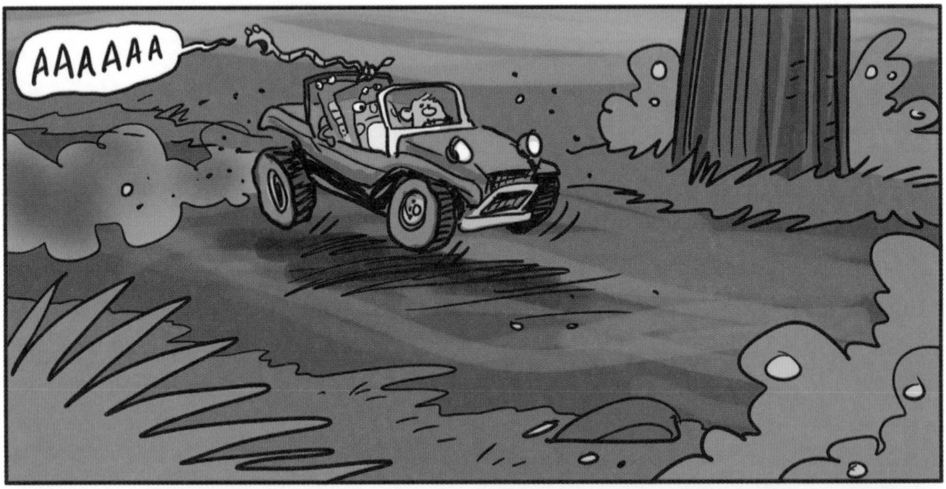
AAAAAA

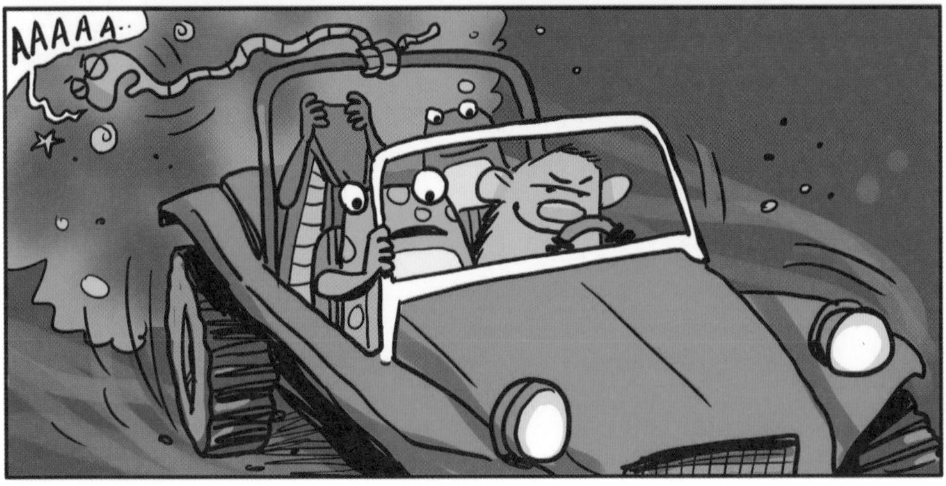
AAAAA..

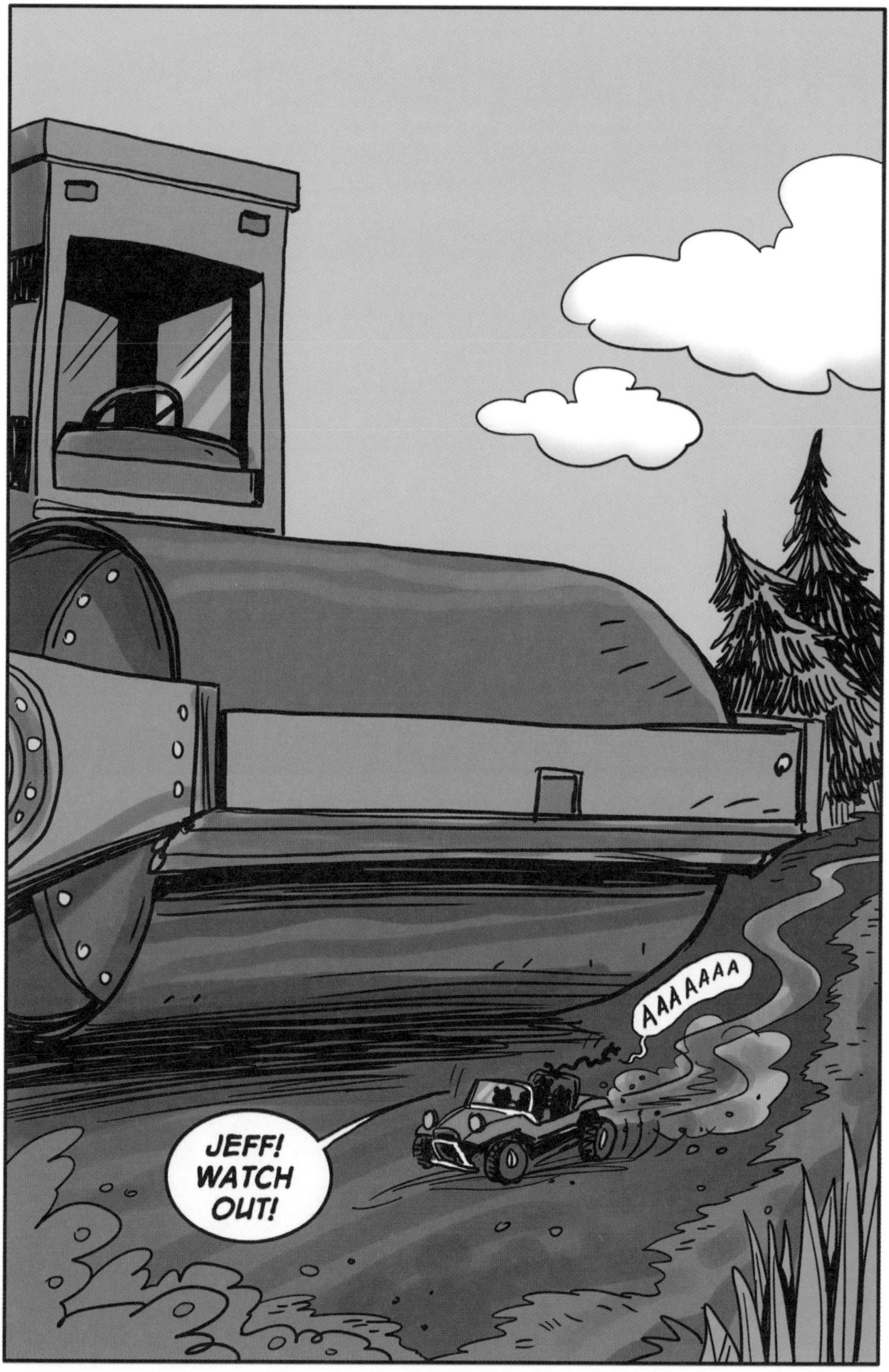
AAAAAAA
JEFF! WATCH OUT!

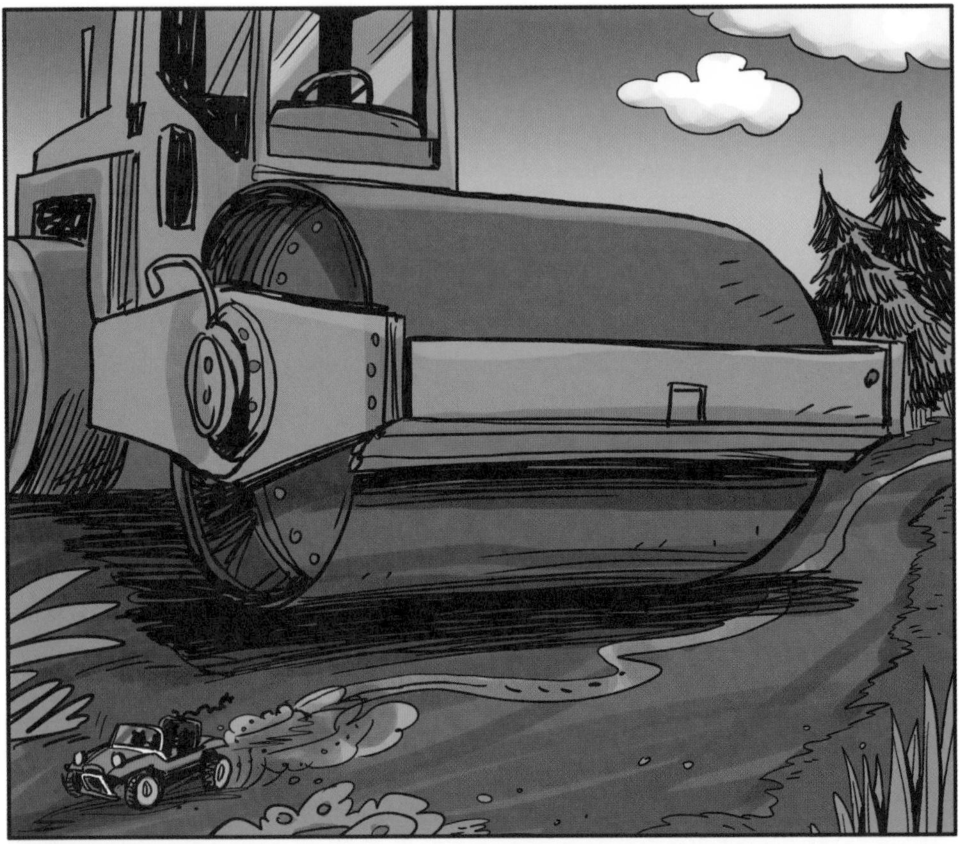

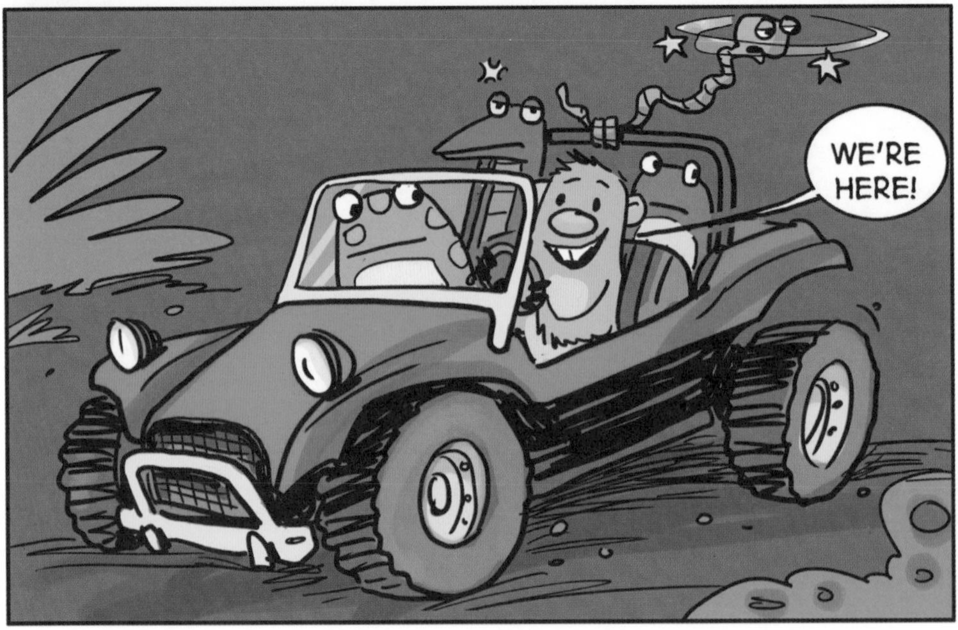
WE'RE HERE!

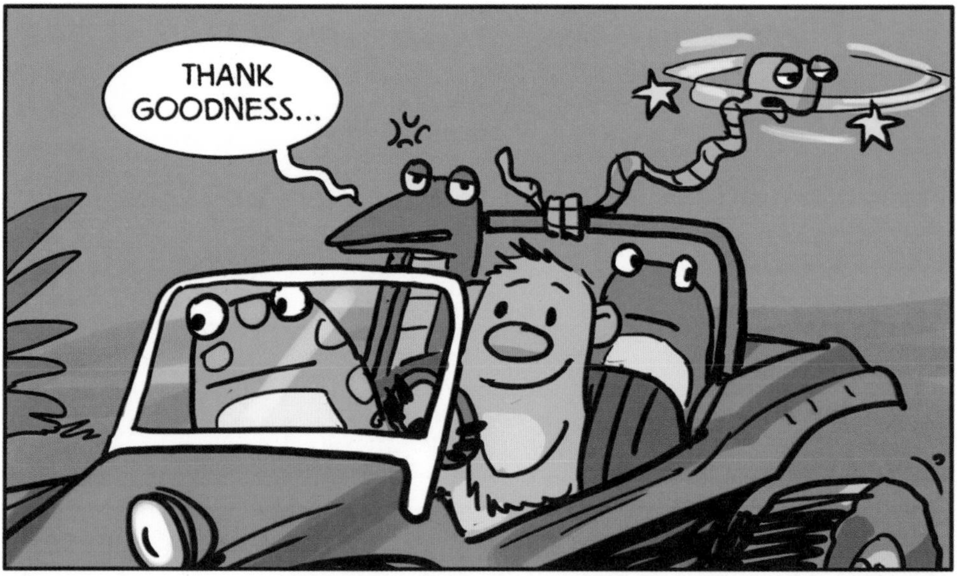
THANK GOODNESS...

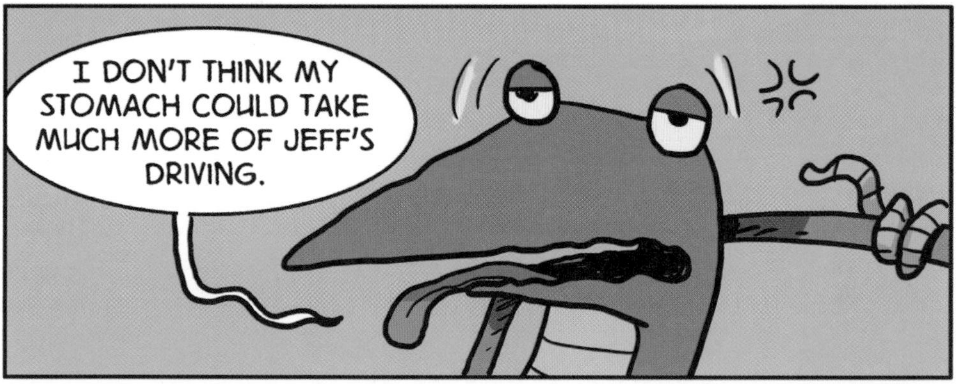
I DON'T THINK MY STOMACH COULD TAKE MUCH MORE OF JEFF'S DRIVING.

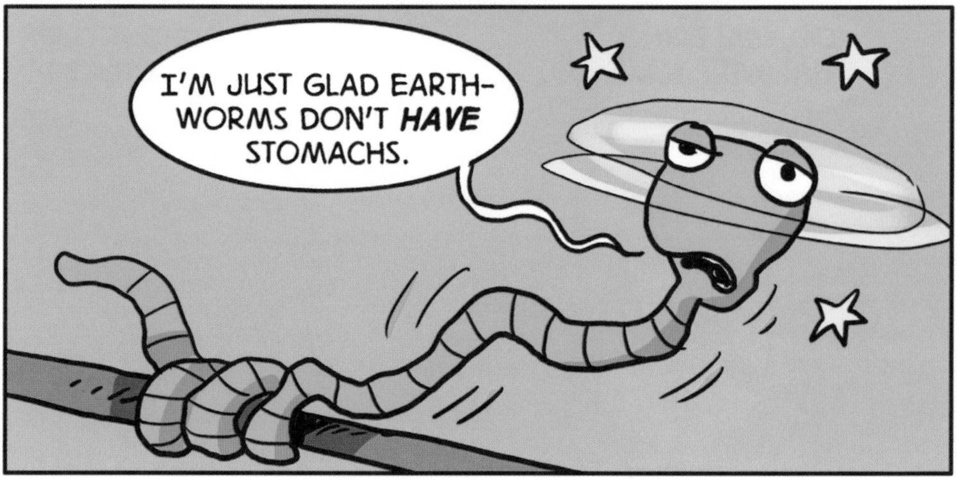
I'M JUST GLAD EARTH-WORMS DON'T ***HAVE*** STOMACHS.

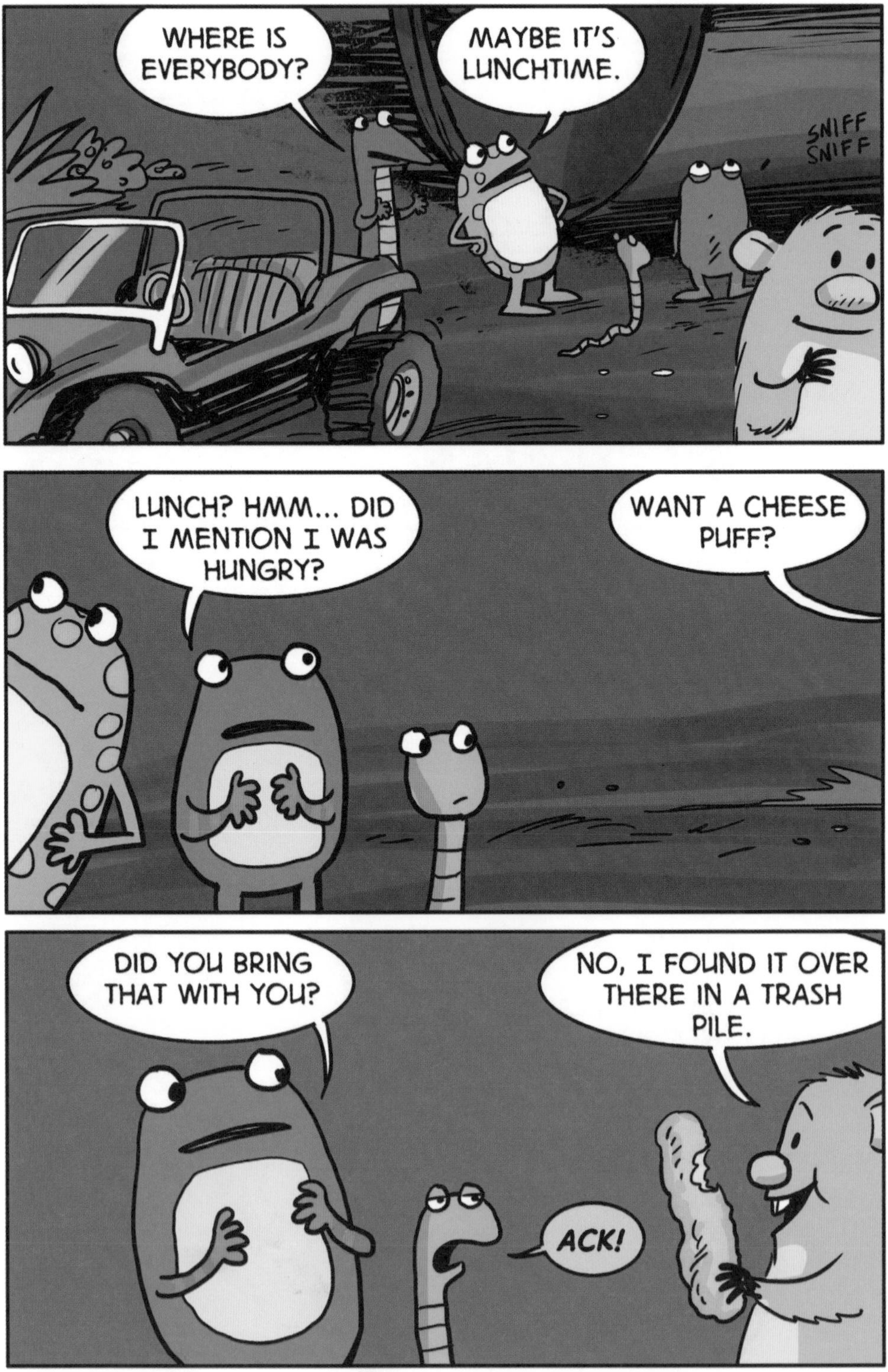
WHERE IS EVERYBODY?
MAYBE IT'S LUNCHTIME.
SNIFF SNIFF
LUNCH? HMM... DID I MENTION I WAS HUNGRY?
WANT A CHEESE PUFF?
DID YOU BRING THAT WITH YOU?
NO, I FOUND IT OVER THERE IN A TRASH PILE.
ACK!

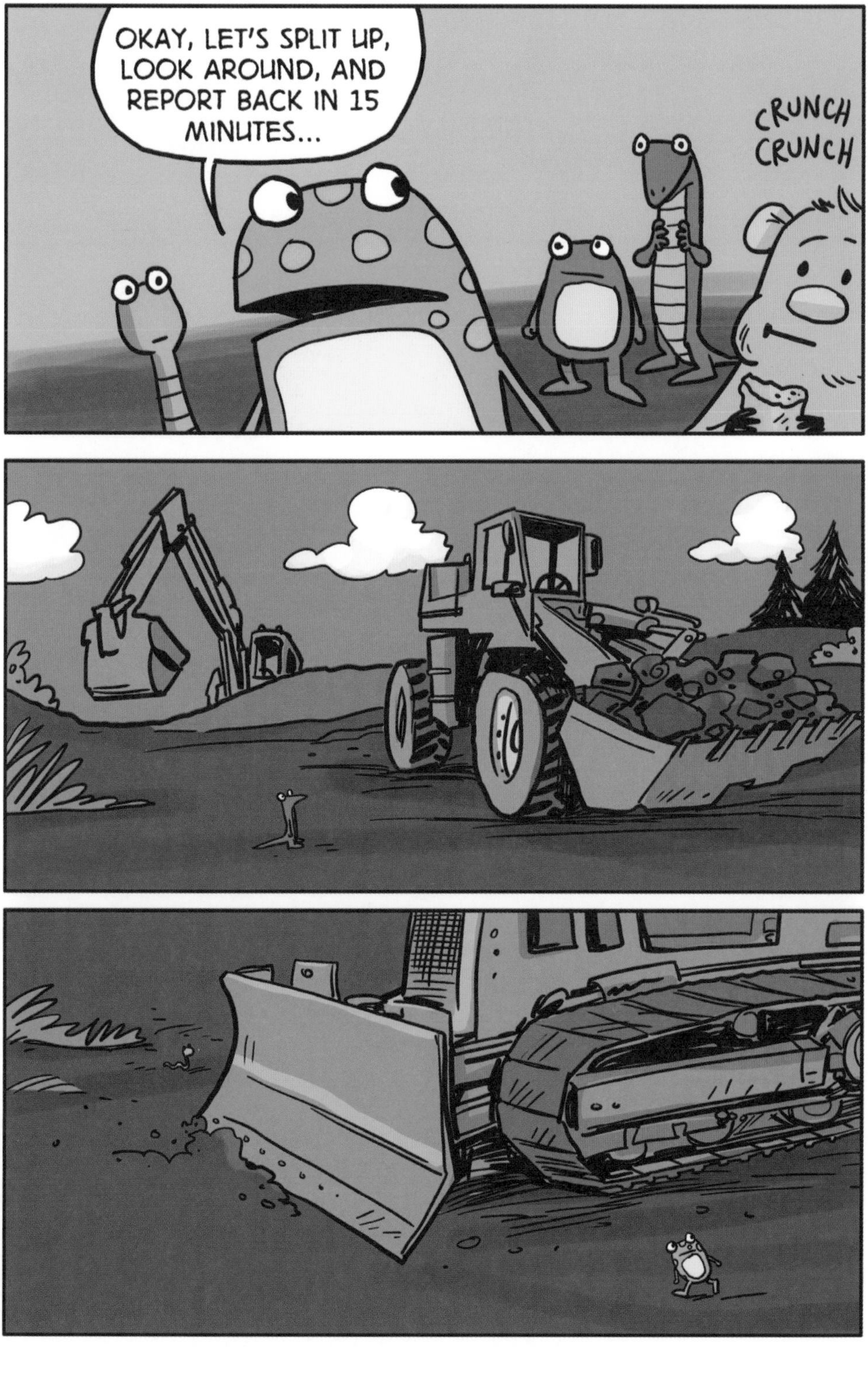
OKAY, LET'S SPLIT UP, LOOK AROUND, AND REPORT BACK IN 15 MINUTES...
CRUNCH CRUNCH

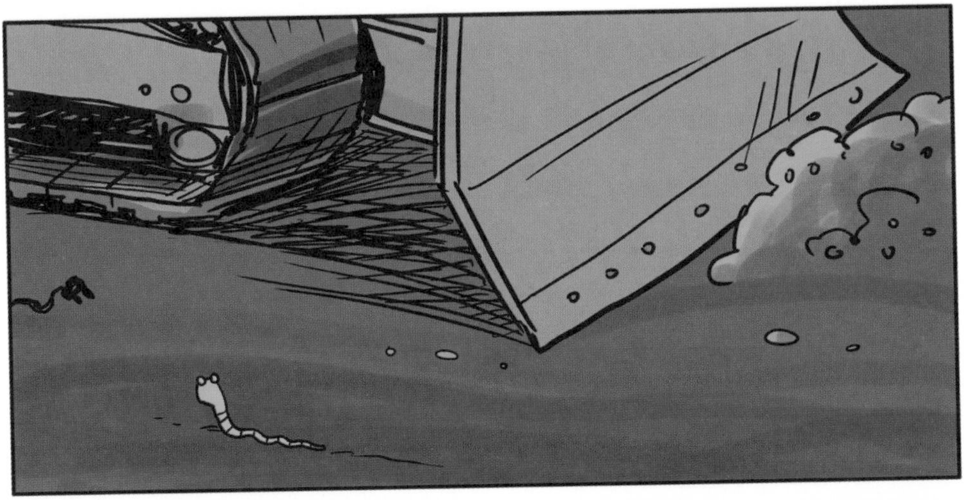

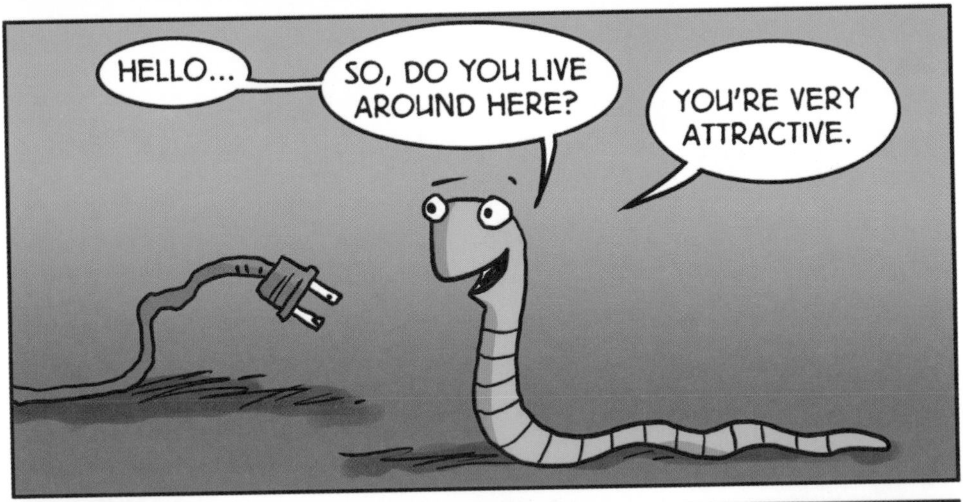
HELLO...
SO, DO YOU LIVE AROUND HERE?
YOU'RE VERY ATTRACTIVE.

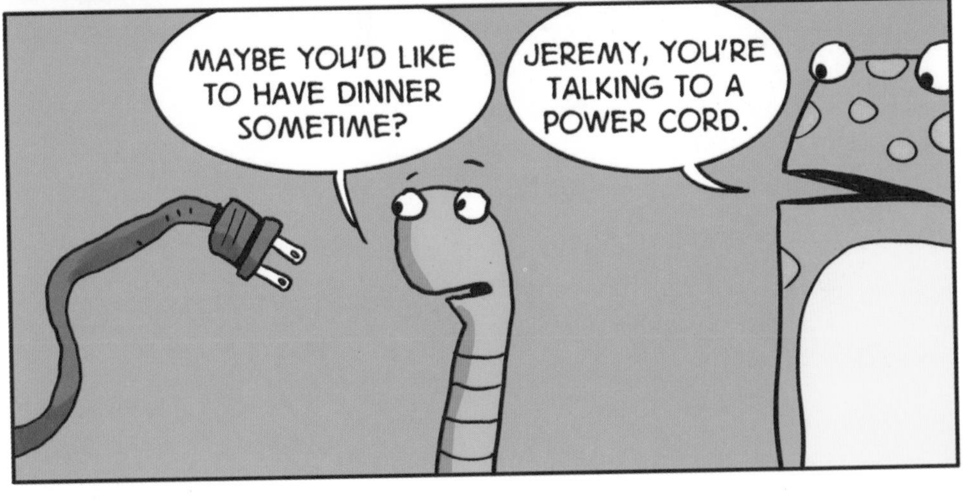
MAYBE YOU'D LIKE TO HAVE DINNER SOMETIME?
JEREMY, YOU'RE TALKING TO A POWER CORD.

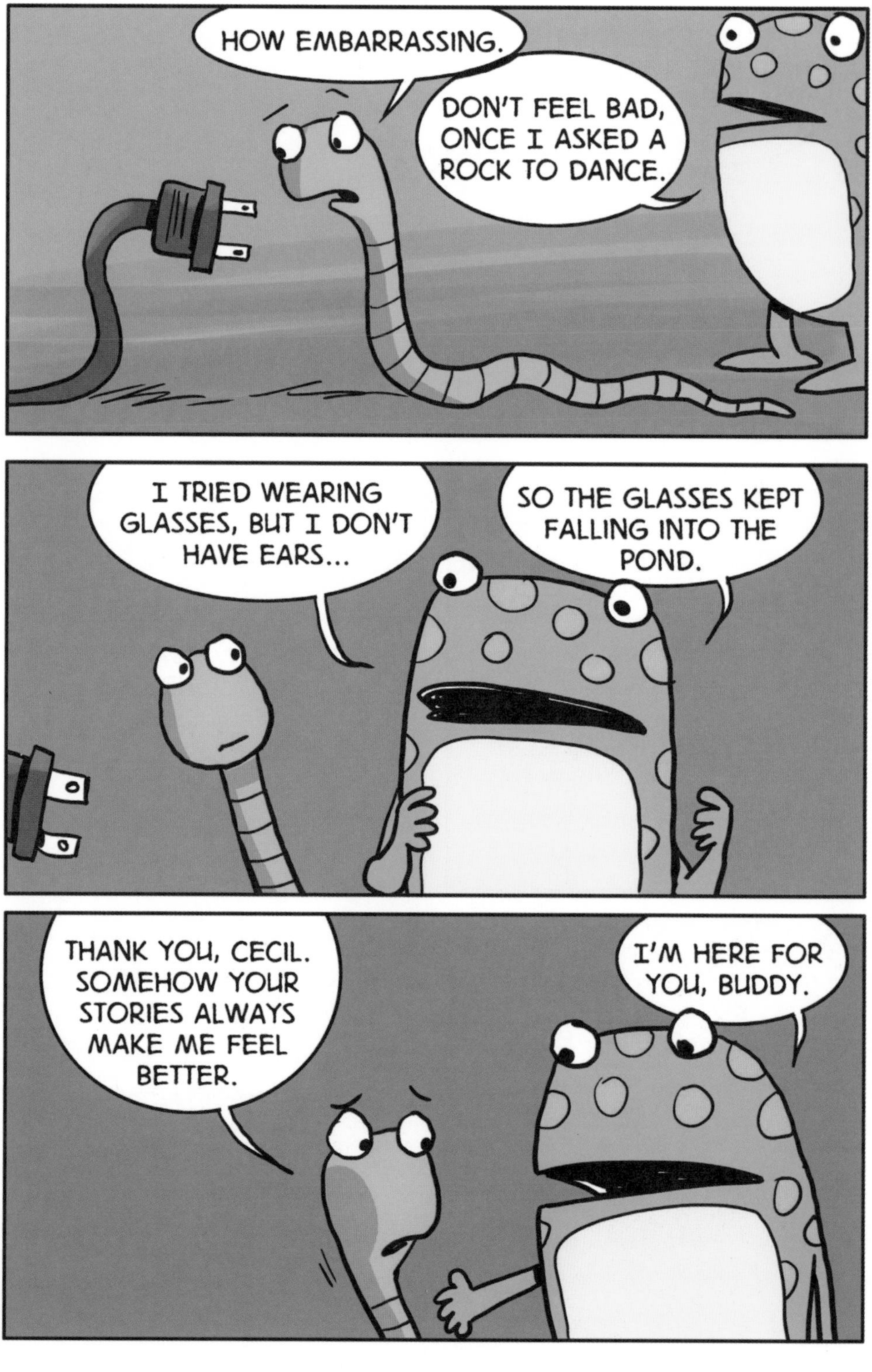
HOW EMBARRASSING.
DON'T FEEL BAD, ONCE I ASKED A ROCK TO DANCE.
I TRIED WEARING GLASSES, BUT I DON'T HAVE EARS...
SO THE GLASSES KEPT FALLING INTO THE POND.
THANK YOU, CECIL. SOMEHOW YOUR STORIES ALWAYS MAKE ME FEEL BETTER.
I'M HERE FOR YOU, BUDDY.

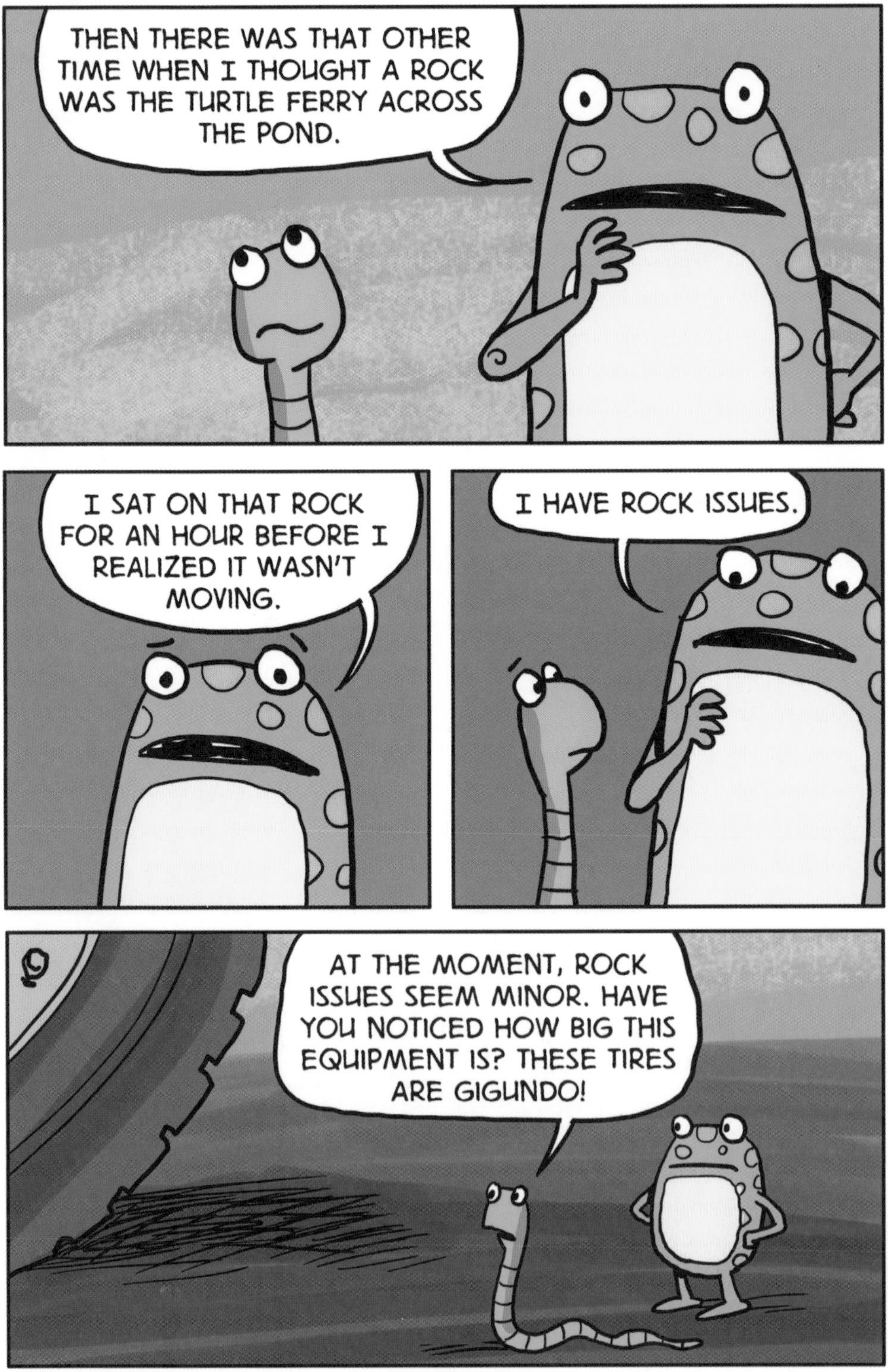
THEN THERE WAS THAT OTHER TIME WHEN I THOUGHT A ROCK WAS THE TURTLE FERRY ACROSS THE POND.
I SAT ON THAT ROCK FOR AN HOUR BEFORE I REALIZED IT WASN'T MOVING.
I HAVE ROCK ISSUES.
AT THE MOMENT, ROCK ISSUES SEEM MINOR. HAVE YOU NOTICED HOW BIG THIS EQUIPMENT IS? THESE TIRES ARE GIGUNDO!

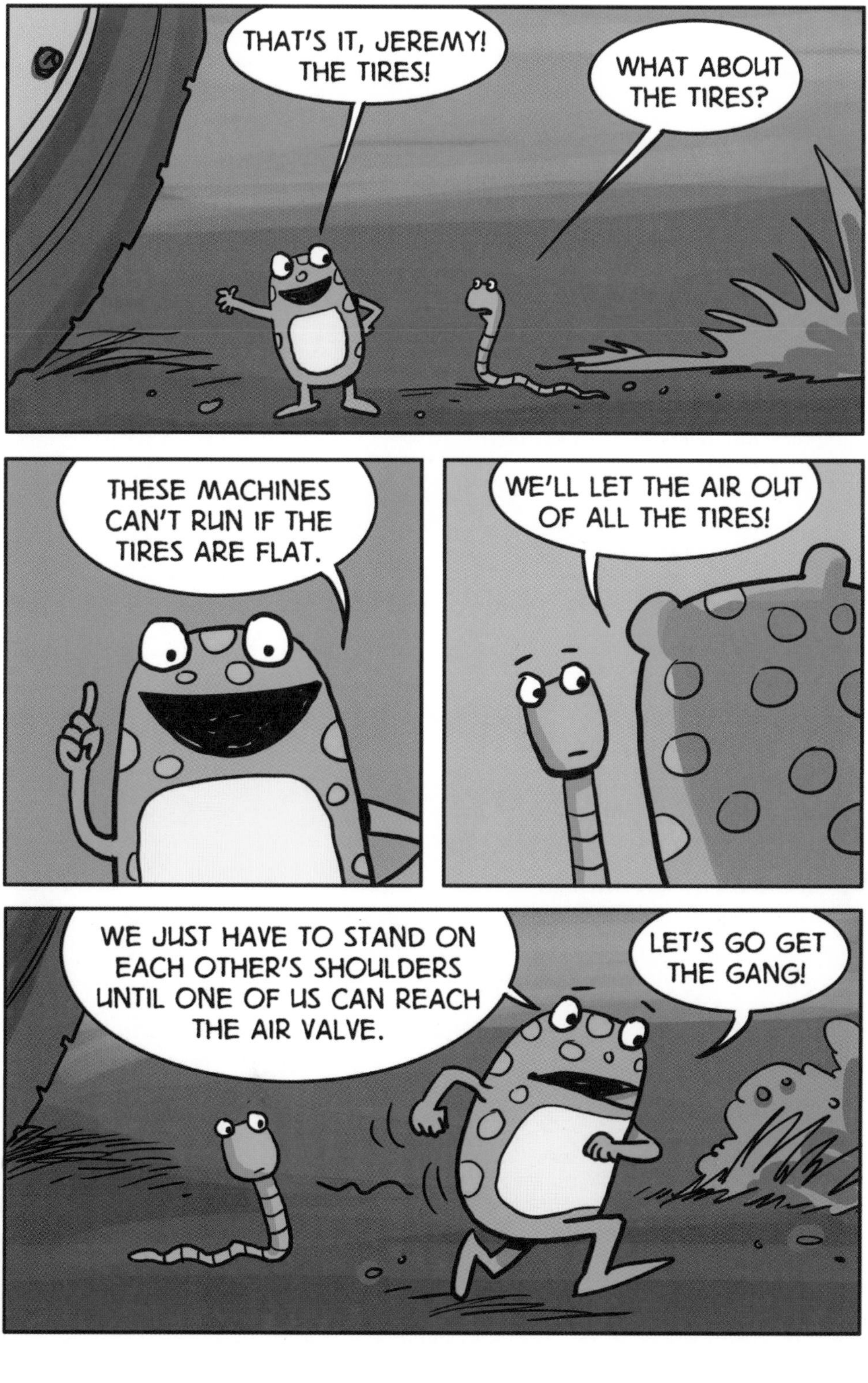
THAT'S IT, JEREMY! THE TIRES!
WHAT ABOUT THE TIRES?
THESE MACHINES CAN'T RUN IF THE TIRES ARE FLAT.
WE'LL LET THE AIR OUT OF ALL THE TIRES!
WE JUST HAVE TO STAND ON EACH OTHER'S SHOULDERS UNTIL ONE OF US CAN REACH THE AIR VALVE.
LET'S GO GET THE GANG!

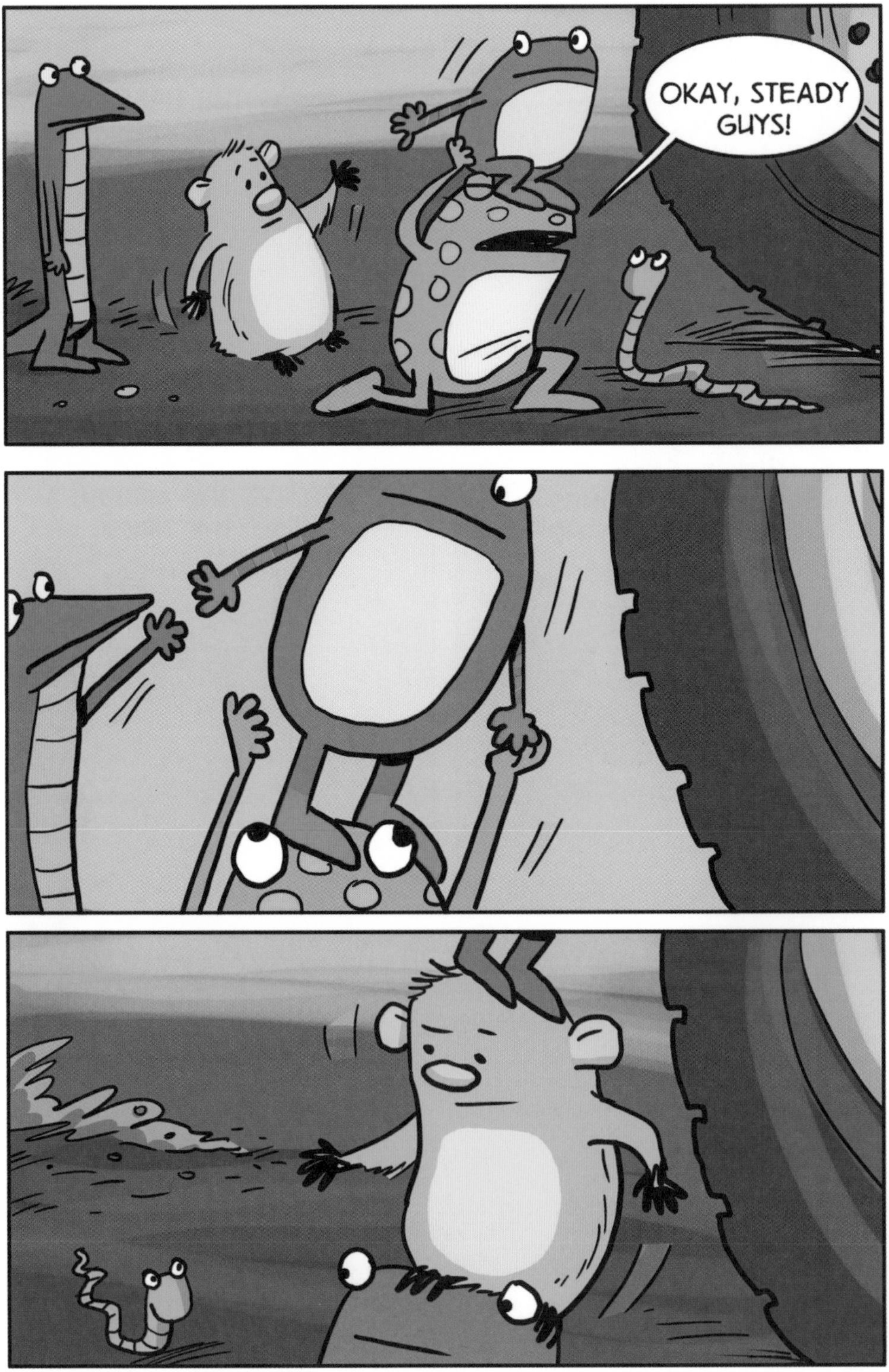
OKAY, STEADY GUYS!

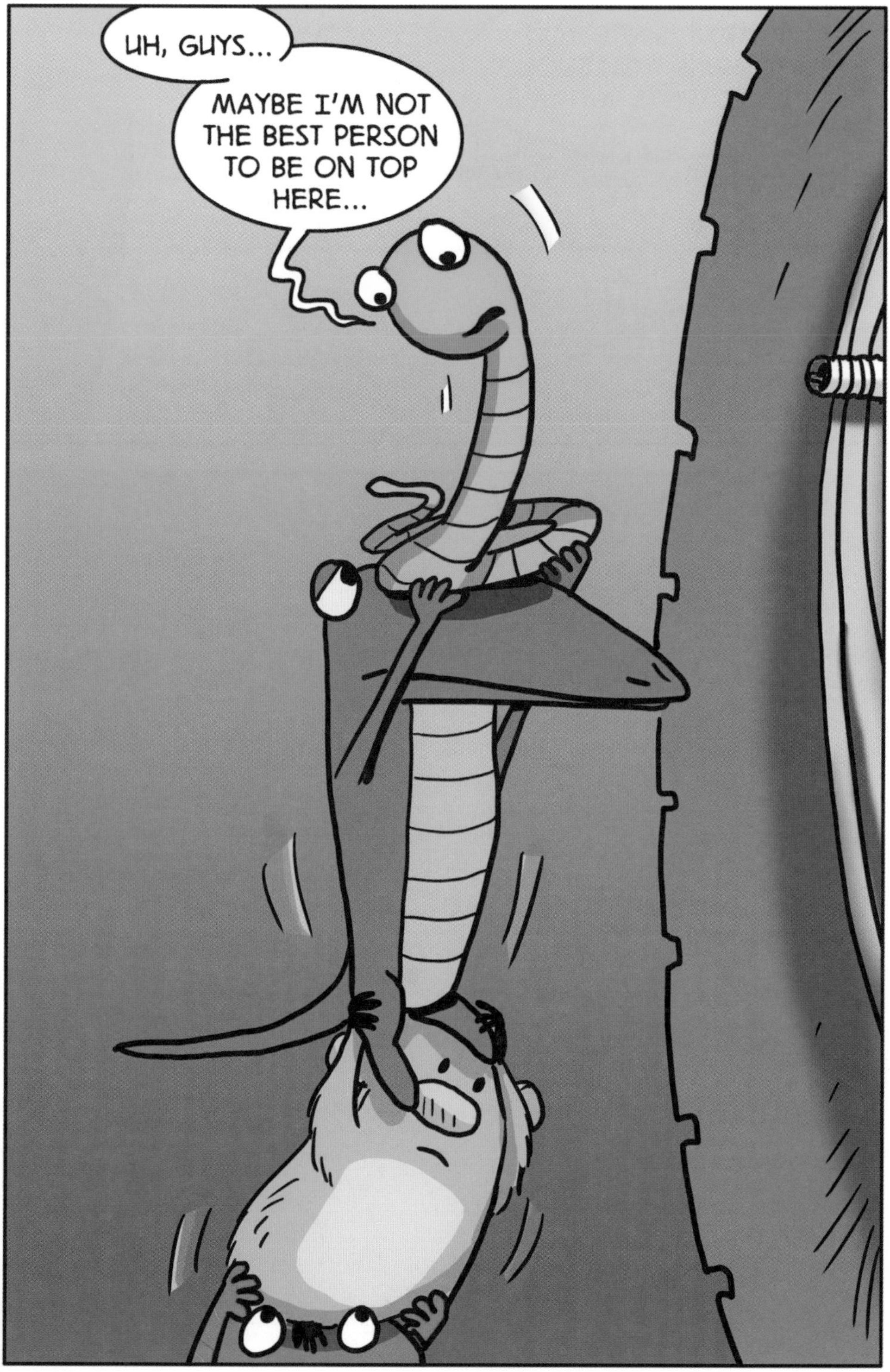
UH, GUYS...
MAYBE I'M NOT THE BEST PERSON TO BE ON TOP HERE...

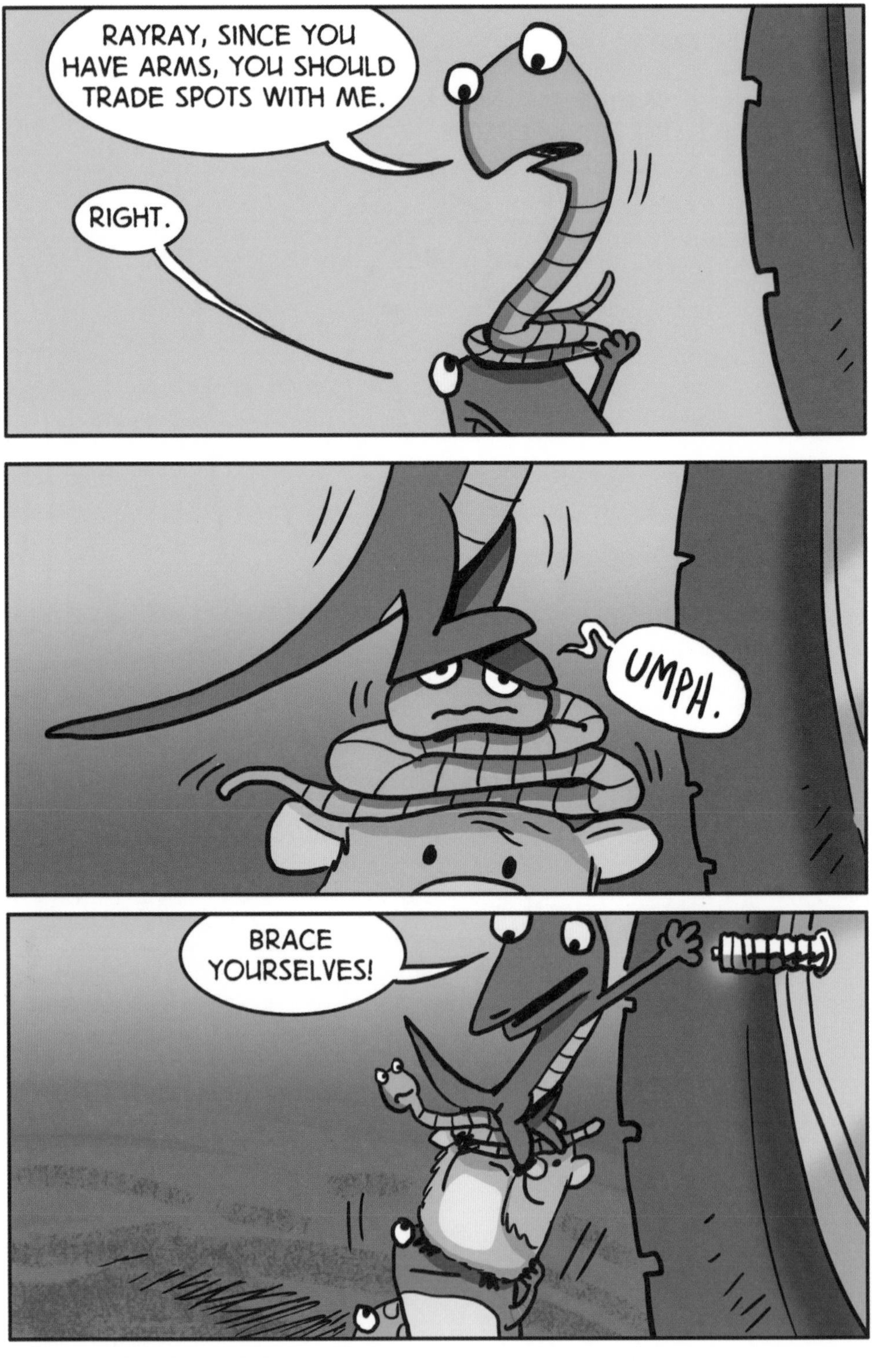
RAYRAY, SINCE YOU HAVE ARMS, YOU SHOULD TRADE SPOTS WITH ME.
RIGHT.
UMPH.
BRACE YOURSELVES!

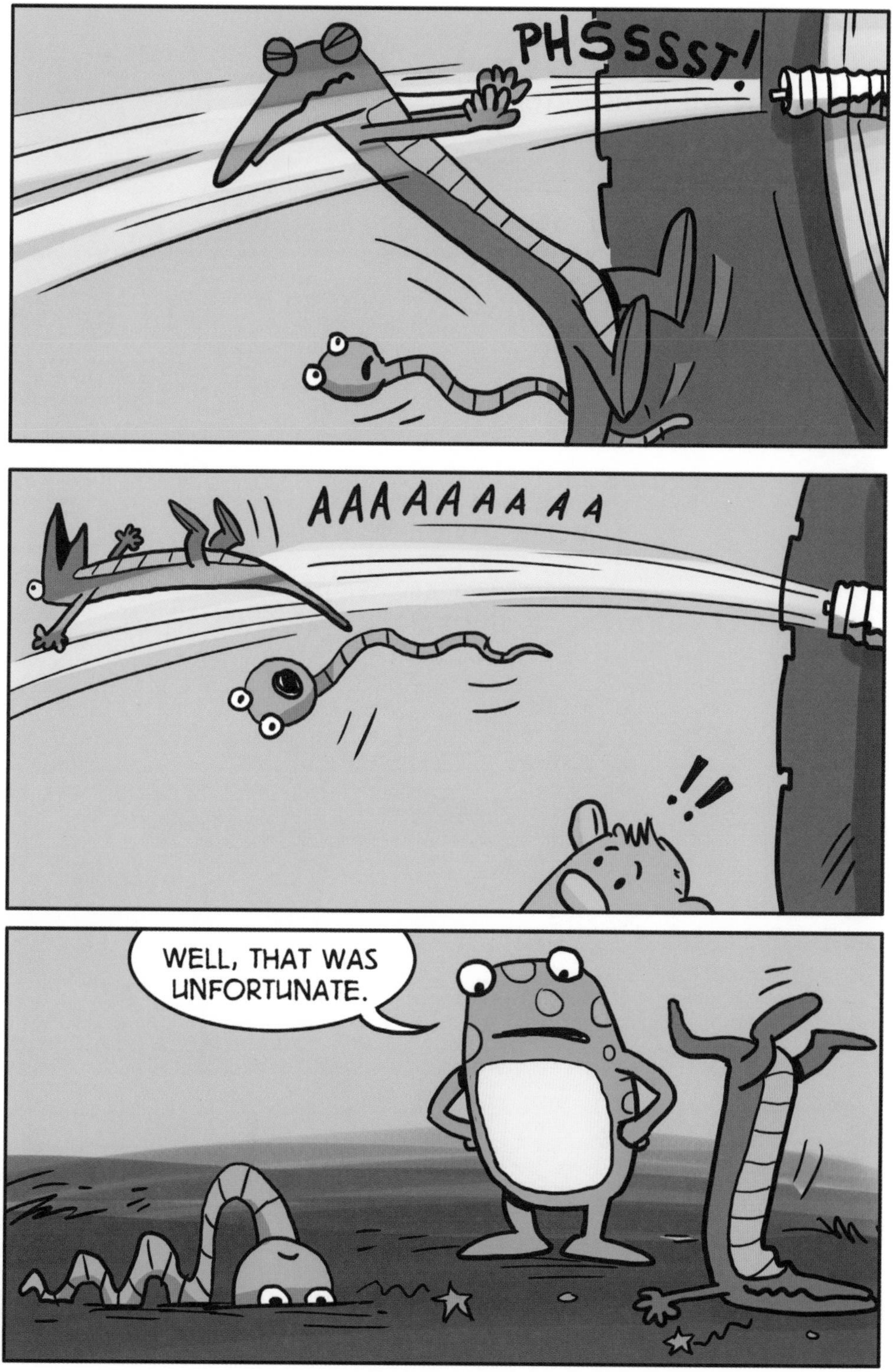
PHSSSST!
AAAAAAA AA
!!
WELL, THAT WAS UNFORTUNATE.

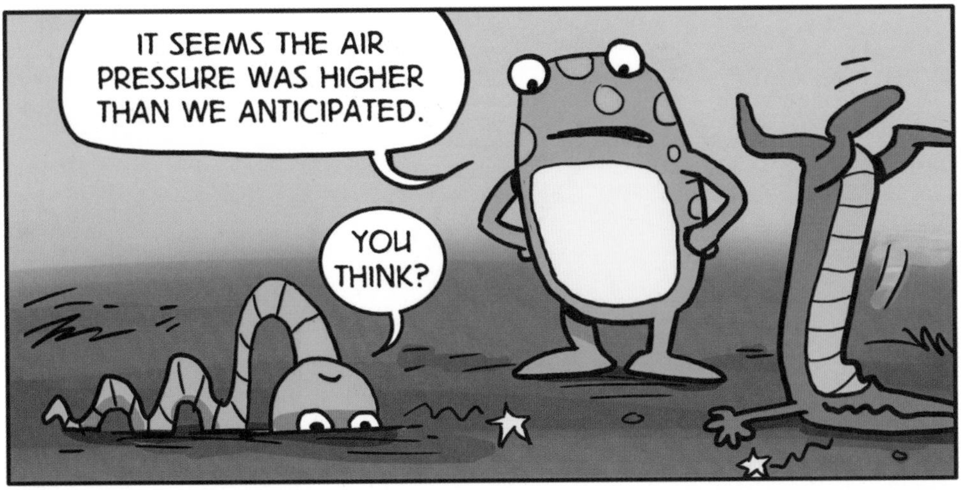
IT SEEMS THE AIR PRESSURE WAS HIGHER THAN WE ANTICIPATED.
YOU THINK?

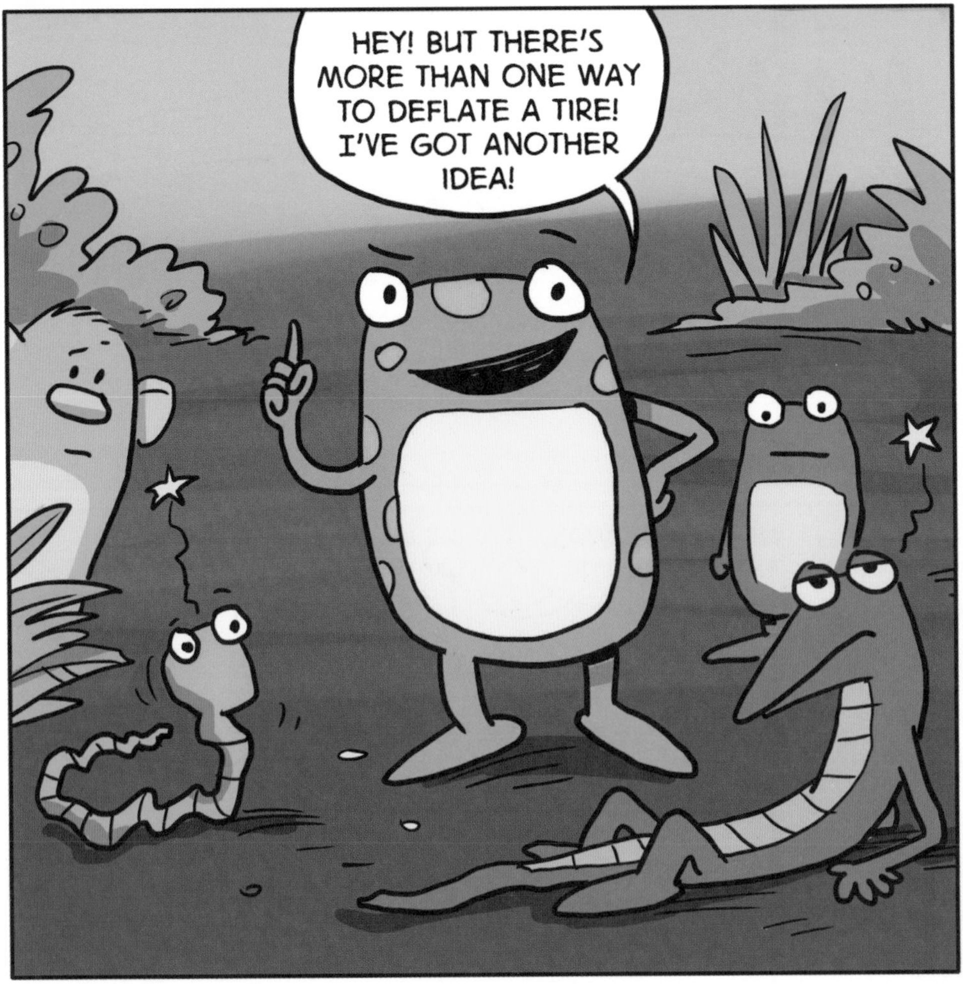
HEY! BUT THERE'S MORE THAN ONE WAY TO DEFLATE A TIRE! I'VE GOT ANOTHER IDEA!

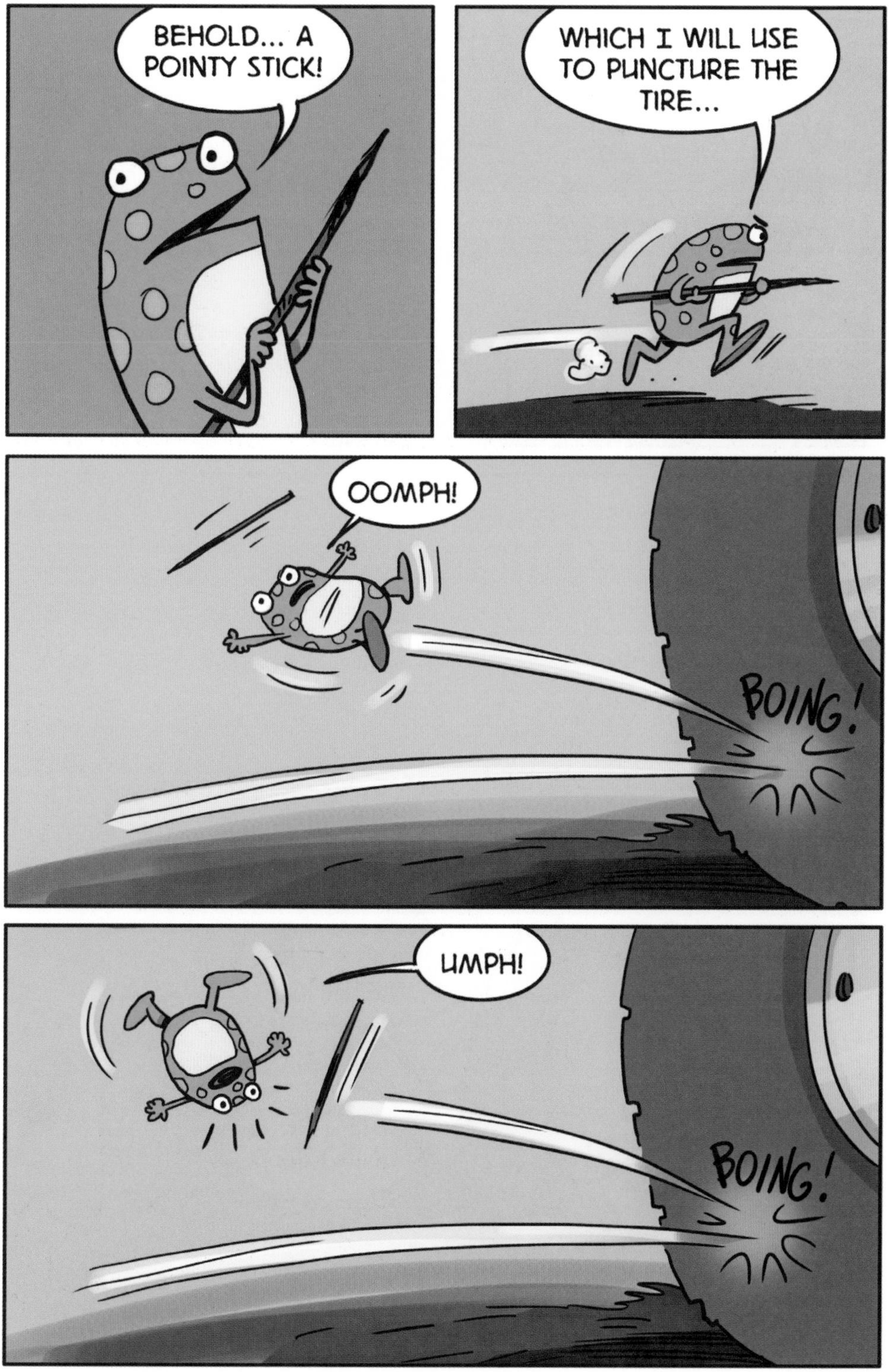
BEHOLD... A POINTY STICK!
WHICH I WILL USE TO PUNCTURE THE TIRE...
OOMPH!
BOING!
UMPH!
BOING!

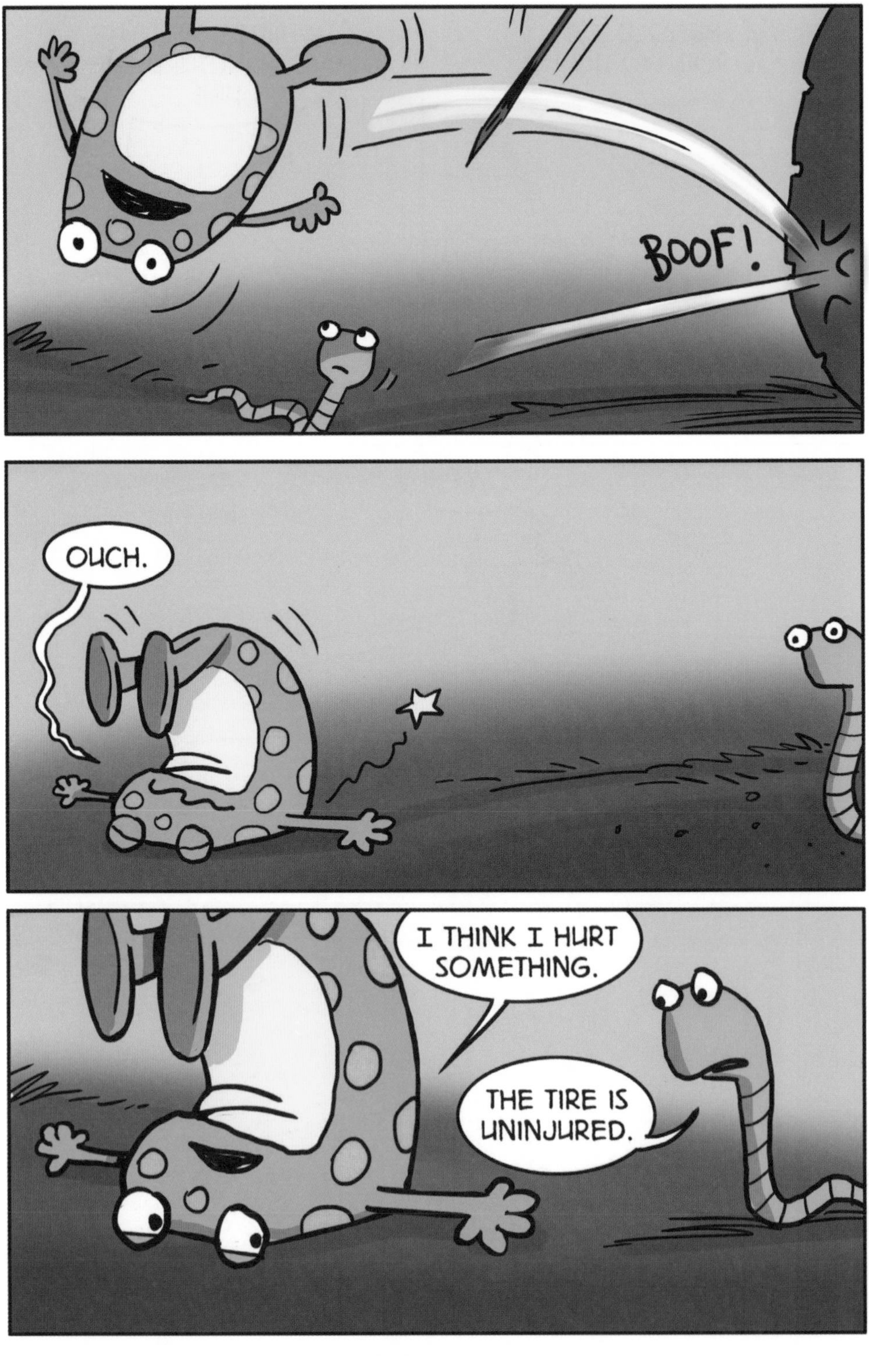
BOOF!
OUCH.
I THINK I HURT SOMETHING.
THE TIRE IS UNINJURED.

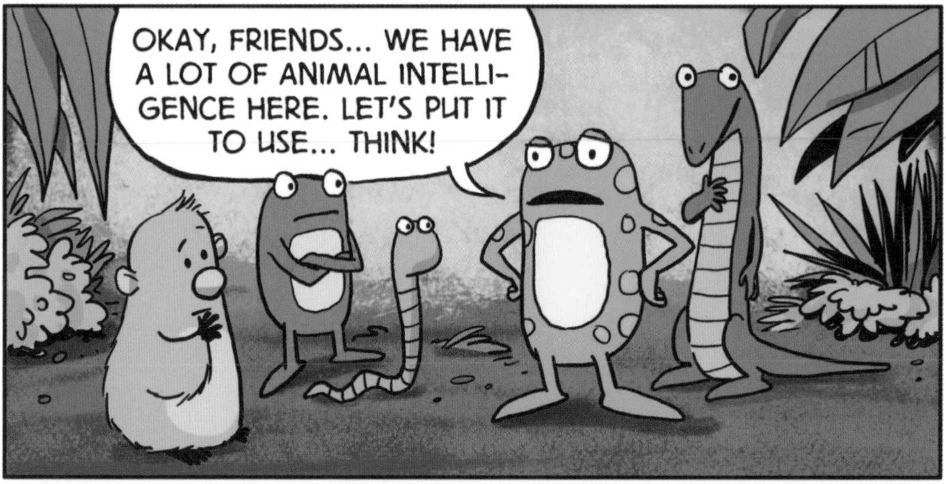
OKAY, FRIENDS... WE HAVE A LOT OF ANIMAL INTELLI-GENCE HERE. LET'S PUT IT TO USE... THINK!

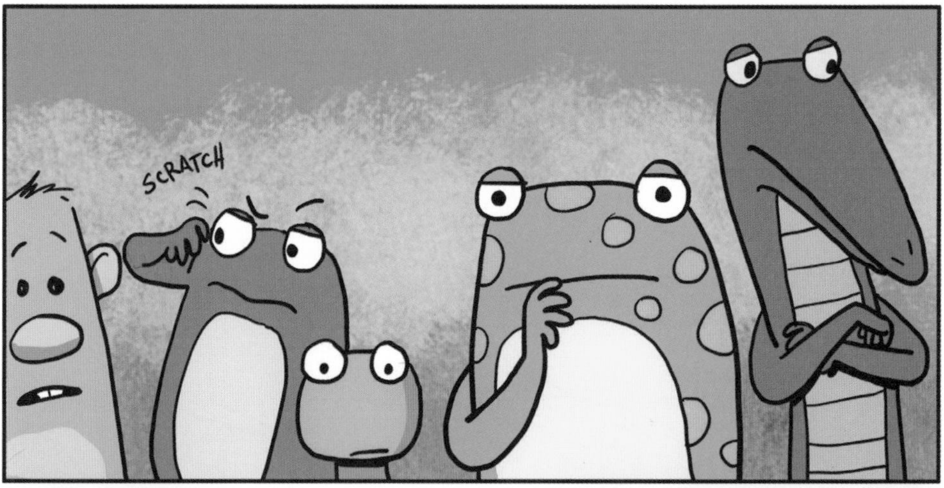
SCRATCH

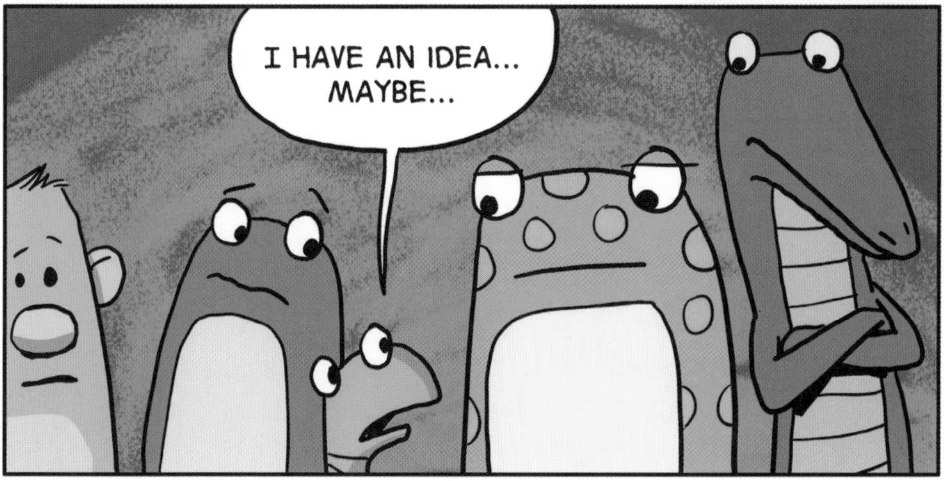
I HAVE AN IDEA... MAYBE...

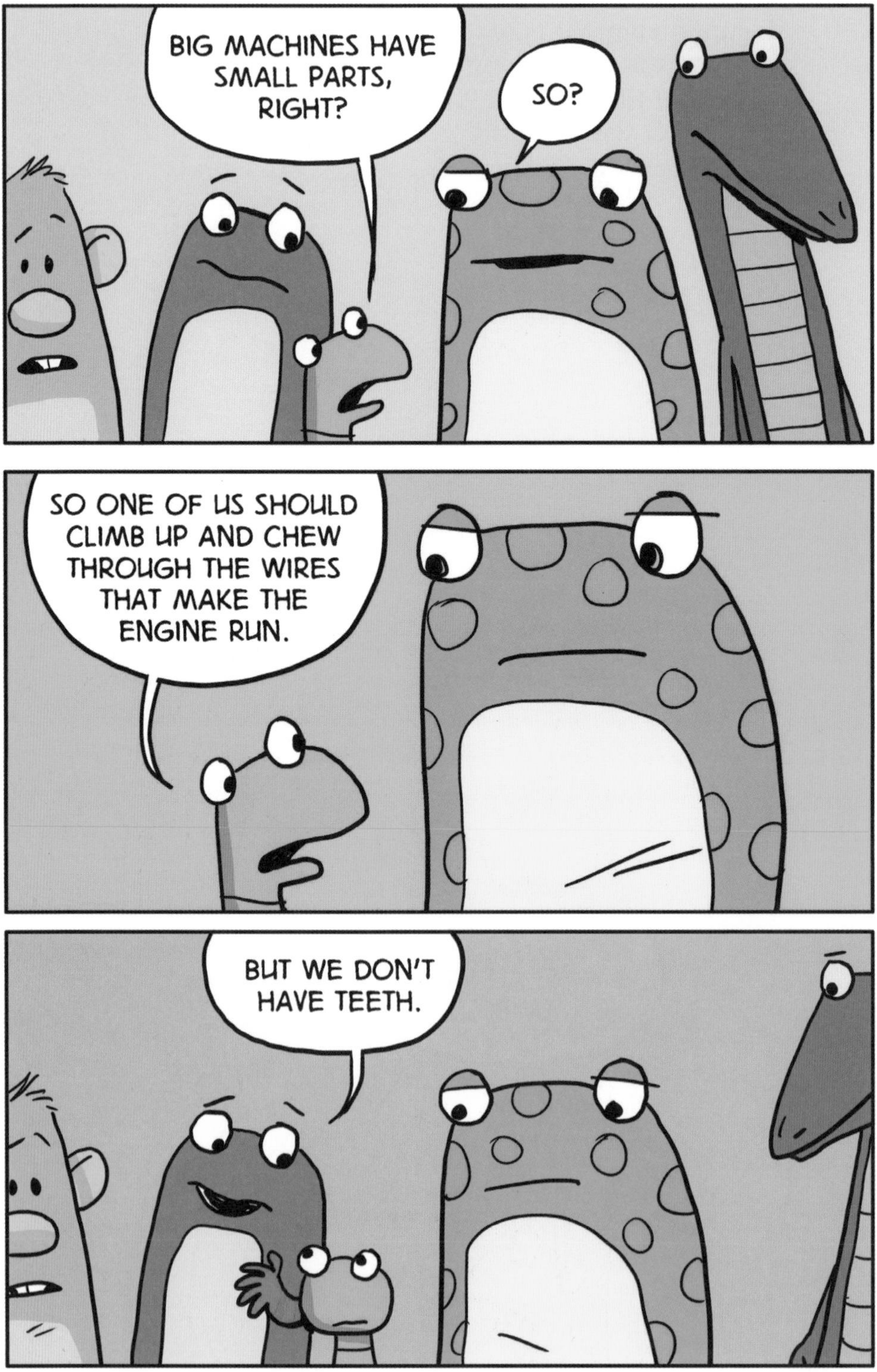
BIG MACHINES HAVE SMALL PARTS, RIGHT?
SO?
SO ONE OF US SHOULD CLIMB UP AND CHEW THROUGH THE WIRES THAT MAKE THE ENGINE RUN.
BUT WE DON'T HAVE TEETH.

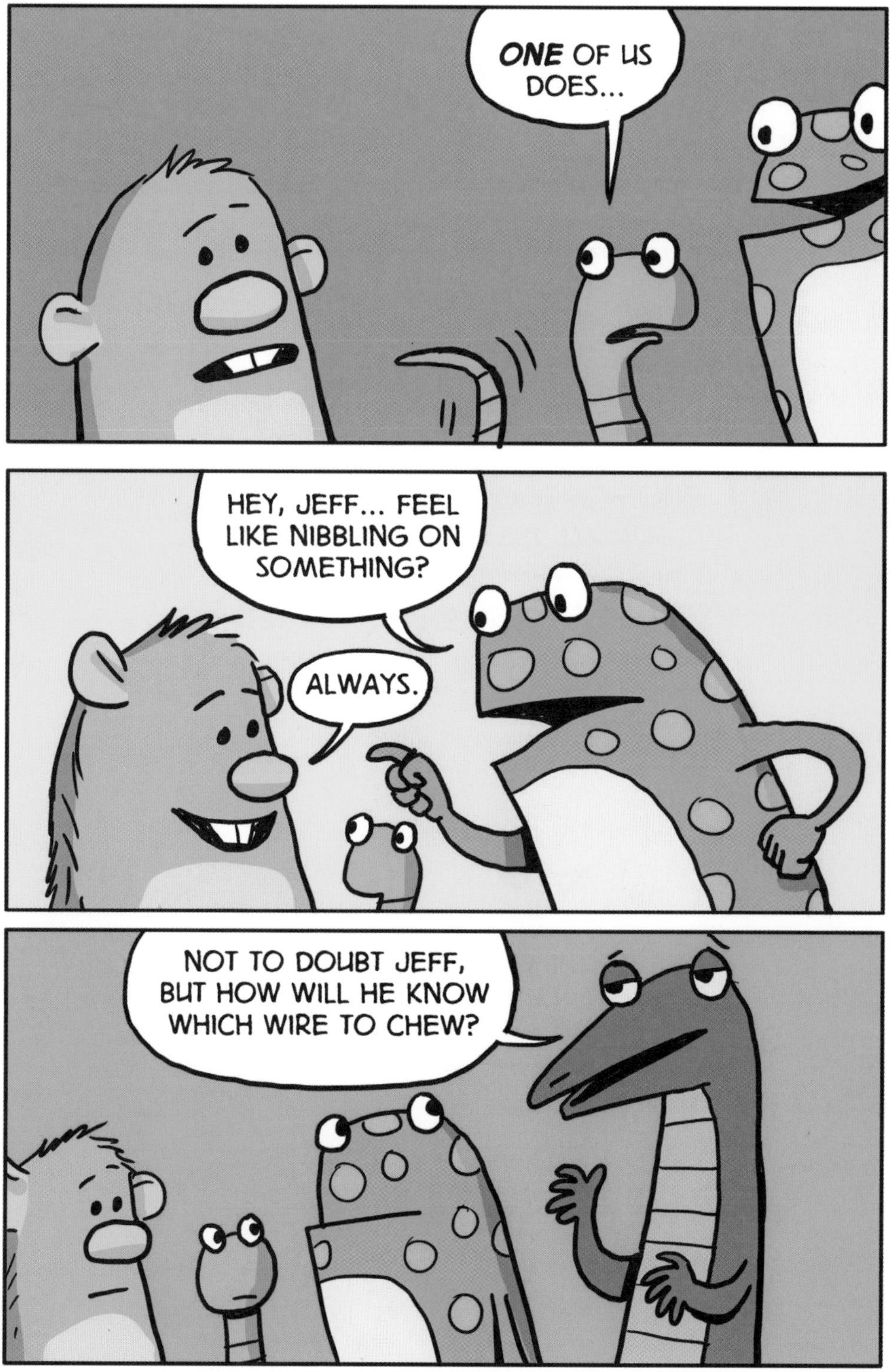
ONE OF US DOES...
HEY, JEFF... FEEL LIKE NIBBLING ON SOMETHING?
ALWAYS.
NOT TO DOUBT JEFF, BUT HOW WILL HE KNOW WHICH WIRE TO CHEW?

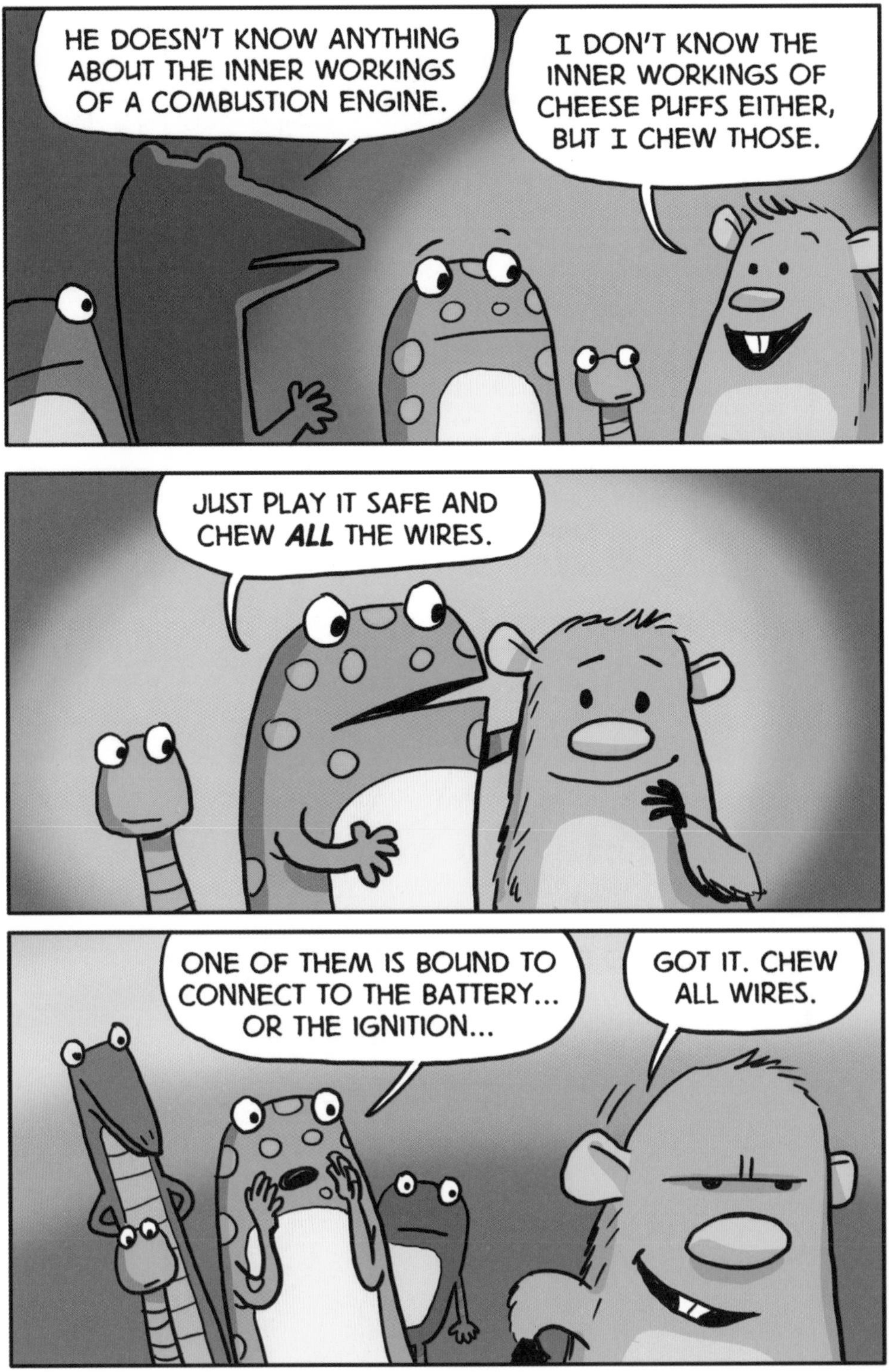
HE DOESN'T KNOW ANYTHING ABOUT THE INNER WORKINGS OF A COMBUSTION ENGINE.
I DON'T KNOW THE INNER WORKINGS OF CHEESE PUFFS EITHER, BUT I CHEW THOSE.
JUST PLAY IT SAFE AND CHEW ***ALL*** THE WIRES.
ONE OF THEM IS BOUND TO CONNECT TO THE BATTERY... OR THE IGNITION...
GOT IT. CHEW ALL WIRES.

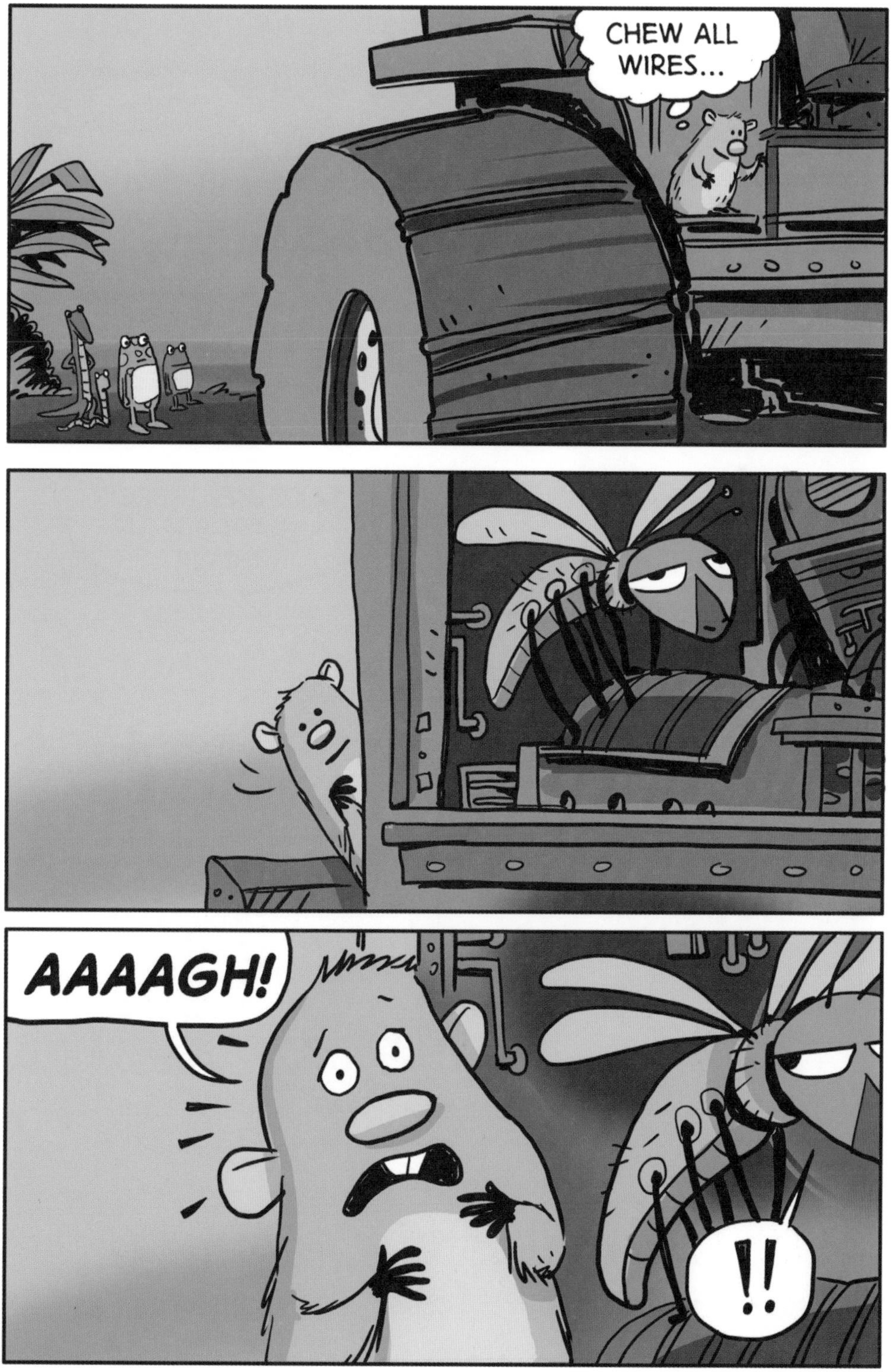
CHEW ALL WIRES...
AAAAGH!
!!

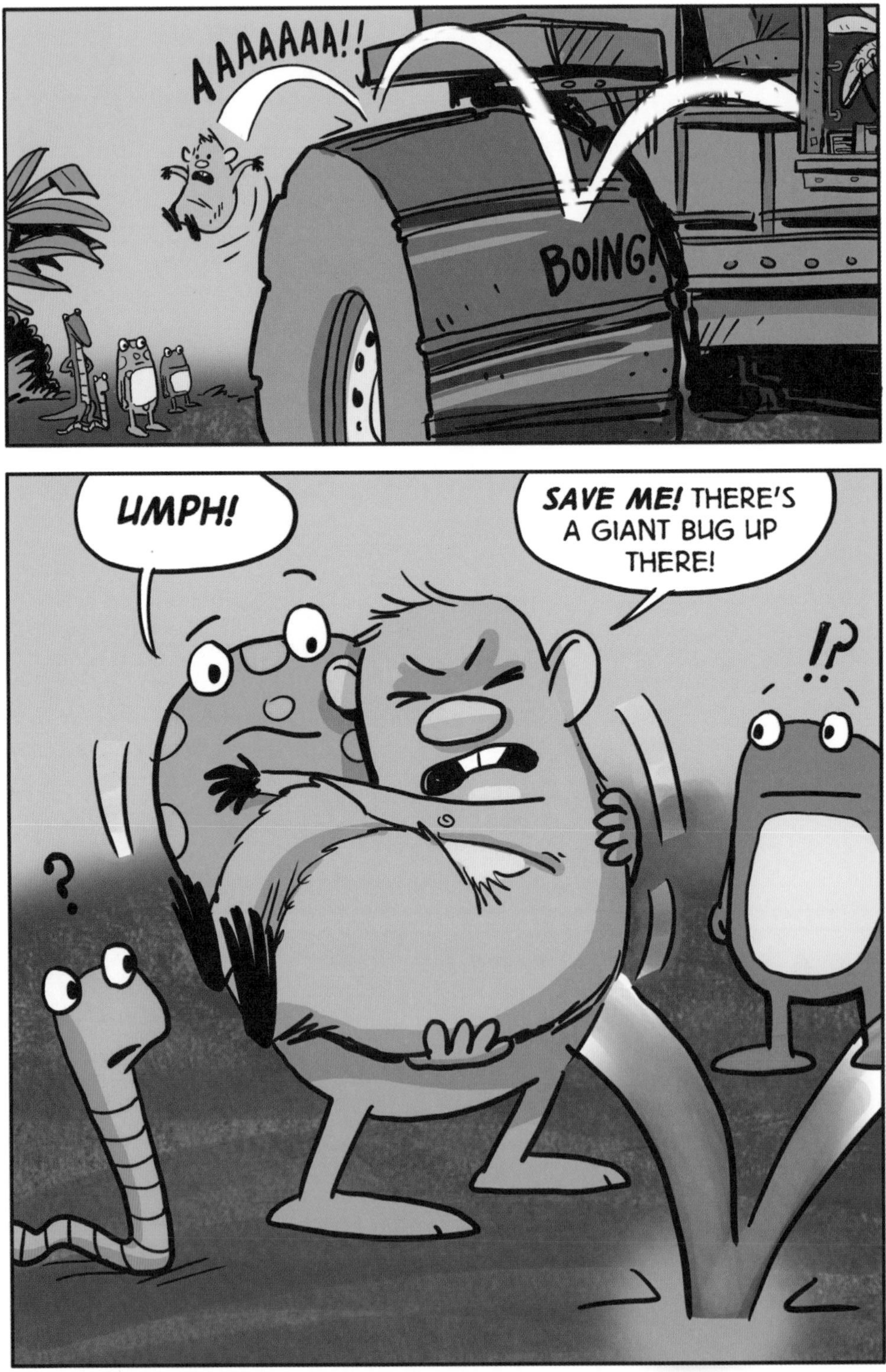
AAAAAAA!!
BOING!
UMPH!
SAVE ME! THERE'S A GIANT BUG UP THERE!
!?
?

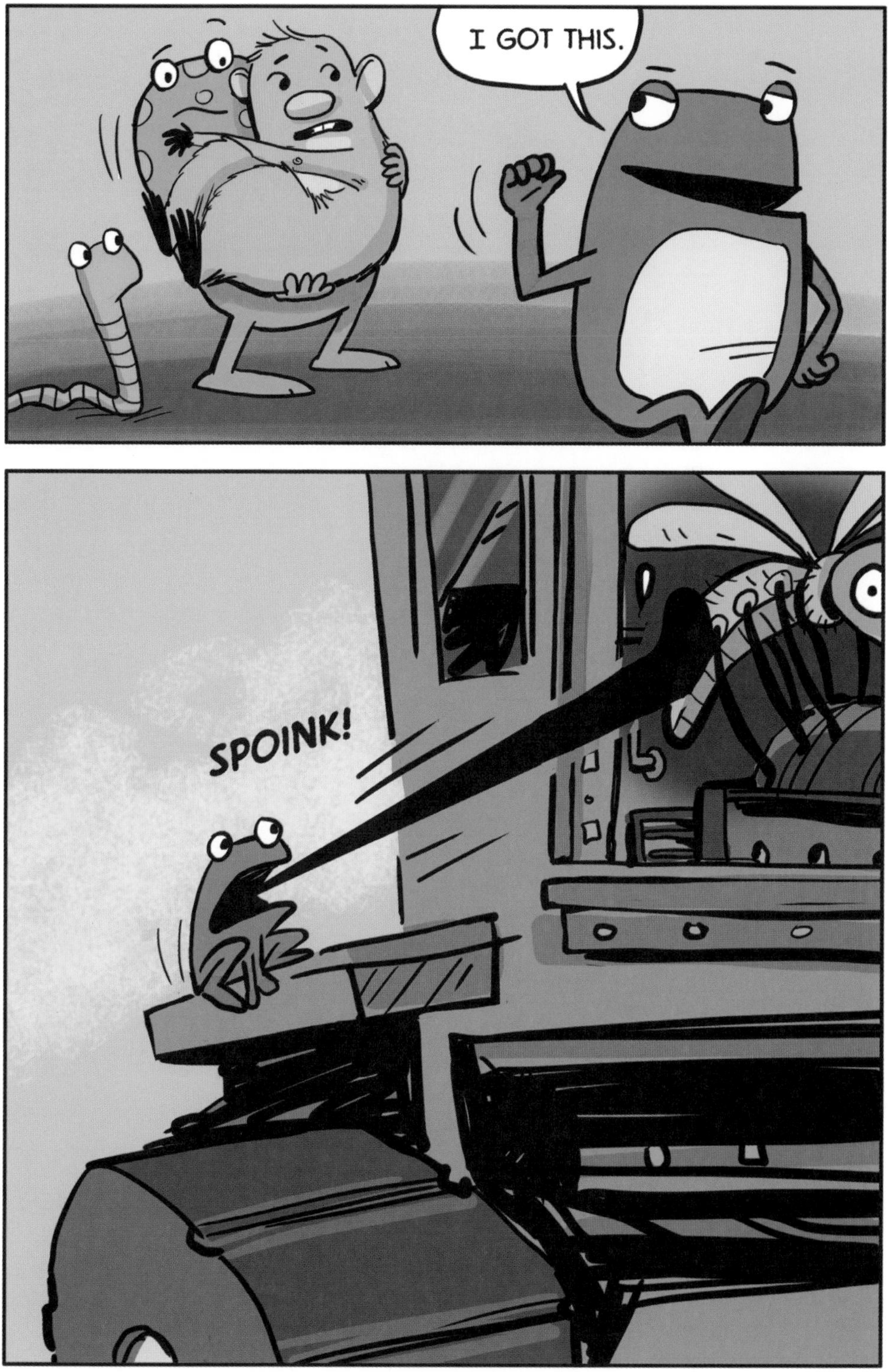
I GOT THIS.
SPOINK!

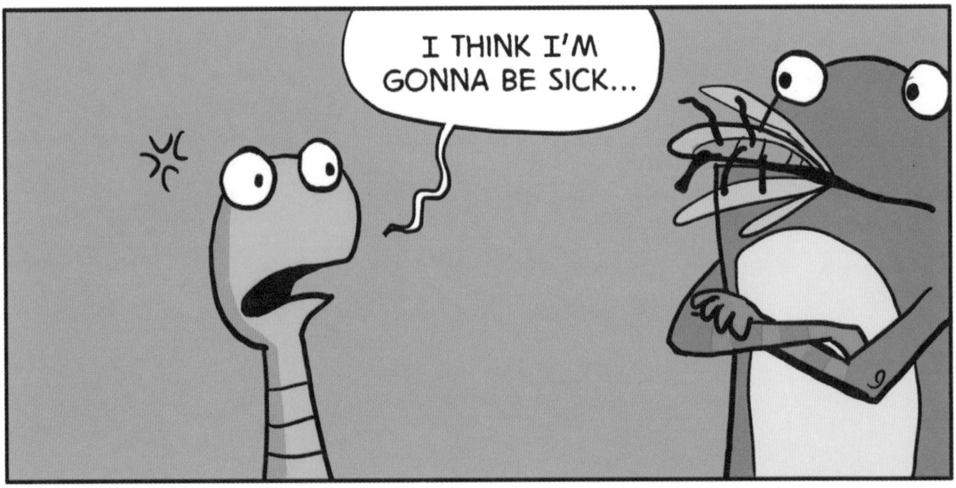
I THINK I'M GONNA BE SICK...

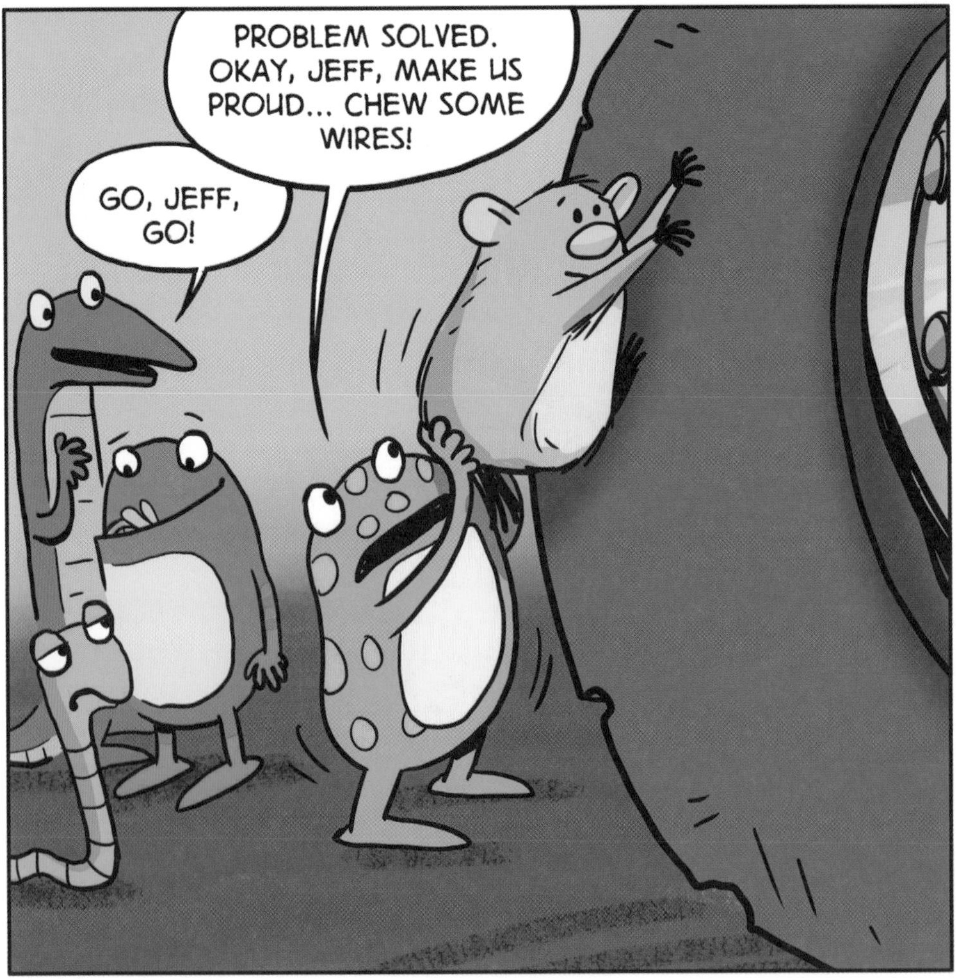
PROBLEM SOLVED. OKAY, JEFF, MAKE US PROUD... CHEW SOME WIRES!
GO, JEFF, GO!

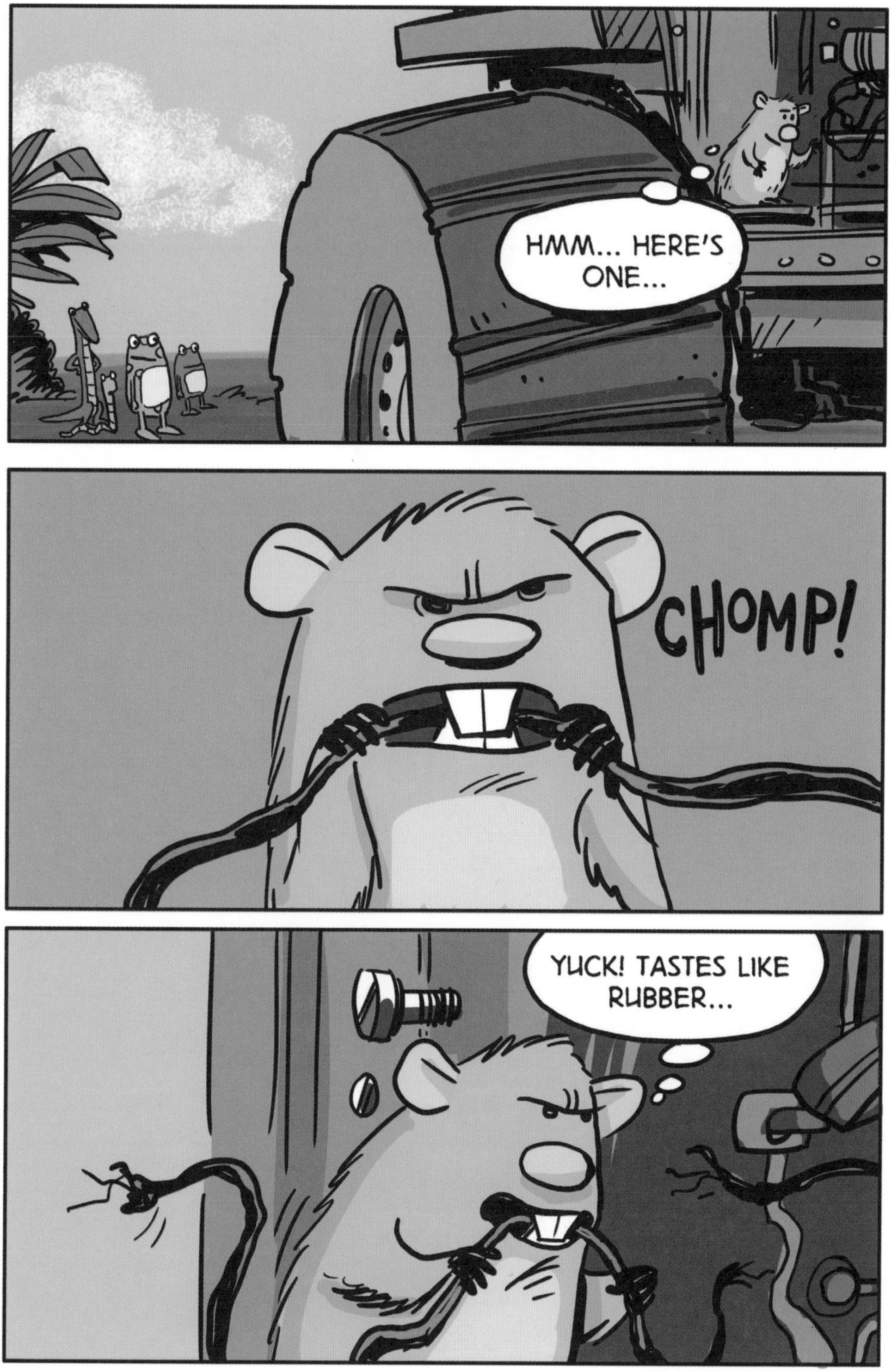
HMM... HERE'S ONE...
CHOMP!
YUCK! TASTES LIKE RUBBER...

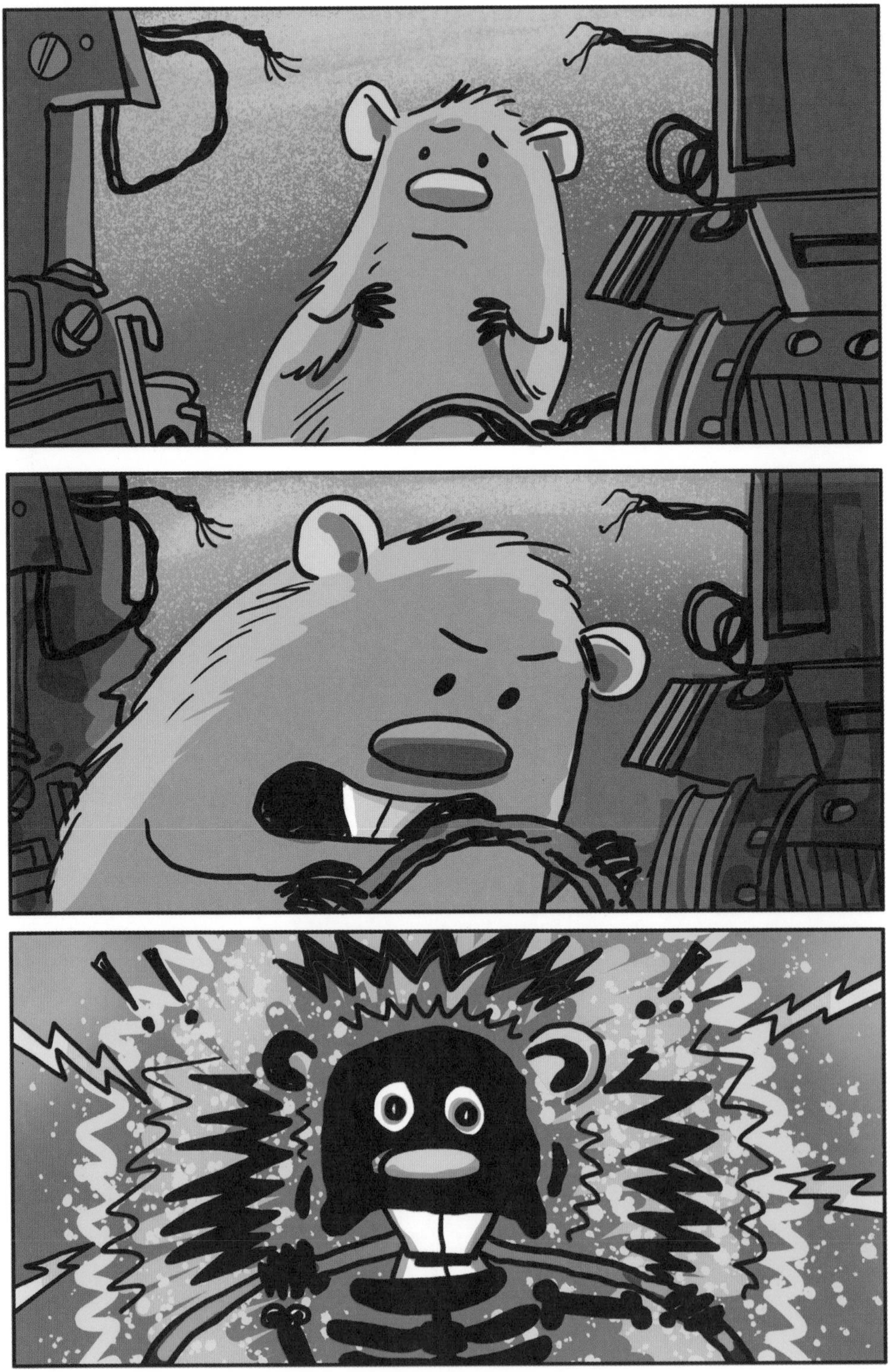

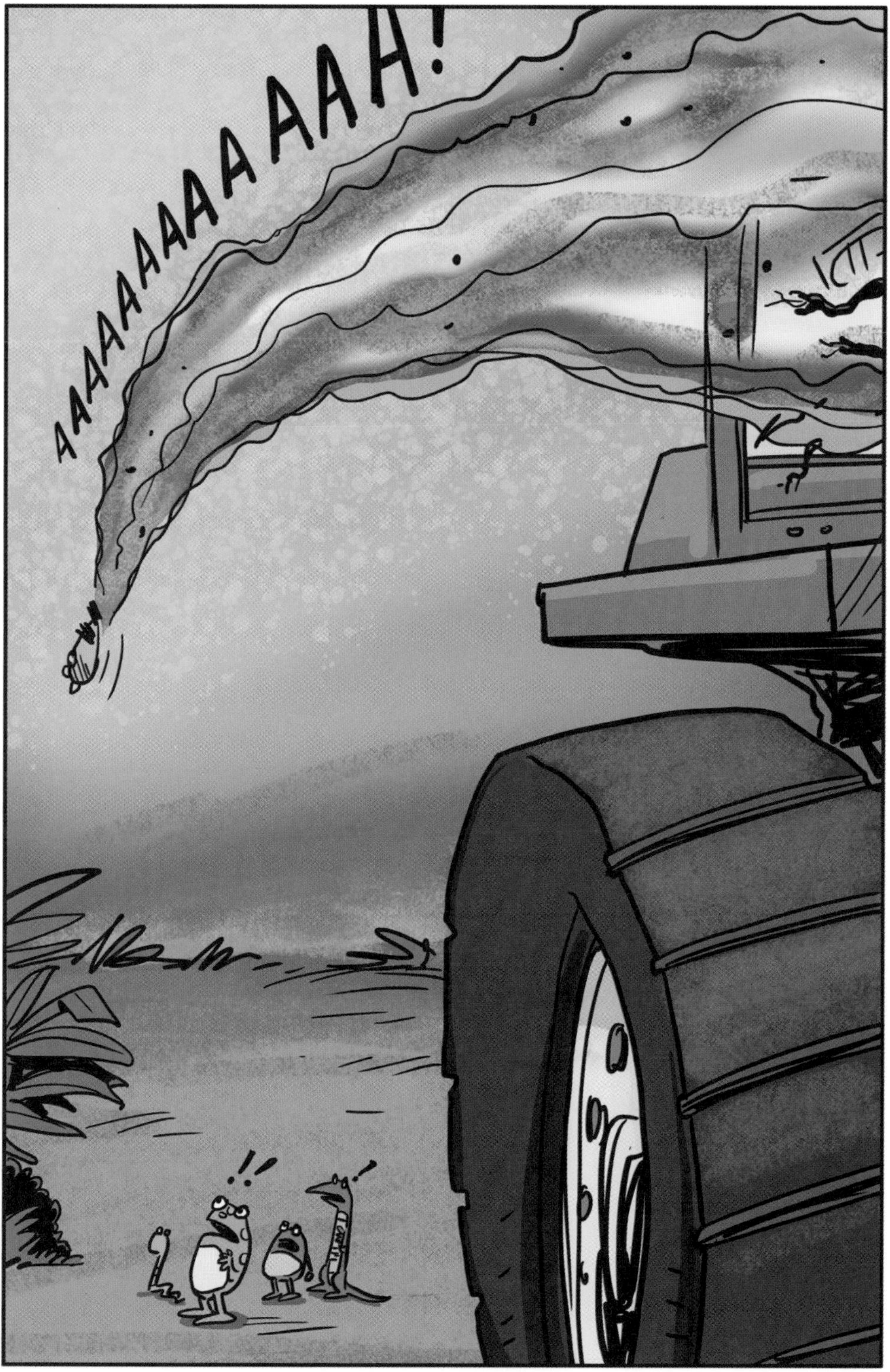
AAAAAAAAAAAH!
!!
!

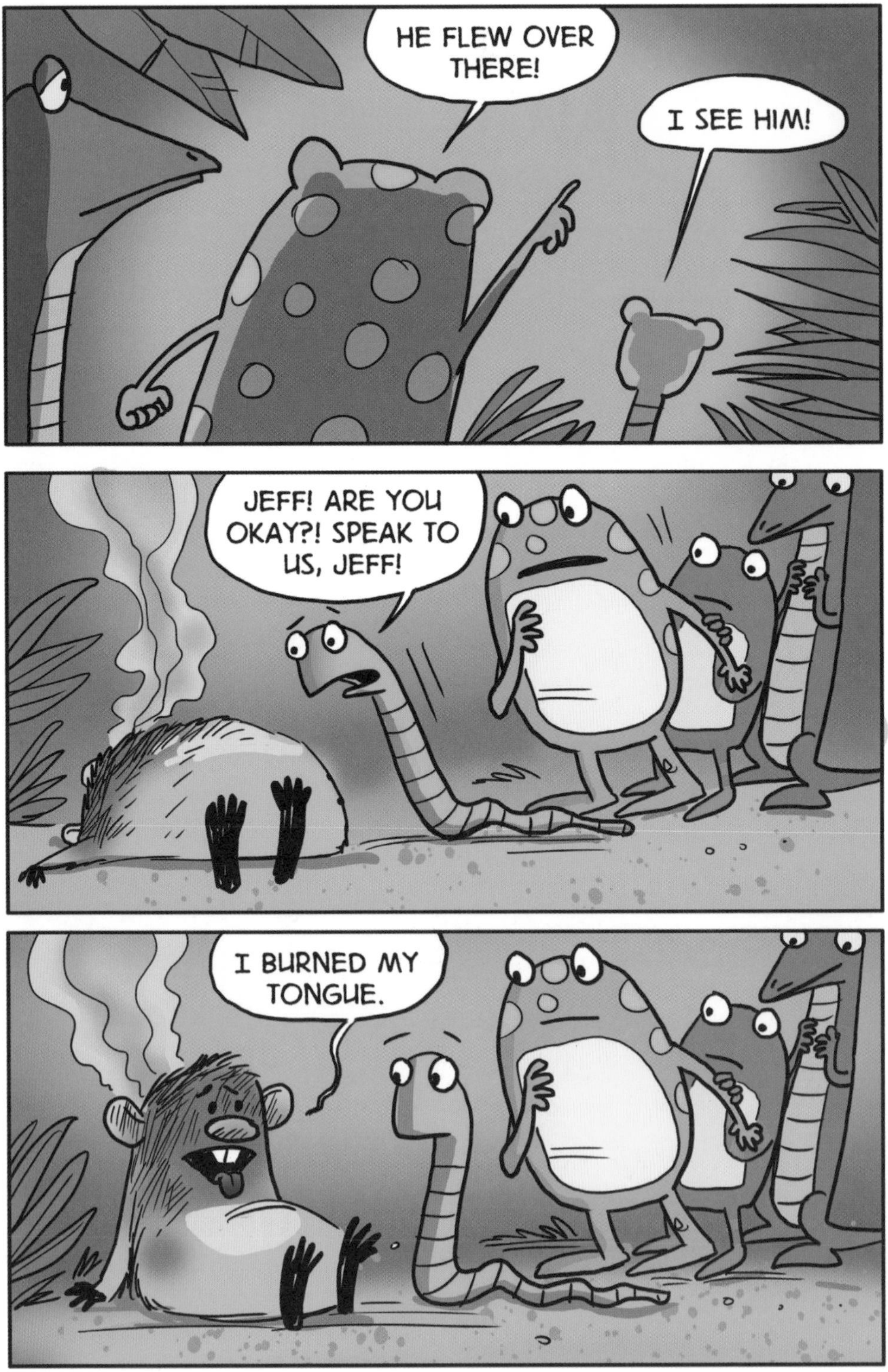
HE FLEW OVER THERE!
I SEE HIM!
JEFF! ARE YOU OKAY?! SPEAK TO US, JEFF!
I BURNED MY TONGUE.

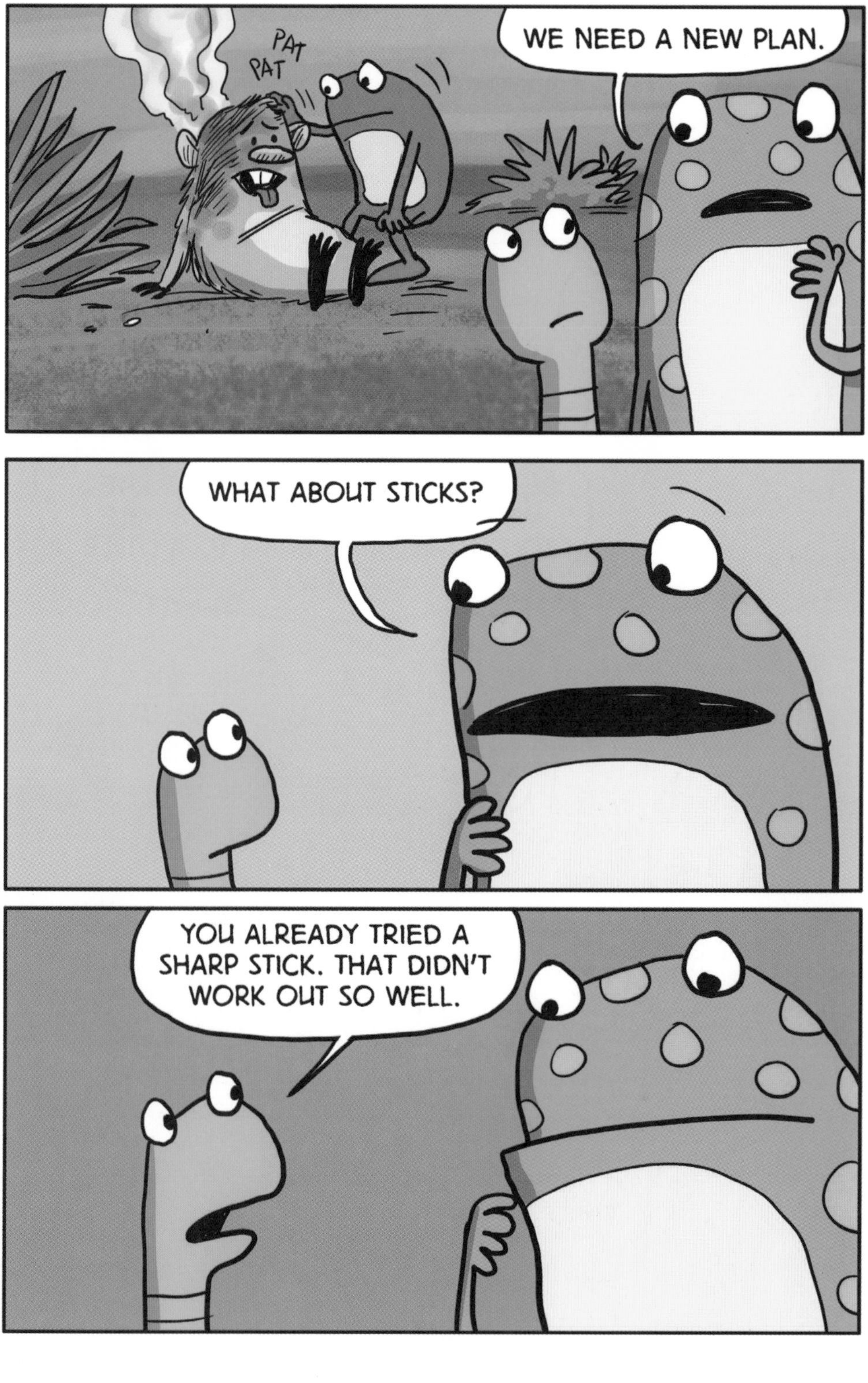
PAT
PAT
WE NEED A NEW PLAN.
WHAT ABOUT STICKS?
YOU ALREADY TRIED A SHARP STICK. THAT DIDN'T WORK OUT SO WELL.

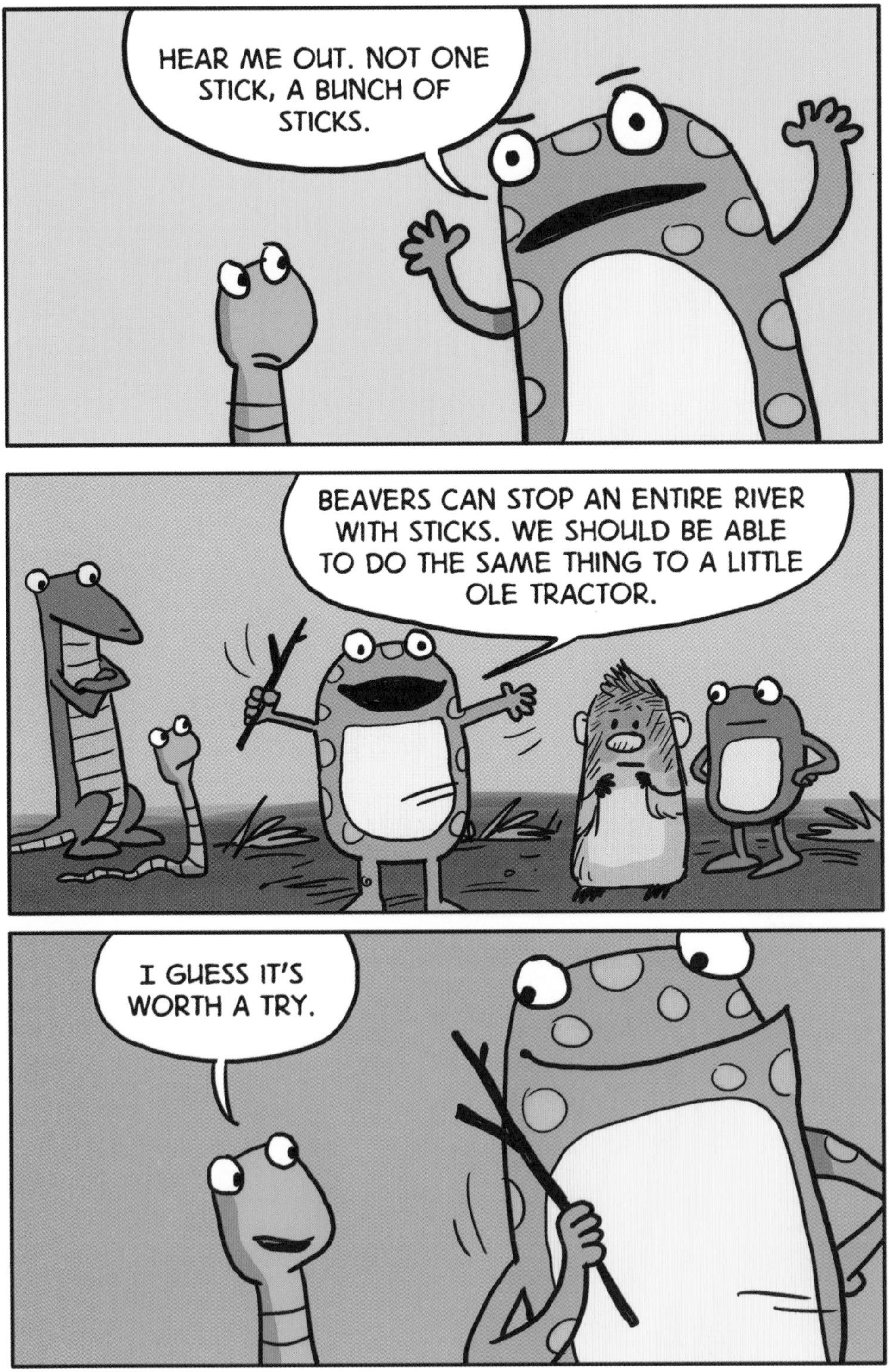
HEAR ME OUT. NOT ONE STICK, A BUNCH OF STICKS.
BEAVERS CAN STOP AN ENTIRE RIVER WITH STICKS. WE SHOULD BE ABLE TO DO THE SAME THING TO A LITTLE OLE TRACTOR.
I GUESS IT'S WORTH A TRY.

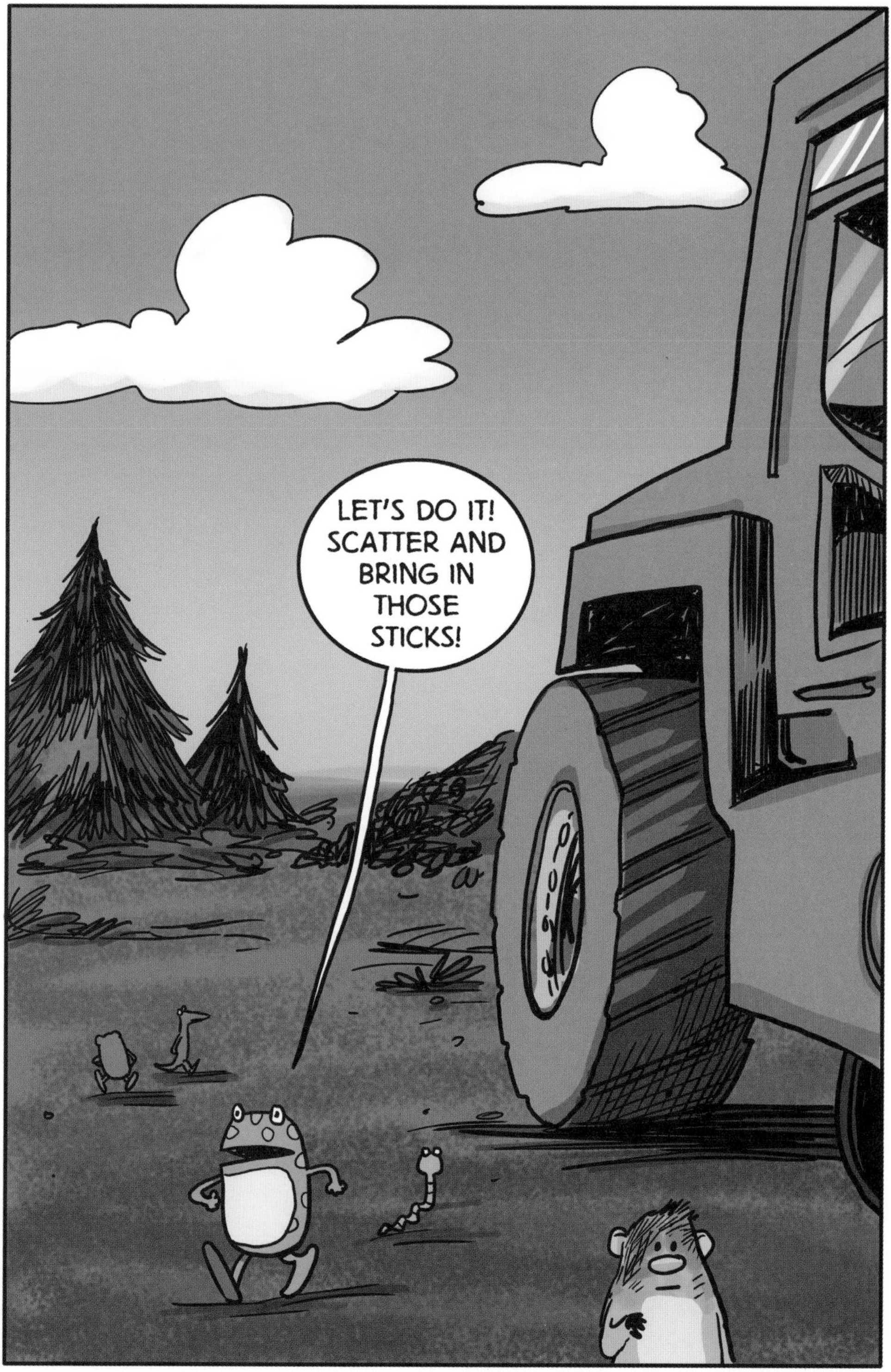
LET'S DO IT! SCATTER AND BRING IN THOSE STICKS!

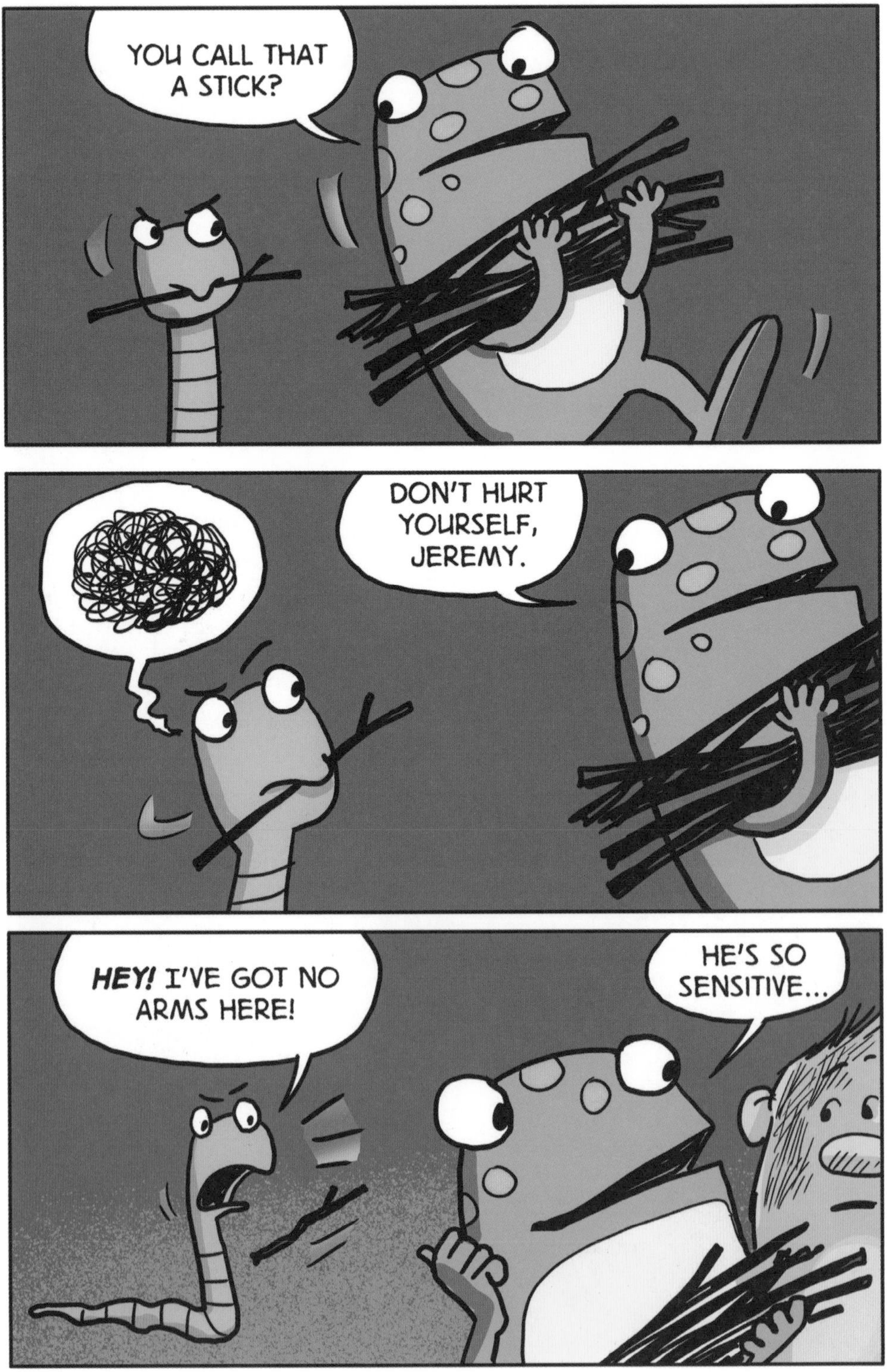
YOU CALL THAT A STICK?
DON'T HURT YOURSELF, JEREMY.
HEY! I'VE GOT NO ARMS HERE!
HE'S SO SENSITIVE...

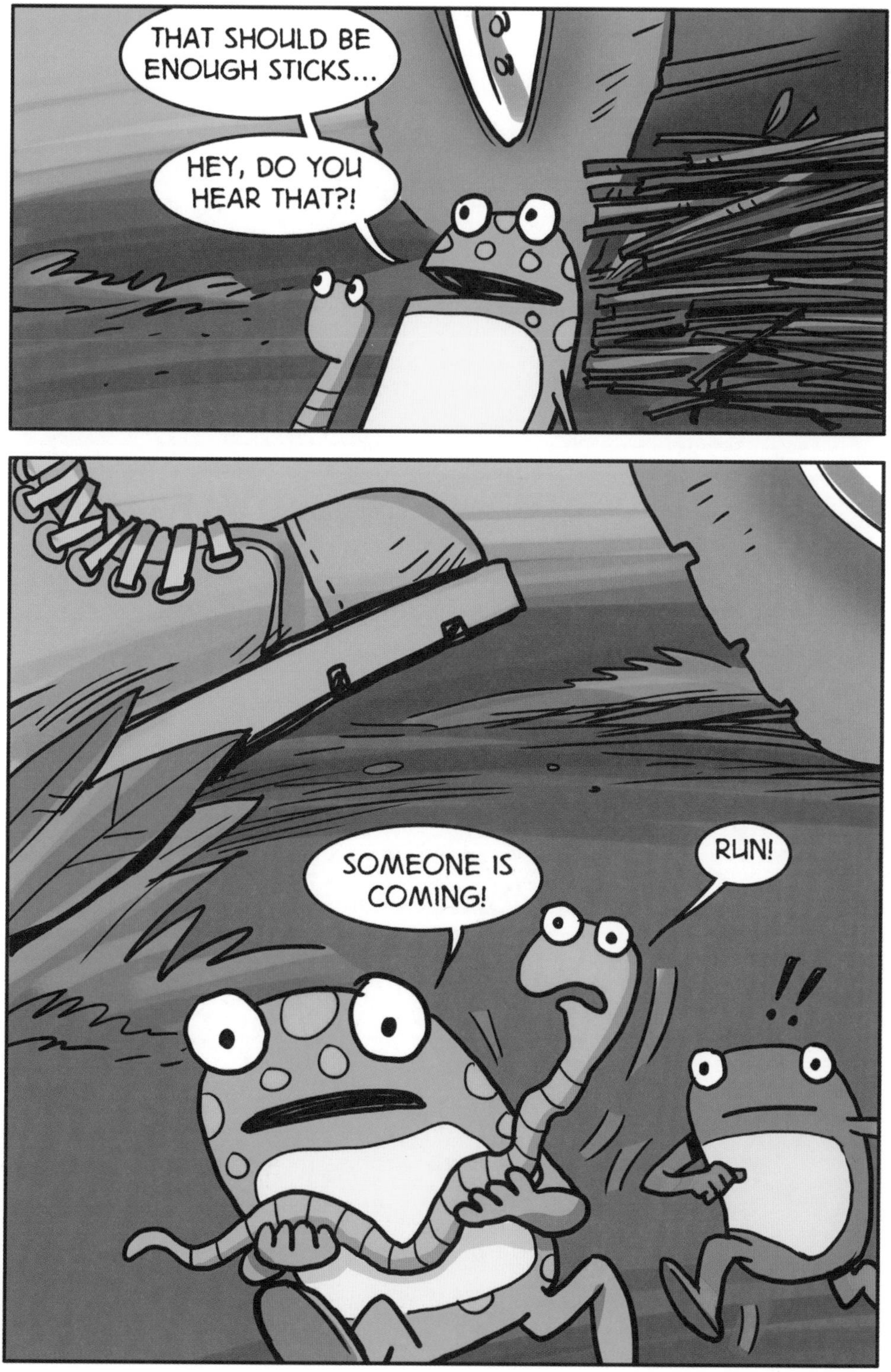
THAT SHOULD BE ENOUGH STICKS...
HEY, DO YOU HEAR THAT?!
SOMEONE IS COMING!
RUN!
!!

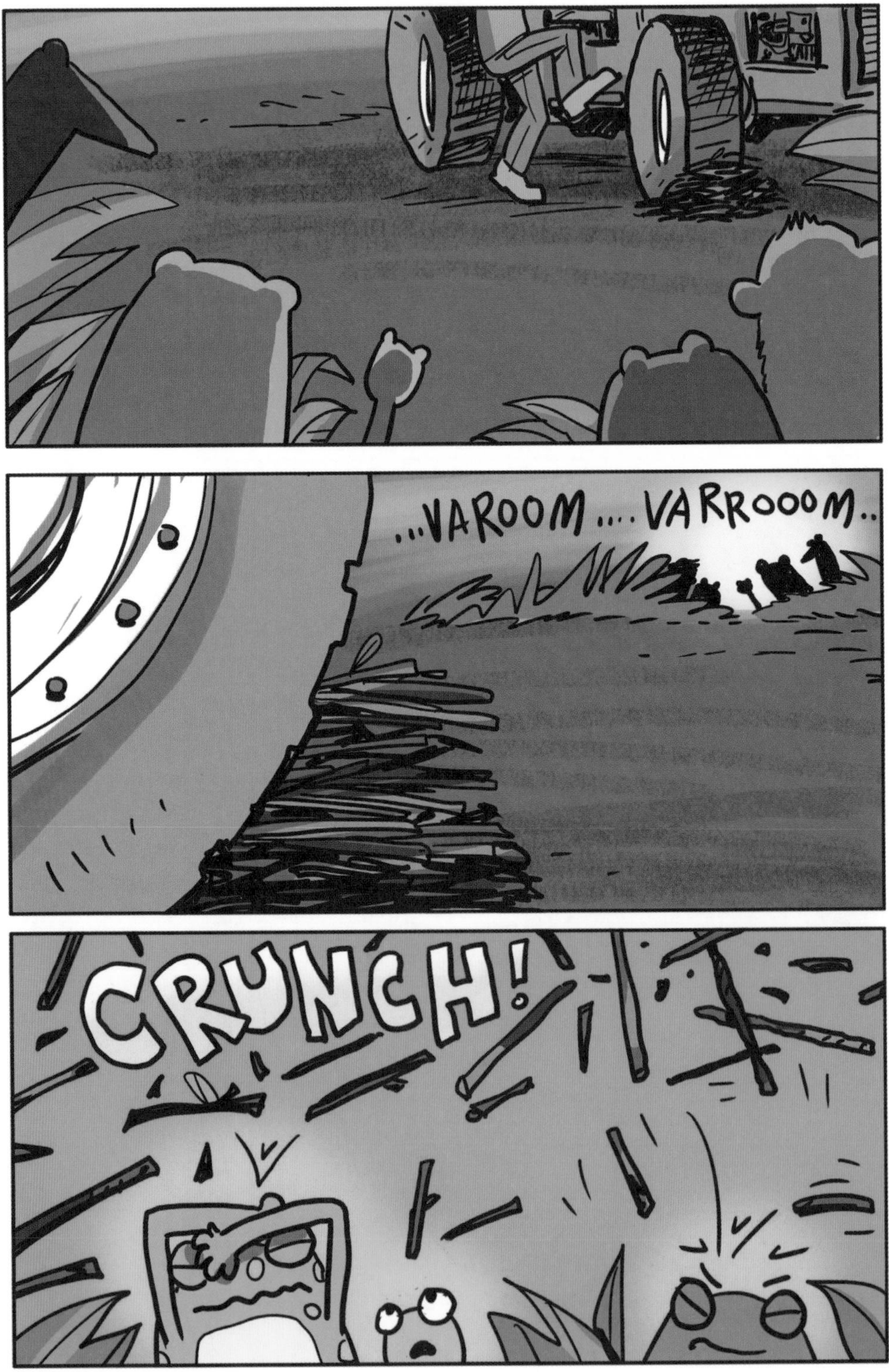
...VAROOM.... VARROOOM...
CRUNCH!

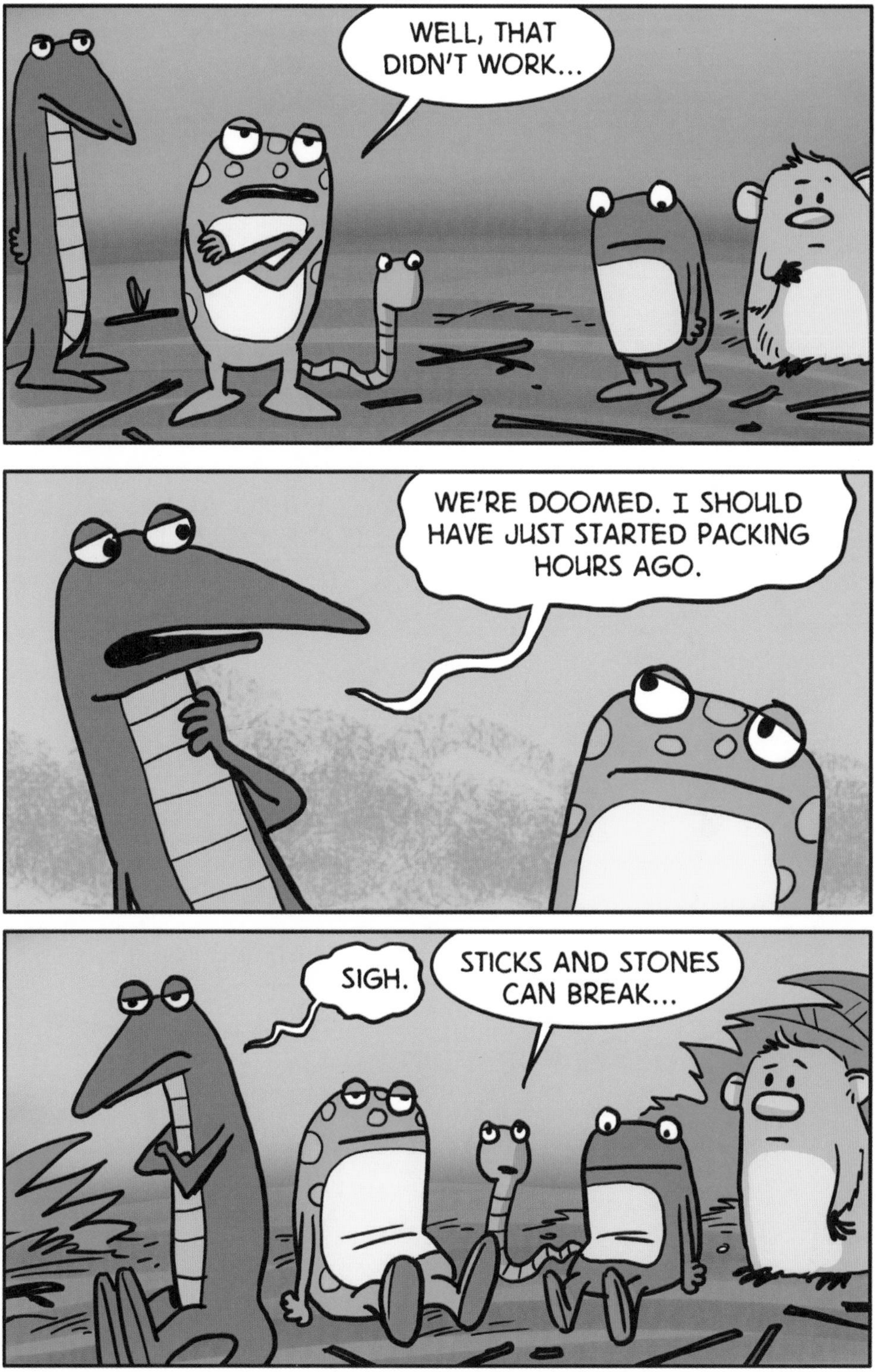
WELL, THAT DIDN'T WORK...
WE'RE DOOMED. I SHOULD HAVE JUST STARTED PACKING HOURS AGO.
SIGH.
STICKS AND STONES CAN BREAK...

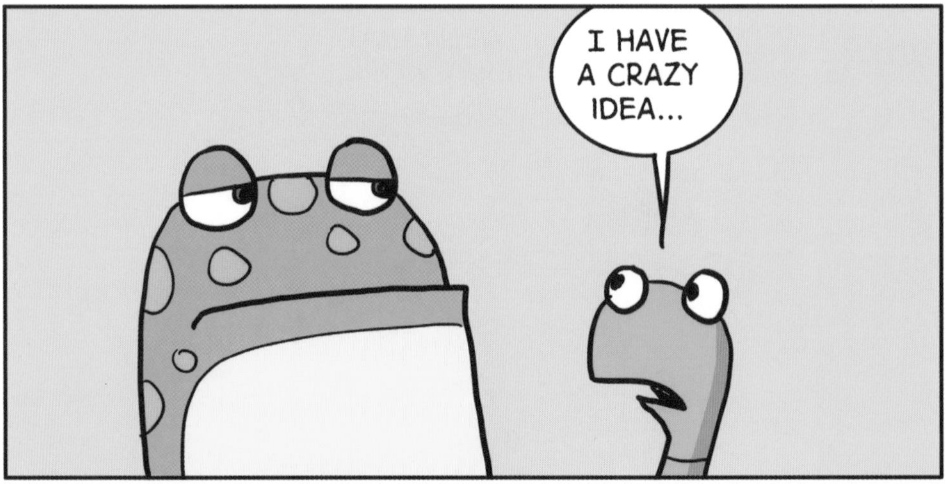
I HAVE A CRAZY IDEA...

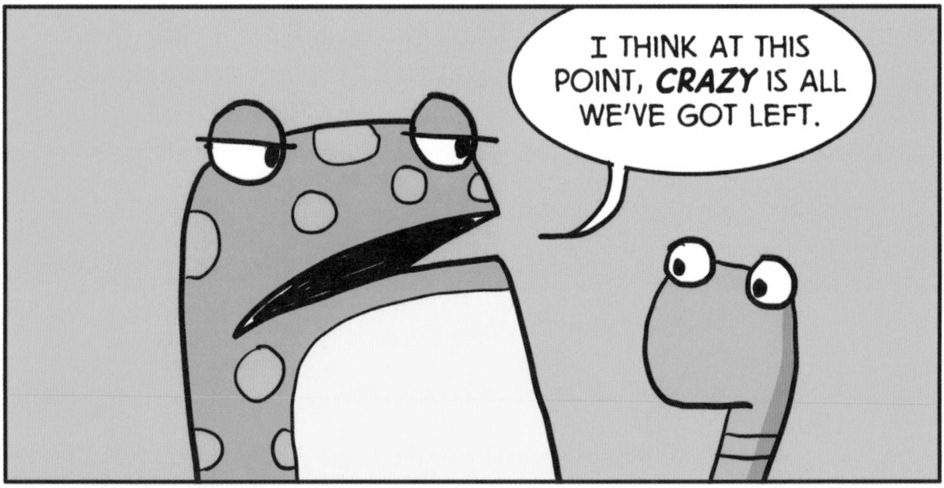
I THINK AT THIS POINT, ***CRAZY*** IS ALL WE'VE GOT LEFT.

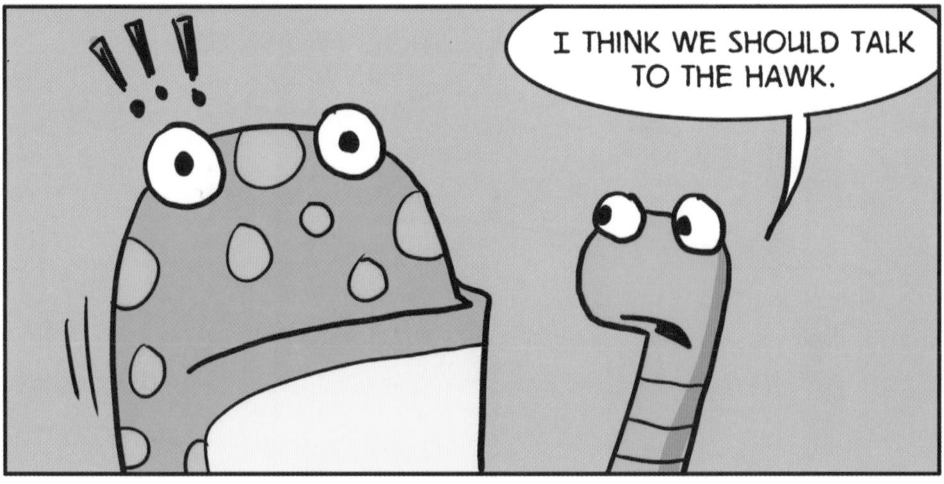
!!!
I THINK WE SHOULD TALK TO THE HAWK.

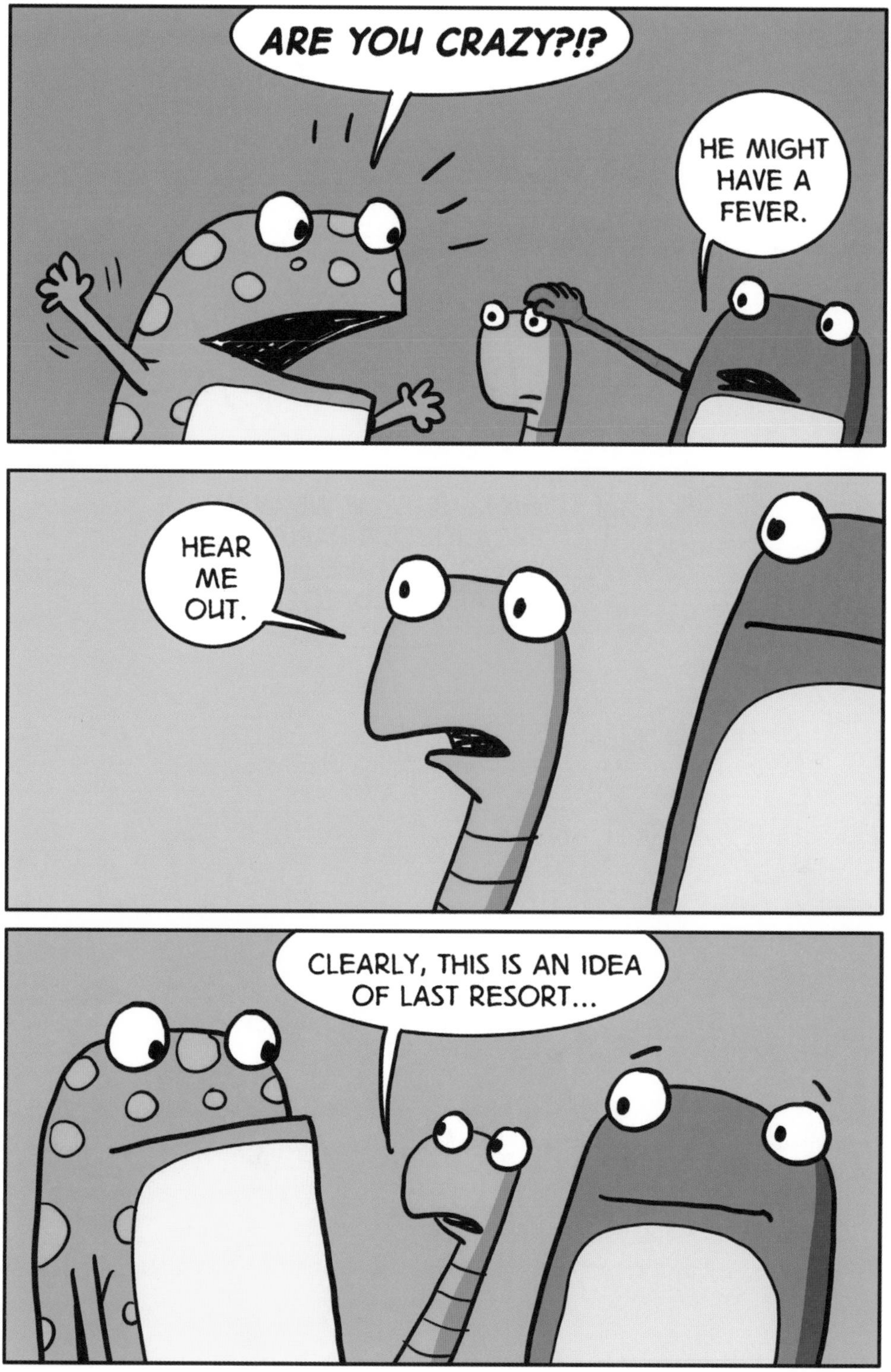
ARE YOU CRAZY?!?
HE MIGHT HAVE A FEVER.
HEAR ME OUT.
CLEARLY, THIS IS AN IDEA OF LAST RESORT...

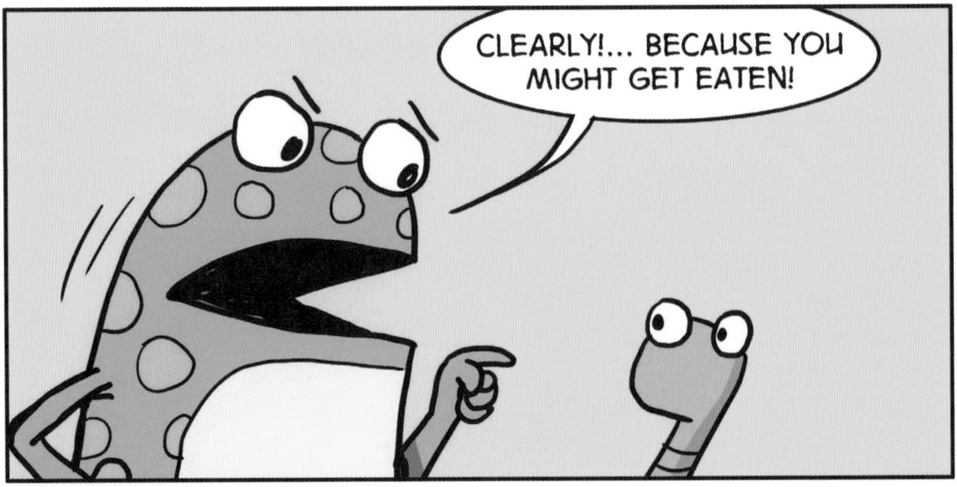
CLEARLY!... BECAUSE YOU MIGHT GET EATEN!

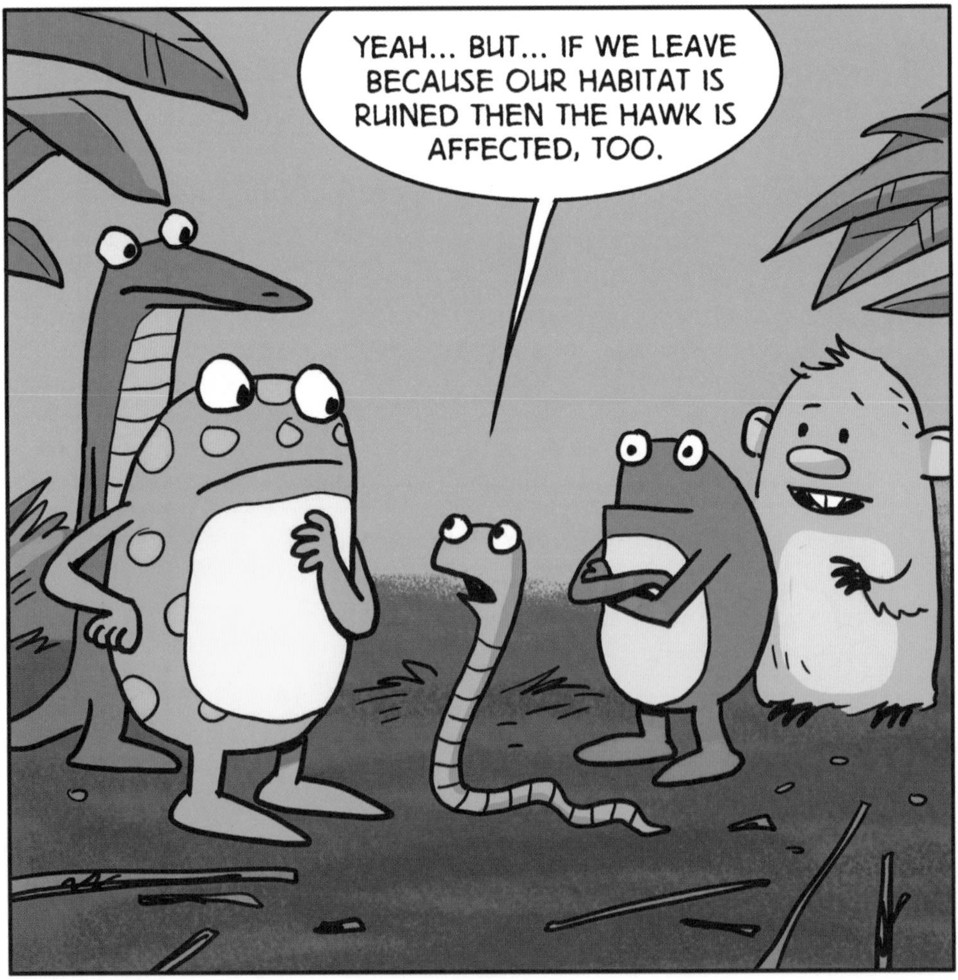
YEAH... BUT... IF WE LEAVE BECAUSE OUR HABITAT IS RUINED THEN THE HAWK IS AFFECTED, TOO.

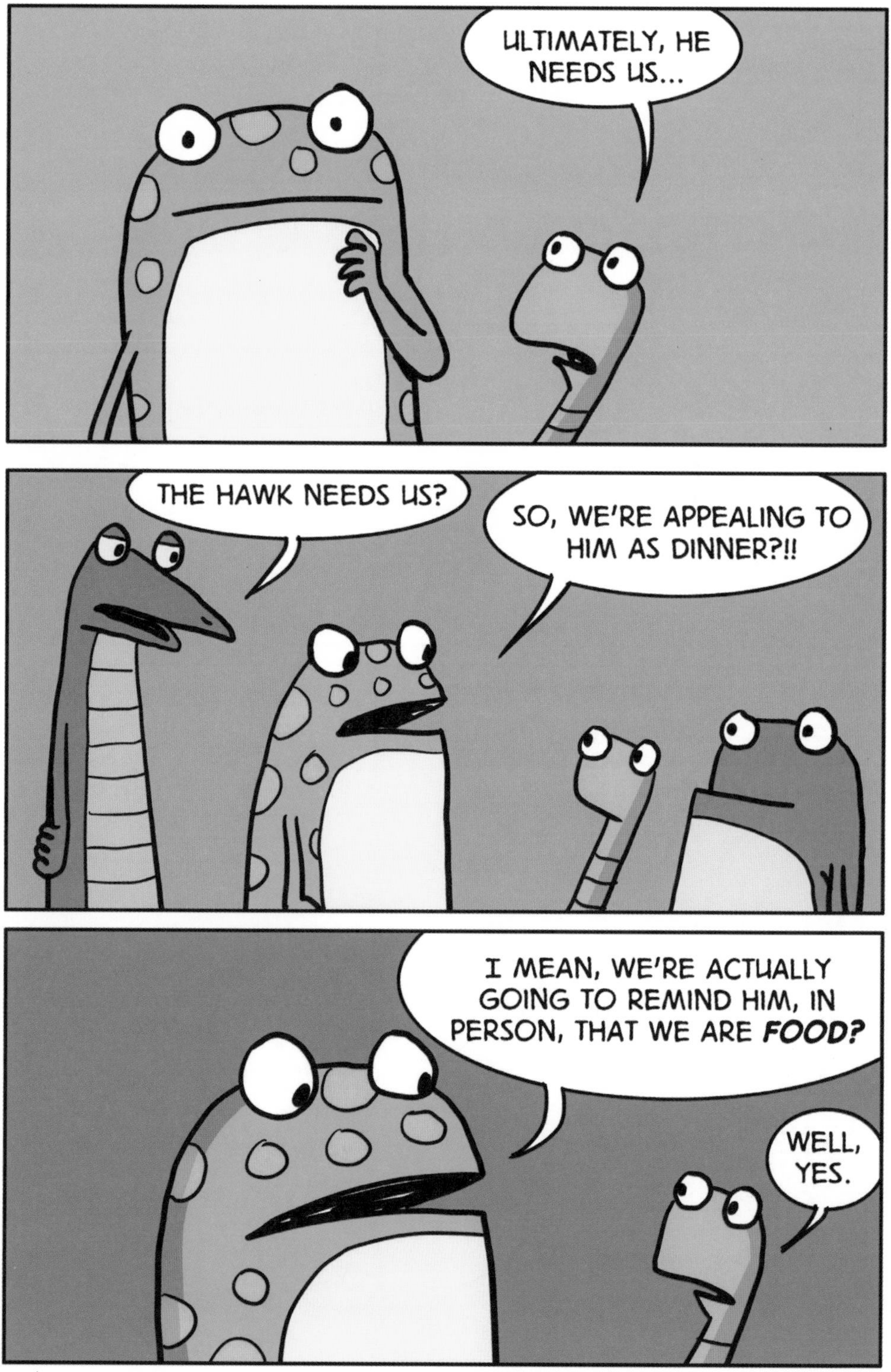
ULTIMATELY, HE NEEDS US...
THE HAWK NEEDS US?
SO, WE'RE APPEALING TO HIM AS DINNER?!!
I MEAN, WE'RE ACTUALLY GOING TO REMIND HIM, IN PERSON, THAT WE ARE ***FOOD?***
WELL, YES.

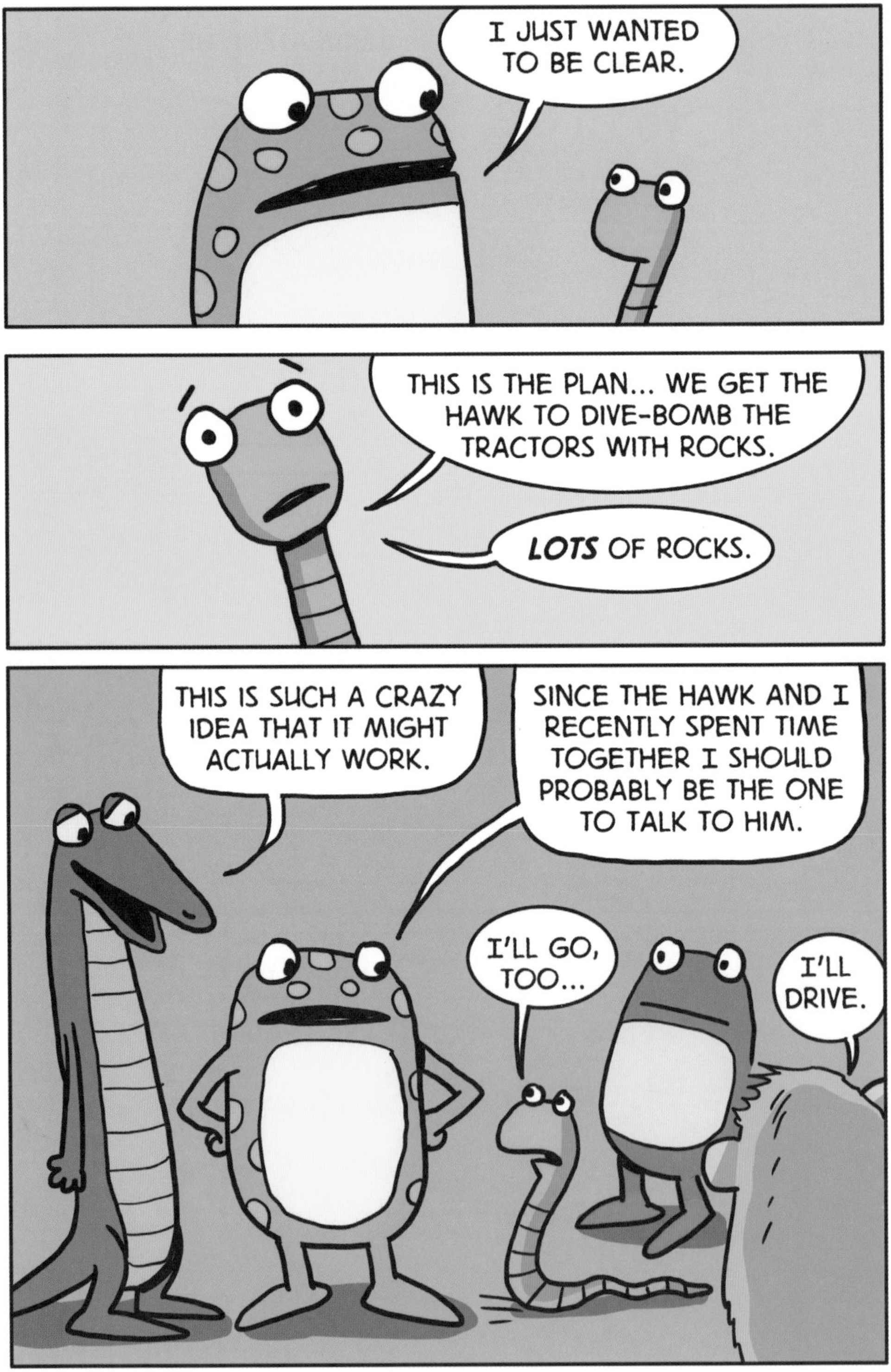
I JUST WANTED TO BE CLEAR.
THIS IS THE PLAN... WE GET THE HAWK TO DIVE-BOMB THE TRACTORS WITH ROCKS.
LOTS OF ROCKS.
THIS IS SUCH A CRAZY IDEA THAT IT MIGHT ACTUALLY WORK.
SINCE THE HAWK AND I RECENTLY SPENT TIME TOGETHER I SHOULD PROBABLY BE THE ONE TO TALK TO HIM.
I'LL GO, TOO...
I'LL DRIVE.

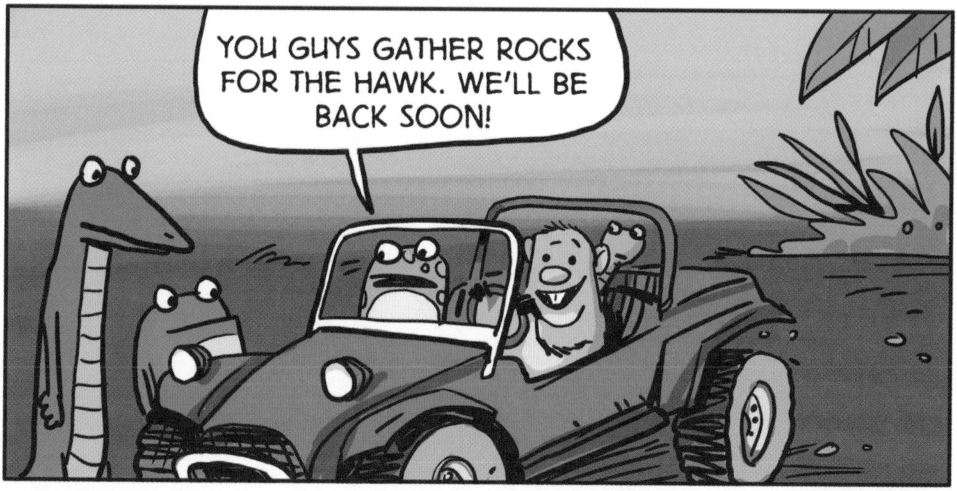
YOU GUYS GATHER ROCKS FOR THE HAWK. WE'LL BE BACK SOON!

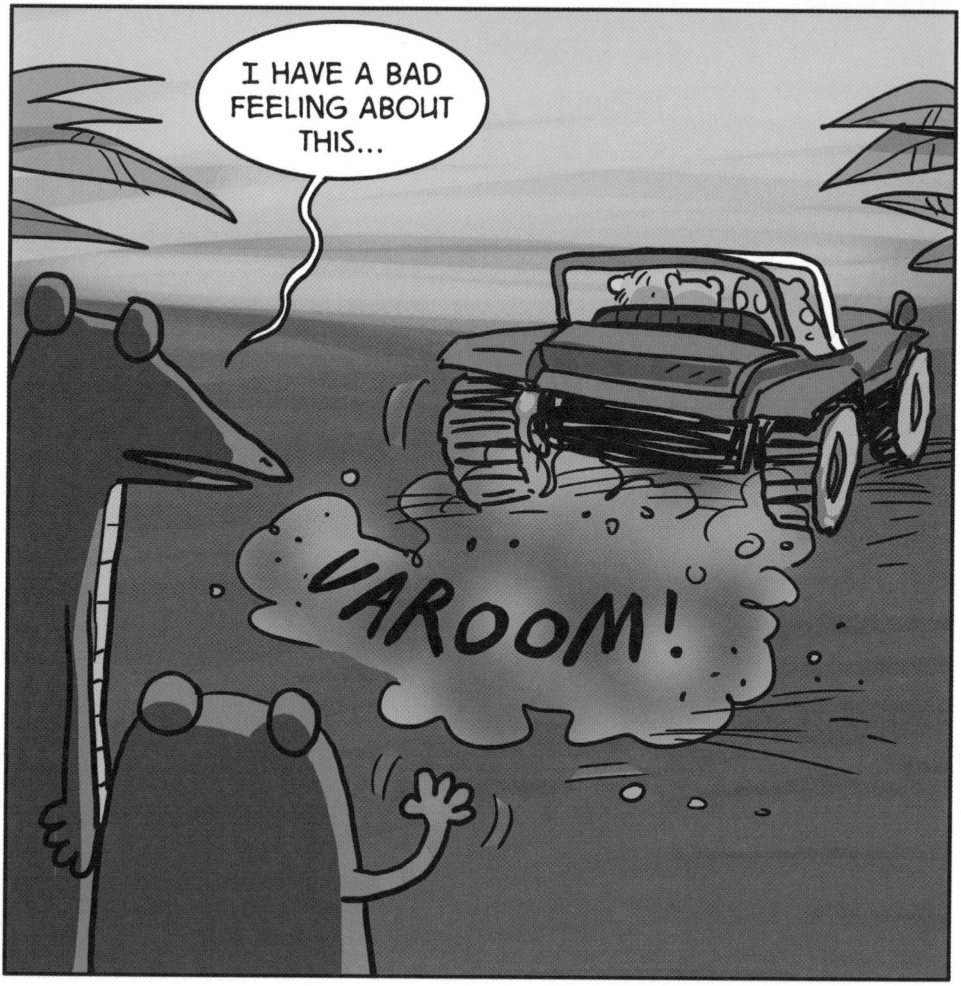
I HAVE A BAD FEELING ABOUT THIS...
VAROOM!

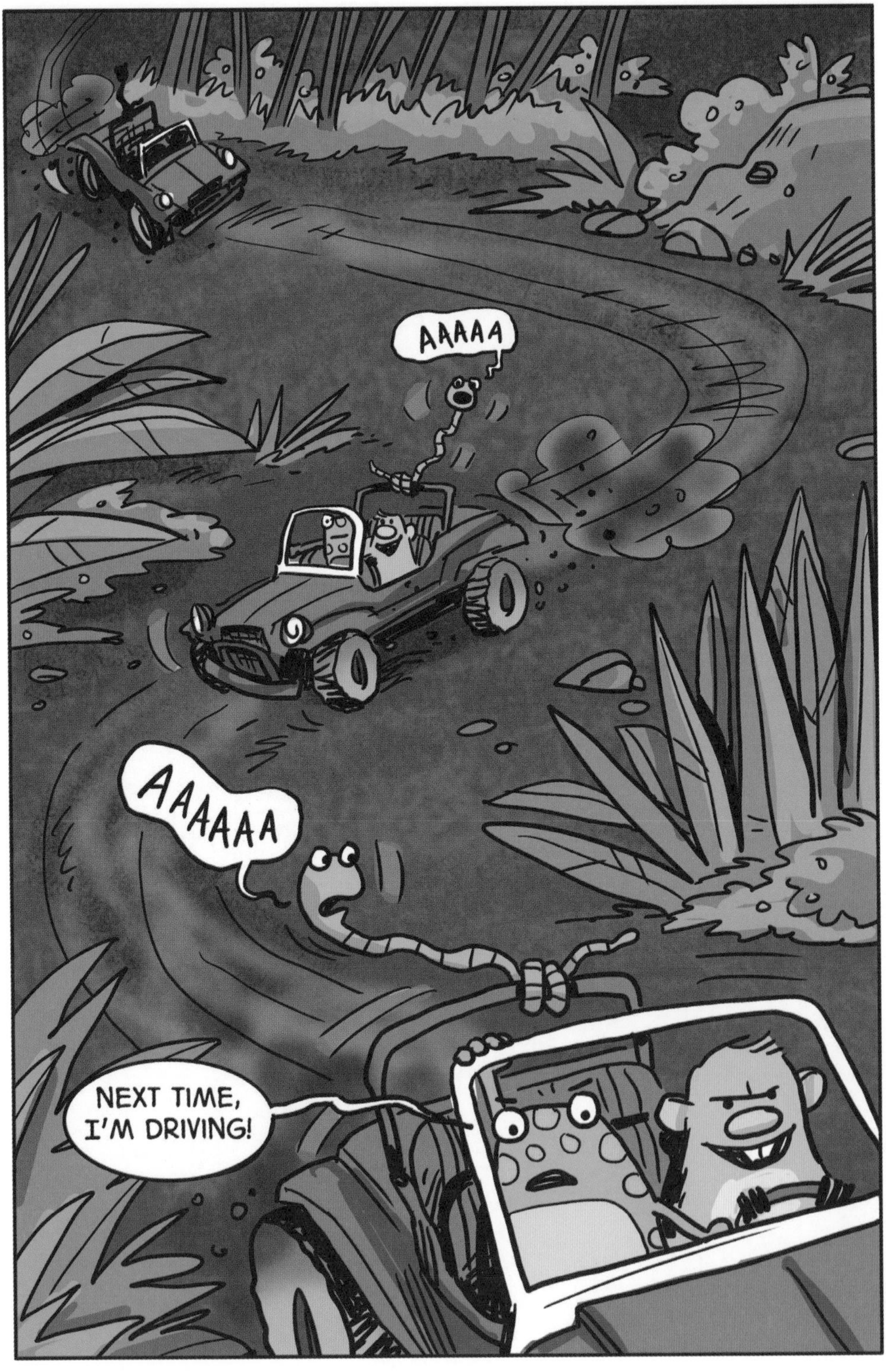
AAAAA
AAAAAA
NEXT TIME, I'M DRIVING!

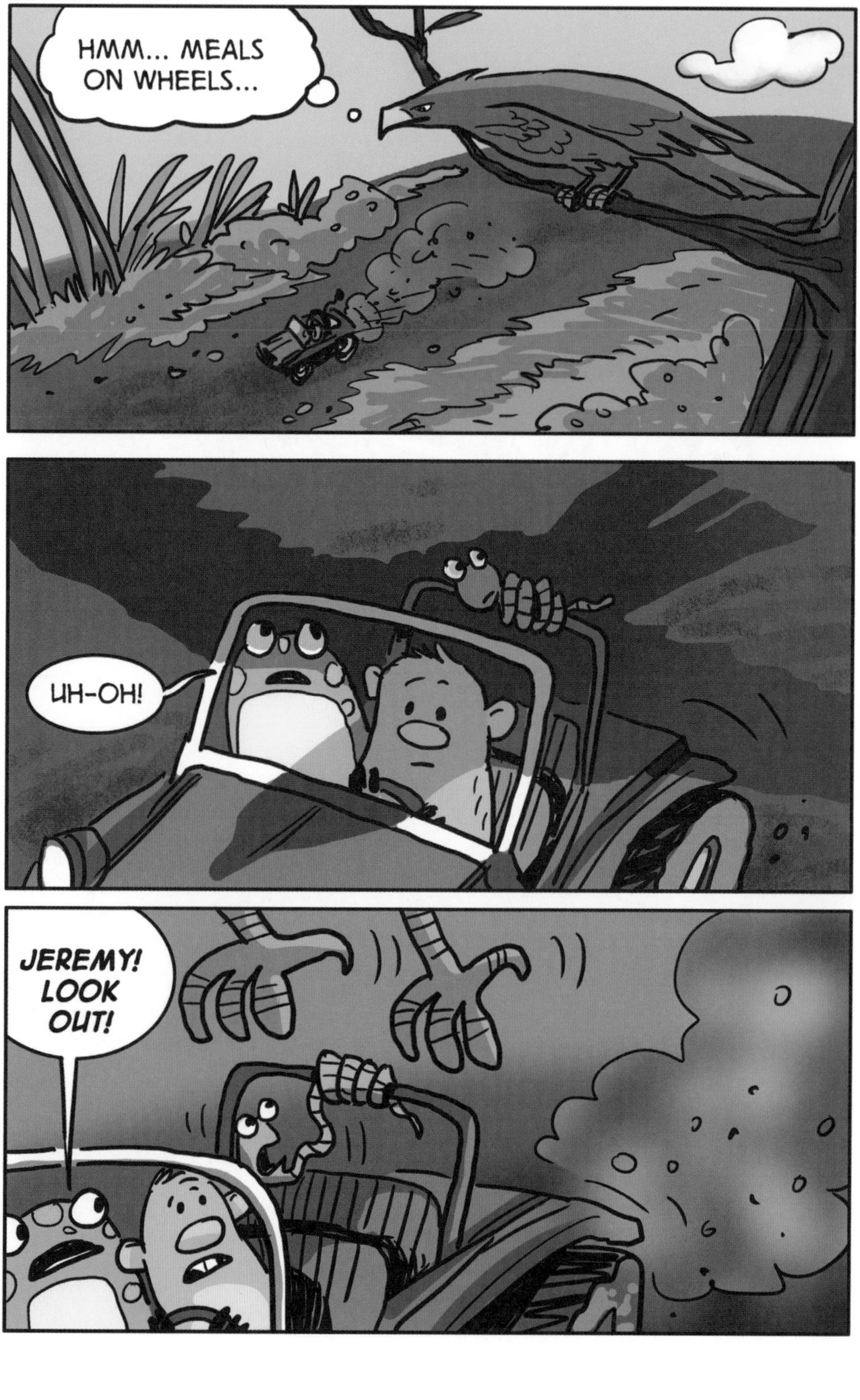
HMM... MEALS ON WHEELS...
UH-OH!
JEREMY! LOOK OUT!

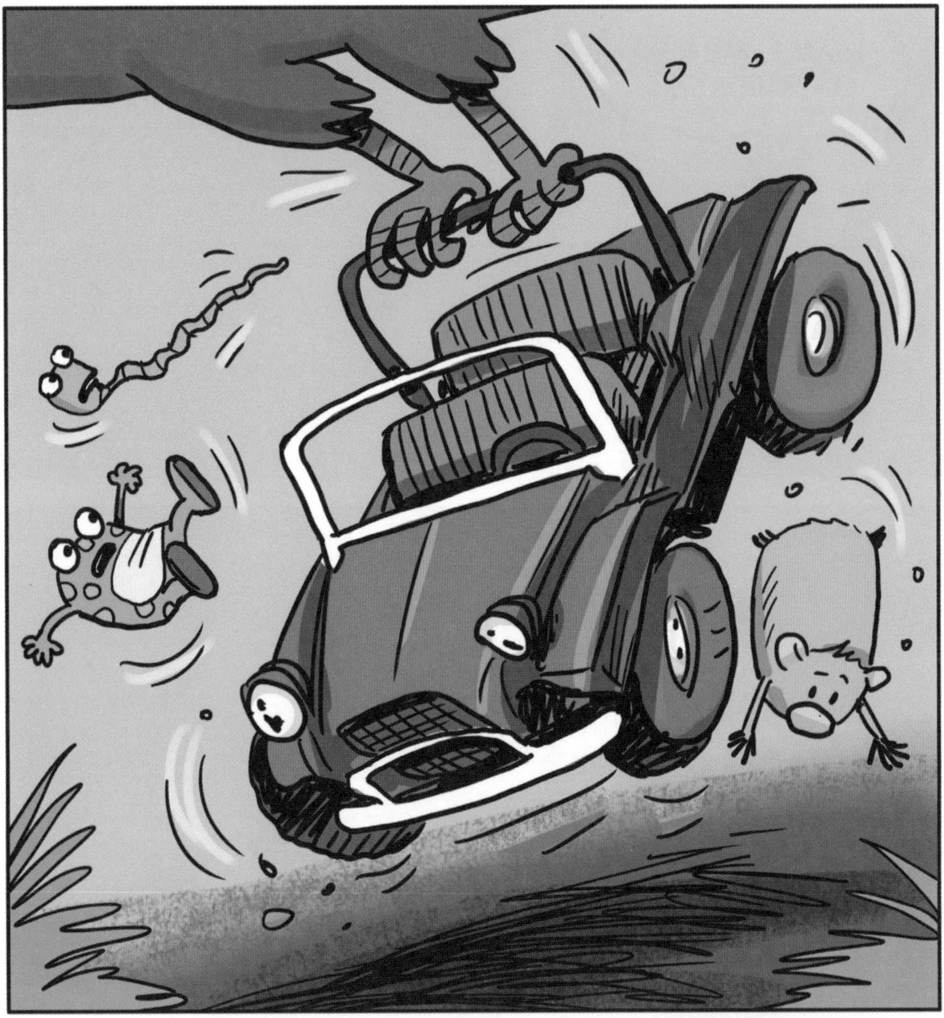

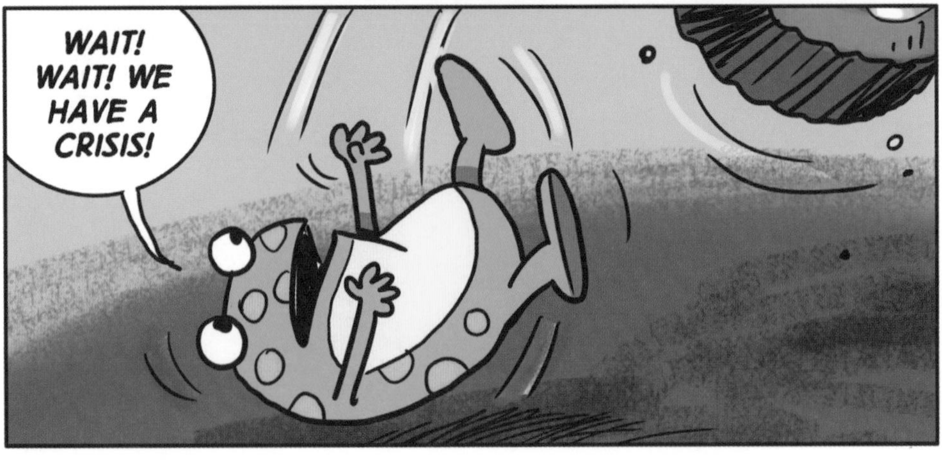
WAIT! WAIT! WE HAVE A CRISIS!

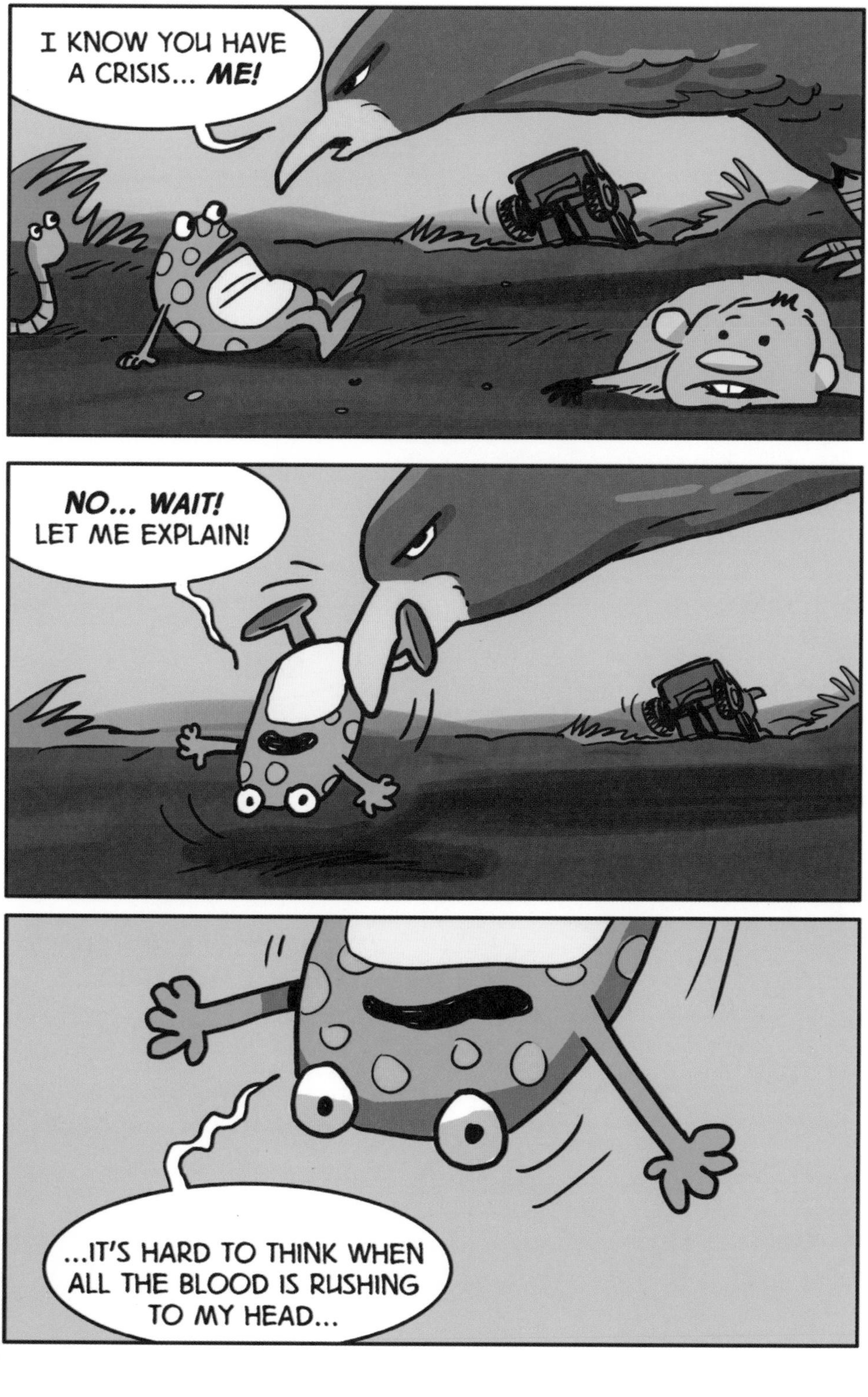
I KNOW YOU HAVE A CRISIS... **ME!**
NO... WAIT! LET ME EXPLAIN!
...IT'S HARD TO THINK WHEN ALL THE BLOOD IS RUSHING TO MY HEAD...

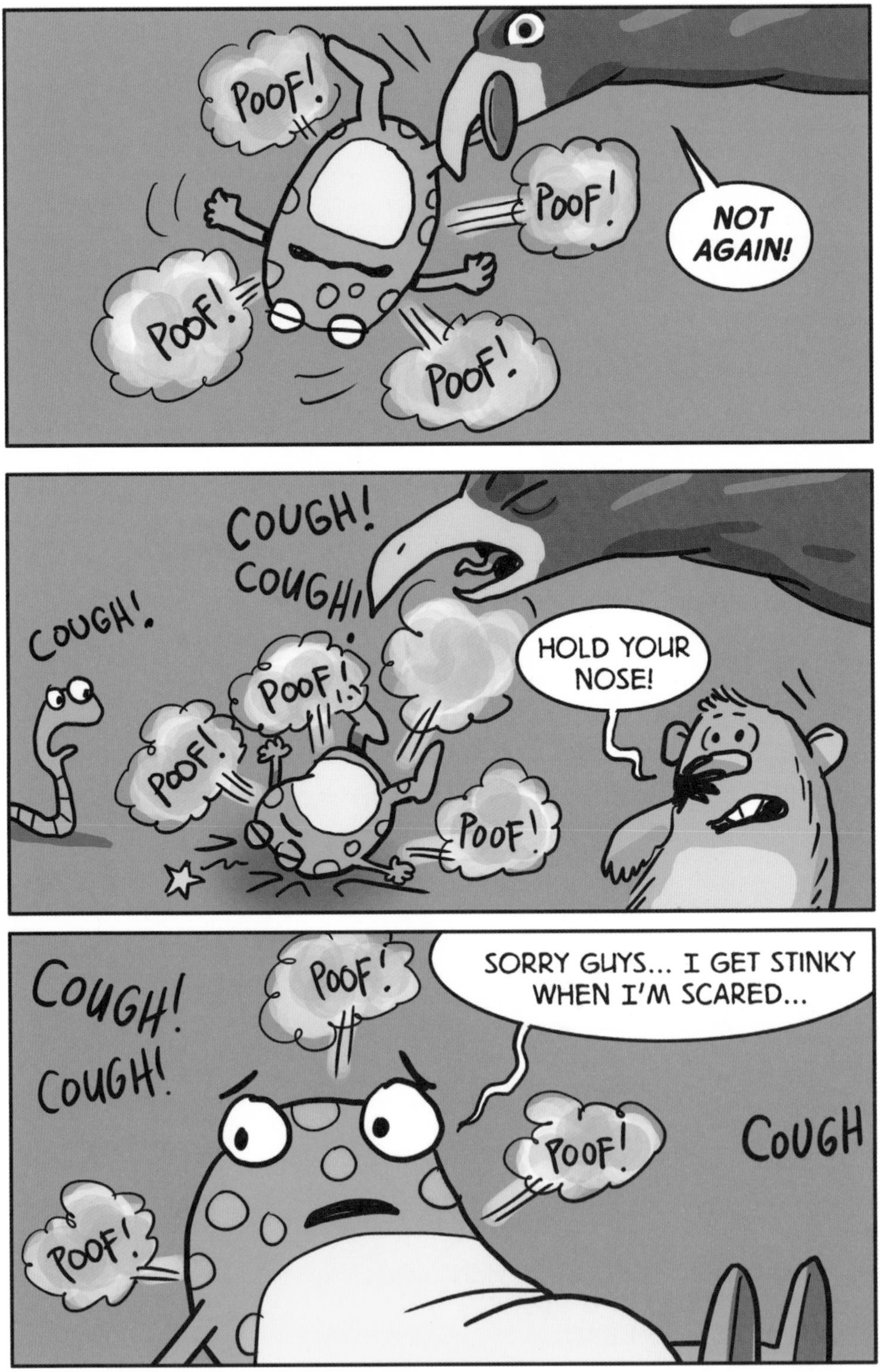
POOF!
POOF!
POOF!
POOF!
NOT AGAIN!
COUGH!
COUGH!
COUGH!
POOF!
POOF!
POOF!
HOLD YOUR NOSE!
COUGH!
COUGH!
POOF!
SORRY GUYS... I GET STINKY WHEN I'M SCARED...
POOF!
COUGH
POOF!

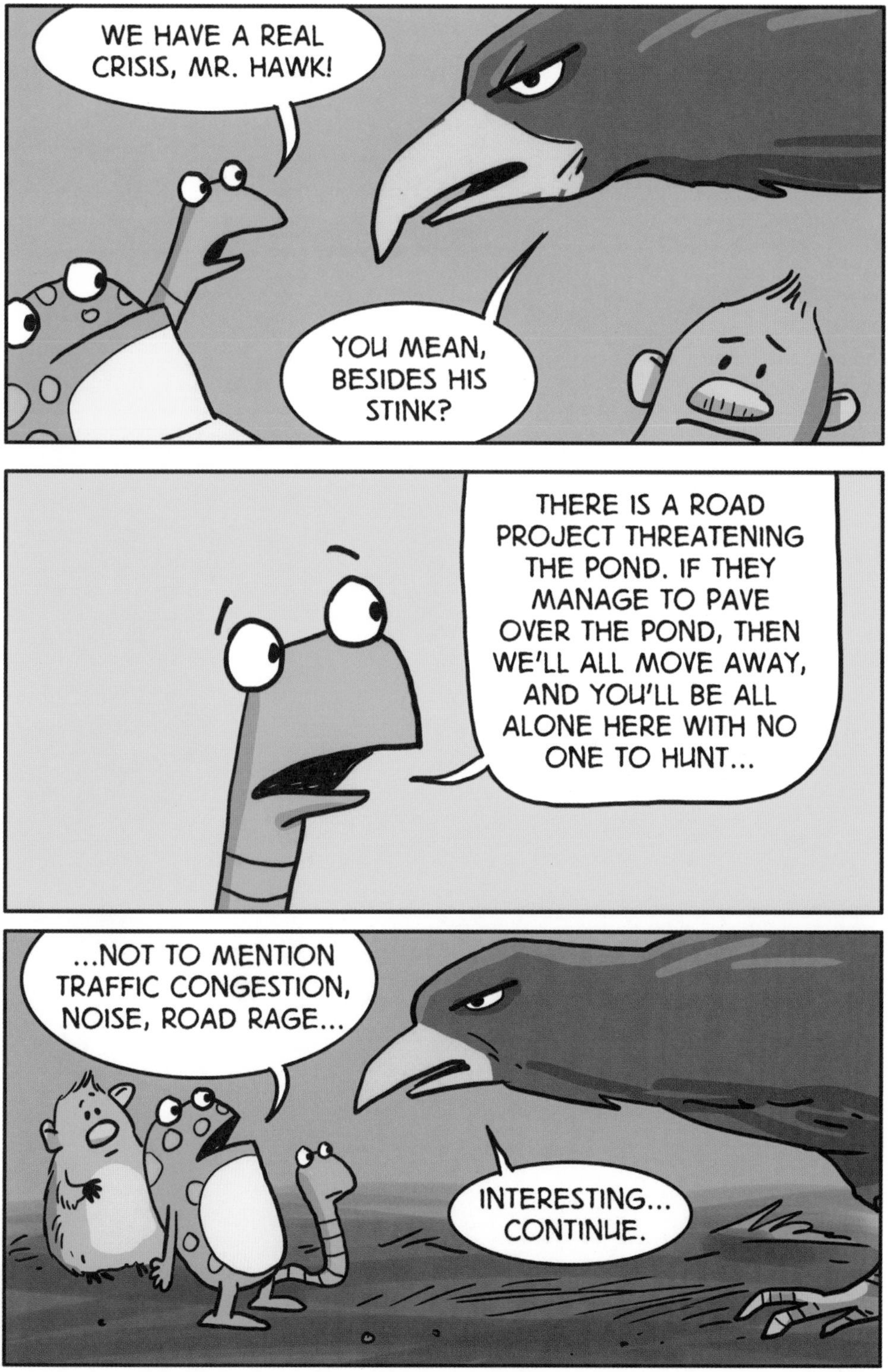
WE HAVE A REAL CRISIS, MR. HAWK!
YOU MEAN, BESIDES HIS STINK?
THERE IS A ROAD PROJECT THREATENING THE POND. IF THEY MANAGE TO PAVE OVER THE POND, THEN WE'LL ALL MOVE AWAY, AND YOU'LL BE ALL ALONE HERE WITH NO ONE TO HUNT...
...NOT TO MENTION TRAFFIC CONGESTION, NOISE, ROAD RAGE...
INTERESTING... CONTINUE.

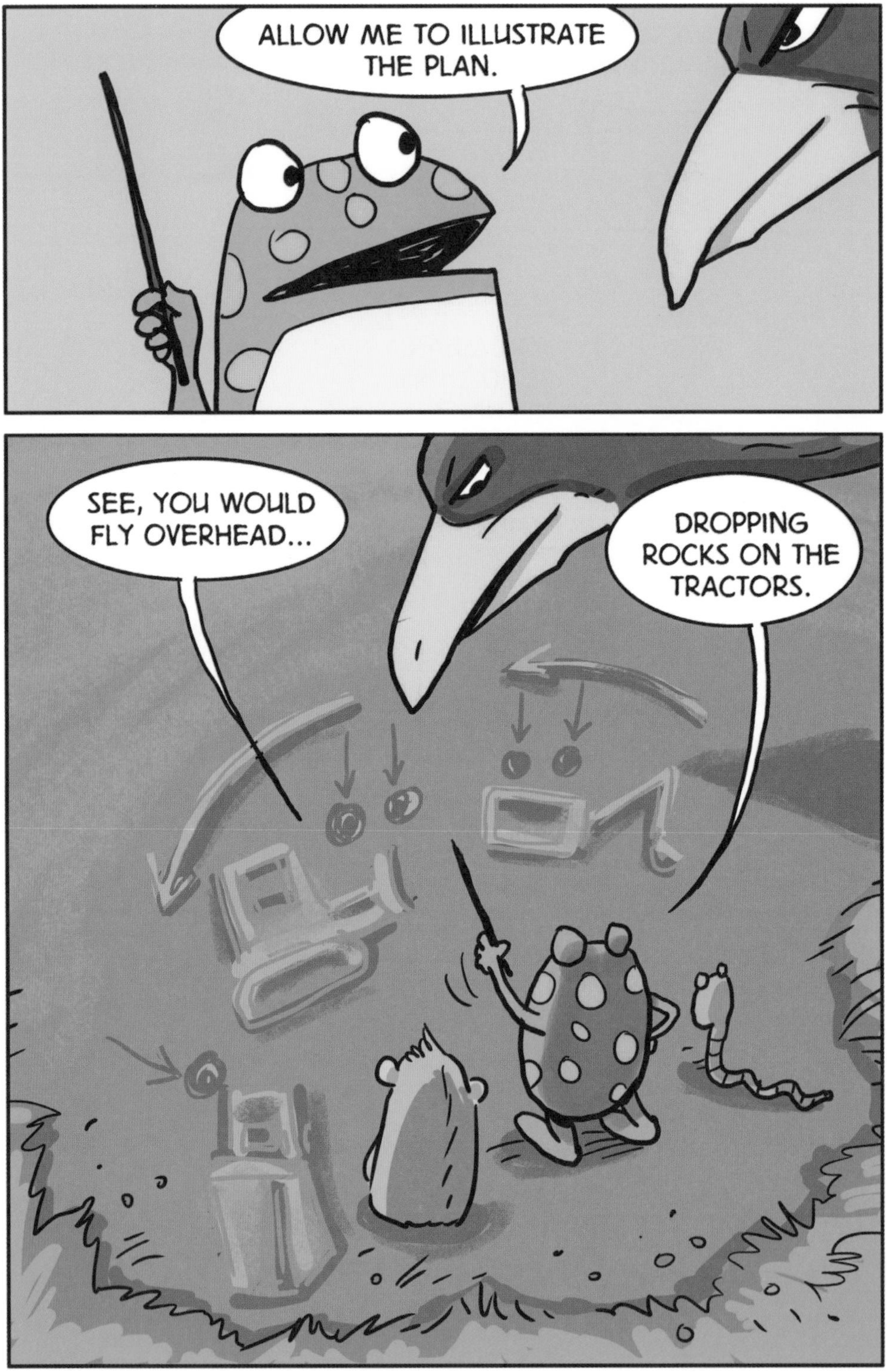
ALLOW ME TO ILLUSTRATE THE PLAN.
SEE, YOU WOULD FLY OVERHEAD...
DROPPING ROCKS ON THE TRACTORS.

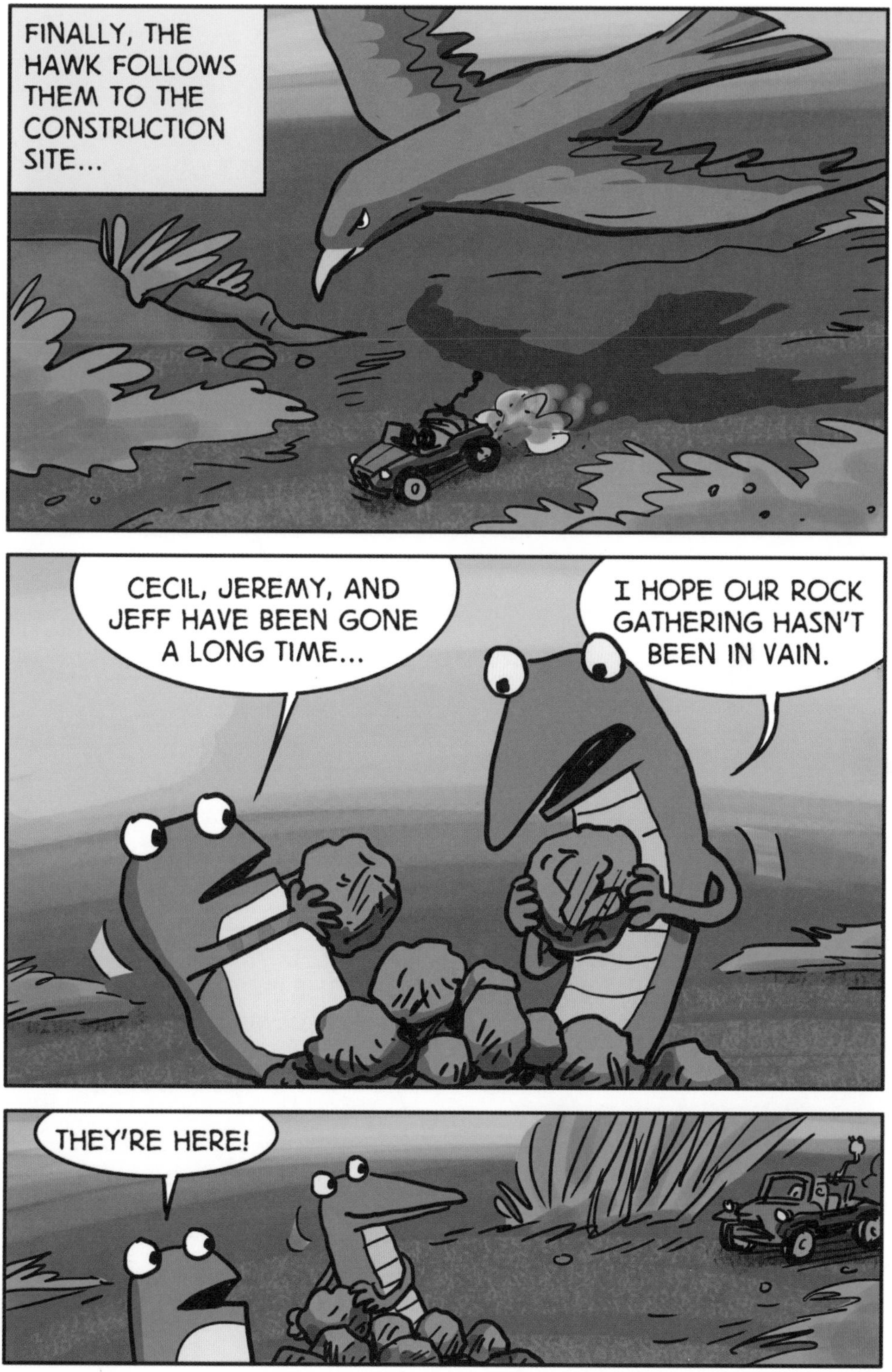
FINALLY, THE HAWK FOLLOWS THEM TO THE CONSTRUCTION SITE...
CECIL, JEREMY, AND JEFF HAVE BEEN GONE A LONG TIME...
I HOPE OUR ROCK GATHERING HASN'T BEEN IN VAIN.
THEY'RE HERE!

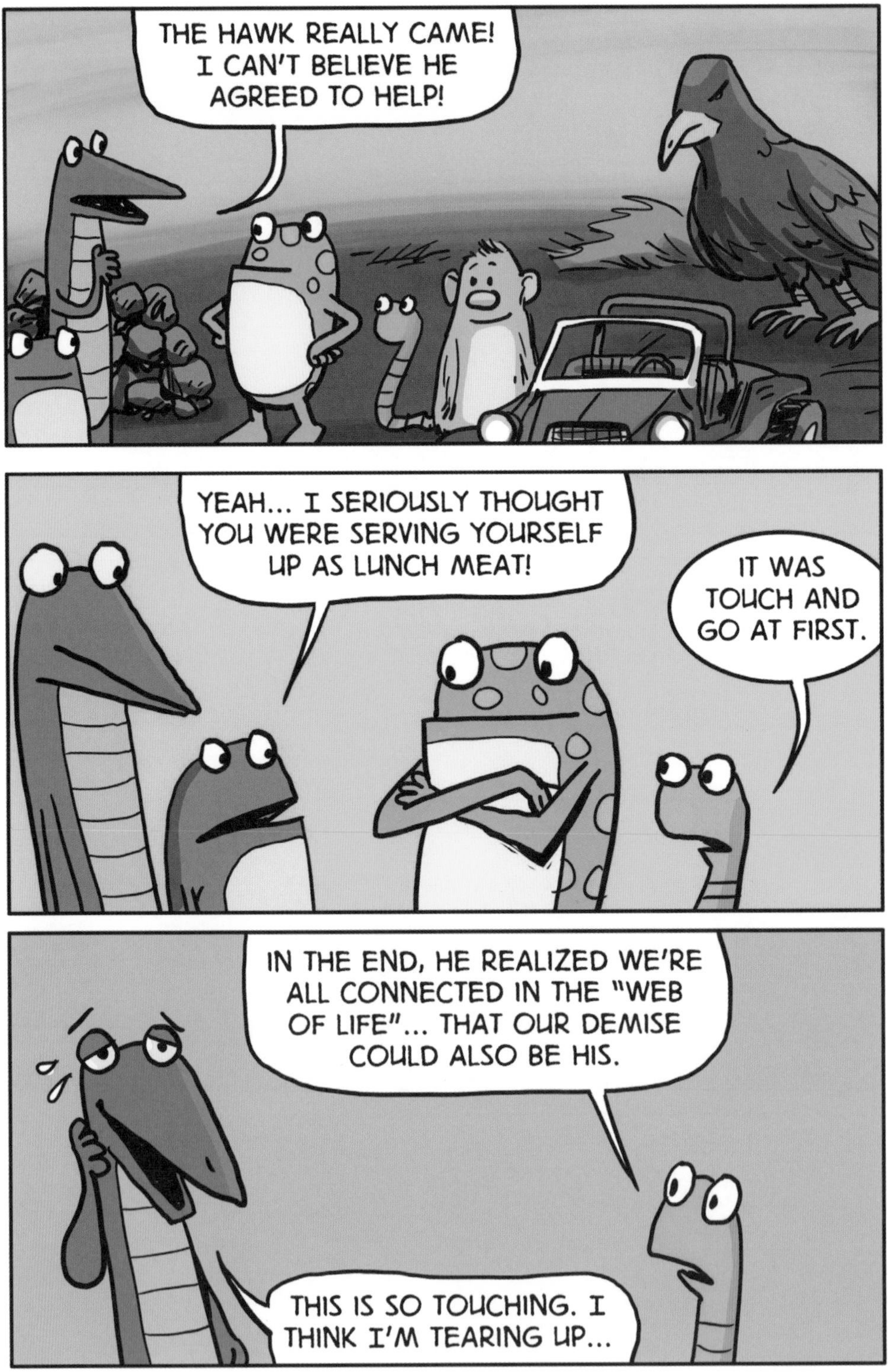
THE HAWK REALLY CAME! I CAN'T BELIEVE HE AGREED TO HELP!
YEAH... I SERIOUSLY THOUGHT YOU WERE SERVING YOURSELF UP AS LUNCH MEAT!
IT WAS TOUCH AND GO AT FIRST.
IN THE END, HE REALIZED WE'RE ALL CONNECTED IN THE "WEB OF LIFE"... THAT OUR DEMISE COULD ALSO BE HIS.
THIS IS SO TOUCHING. I THINK I'M TEARING UP...

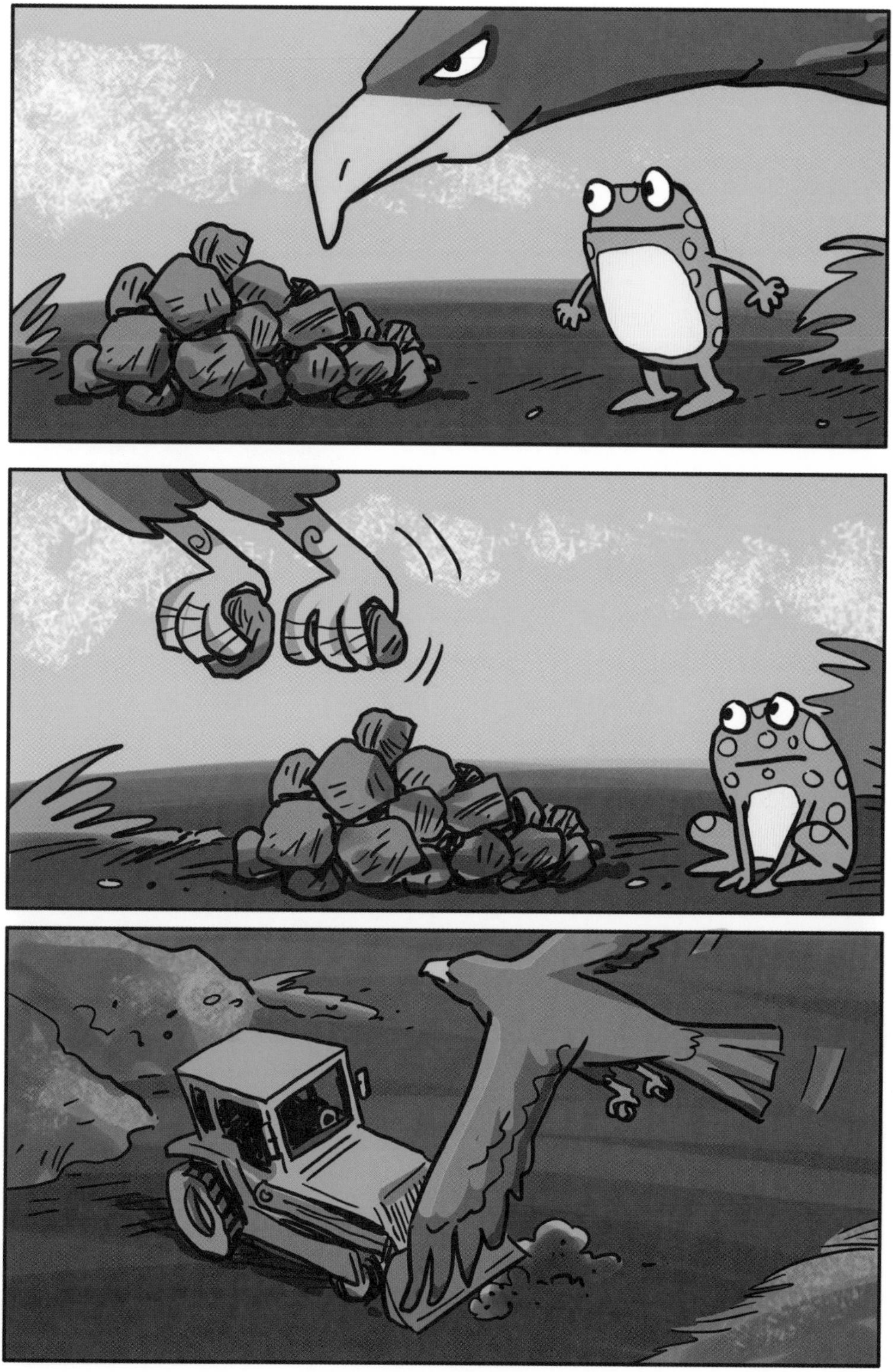

ROCKS AWAY!
BOOF!
BONK!
!!
YIKES!

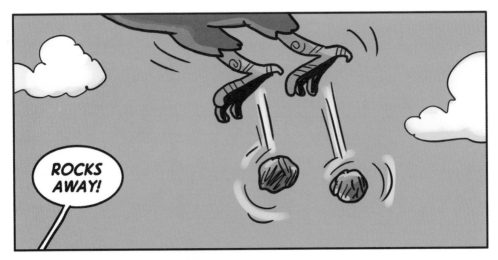

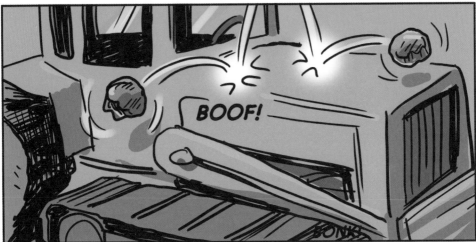

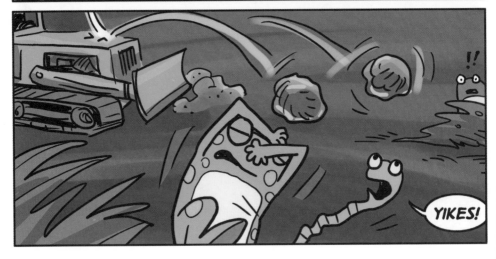

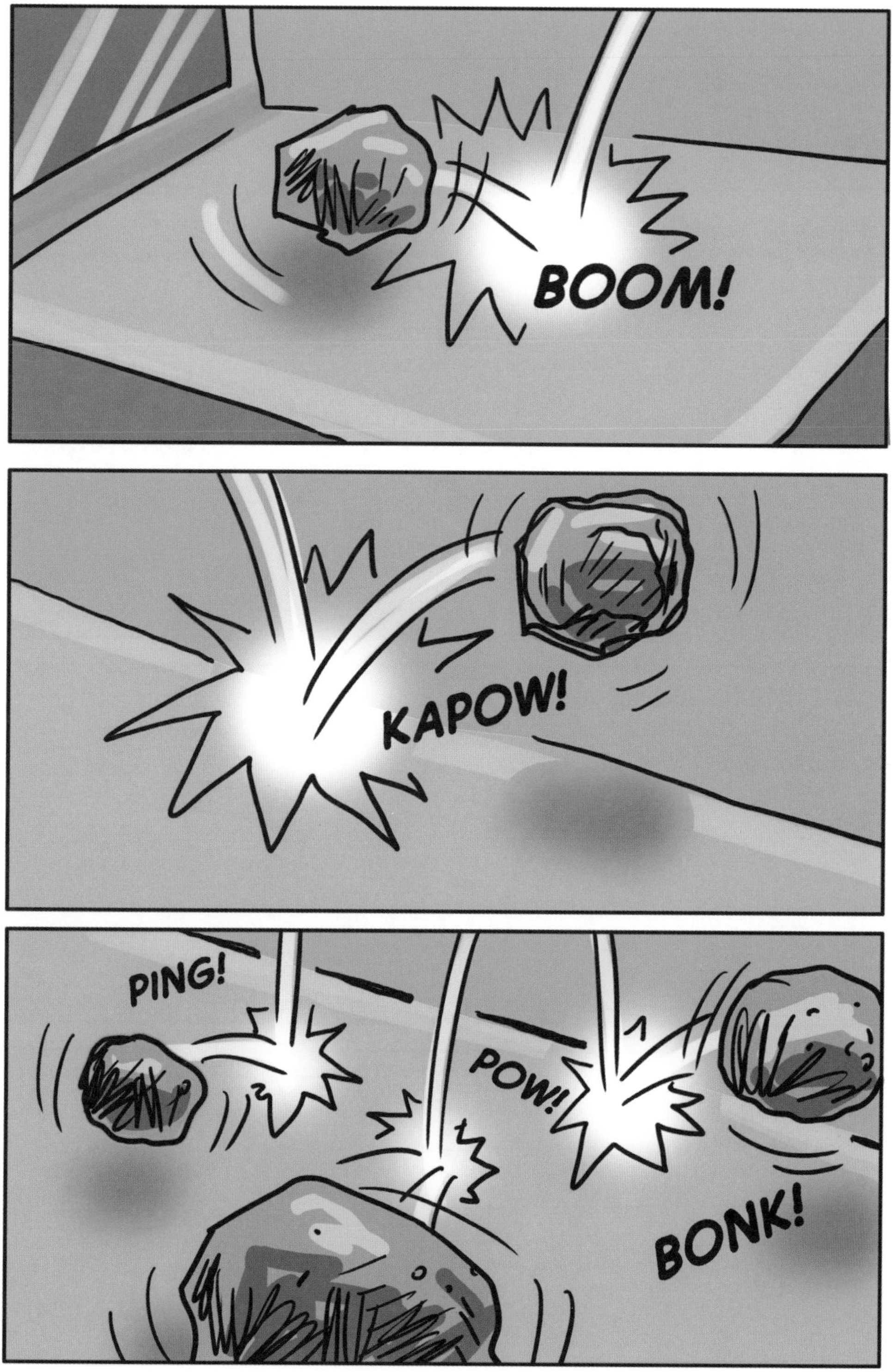
BOOM!
KAPOW!
PING!
POW!
BONK!

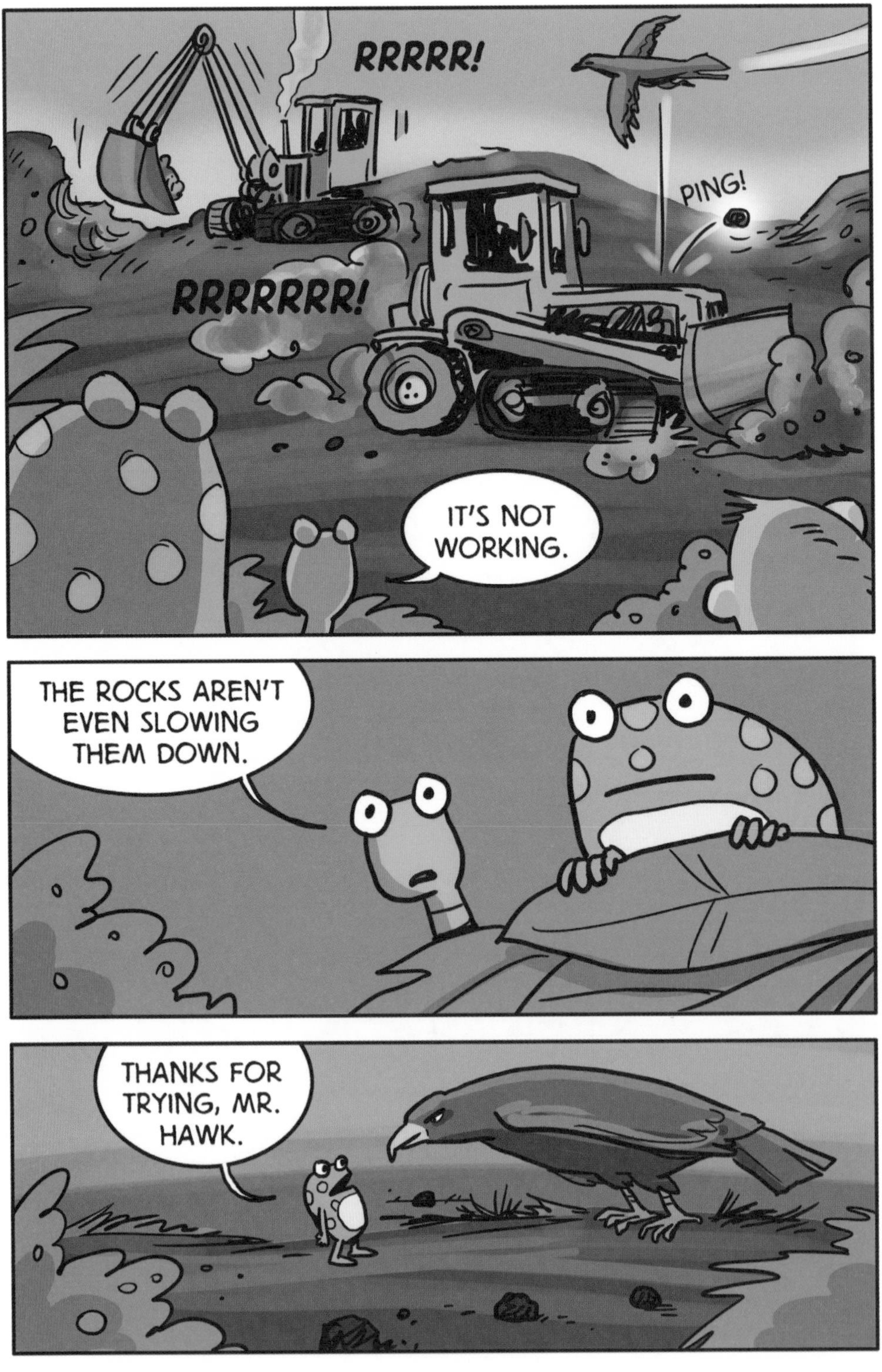
RRRRR!
RRRRRRR!
PING!
IT'S NOT WORKING.
THE ROCKS AREN'T EVEN SLOWING THEM DOWN.
THANKS FOR TRYING, MR. HAWK.

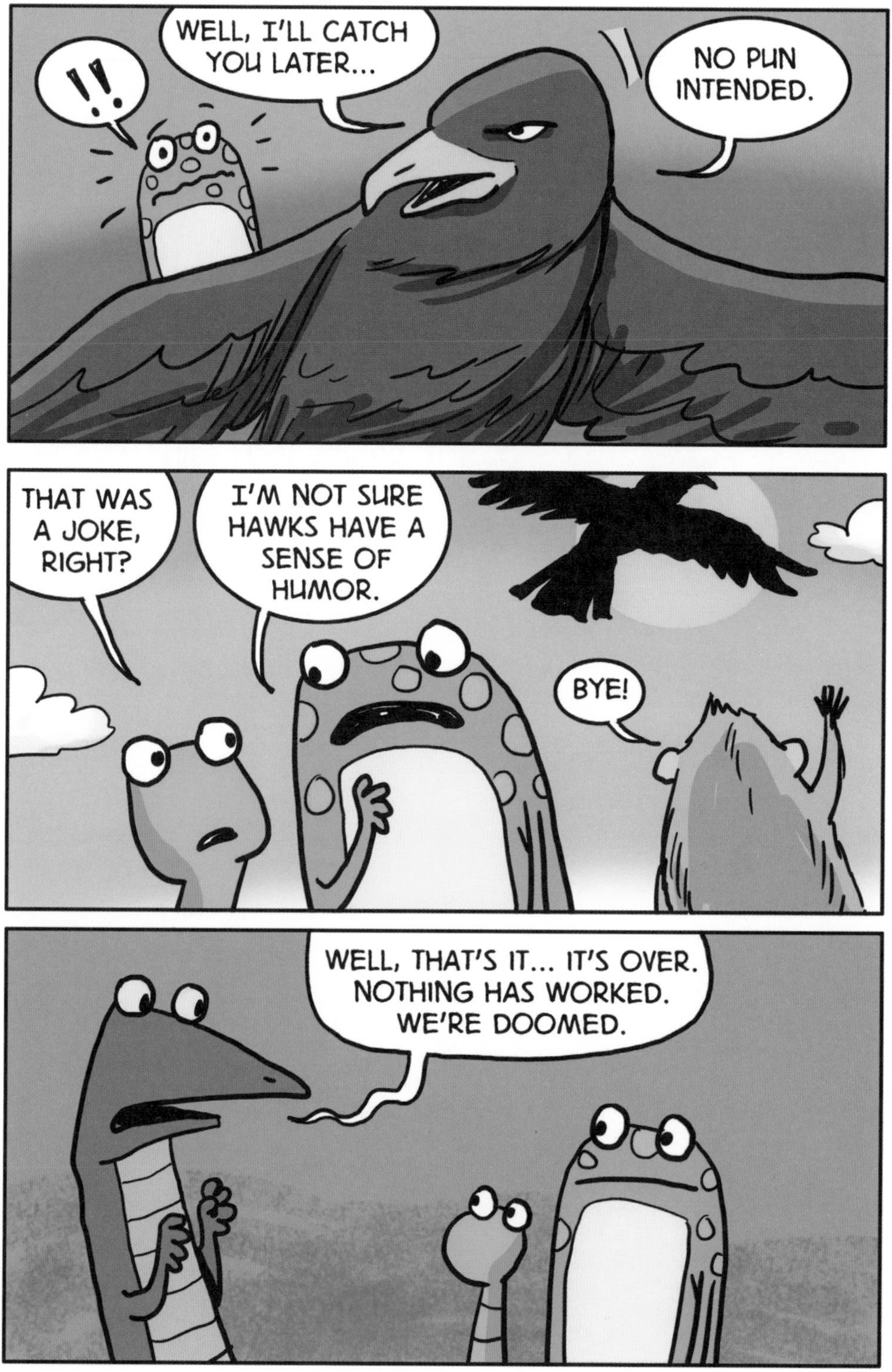
!!
WELL, I'LL CATCH YOU LATER...
NO PUN INTENDED.
THAT WAS A JOKE, RIGHT?
I'M NOT SURE HAWKS HAVE A SENSE OF HUMOR.
BYE!
WELL, THAT'S IT... IT'S OVER. NOTHING HAS WORKED. WE'RE DOOMED.

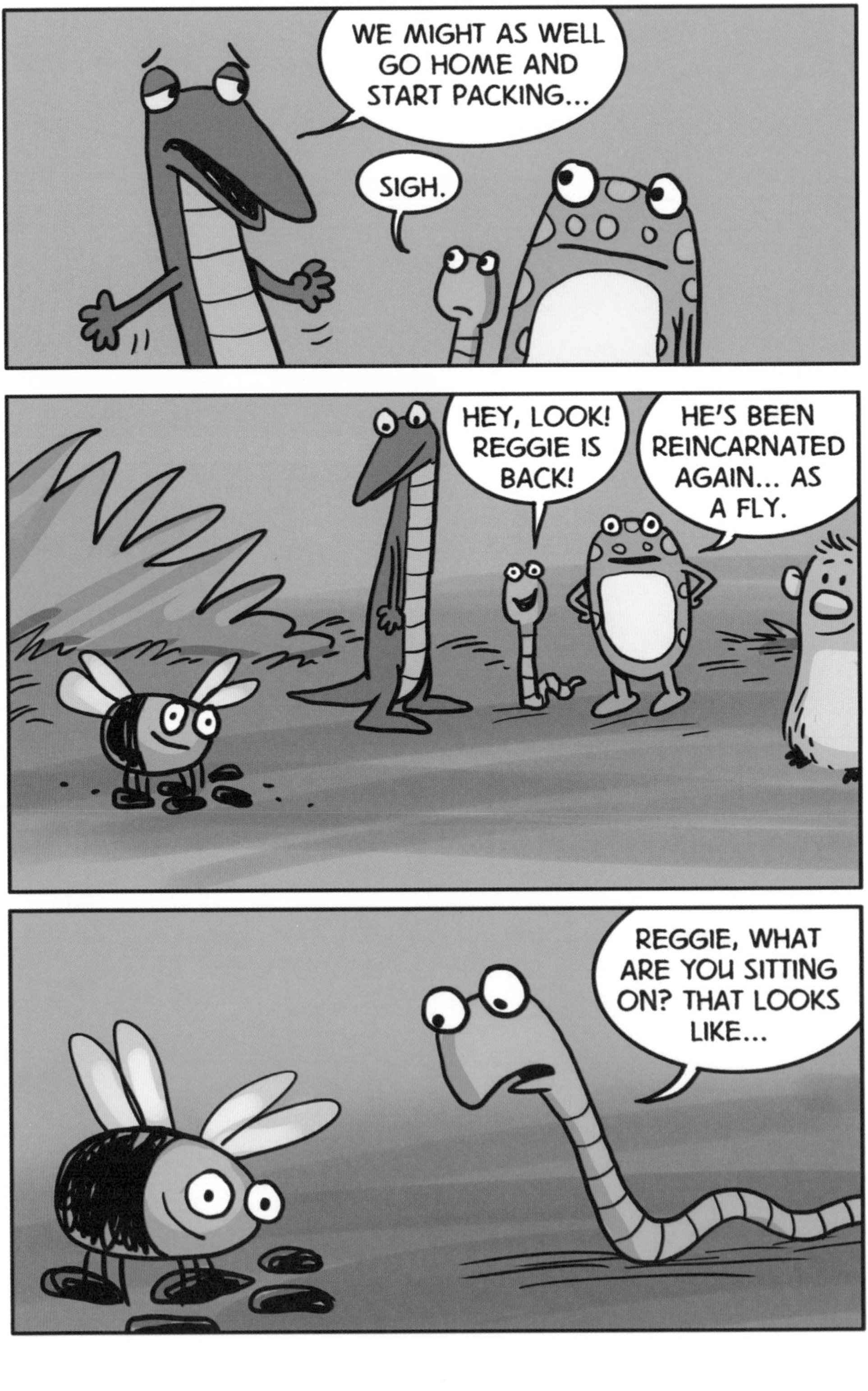
WE MIGHT AS WELL GO HOME AND START PACKING...
SIGH.
HEY, LOOK! REGGIE IS BACK!
HE'S BEEN REINCARNATED AGAIN... AS A FLY.
REGGIE, WHAT ARE YOU SITTING ON? THAT LOOKS LIKE...

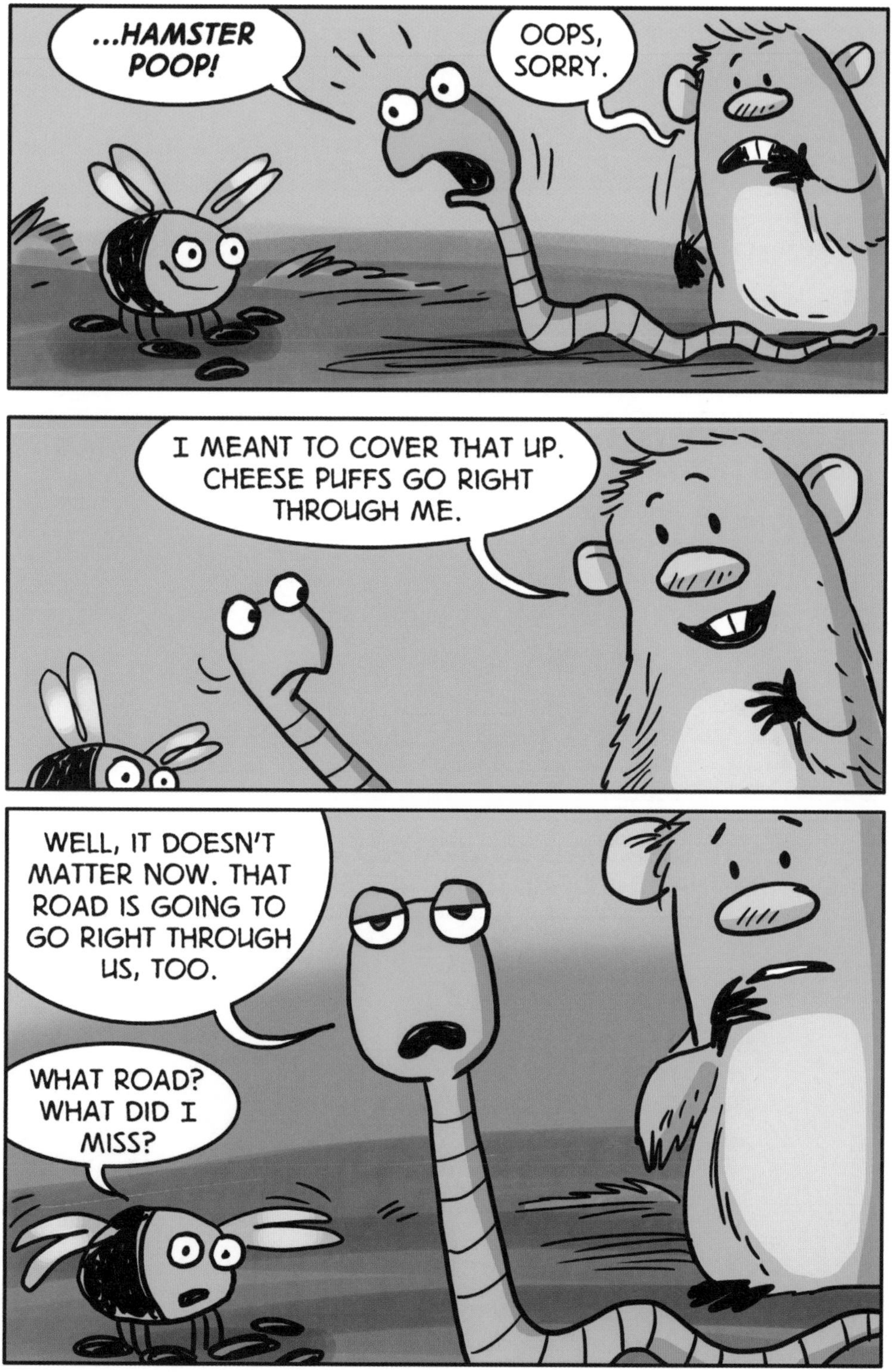
...HAMSTER POOP!
OOPS, SORRY.
I MEANT TO COVER THAT UP. CHEESE PUFFS GO RIGHT THROUGH ME.
WELL, IT DOESN'T MATTER NOW. THAT ROAD IS GOING TO GO RIGHT THROUGH US, TOO.
WHAT ROAD? WHAT DID I MISS?

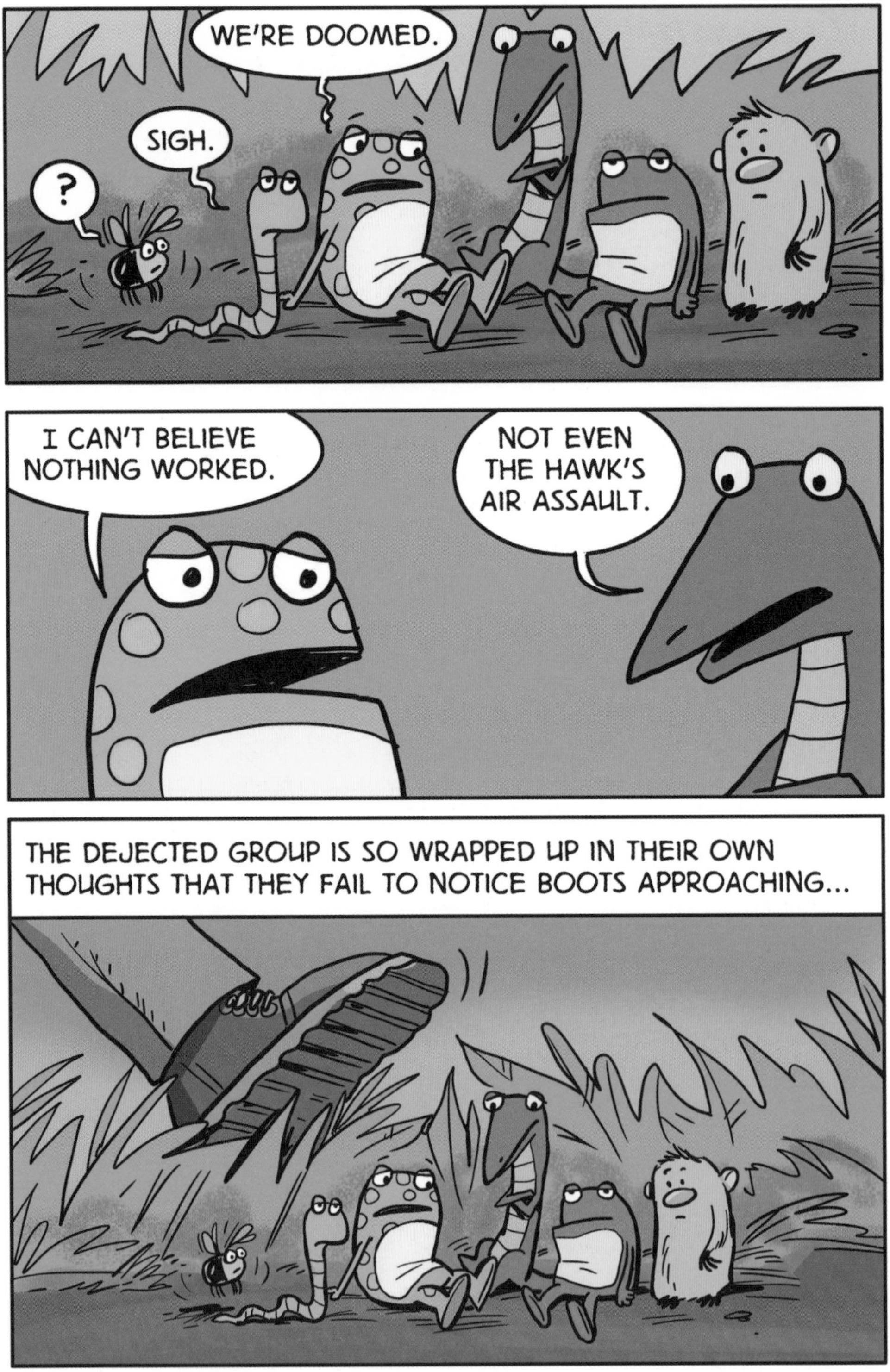
?
SIGH.
WE'RE DOOMED.
I CAN'T BELIEVE NOTHING WORKED.
NOT EVEN THE HAWK'S AIR ASSAULT.
THE DEJECTED GROUP IS SO WRAPPED UP IN THEIR OWN THOUGHTS THAT THEY FAIL TO NOTICE BOOTS APPROACHING...

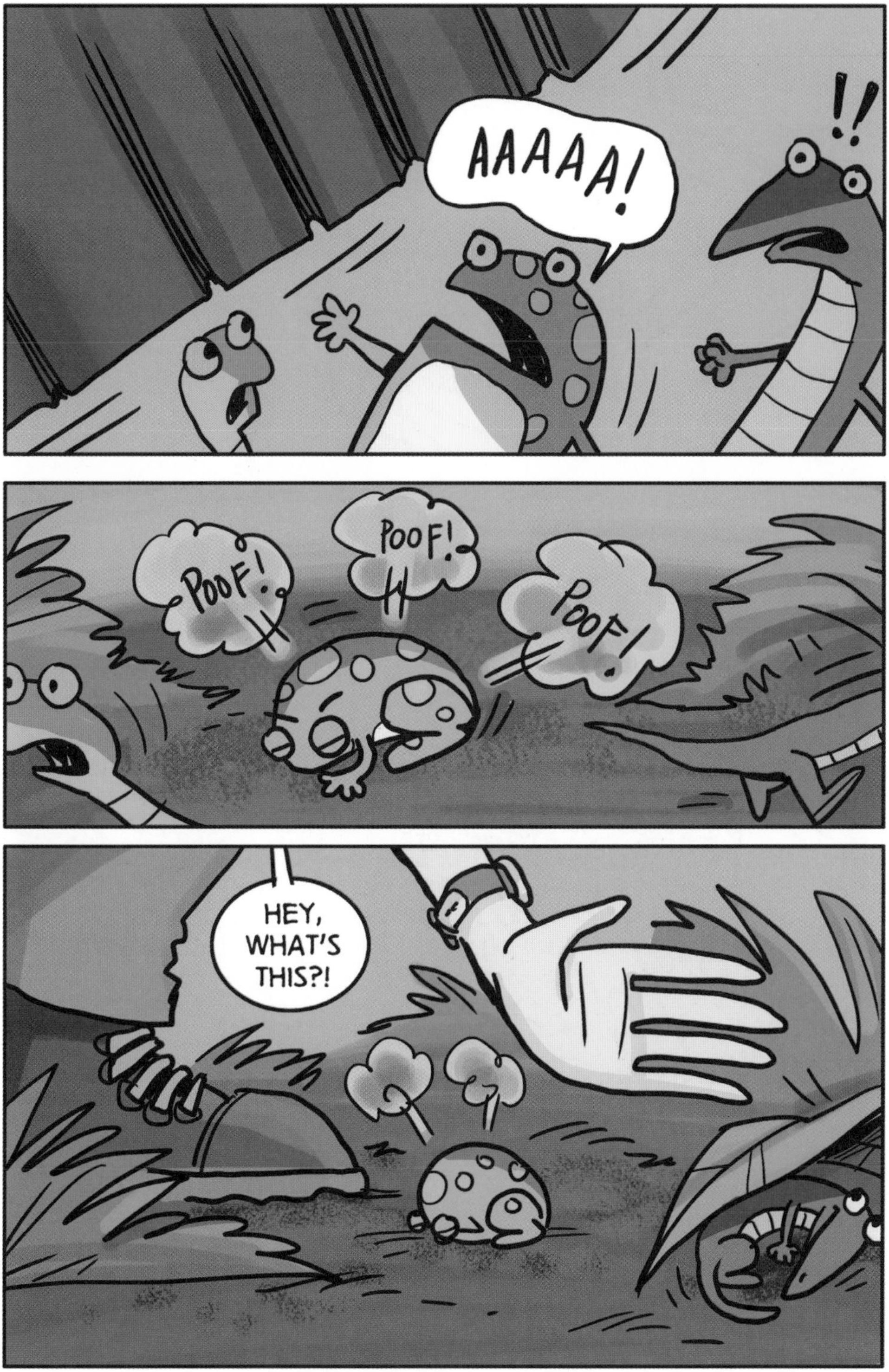
!!
AAAAA!
POOF!
POOF!
POOF!
HEY, WHAT'S THIS?!

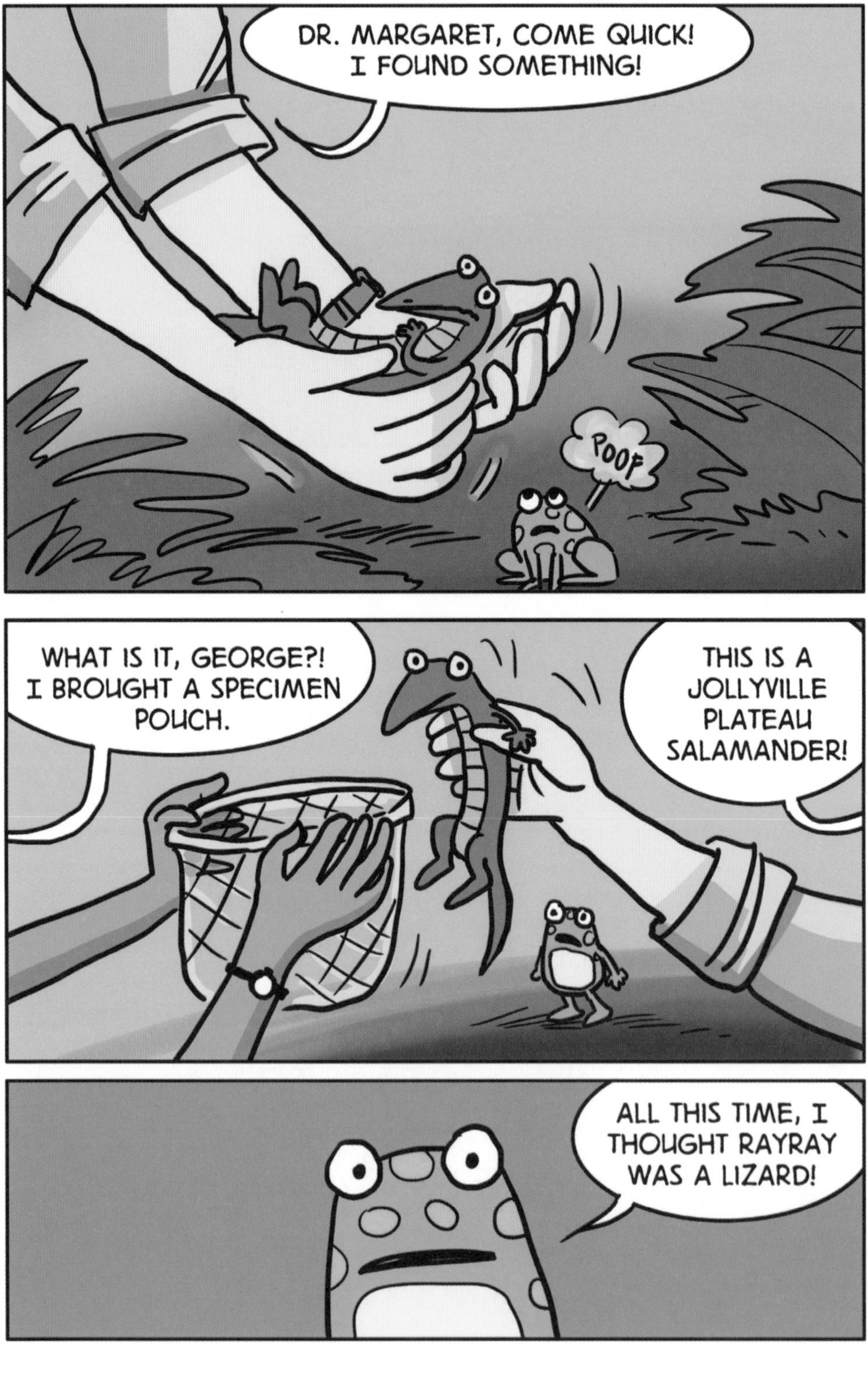
DR. MARGARET, COME QUICK! I FOUND SOMETHING!
POOF
WHAT IS IT, GEORGE?! I BROUGHT A SPECIMEN POUCH.
THIS IS A JOLLYVILLE PLATEAU SALAMANDER!
ALL THIS TIME, I THOUGHT RAYRAY WAS A LIZARD!

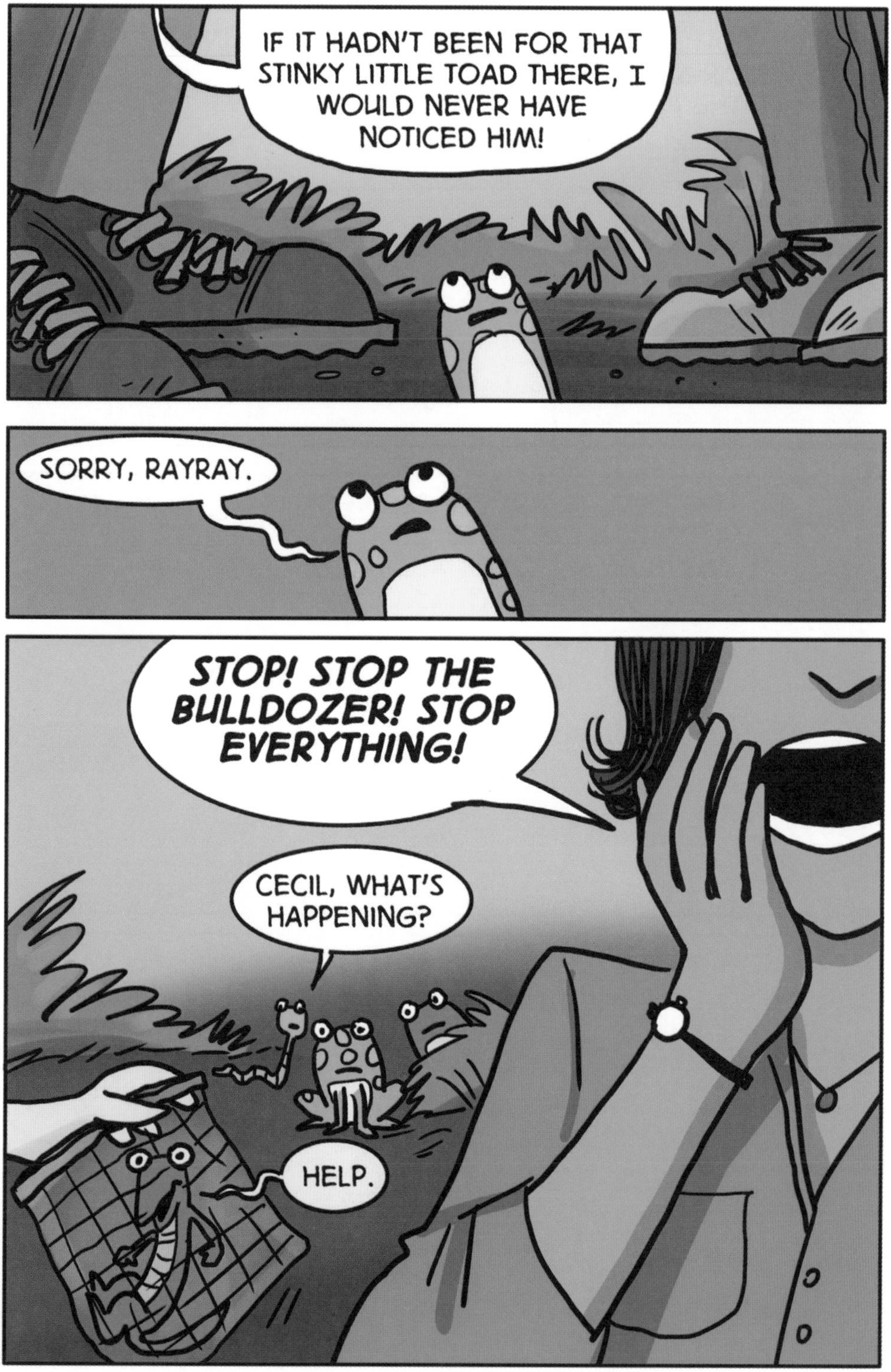
IF IT HADN'T BEEN FOR THAT STINKY LITTLE TOAD THERE, I WOULD NEVER HAVE NOTICED HIM!
SORRY, RAYRAY.
STOP! STOP THE BULLDOZER! STOP EVERYTHING!
CECIL, WHAT'S HAPPENING?
HELP.

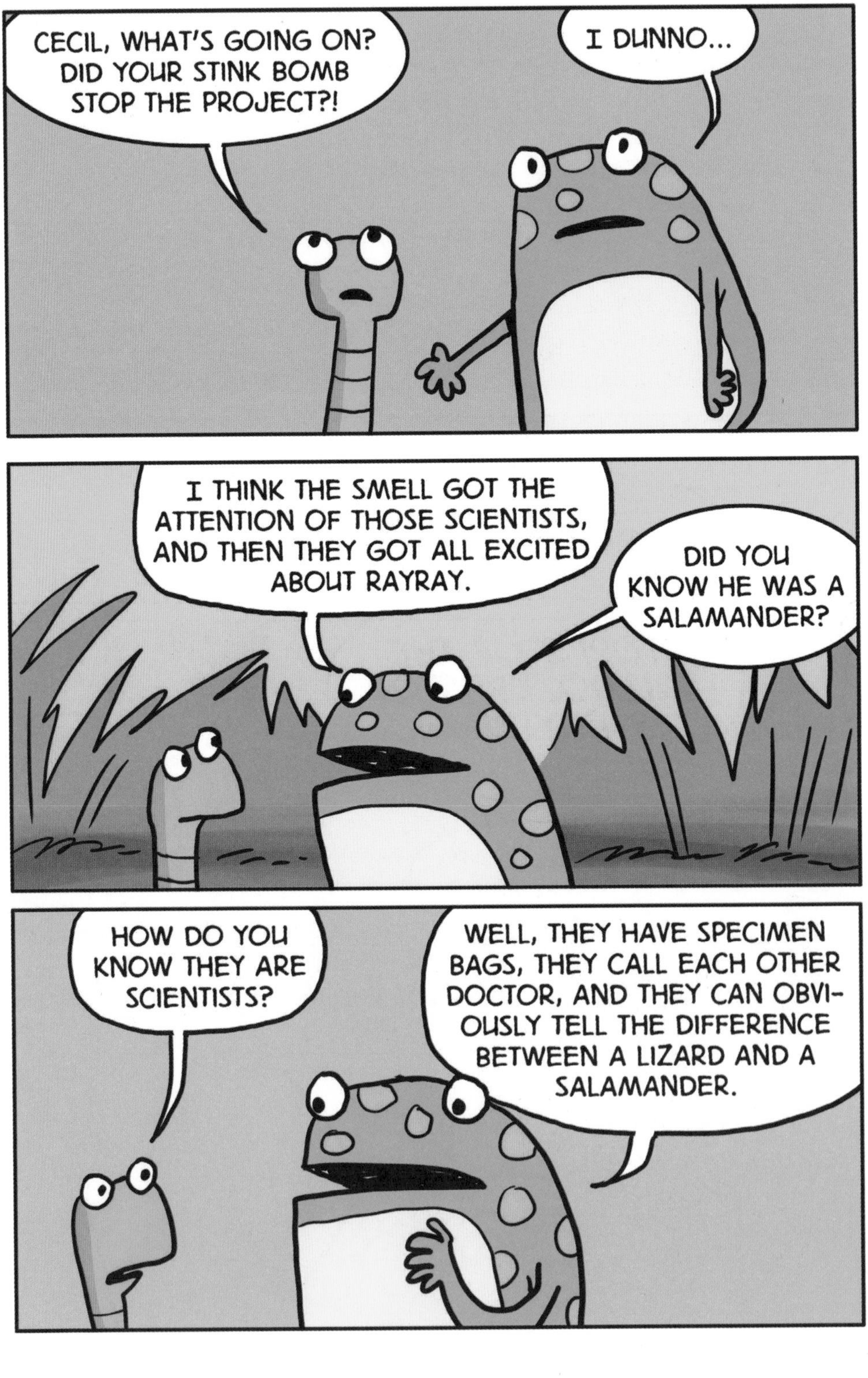
CECIL, WHAT'S GOING ON? DID YOUR STINK BOMB STOP THE PROJECT?!
I DUNNO...
I THINK THE SMELL GOT THE ATTENTION OF THOSE SCIENTISTS, AND THEN THEY GOT ALL EXCITED ABOUT RAYRAY.
DID YOU KNOW HE WAS A SALAMANDER?
HOW DO YOU KNOW THEY ARE SCIENTISTS?
WELL, THEY HAVE SPECIMEN BAGS, THEY CALL EACH OTHER DOCTOR, AND THEY CAN OBVIOUSLY TELL THE DIFFERENCE BETWEEN A LIZARD AND A SALAMANDER.

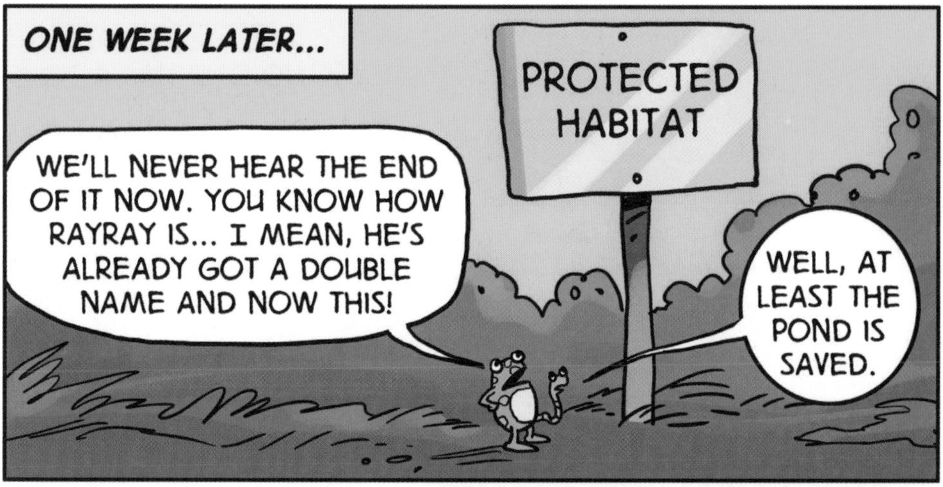
ONE WEEK LATER...
PROTECTED HABITAT
WE'LL NEVER HEAR THE END OF IT NOW. YOU KNOW HOW RAYRAY IS... I MEAN, HE'S ALREADY GOT A DOUBLE NAME AND NOW THIS!
WELL, AT LEAST THE POND IS SAVED.

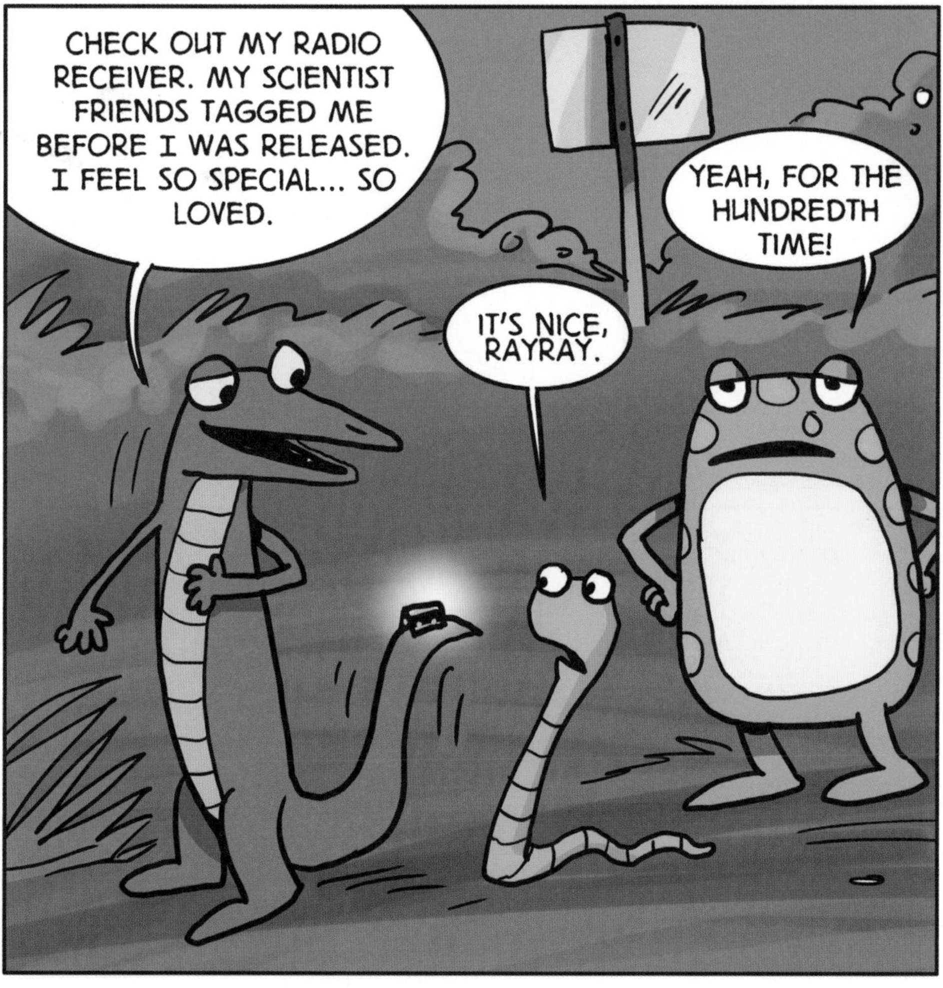
CHECK OUT MY RADIO RECEIVER. MY SCIENTIST FRIENDS TAGGED ME BEFORE I WAS RELEASED. I FEEL SO SPECIAL... SO LOVED.
IT'S NICE, RAYRAY.
YEAH, FOR THE HUNDREDTH TIME!

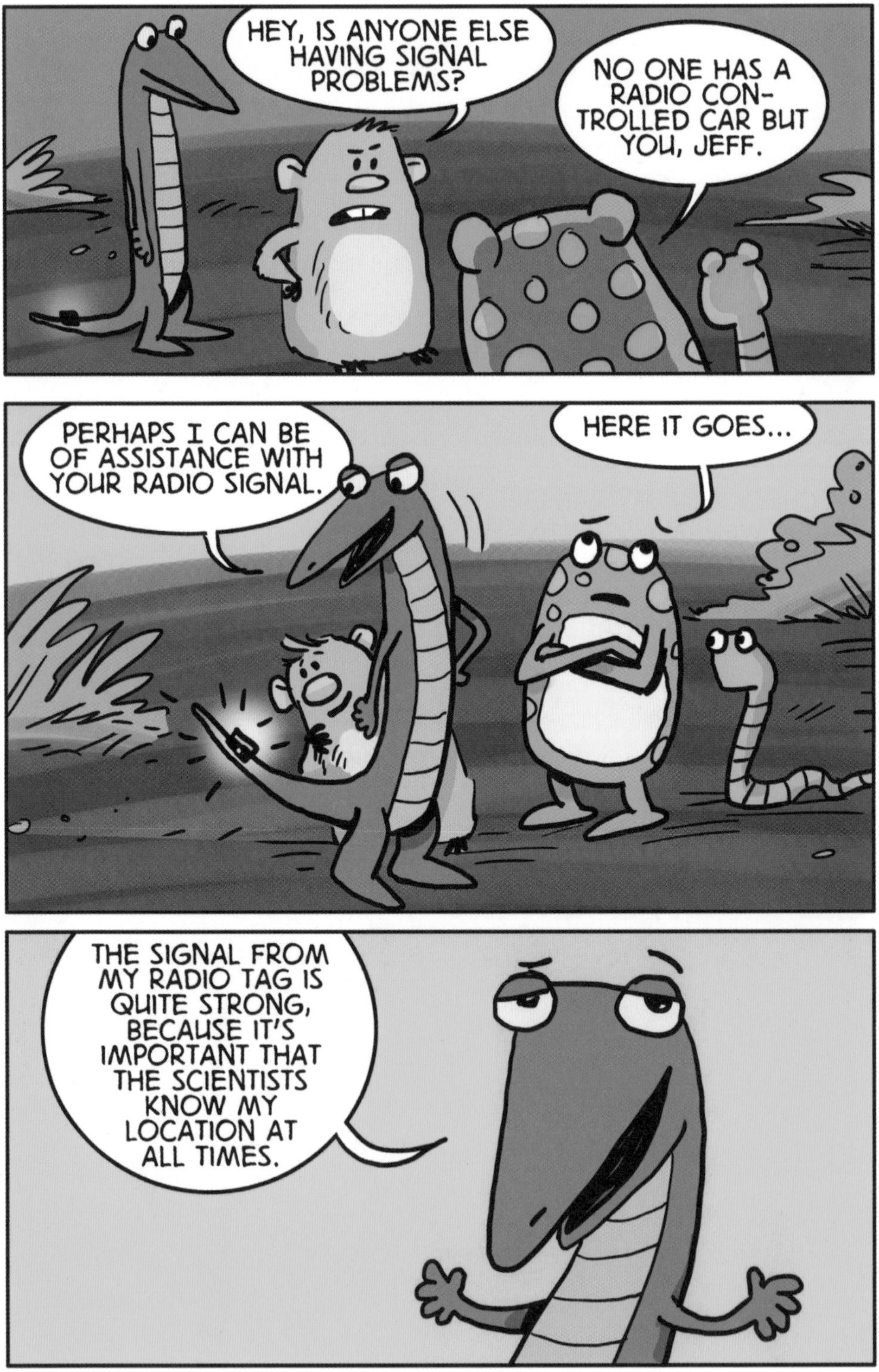
HEY, IS ANYONE ELSE HAVING SIGNAL PROBLEMS?
NO ONE HAS A RADIO CON-TROLLED CAR BUT YOU, JEFF.
PERHAPS I CAN BE OF ASSISTANCE WITH YOUR RADIO SIGNAL.
HERE IT GOES...
THE SIGNAL FROM MY RADIO TAG IS QUITE STRONG, BECAUSE IT'S IMPORTANT THAT THE SCIENTISTS KNOW MY LOCATION AT ALL TIMES.

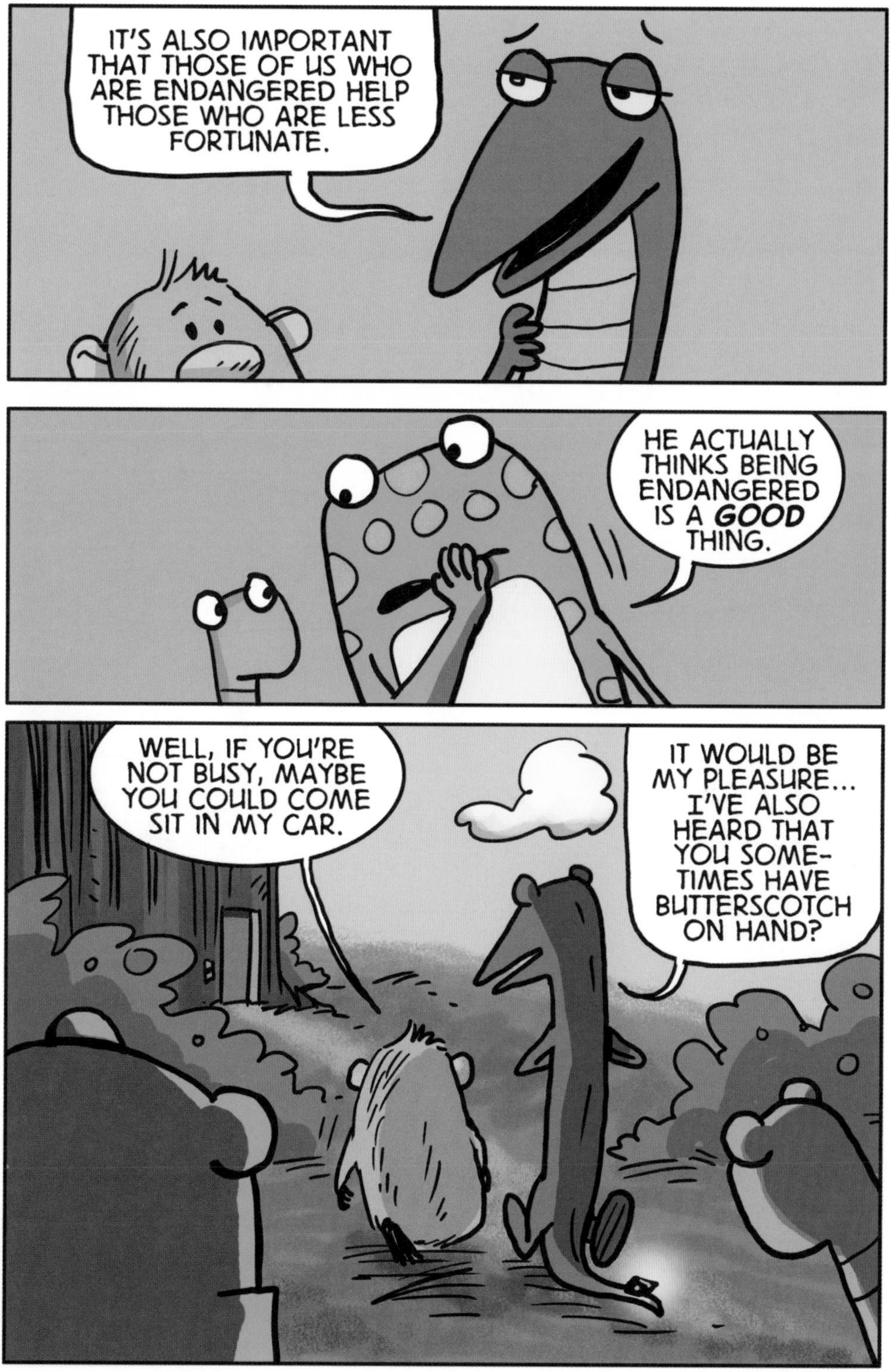
IT'S ALSO IMPORTANT THAT THOSE OF US WHO ARE ENDANGERED HELP THOSE WHO ARE LESS FORTUNATE.
HE ACTUALLY THINKS BEING ENDANGERED IS A ***GOOD*** THING.
WELL, IF YOU'RE NOT BUSY, MAYBE YOU COULD COME SIT IN MY CAR.
IT WOULD BE MY PLEASURE... I'VE ALSO HEARD THAT YOU SOMETIMES HAVE BUTTERSCOTCH ON HAND?

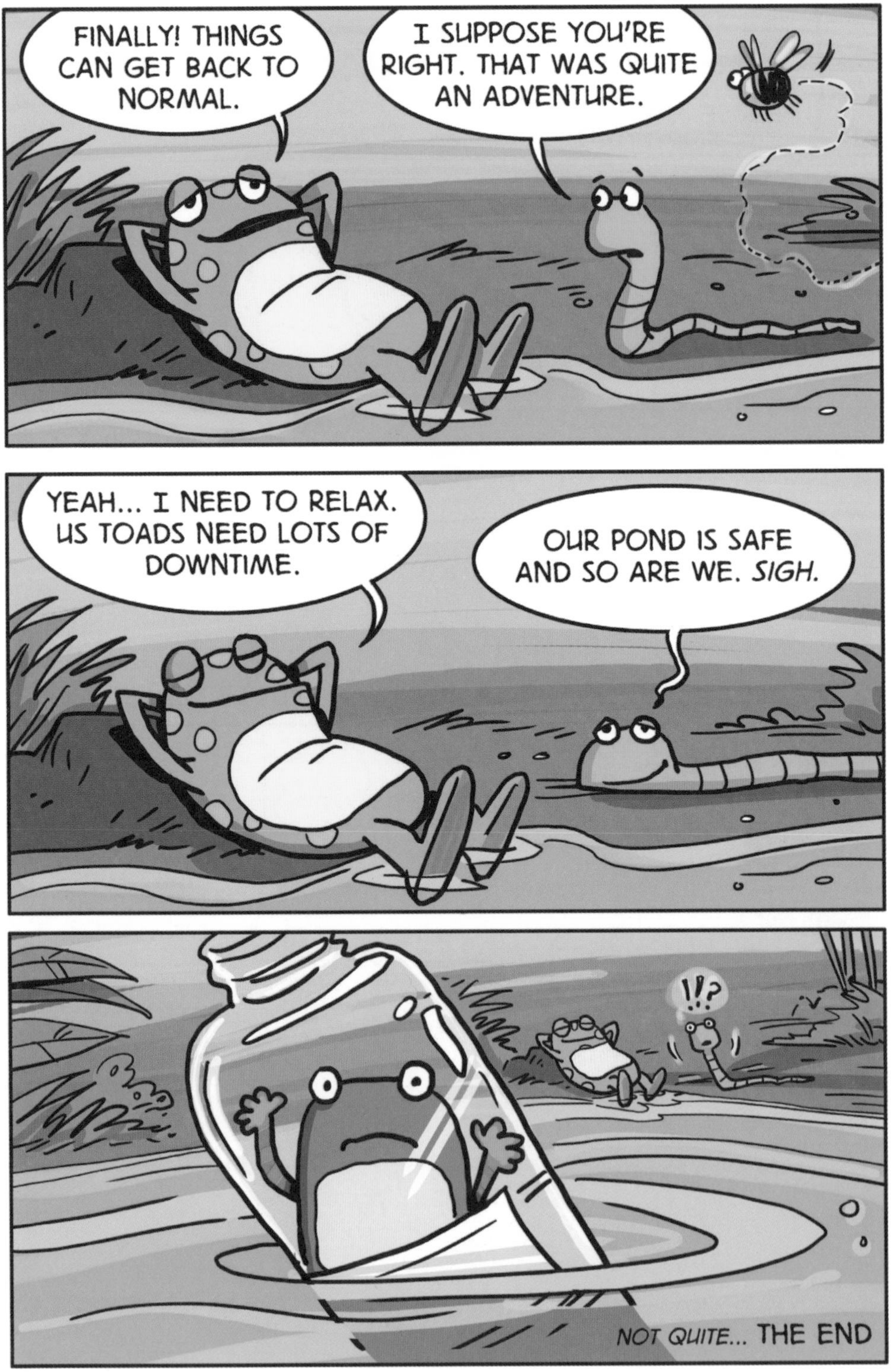
FINALLY! THINGS CAN GET BACK TO NORMAL.
I SUPPOSE YOU'RE RIGHT. THAT WAS QUITE AN ADVENTURE.
YEAH... I NEED TO RELAX. US TOADS NEED LOTS OF DOWNTIME.
OUR POND IS SAFE AND SO ARE WE. *SIGH.*
!!?
NOT QUITE... THE END

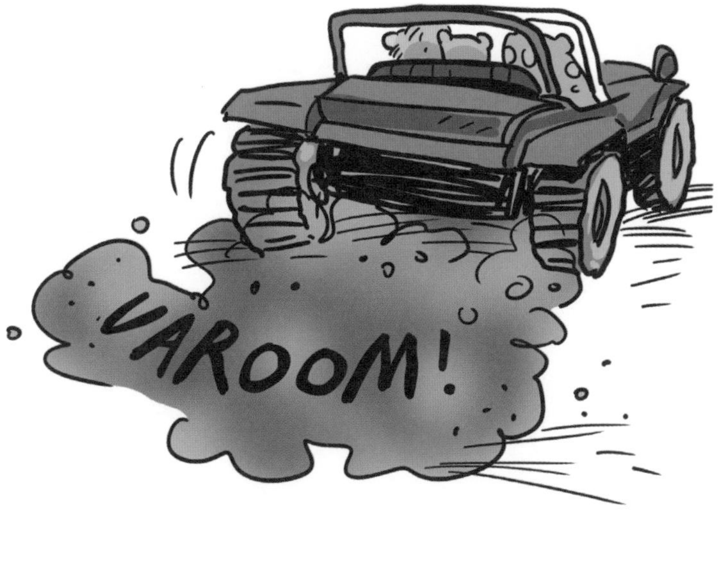
VAROOM!

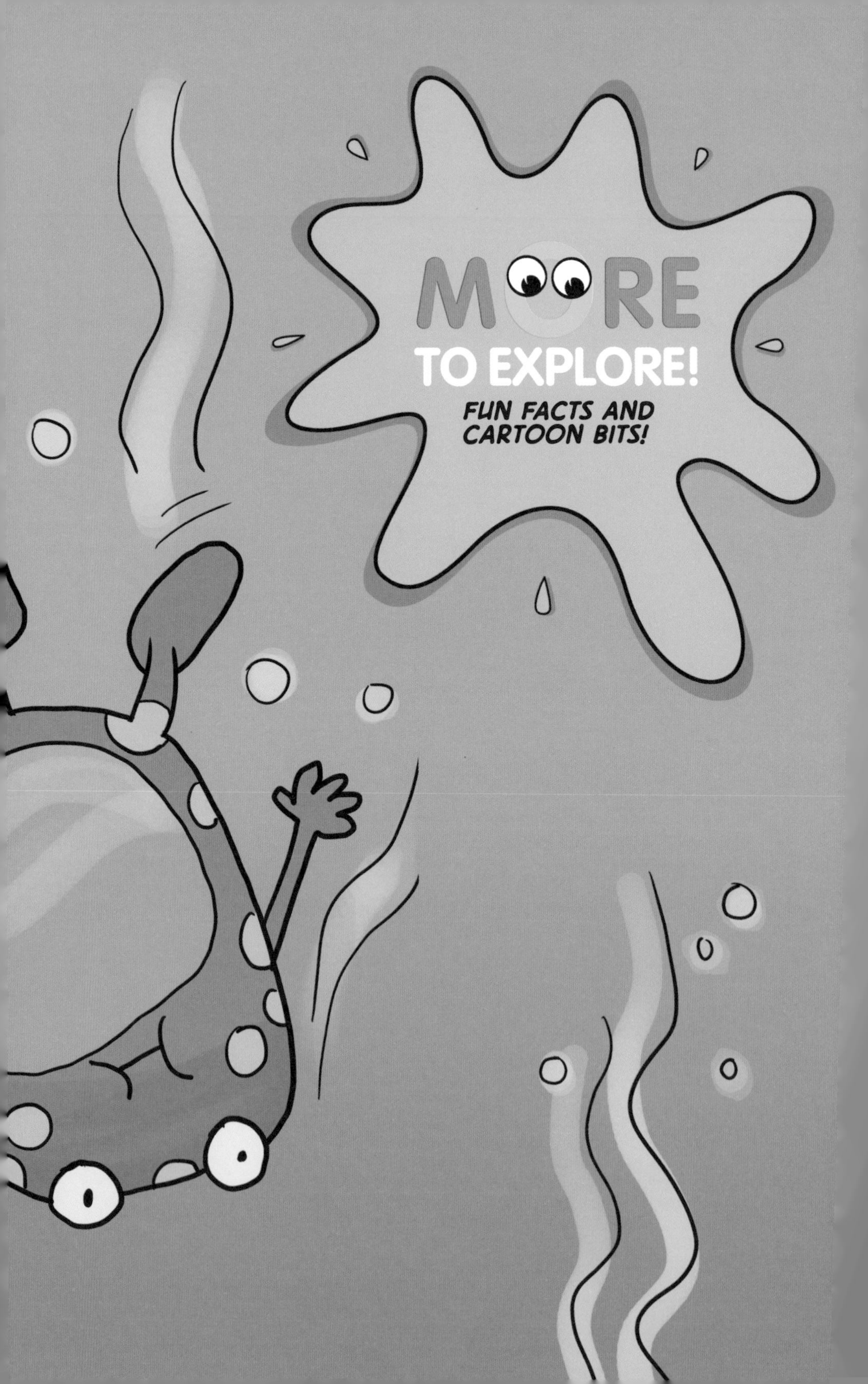
MORE
TO EXPLORE!
FUN FACTS AND CARTOON BITS!

STINKY CECIL IN "ROCK ISSUES"

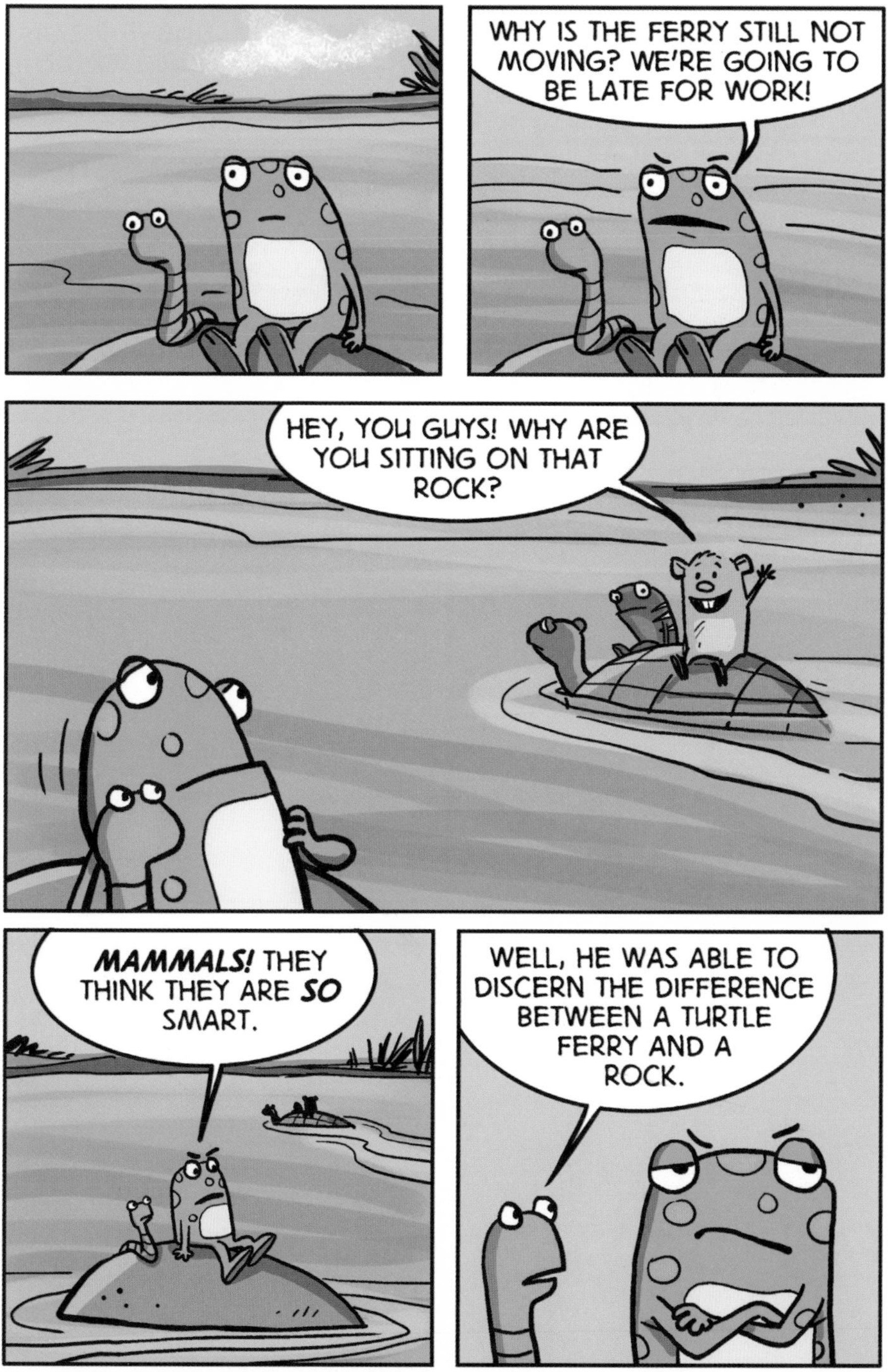
WHY IS THE FERRY STILL NOT MOVING? WE'RE GOING TO BE LATE FOR WORK!
HEY, YOU GUYS! WHY ARE YOU SITTING ON THAT ROCK?
MAMMALS! THEY THINK THEY ARE SO SMART.
WELL, HE WAS ABLE TO DISCERN THE DIFFERENCE BETWEEN A TURTLE FERRY AND A ROCK.

STINKY CECIL IN "BABYSITTING BLUES"

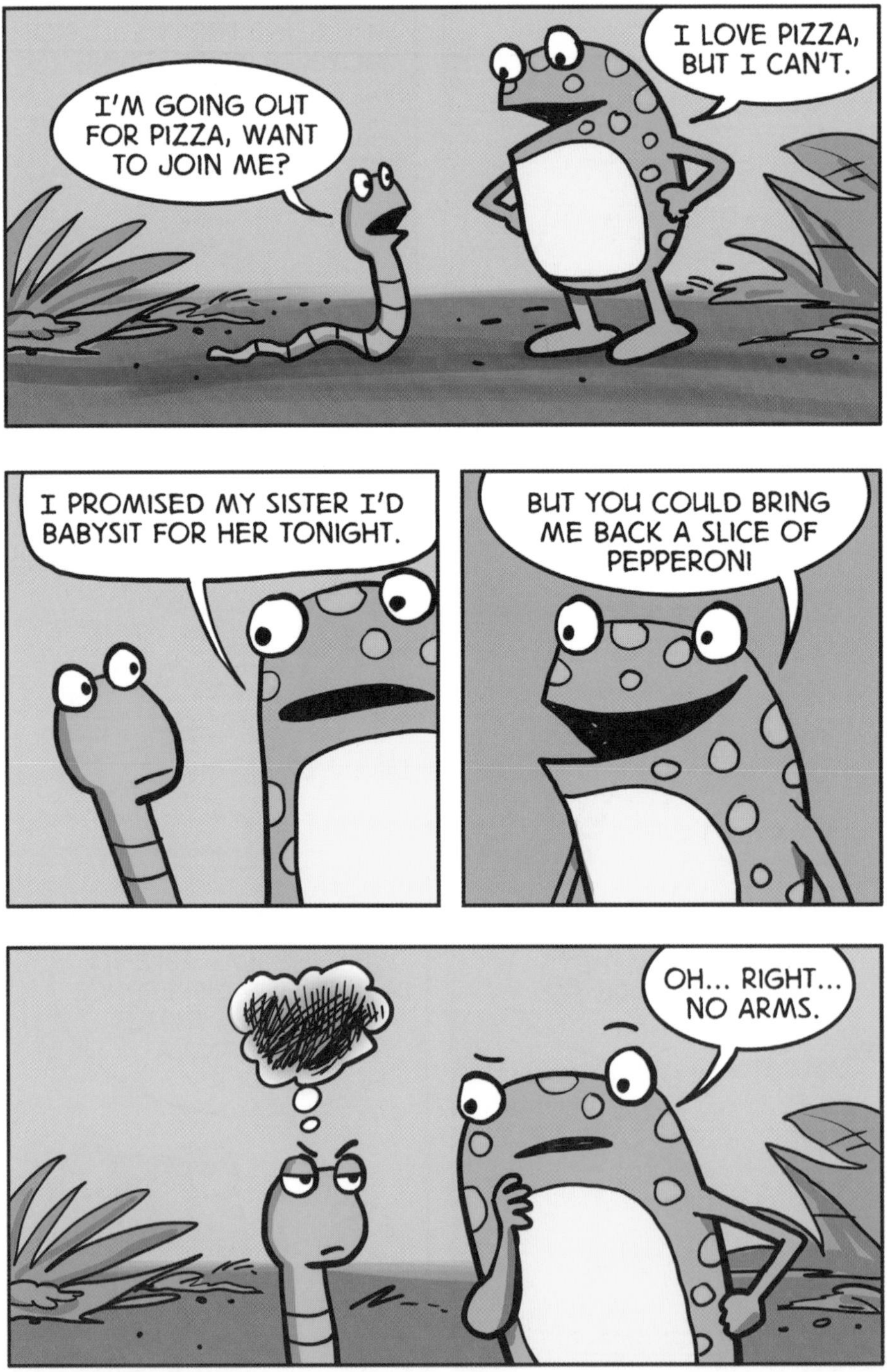
I'M GOING OUT FOR PIZZA, WANT TO JOIN ME?
I LOVE PIZZA, BUT I CAN'T.
I PROMISED MY SISTER I'D BABYSIT FOR HER TONIGHT.
BUT YOU COULD BRING ME BACK A SLICE OF PEPPERONI
OH... RIGHT... NO ARMS.

WELL, I BETTER GET GOING. HAVE FUN JEREMY, AND I'LL SEE YOU TOMORROW.
LATER
OKAY, KIDS, UNCLE CECIL IS IN THE HOUSE!
WHO WANTS A BEDTIME STORY?
THE FROG PRINCE
ME! ME! ME! ME! ME! ME! ME! ME! ME! ME! ME! ME! ME! ME! ME! ME! ME! ME! ME! ME! ME! ME! ME! ME! ME! ME! ME! ME! ME! ME! ME! ME! ME! ME! ME! ME!
THE FROG PRINCE

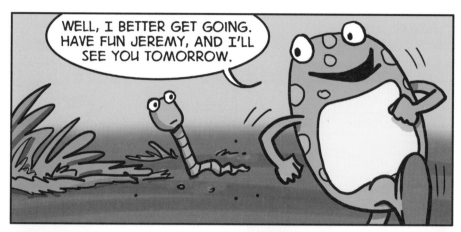

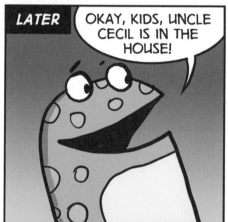

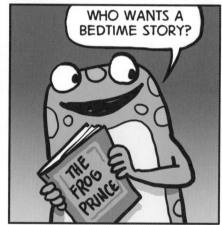

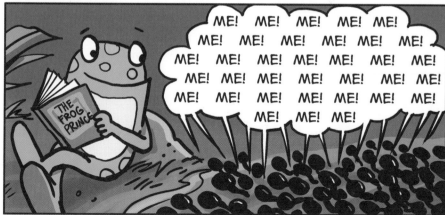

FUN FACT: TOADS CAN LAY BETWEEN 4,000 AND 8,000 EGGS!

ABOUT THE AMERICAN TOAD

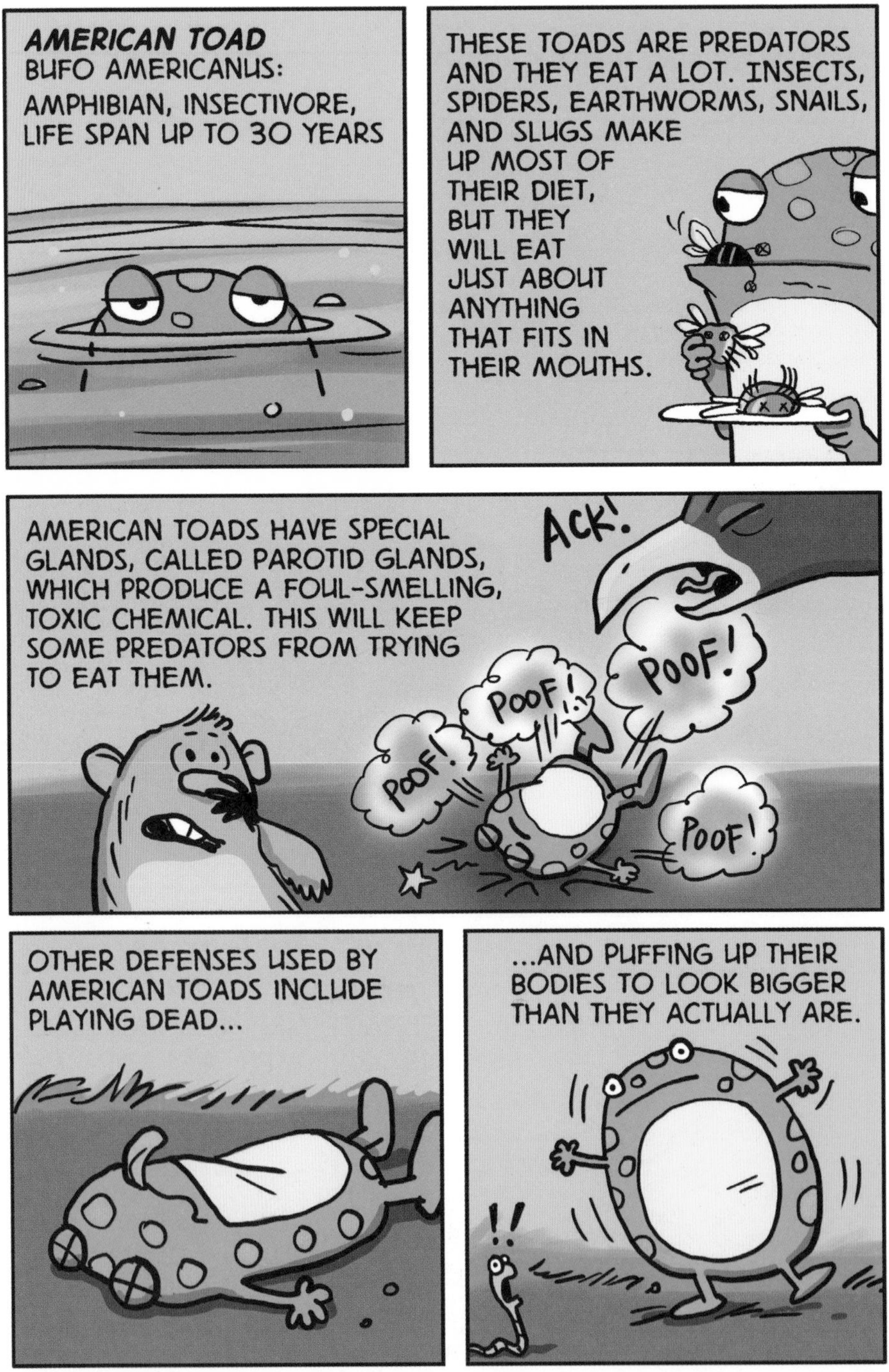
AMERICAN TOAD
BUFO AMERICANUS:
AMPHIBIAN, INSECTIVORE, LIFE SPAN UP TO 30 YEARS
THESE TOADS ARE PREDATORS AND THEY EAT A LOT. INSECTS, SPIDERS, EARTHWORMS, SNAILS, AND SLUGS MAKE UP MOST OF THEIR DIET, BUT THEY WILL EAT JUST ABOUT ANYTHING THAT FITS IN THEIR MOUTHS.
AMERICAN TOADS HAVE SPECIAL GLANDS, CALLED PAROTID GLANDS, WHICH PRODUCE A FOUL-SMELLING, TOXIC CHEMICAL. THIS WILL KEEP SOME PREDATORS FROM TRYING TO EAT THEM.
ACK!
POOF!
POOF!
POOF!
POOF!
OTHER DEFENSES USED BY AMERICAN TOADS INCLUDE PLAYING DEAD...
...AND PUFFING UP THEIR BODIES TO LOOK BIGGER THAN THEY ACTUALLY ARE.
!!

ABOUT THE COMMON EARTHWORM

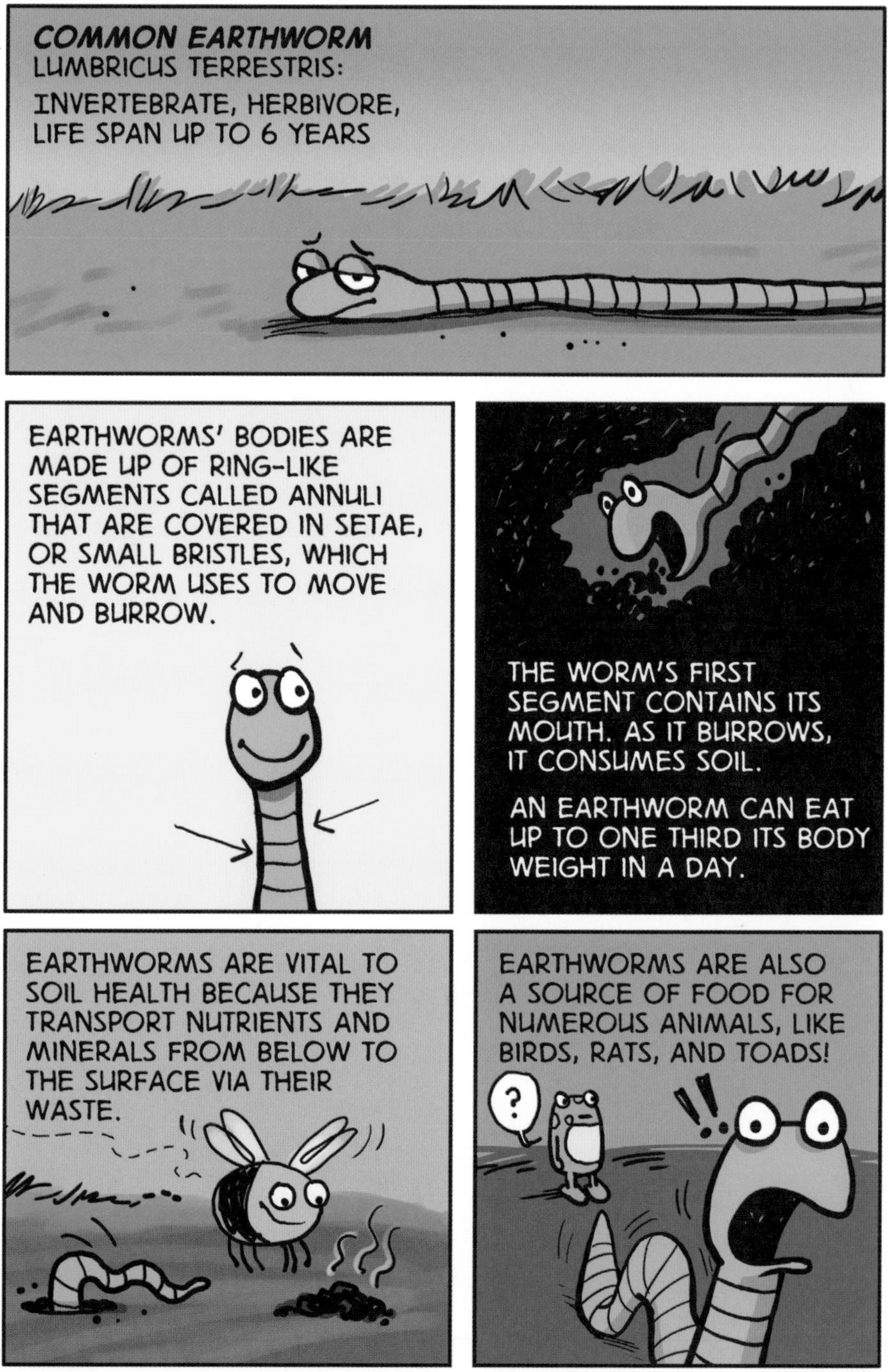
COMMON EARTHWORM
LUMBRICUS TERRESTRIS:
INVERTEBRATE, HERBIVORE, LIFE SPAN UP TO 6 YEARS
EARTHWORMS' BODIES ARE MADE UP OF RING-LIKE SEGMENTS CALLED ANNULI THAT ARE COVERED IN SETAE, OR SMALL BRISTLES, WHICH THE WORM USES TO MOVE AND BURROW.
THE WORM'S FIRST SEGMENT CONTAINS ITS MOUTH. AS IT BURROWS, IT CONSUMES SOIL.
AN EARTHWORM CAN EAT UP TO ONE THIRD ITS BODY WEIGHT IN A DAY.
EARTHWORMS ARE VITAL TO SOIL HEALTH BECAUSE THEY TRANSPORT NUTRIENTS AND MINERALS FROM BELOW TO THE SURFACE VIA THEIR WASTE.
EARTHWORMS ARE ALSO A SOURCE OF FOOD FOR NUMEROUS ANIMALS, LIKE BIRDS, RATS, AND TOADS!
?
!!